THE WAKING OF GREY GRIMM

BOOK 1 IN THE MAZE

TONY BERTAUSKI

BERTAUSKI STARTER LIBRARY

FREE!

---

bertauski.com

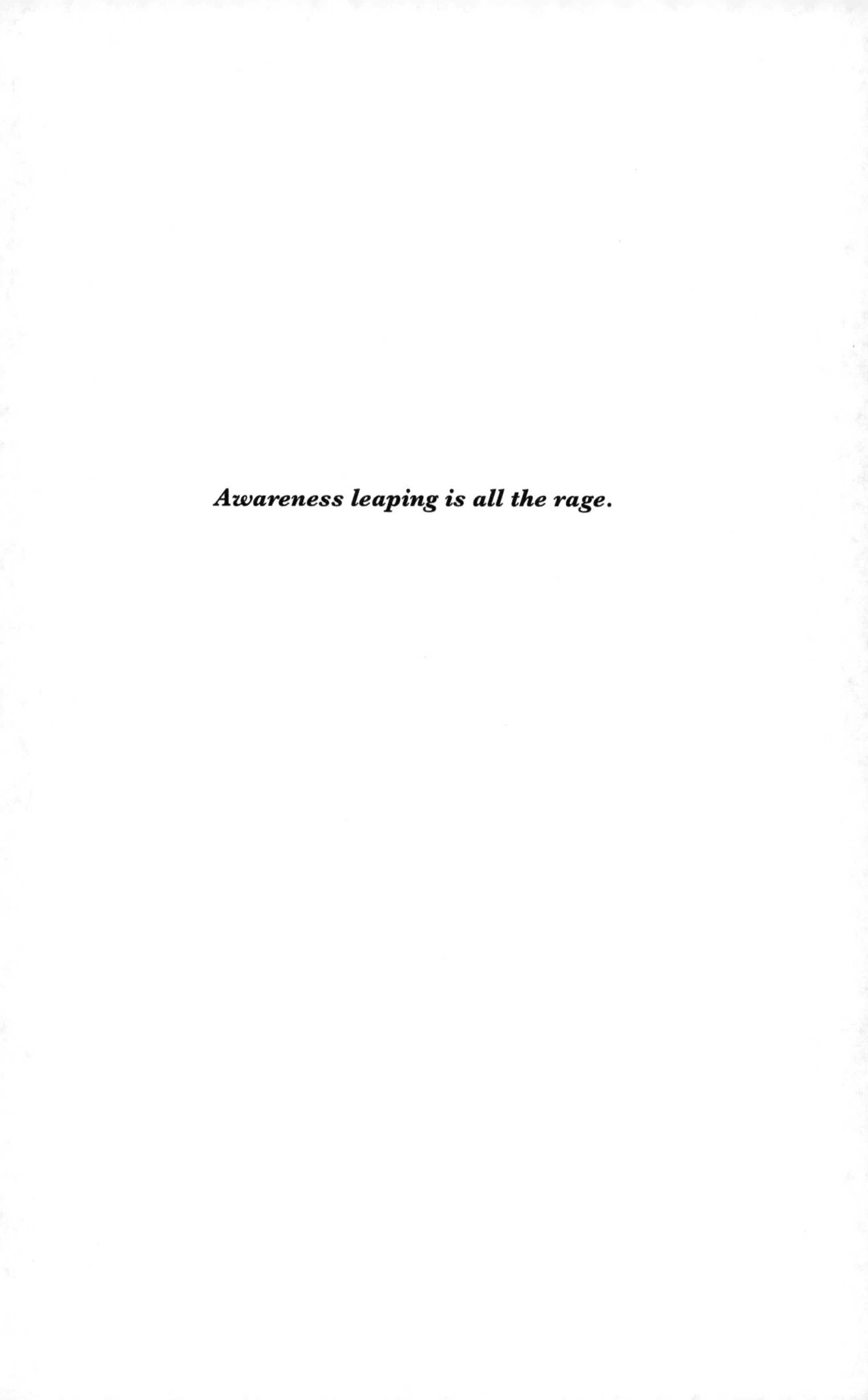

Awareness leaping is all the rage.

INTERVIEW WITH GREY GRIMM

"He wants to talk to you," Andrew says.

Freddy drops his pen. The feed on his monitor shows a kid in a hard-backed chair. He's got shaggy hair and a smooth chin. Freddy would've guessed the kid is fifteen years old, but he knows he's eighteen.

"Why's he here?"

Andrew taps his forehead. "He was in it."

Freddy sighs. Ten-year-olds, grandmothers, or paraplegics, it doesn't matter who you are. Mention the Maze and you get a free conversation with authorities.

Especially this kid.

His mom was fished from a submersion tank six months ago. The stink of the thick bubbling goo was as bad as a summer corpse—like oil scraped from the skull of a beached whale. Kid's mom was just another donation to the Maze, a puckered human shell in a giant egg jar.

She was in the high-rent district, an abandoned warehouse with amenities. It was the biggest bust in quite some time. No telling how long they'd been operating. Then again, no one ever did. Maze operators were like fire ants: kill the mound and another pops up.

Feds flew in to photograph her pickled husk; they pulled samples, led interrogations, confiscated equipment and went home. Nothing came of it. Never did.

Why don't they just legalize the thing? Prohibition didn't stop booze. Weed laws only filled prisons. The Maze and all its promises are here to stay. Freddy is sick of the resistance. He just wants it to stop. They all do. If Sunny Grimm wanted to skinny dip in a vat of whale jizz, that was her right.

Freddy opens the interrogation room. The heavy door latches behind him. He stops and stares, but not to intimidate him. Kid looks like he should be tagging brick walls, not confessing to Maze activity.

He sits in the hard chair across from him, reaching deep for the politically correct opener. It comes out partially hollow, mostly rehearsed. "Sorry about your mother. You're a kid; this isn't fair. You don't deserve this."

"She's gone," Grey says, "because of me."

"All right." Freddy leans back. "Did you kill her?"

He doesn't shake his head. Freddy gives him time to find an answer because his mom is dead and that's what he should do.

"She's gone because you were in the Maze," Freddy finally says. "Is that it?"

"I was the one that called you."

An anonymous caller tipped off the warehouse operation, leading them to the tanks and Sunny Grimm's marinated body. The place was unlocked when they arrived. The evidence waiting. There was no trace of who called or why.

"If you were involved, you're admitting to a felony. You realize that."

He stares at the kid's forehead. It's not a sweeping glance or polite gander. He lets him know he's looking for a dot or hole.

"Did you punch in?" Freddy says.

"I didn't say she was dead."

"Her body says different, Grey."

The kid's not bothered. He even smiles. Maybe he did off his mom. Then he volleys back.

"I was in the Maze, Kaleb. You were, too."

Kaleb? Freddy looks around the interrogation room. No one knew his middle name, not even Andrew. But that wasn't what crawled up his spine. *You were, too,* he said.

"You were in the Maze?"

"You know about parallel worlds?"

"No."

"The Maze is an alternate reality that looks exactly like this one. It has this desk, these walls, this building and the streets outside. All the same people living dull lives and frustrations. Including you, Kaleb."

"Stop using my middle name. Whatever you think happened, didn't. Your mom didn't make it back and I wasn't there. Those are facts in this reality. So are the laws."

"How do you know you weren't there?"

"Because I know."

"Your memories aren't the best proof, Freddy."

Freddy shakes his head. He's had about enough of the first name and middle name act. "What are you doing here, Grey?"

Grey sits rigid, looking thoughtful. "We live in a networked world," he says. "Satellites, security cameras, electronic eyes are everywhere, no corner left alone. It's all uploaded somewhere, collated and stored. I suppose the Maze builds a parallel world with this data, a virtual environment that simply pieces together a three-dimensional reality indistinguishable from this one."

He knocks on the table. A private grin breaks out.

"Every speck of dust is accounted for, every mannerism, every piece of litter and drop of dew. Maybe it's some sort of quantum absorption, an essential snapshot of this world of flesh and bone and everything in it—you, me, our thoughts and beliefs. Because you were there, Freddy. You just don't know it."

For a moment, he looks like a kid filled with wonder, seeing the world for the first time, like he knows how the universe works. He's just an eighteen-year-old kid who just lost his mother. Instead of cursing God or running away, he's nodding along like death is just a doorway to a room full of virgins.

Freddy looks up. The interrogation room recorded every conversation. It would be enough to convict him, but he won't do it. There's no proof, really. Honestly, he just doesn't want to do it.

It won't stop the Maze.

"I'm only going to say this once and I hope you listen. This isn't the conversation you want to have in this room. Your mom took the dive, Grey. She did it, not you. I'm sorry, I really am. But you need to go home, make amends with your dad, talk to a therapist or priest or girlfriend. Anywhere but here."

Grey drums his fingers. A darker pall falls over him.

"Someone is guilty," he says. "That's why I'm here."

PART 1

LOST IN REALITY

[1]

Sunny

After the Punch

Henk can't find out.

Sunny Grimm found her son comatose, and her first thought was to keep it from her ex-husband.

Priceless.

She came home with groceries. Dirty dishes were in the sink, the orange juice was left out. The mail was on the kitchen island, along with half a dozen dead cans of energy drink. He had a list of chores that was still there, stuck on the refrigerator, held in place by a yellow flower magnet. And all he did was grab the mail.

She didn't bother setting down the groceries. Instead, she went to his bedroom and kicked the door open, expecting to find him hunched over a laptop or dumping his brain in that virtual reality headset, slack-jawed and stupid. This would be the last time.

She was right about that.

The gunshot sound of the door smacking the wall would make

him scream. He'd start promising to clean up, like always, swear that he lost track of time, like always. He didn't know her shift was over. Was it morning already? Sunny was going to break some shit.

She dropped the milk instead.

There was a thing around his head. It wasn't a chunky headset or VR goggles. It looked new and dangerous. She'd never seen it before. A ghostly shiver pulled the short hairs on her neck.

"Grey?"

His arm was tacky; his shirt sour. His chest was slowly rising and falling, long and methodical. She hesitated to touch him, afraid his flesh would be room temperature. Instead, he was feverish.

"Grey? Honey?" she whispered. "What are you doing?"

She tapped his chin, traced his cheeks. His eyes didn't jitter beneath the lids; lips didn't twitch. That thing around his head, she didn't know what it was—a hefty knob centered between his eyes, his brown hair curling around a thick strap holding it snug. A cable was plugged into the knob and ran beneath the bed. Black equipment was hidden in the corner, lights blinking, drives breathing. She didn't know what the box was or the thing on his head, but she knew the symbol embossed on them.

"No. No, no, no."

She held up her phone, thumb over the glass. She'd heard rumors about the symbol, that it was not wise to search about comatose teenagers and malicious knobs connecting their foreheads to modded computers. People listened closely to those searches. What people, she didn't know. The police, the feds, or someone worse, it didn't matter.

She needed that thing off his head.

She deconstructed his bedroom, kicking dirty clothes, pouring desk drawers on the floor, turning over milk crates and boxes of discarded gear. His desk was cluttered with empty cups and plates with dried ketchup. A pile of papers of a scattered research project on something called Foreverland.

A wristwatch was balanced on a tin box, the digital numbers

turning over. Masking tape was wrapped around the band, small letters stenciled in black marker. *For Mom.* It was how he labeled his presents. Last Christmas it was a cuckoo clock in a plastic bag, tape pressed on the side.

For Mom.

The tin box rattled onto the floor. It was his old vape pen holder with weird stickers of a serpent eating its own tail. The vape pen was on the desk, a shiny metal pipe that looked dangerous. She thought he'd quit after her nuclear meltdown a year ago.

She paced the room and dialed. "Pick up, Donny. Pick up, pick up, pick up—"

"I'm off the clock, Grimm."

"Donny, come over, now." She could hear him sucking on the long end of a hookah. "Donny?"

"I'm waiting for the punch line." His words were smoke-filled.

"I need you here, now."

"Use a hairbrush or a showerhead or whatever works down there, Grimm."

"Stop—" Her hair was too short to grab. "Just listen to me. I'm calling you a car."

"Why?"

"I don't want to *talk* about this on the phone." Her lips pulled into a thin line.

"Why can't you talk?"

"What don't you understand, Donny?"

"You're on the phone talking and you can't talk is what I don't understand."

She breathed into the phone, a wounded animal not to be mistaken for one in heat. Donny would be the last person to call to get laid.

"Goddamn it." He sighed.

Sunny killed the connection. She picked up the half-empty milk jug and closed the bedroom door to put the groceries away and start some coffee. Pretending her son wasn't a breathing funeral display, she lit a vanilla-scented candle and went for the aspirin above the stove.

The time was flashing three o'clock.

The mail was on the counter. An empty package was left open, the address label ripped off. No return address. No invoice, no instructions.

She went back into his bedroom, hoping this was a dream, that he'd be sitting at his desk. She would hug him even if he was packing a bong. Everything needed perspective. She came back to the kitchen with his phone, laptop and the silver pipe. A tiny light glowed as she sucked a blue cloud of cherry menthol. The urge to vomit swelled in her throat.

She took another hit.

His browser history was clean. The email log was empty. His phone was locked and she didn't know the code. It wouldn't matter. What was she going to do, call a random friend?

Hi, this is Sunny Grimm. Grey's mom. Yeah, have you guys been experimenting with awareness leaping wetware in, say, the last twelve to twenty-four hours? Oh, Grey is sleeping, I just thought I'd ask. No worries. Please don't tell your parents or call the police.

Who was she kidding? Grey didn't have friends except for Rachel and she hadn't been around lately. Her son was a loner bored with school. He wasn't much crazy about people in general.

Nut, meet tree.

It was all the same reasons Sunny had quit medical school. Well, she'd stopped going in the first semester, so she was hardly a med student. It was a career plan that didn't make much sense for her. She needed something that minimized human contact, someplace she could get paid to push a button. She had lowered the bar until it lay on the floor. Sound choice-making was not a skill set she'd acquired.

Sunny did everything on her own because no one did anything for her. Never had.

Maybe she deserved it.

The world isn't going to hell. It's already there.

She cleaned her face, washing off the smell of third shift, a plastic odor that followed her home. The yellow bandana around her neck smelled salty. Three stories below, the asphalt shone with brake lights. Her streaked reflection looked back through a haze of cherry menthol. What few tears survived childhood had dried up in a sexless marriage.

The sky cried for her.

Her eyes stared from sunken pockets, verdant green with light spokes radiating from large pupils. Her graying hair was cut near the scalp. A horizontal scar was high on her forehead, just below the hairline—a jagged gash that was more Jack Rippperish than Harry Potterish. It was where her uncle dropped her, or where she fell off her bike, or was bitten by a dog. No one really knew.

She vaped and watched cars pass through watery lines as she strapped the digital watch on her wrist, leaving the masking tape in place. The old pawnshop cuckoo clock Grey had bought her for Christmas was stuck.

She didn't bother winding it.

Donny arrived thirty minutes later. Or maybe it was an hour. Time was warped from the heat of desperation, stretched and pummeled until it stood still or raced past. Sunny watched him through the distorted window, rain slashing his grizzly frame crawling out of the compact automobile.

He grunted when she opened the front door.

Sunny stepped aside, eyes pried wide, heavy words stuck on the back of her tongue. She pointed at the bedroom. Donny, half-lidded and unshaven, smelling of spiced apple and peppermint, dragged his feet through the apartment. He was weary when he arrived, grumbling when he walked inside. He never went straight home after third shift, not even after a double. It was straight to the café for a hookah to calm the nerves. Now he was wide-eyed. Almost hyperventilating.

"Holy shit."

He stood in the doorway, fingers fluttering over his mouth. Somewhere in those thick whiskers, his tongue darted over his lips, something he did when he was in trouble at work.

He hit a soggy spot of milk, looked at his shoe, and kicked a pile of clothes. She told him to look under the bed. A few minutes later, he came out with a velvet bag with a loose gold drawstring.

"Where's the box?" he said.

"Box?"

He pointed at the mail. Sunny stepped away. He studied the torn label, turning it over. The velvet bag in his hand was empty. No tag, no logo.

"You better sit down."

"What the hell is going on, Donny?"

He took the pipe from her and sucked on it hard. Thin clouds streamed from his nostrils. He nodded, pulling a deeper drag.

"A punch, Grimm."

"What?"

"That thing around his head..."

She knew it. Just needed to hear someone say it out loud, confirming this wasn't a dream. Awareness leaping was more alluring than any drug invented by God or human, a new addiction that never gave back its victims. Twelve-step programs didn't exist for it.

Wealthy addicts used submersion tanks and respirators, sensory manipulators that drew them into a lucid dream as real as the rug under her feet. When the dream was over, they were hoisted out and returned to the skin. Some claimed it was nothing more than a recreational addiction. A good time. Drinks with friends, a day trip to fantasyland.

Most people couldn't afford tanks. There were places that leased trips, but those were inaccessible and legally questionable. There were other ways to get there, one-way tickets that transported the awareness through a cable and left the body behind.

Heart still beating.

"How can this be?" she whispered.

"It's automated." Donny tapped the package. "Grey must've known someone to have it shipped to him. You don't just order this online. Even if you get one, it's the access—"

"That's not what I mean." She raked her scalp. "This is my fault. This is all my fault. I never should've—"

"He's eighteen, Grimm. He's not a kid."

She started walking. The urge to destroy the apartment tremored in her joints; the compulsion to drive her elbow into something clenched her fists. She needed something to blame, something to punch.

Besides herself.

"What are we going to do?" she said.

"Not be hasty, that's one. You were right not to talk about it on the phone. That's a hot word." He tapped his forehead, referring to the symbol on Grey's forehead more than the punch. "The government listens for it. And don't search about this on the Internet just yet."

"And just sit here?"

"For now, yeah. You can search his room—"

"For what, Donny? An off switch? A fucking suicide note?"

"Keep your voice down." He handed her the pipe. "Listen, this is illegal. You need to think about every move you make right now. It ain't easy to escape. Come up with some generic search words for an Internet search, something that sounds like research or game play."

"It ain't easy to escape? Escape what, Donny? What are you talking about?"

"What do you think I'm talking about?" He jabbed at his forehead, referring to the punch that had emptied her son's head.

"Oh, God. I'm a horrible parent, a terrible mother. Oh God, oh God—"

"You're not a terrible mother, Grimm. You can't isolate him from the world. He was going to do something like this sooner or later.

They all do, they're kids, stupid as hell. I'm surprised he made it to eighteen."

She rubbed her face, a spring suddenly welling up. She swallowed it back and clenched her teeth. "I just want him back. I don't give a damn what happens to me, just... we got to get him out, find help."

Donny sighed. He didn't answer that. *Because people don't come back from this.*

"What am I going to do?"

"I know someone from the Glass Jar," Donny said.

"The gay bar?"

"Yeah, the gay bar. Let me make a call. Keep this quiet for now, see what our options are, all right? Stay off the computer and phone until we get some answers."

She nodded blankly.

"People make it out, Grimm. They do."

That was what you tell people to help them shoulder the impossible weight of hopelessness. Donny would talk to someone and Grey would make it back to the skin and everything would go back to normal. Sunny would sit down with her son, tell him how worried she was, how he needed to live a better life, a happier life. He needed to stop doing bad things.

Because that's exactly how parenting works.

Donny made a call, speaking in hushed tones. At one point, he giggled and made a promise, bargaining for counsel on behalf of Sunny. It sounded more like a date. They ripped through all the ecig fluid waiting for whomever he called. Donny went back into Grey's bedroom in search of more.

A second pot of coffee was cooling when someone tapped on the door. He was short, very short, and wearing a beret that was stupid. His facial hair was tightly clipped. Sunny was hunched on the kitchen stool, her knee fueled on adrenaline and several charges of ecigs. Donny helped him with his coat and held his beret, introducing him to Sunny.

Neither of them said anything. Not even a nod.

Then the short, stout man walked like a royal asshole into the bedroom and tiptoed around the dirty clothes. From the kitchen it looked like he was studying an abstract sculpture, as if he were there on behalf of a collector. Then he blurted into the hand holding up his chin, "Is he an idiot?"

The stool fell behind Sunny. She launched herself at the bedroom. Donny roadblocked the doorway, hands up. His little friend had squatted down to examine the black knob on Grey's forehead, peering from three angles, leaning in to give it two quick sniffs.

"No stent, no medical support. No bedsore prevention." He wiped his palms on his thighs. "This is suicide."

Sunny shoved into the room and snatched the back of his sleeveless vest, the tendons springing from her wrist. She was aiming for his ponytail but had a firm grip on the slick fabric, not sure what to do next. On his toes, he was almost to her chin.

"Donny," he said, "calm your friend."

"Ax?" she said. "Your name is Ax?"

"You can let go, Mother. I'm here to help."

"Then stuff the snipe and tell me what the hell to do."

Donny put his hand on Sunny's arm and lowered his friend with the fake name to the carpet. She retreated to the doorway. The little man cleared his throat, brushed the wrinkles from his vest and fluffed his ponytail.

"I'm sorry for being so blunt," he said. "I didn't think there was time for sweet talk. What your son did was stupid."

"Just tell me what to do."

"Right." He looked around the room. "You did the right thing, by the way. This is illegal, I'm sure you know. He's in your house, under your supervision. All of this equipment will get you fined, maybe worse."

"I don't care."

He squatted by the bed. "How'd he get the needle?"

"The needle?"

"The one that is currently in his brain."

Needle. So far it was just a knobby strap that kidnapped her son. The image of a needle piercing his forehead kicked at the back of her knees.

"I… I don't know. I've never seen it before."

Ax looked up at Donny.

"It came in the mail," Donny said.

"The mail? Curious." Still on his haunches, he bounced on the balls of his feet. "Shipped here, then?"

"The address was ripped off," Sunny said.

"Why would he hide the address?"

"Does it matter?" she said. "Focus on right now. What are we going to do?"

"You keep saying *we*."

"Me, goddamnit! Me! What am *I* going to do?" She kicked the door against the wall. She'd been asking that cursed question all her life. *What am I going to do now?*

"Can you get me some coffee?" Ax said.

"No."

He looked up. Donny went to the kitchen. He came back with a mug of tepid coffee and a splash of creamer. Ax pulled a chair from Grey's desk to sit, but not before wiping it with a balled-up shirt. He pushed a few items on the desk with a pencil and tapped the tin can with the stickers, the snake eating its tail.

"It's called a punch," he said.

"I know what it's called."

"Well, then you know in order to get one, you have to be invited. They don't sell them online."

Sunny crossed her arms.

"It arrived in a plain box, right? Inside was a velvet bag and that was it." He sipped. "You won't find a return address, no way to track it. I'll give your son this, as idiotic as that is right there, he was smart enough to know someone with enough connections to the…" He tapped his forehead like Donny had done. This time he didn't mean the needle. *The symbol.* "Are you rich?"

"Does it look like it?"

"Then you must know players."

"Players?"

Ax sniffed a quick glance at Donny. His uppity nature was going to get his head buried in the wall.

"Players," he said slowly, "means the *game.*"

He touched his forehead again. Even in conversation, he didn't want to say it out loud, as if someone could be listening to them in her shitbox apartment.

"You don't sign up to play the *game,* Ms. Grimm. You don't log on or make an account. You have to be invited. You have to know people to invite you. And then you need lots of money to accept the invitation. You see a pattern?"

"You think..." She swallowed. "He's in the *game*?"

She wasn't going to touch her forehead. Up to that point, she'd assumed he was just awareness leaping with some insidious gear, one that licked the frontal lobe with a surgical steel tongue. *But the game?* She'd ignored the symbol, hoping it was just gear.

She could hardly stand.

"If it was something else, like a VR headbox or channel glasses, you know, something he could just take off, then of course he wouldn't be in the game. But he's got a needle in his head, Ms. Grimm. That's total commitment. I don't smell any gel, so he didn't sterilize. He just strapped on and punched in before you got home. Before you could talk some sense into him, I'm guessing."

"Why would he do this?" she whispered to herself.

"For the money, I suppose."

"What?"

"Immediate family collects the player's winnings, win or lose."

"You think I care about money?"

The grim line drawn between her lips erased any sharp retorts that he was entertaining. Instead, he scooted to the edge of the chair, leaned forward and spoke in a softer tone.

"He's not there anymore. We can't just peel the straps off and uncork him like a bottle of wine. That needle sucked him out of his body, through that cable and into some distant network. That's not a short trip. What I'm saying is I don't think he planned on coming back, Ms. Grimm."

"Where is he?"

Ax flicked a glance at Donny.

"Stop looking at him or I'll hang you on a hook. Where's my son? If he's not in his body, where is he?"

The little man didn't answer. Donny sighed.

She swallowed a hard knot. "Are you saying he... he's in the Maze?"

"Don't say that." Ax pointed a stubby finger. "That's the last time you say it out loud, you understand? You want that thing off his head, then you need to be very careful. You start asking questions, start throwing around words, people start listening. You think this *game* has been around for all this time because people are nice?"

He put the mug on the desk.

"I'm sorry, but your son chose to go down a very dark alley, Ms. Grimm. He's not a child; he didn't get kidnapped or lost. He sought that thing out, talked to the right people, had it shipped, put it on his head and went there knowing exactly where it would take him and what reward it would get him. Or get you, I should say."

"What did you say?"

Donny intercepted her before she took a step. The little man retrieved his coffee without flinching.

"I'm not insinuating you had anything to do with this, Ms. Grimm. Others might not see it that way, being that you will inherit a small fortune from your son's mischief."

"No one has contacted me."

"Yet. There are a lot of moving parts to fall in place. Investors reward the players handsomely. It's an illegal game, a felony in most countries, but it doesn't stop them from making money. There is a rich undercurrent beneath the Internet of all things, Ms. Grimm, one where you can get anything or anyone to do what you want. Currently, access to watch the game is highly coveted."

Donny put his arm around her. She walked off, didn't want to be touched, and stood over her boy, her eighteen-year-old son, lying in the bed where he grew up.

"This is his fault, just so we're clear," Ax said. "Your son did this. No one can be forced to play. Only the willing enter the game, Ms. Grimm. He made the choice."

"I know," she said. "I know."

Donny muttered to his friend. She imagined he was gesturing for him to tone it down. He'd heard that tone from her before, when she'd just had enough, was on the verge of dropping everything and walking out, leaving her car in the garage and just walking until her legs gave out. Or drilling the first dipshit to say the wrong thing.

"Look," Ax started, "this *game*... it's complicated. I don't know how much you know or how much you want to know, but I suggest you don't go looking. It's a gambling empire, but instead of taking your mortgage, it eats your mind, a modern-day version of feeding peasants to the lions, only worse. At least the peasants died. People in the game don't come back the same. Your boy has decided it was worth the risk. Maybe it's better he doesn't survive. You won't like who comes back."

"The one who wins comes back," Donny said.

"There's a... a winner?" she said.

"He's not going to win, Ms. Grimm."

She brushed her son's hair, careful not to touch the knob. "So what do I do?"

"Not the police," Ax said. "The people that run the game are everywhere. They have ears in the government and spies in law enforcement. Personally, I think they were behind making the game illegal, lending it a certain edge of danger that cranked up the demand. The authorities bust a lab every now and again, but that's just for show. If you go to the police, they'll only make it harder for you. There's even a chance they've been listening to us ever since you blurted out the word."

Maze.

"Is that why you're using the name Ax?" she said.

He shrugged.

She chuckled drily. Life was like this. The best she could hope for was a long, boring life and to die without drama, without happiness or sadness. She had found peace working at a manufacturing plant, chose third shift so she didn't have to see many faces, hired Donny because he was gay and there would be no chance of romance.

Maybe I deserve this.

"So what then?" she asked.

"I know a place you can get started, but you'll need to do it now. Your boy isn't going to last long like that unless you know how to insert an IV."

"Where?" She towered over him.

"You'll need money."

"Okay."

"Lots of it."

"Are you fleecing me, Ax?"

"I don't want the money. I'm just pointing the way."

"You're not taking a cut?"

He jumped out of the chair and wandered past Donny with the mug hooked on his finger. "If I wanted a cut," he called from the kitchen, "I would've already taken your money. I'm just telling you the truth about your boy. And I want nothing to do with this after I leave."

A scribble of a pen, the tearing of paper. He returned with a scrap folded between his fingers.

"I only came here as a favor." He looked up at Donny.

Then he left the apartment, taking the black umbrella propped on the wall and quietly closing the door. He was whistling as he left.

Sunny deflated, the paper still folded on the desk.

"Do you need money?" Donny asked.

"No. You've already done enough."

"I don't mind—"

"No, Donny. No, thank you."

She toyed with the paper, needed to make a decision, needed to get moving. The clock on the stove wasn't working, but the one on her son's forehead was ticking.

"Maybe you should tell Henk," he said.

Another dry chuckle. The police was a better idea than her ex-husband. Everything was a better idea. She wanted Henk out of her life no matter what. So did her son.

"Maybe we should go to the police?" he said.

"*We?*"

"Ax is a little over the top, likes a good conspiracy. It's just, he's short and gay, likes to push buttons. You know the type. The police aren't going to arrest you, Grimm. I know a lawyer."

She opened the note and read the address. "Can I ask a favor?"

"Yeah."

"Will you stay with Grey? You can sleep in my room, get some rest. I just want someone here in case he, uh..."

"Of course." He pulled her against him, the curly hair poking out from his open collar tickling her cheek. "It'll be all right, Grimm."

No, Donny. It's not all right. It never was.

[2]

Sunny
After the Punch

Sunny took cover beneath an uptown pawnshop. The rain raised gooseflesh along her arms. The buildings disappeared in a gray pall that continued to weep.

Cars honked as her driver pulled back into traffic. Puddles crashed on the sidewalk in waves. She huddled against the wall with a shred of paper damp in her palm. The address matched the storefront across the street. Ax had written a name as well, which she had assumed was a person. Maybe it was a business or a studio. There was no name on the glass wall that exposed the room inside. There was just a number stenciled in white.

511.

Track lights illuminated off-white walls. From this side of the street, it looked like an empty dance studio.

Why was she listening to a guy named Ax? And how would he

know the survival odds of someone with a needle in their head? The fact was this: he couldn't know less than Sunny.

Desperation makes fools of us all.

Branches sagged on street trees trapped in sidewalk planting boxes. The traffic was as relentless as the rain. She timed her escape and hit a small gap in traffic. She leaped beneath the blue 511 awning and shivered outside the door, shaking the rain off her head like a dog. Her work shirt stuck to her back.

The glass door provided a view of the open room. Half a dozen products were stationed along the walls. There was no name on the door, just the number. No bell when she opened it, no buzzer or signal. Just the silent swish of the hinges. The door sealed out the traffic behind her. Her shirt dripped on the bamboo floor.

"Hello?"

A white door was on the far side of the room. Two of the walls displayed tech gear and ongoing video adverts for surgical implants and sensory augments, the kind that were susceptible to hacking and body-jacking, the sort of thing a vendor wouldn't admit to.

The wall to her left displayed the address in raised, backlit numbers and letters that matched the sopping paper scrap in her hand.

"Can someone help me?"

Her shoes squished. There was only one other item in the room. Not a desk or register, just a simple stand that held a stack of postcards. The address, once again, was printed in the center, the font small and thin.

511 South Forest
Find a way to please yourself.

THE CARD WAS THICK, the corners sharp. No information was on the back except for thick, random lines, like the printer had made a mistake. It contrasted with the minimalist design, everything so orderly and planned.

The white door opened.

A woman closed it quietly and carefully. Like the card contrasting with the room's décor, the woman's black skin was sharply displayed against her ivory white dress. Lips painted red as her nails, she approached with long, even steps.

"Do you have an appointment?" she said with an accent.

Sunny cleared her throat. "Micah," she whispered.

The woman didn't answer, didn't step away. She only cocked her head with a silent question. Sunny took her hand, the fingers long and slick with lotion, and pushed the damp wad of paper into it.

"Are you Micah?"

The woman didn't respond.

"I need help." Sunny's whisper bounced around the room. "Someone told me... he said Micah could help me."

The woman slowly opened the paper, staring for several seconds before folding it four times and placing the tight square in Sunny's hand.

"Is he here?" Sunny asked.

A smile haunted the woman's painted lips.

"What do you... do you want something?" Sunny stepped closer and leaned in. "I have an eighteen-year-old son that's in trouble. He has taken a, uh, a punch to play a... play the *game*."

The woman twitched.

"Can you help me?"

There was no response. No rejection. Barely a recognition of what she was saying. Sunny dug into her pocket.

"He said it would cost me. I don't have money right now, but I can get it. I do have these though."

She pried open the lid. Holo lenses floated in clear solution. They belonged to her employer—circuited contact lenses that enhanced her vision and retrieved information. If someone else put them in their eyes, such as non-coded personnel outside the company, they would shut off and a signal would be sent to her superiors. She would be fired. They weren't cheap and the right people could recode them.

"Use this as a down payment, please. I just need to talk to someone. My son needs help."

The woman cupped her hand, snapped the lid closed and pushed the offering back. Her eyes were severely lined. She turned with the same even stride and walked back to the white door.

Sunny continued to drip.

She waited for her to return as the cold soaked past her flesh and into her bones. The shivers turned into shakes. Traffic silently passed outside, puddles swelling on the sidewalks. She turned around when the sound of an opening door echoed in the open room, but the door was still closed. No one had returned to help.

When she turned back toward traffic, the ghostly image of an old homeless woman looked at her, a plastic chrysanthemum tucked in her hat. She was desperate for help, begging for attention, as if she had something to say and just needed to be heard. *Please listen.*

Sunny Grimm was looking at her reflection.

She was lifeless. A haunted ghost trying to escape the present, running from a damaged past that rattled like tin cans. Her history was a long train of railroad containers following her to the end, each day getting longer and heavier. If she could just pull the lynchpin and leave them behind, start a new life, lay a set of tracks in another direction, one that wasn't heading for a cliff.

She would never look back.

Was that what Grey felt? Did he feel the weight of his family inheritance, the genetic disposition that brought so many of her relatives to their knees? Her father ate a bullet. The father before that used a rope.

Is that why he took the punch? Is he trying to unhitch the past and lay new tracks?

Maybe he wasn't in the Maze, just using the punch to change his life. There were transformative therapies that reorganized thought patterns and turned off self-destructive genes. They were known to be invasive and effective, but none that came in a do-it-yourself kit.

But the symbol...

She dialed a number. The call ticked over to Donny's voicemail. He would be crashed on the couch by now. It was well past bedtime.

Sunny walked to the white door and quietly turned the handle. It wouldn't open. When another ten minutes passed, she knocked. Politely, at first.

"I need help," she called. "I need to see Micah."

The thick door absorbed her blows. She kicked it.

"Help me, someone. He's all alone. He doesn't have much time and I need help. He's in the Maze. Someone told me you can help my son. I need to know if—"

The door pushed back.

The woman stepped out forcefully, a long cool breeze exhaling from behind her like that of a concrete warehouse. It was pungent, clawing at her sinuses, stinging her throat. Sunny's eyes itched and she was suddenly nauseous.

It seems so familiar.

"I'm sorry, you've been misinformed." Her accent was thick, South African maybe. "There is no Micah for you to see. We have no affiliation with black-market wares. We are a federally licensed retailer of sensory augments."

"He said you could—"

"If what you say is true, you need to go directly to the police. Go there now because this is very serious. Your son will need help as soon as possible."

"He'll be in trouble."

"There's more at risk than legal trouble, ma'am."

Sunny backed away. It was suddenly clear how stupid she was. Why would she listen to a stranger like Ax, let him fill her head with conspiracy and urban legend, wasting precious time on secret societies?

Sunny backed into the pedestal. Stiff white cards sprayed over the bamboo floor, some sticking in small puddles. Random black lines bled across the backs of them. She ran onto the sidewalk before the South African woman insisted she clean them up.

The rain soaked her once again.

Sunny dialed as she ran down the sidewalk. First for a car to pick her up, then Donny. When he didn't answer, she called the police. She would take them to the apartment; she would show them her son and the punch.

The symbol that would betray them both.

She was ready for that, prepared to accept the consequences, fines that left her homeless or a stretch in jail. She'd take the police to her apartment, give herself up for her son. Only they wouldn't find him when they got there.

There's more to risk than legal trouble.

[3]

SUNNY
After the Punch

THE BED WAS EMPTY.

The room was still the same—dirty clothes and tipped boxes, the desk buried beneath papers, the tin box where she left it. The pillow was fluffed, the corners tucked in as if no one had ever lain on it, no one had ever slept in it. No one had used a punch.

The second she walked in her apartment, she knew it. It felt different. Smelled odd. It was the same scent that had wafted out of the back room of 511, the nasty sting in her nose.

The kitchen was still a mess. The orange juice was on the counter, the empty box and velvet bag. She thought, for a moment, this was all a joke, that Grey had woken up to peel that thing off his head and together he and Donny went for breakfast. Maybe they'd left a message or sent a text she never received.

Donny still wasn't answering the phone.

This is a dream. She propped herself in the doorway. *A fucking nightmare.* The seconds fell around her like radioactive snowflakes, stripped her of hope, and left her naked and exposed.

Grey's phone was on the desk. His phone never left his pocket or his hand, and there it was on the desk, squared in the corner, screen black. She thought she'd left it in the kitchen. Maybe Donny put it there. It requested a passcode when she touched the screen.

How long have I been gone? Hours felt like days, even years. Already the memory of her son was fading, the details of his face dusty with time.

"Ma'am?" Officer Blake stepped into the room. "Is there anything else?"

Sunny couldn't even shake her head.

"You need to understand the severity of filing a false report—"

"It wasn't false. He was here, in his bed. This is all..."

"Okay. We can still file a missing persons report, but you'll have to come back to the station. Unfortunately, the rest of your story just doesn't hold up. There's no evidence your son was tampering with the Maze."

Sunny scrambled to the bed. The computer beneath it was gone. No lights, no cable. *No evidence.*

"Maze activity is a felony. If your son was involved in any way, he can be prosecuted. You'll be held accountable, too, Mrs. Grimm. This is your apartment."

She leaned on the bed, unsure if she could stand.

"Mrs. Grimm?"

"I understand."

Officer Blake looked at his partner then back again. "You want to file a missing persons report?"

"No. No, he might be at a friend's house. I'm... I'm sorry. I panicked this morning. I work a lot of late shifts and..." She rubbed her face. "Maybe I wasn't seeing things right."

"You sure it wasn't a VR headset?" the partner called from the kitchen.

"Yeah, maybe," she said. "I don't know."

"We'll have to include this in our report," Officer Blake said.

"Of course."

"Sunny Marie Jones?"

"What?"

"That's your name." His thumbs were poised over his phone.

"No, Jones is my maiden name... I gave all that information at the station."

Officer Blake cleared his throat and nodded at his partner. He said something, maybe it was goodbye or his contact information. Sunny didn't process anything but the front door closing. And the crushing silence.

The apartment spoke loud and clear.

She knew what she had seen that morning. She wasn't dreaming, wasn't hallucinating. She didn't need a note to explain what had happened since she left that morning. The ominous warnings were clear. *There's more to risk than legal trouble.*

And now Donny was involved.

She wouldn't forgive herself if something happened to him. She didn't know much about the Maze, just that it was a black-market sport that dealt with virtual realities that destroyed the losers and sometimes the winners, a virtual game of Russian roulette.

Grey's phone vibrated. The screen lit up. It was a text.

You all right? It was his girlfriend, Rachel.

Sunny swiped the text. She didn't need a passcode to reply, but her thumbs hovered in place. *Where is he? Do you know about the Maze? Did you break up? Is he okay? What the hell is happening?*

The phone went blank. The text vanished. Her opportunity to reply had passed. She didn't know Rachel's phone number, didn't have it in her phone. And Rachel was his only friend.

That she knew of.

Sunny tried to grab her hair. It was why she had started shaving it, to keep from pulling it out on bad days. She began pacing. The floor rocked with turbulence, as if the building was hitting air pockets. She needed food. Needed sleep. Needed a moment.

There was no time for any of that.

The window was cold. The spatter of rain rattled in her head. The cops were still parked at the curb, standing at open car doors.

Grey's phone vibrated again.

She ran to the bedroom, would answer Rachel this time, write all the questions in one long text and hit send. But it wasn't from her. An unknown sender's message was simple.

Leave the apartment now.

She almost dropped the phone. *Who is this?* she texted back. Before hitting send, she added, *Where is my son?*

Sunny waited for an answer. The logo suddenly appeared. The phone spontaneously shut off. She pushed the button, held it down, and shook it. It had plenty of charge a minute ago, but she plugged it in anyway.

It was dead.

She had to call Henk. She was an incompetent mother, a head case, an emotional plane crash. Fine. She just wanted her son back, wanted him safe. Even if her ex-husband claimed a victory, let him have it.

But her phone was dead, too. "What the hell?"

The police were in their car now. Turn signal on, they merged into traffic. Another car quickly filled the empty spot. A black umbrella emerged from an open door.

Sunny paced again, her breath coming in short stabs. The floor continued to sway, the swales deep and mysterious. She was going under a wave of panic, drowning in a sea of dreaded emotion. She just needed a moment to think, clear her head, see a direction. The police were no help. Micah and 511 weren't either. And Donny. *Where are you, Donny?*

A soft rap on the door.

She stopped too suddenly and almost crumpled. There was silence and rain. Then another knock.

Sunny tiptoed to the door, she didn't know why, and peeked through the eyehole. A short old woman was getting ready to knock again. She was hunched over from a lifetime of gravity, a floral silk scarf around her head and dark sunglasses the size of coasters.

Sunny looked around the chain lock. "Yes?"

"I'm sorry to bother you, dear, but you have a call."

"What?"

"There's someone on the phone."

Sunny didn't talk to her neighbors much. This wasn't the sort of building where people mingled. But in all the time she'd lived there, the apartment across the hall was always quiet. She'd always thought, for some reason, it was empty.

The door was ajar. A Siamese cat watched from inside the dark apartment, a little bell around its neck.

"Did you see anything this morning? Did anyone come to the apartment while I was gone? Did you see anyone leave?"

The old woman's cheeks turned a paler shade. "Um, no."

She seemed unsure if the old woman understood the question or just didn't hear it. She shuffled a stack of mail and dropped an envelope. It fluttered into the narrow slot of Sunny's open door.

She picked it up. "You're Mrs. Jones?"

"I am."

"Have you seen anyone strange on the floor?"

"There's someone on the phone, dear."

"I'm sorry?"

"Someone called for you."

Sunny swallowed a knot before it broke open. She opened the door and looked in both directions, placing the fallen envelope in Mrs. Jones's knobby hands. "Someone called... *for me*?"

"They want to talk to you."

Mrs. Jones tightened the scarf around her head and pulled it behind her dark glasses. Sunny held onto the door and looked down the empty hallway, half expecting it to shrink.

"Who is it?" Sunny asked. "A man or a boy?"

She was afraid to let go, afraid the door to her apartment would slam shut and never let her back in. Everything was about to change. Her life would be completely closed.

There's nothing back there anyway.

That was what it felt like. Someone had turned her life inside out. She could move on now, start a new life.

If they just didn't take my son.

Mrs. Jones scooped up the Siamese and waited. Sunny started across the hall, a sneeze greeting her inside the thick air. Heavy drapes blocked the sunlight. What little light seeped around the edges was diffuse.

Half a dozen lamps shed yellowish light on the clutter. Cat hair floated through the brightest spots. The couches were hidden beneath discarded magazines and old newspapers, boxes of empty tissues and piles of knitted scarves. Somewhere a vanilla-scented air freshener was battling a litter box.

"The phone is in the kitchen." Mrs. Jones scratched the Siamese cat. "It doesn't stretch in here."

It was a phone as vintage as the old woman. The spiral cord was knotted worse than a ball of yarn. Sunny held her face near the receiver.

"Hello? Grey, is that you?" The silence was final. "Hello? Who's there?"

Only her voice answered back. She turned to Mrs. Jones and asked, "Was it a man that called?"

"It was someone."

"Like my son?"

"It was sort of soft but short. I think you were calling from far away."

You? Mrs. Jones was the cat lady they wrote about on postcards, the one with an endless selection of scarves to wrap around her head. A person that wasn't quite in touch with the world outside.

"Far away?" Sunny said.

"The voice was small. It used to be that way when I was little, when someone called from across the country. Their voice was very small. I used to pretend it was someone calling from the future."

The Siamese purred as she stroked her belly, the bell jingling on its collar. Two more cats entered the room, rubbing beneath the old woman's robe. She told them to be patient, it wasn't their turn.

There was a knock on the door.

Mrs. Jones didn't hear it, her arthritic fingers crawling through the Siamese's fur. Once again, Sunny walked on her tiptoes and stood near the door. The knock came again, but not on Mrs. Jones's apartment. Looking through the spyhole, a man was at her apartment. His overcoat was black and beaded with rain. A hood was pulled over his head.

His shoulders were broad, the gloved hand thick; he rapped on apartment 300, Sunny's apartment, where the door would swell in the summer and the bottom was scuffed from kicking it open.

She assumed it was a man.

Sunny's hand rested on the doorknob. He might know something about Grey. Or maybe he took him and was here to offer a way to bring him back. She was about to open the door—

"They said to stay." Mrs. Jones had fallen on the couch.

"What?"

"The one on the phone. They said to stay here."

"Why didn't you tell me that?" Sunny whispered.

Despite the claustrophobic apartment, Sunny's mind had cleared. When she walked back to the door, the floor didn't teeter. The man was gone. Two damp footsteps faded at the foot of the door.

"Did they say anything else?" Sunny repeated the question while spying on the empty hallway. She thought the old woman might have fallen asleep.

"Find me."

Sunny turned. "What?"

"That's what they said. Find me."

Ice water flooded her legs. She made it to the empty couch before collapsing on a heap of knitted scarves. She would wait a few minutes on the couch. Maybe the person would call back. The dregs of third shift caught up with her. The room entered a cycle that spun her into a dead sleep.

SHE DREAMED OF NEEDLES.

Big dull needles prodded her to run on legs too fat, too numb. If she could reach up and pull the needle from her head, the one that pierced the frontal lobe, she could wake up.

Or maybe leave the needle in. Because that's where he is. He's inside the needle. And I need to find him.

Sunny rolled into the pain and stared at fatigued green fabric, breathing through a coarse blanket filled with dust mites and a layer of shed fur. Knitting needles were driving into her side. They clattered on the carpet.

The lamps were off.

A nightlight drove shadows across the littered floor. The pale light of early morning slipped past the thick drapes, the patter of rain against the window. Sleep still dusted her mind, blotting out the past and sun-bleached memories. She was steeped in dullness as cats stirred somewhere. There was a distant memory of the digital watch beeping in the middle of the night, the masking tape pulling at the hairs on her wrist.

As the pale light faded around the window to become fully gray, the details of the cramped apartment reminded her where she was.

And why.

A clock sat on a bookshelf loaded with DVDs and empty picture frames. It was three o'clock, but the diffuse light looked more like early morning. She'd slept through the night.

She'd missed her shift.

Her supervisor would have called her phone, which was in her apartment. And dead. His message would go straight to voicemail, where it would wait for eternity. Maybe he would ask Donny what happened and he would tell him and they would forgive her.

But Donny won't be there, either.

Hopelessness smothered her. Mrs. Jones would find her corpse when digging for her needles. She would call the police and they would bury her without a tear.

"What do you want from me?" she said.

She didn't believe in an all-seeing entity, not Greek or Roman or Christian, because if there was a God, then she had no reason to bend a knee to his cruel sense of humor. She didn't deserve this. Still, she was talking.

So she must believe in something.

She could call Henk, find Grey's girlfriend or try the police again. But none of that would explain the phone calls, the prescient demand to come to Mrs. Jones's apartment when someone came looking for her.

She dug into her pocket and opened a wadded piece of paper. Micah wasn't available and the South African woman wasn't about to speak with her again. But Sunny knew where she could get more answers. With the right amount of prodding, someone could tell her who Micah was and why she needed to find him.

She peeked through the spyhole before opening the door. She walked through her apartment, where everything was exactly the same, the hopeful glimmer this was all a dream going to its final resting place. Sunny left nothing behind that mattered. Grey was out there.

A short, little man was going to help find him.

[4]

Hunter
After the Punch

A white-haired woman sat in the office.

The detective was typing, taking her statement or just flat out ignoring her.

Hunter shook his umbrella and tucked it into his leather bag. He checked the time, ignored the unread emails and scrolled through the weather back home, where it wasn't raining.

The plane ride had been bumpy; the seat wouldn't recline. He felt he'd been away from home too long, even though he'd just arrived in this sad city. His phone buzzed.

Who is this? was the text.

The number seemed familiar, but there was no texting history. He was about to respond (*You texted me. Who are* you?) but then decided to block it. Spammers knew how to bait a conversation.

"Help you?" an officer asked.

"Waiting for the, uh... for him." Hunter gestured at the office. The old woman was gone. She'd slipped out without notice.

"He expecting you?"

"Probably."

Hunter hiked the leather bag on his shoulder and made his way to the open door. He lightly knocked.

"Yes?" the detective answered.

"Hunter Montebank. FBI, cybercrime." He cleared his throat. He'd been doing this job forever, but sometimes he just didn't know how to start or what he was doing. Like it was day one. "We, uh, spoke this morning."

The sign on the desk said Fred Billingsly, but he liked to go by Freddy. Hunter wasn't sure how he knew that, must've overheard a conversation when he arrived, one of those details he absorbed and couldn't remember.

Freddy pointed at a chair while he cleared a space on his desk. A yellow envelope fell on the floor, one that appeared to be a birthday card. It was addressed to Fredrick Kaleb Billingsly in big loopy cursive. The same handwriting was in the upper left corner. It was from Mom.

Hunter was about to wish him happy birthday, but instead he said, "Lovely city. Does it ever stop raining?"

An awkward minute passed. "Do you know where you are, Mr. Hunter?"

"The saddest city in the world?"

It wasn't clear what Freddy meant by that. Hunter assumed it was a veiled reference to his race. His birth parents were Asian, but his adoptive parents were Caucasian. Both had abandoned him. The only good thing his adoptive parents did for him—the word *parents* a very loose description—was establish his citizenship. Other than that, he was twice abandoned.

Oddly enough, not the worst thing about his youth.

"What can I do for the federal government?" Freddy said.

Hunter dropped the leather bag and looked through the pockets.

He was cold when he arrived. Now he was breaking a sweat. He took off his ball cap and dabbed his forehead.

"Formal attire?" Freddy asked.

Hunter put the salty cap back on. "Travel wear."

Freddy leaned back, hands laced behind his head. Boredom lay in his eyes. Hunter found his pad of paper, but the pen must've fallen out. He patted his pockets and pointed at a cup of pens on the desk.

"A bit old-fashioned for a technology cop," Freddy said. "Can I see your ID?"

"I'm not a cop. I'm just here to gather intel and send it up the ladder."

"The government really does care."

Hunter wasn't that old, he just looked it. An honest mistake. One that Hunter had stopped correcting years ago. Time was relative in matters of maturity. Hunter's closest friends knew a lot of living could get done in a short amount of time. Time was a human invention. Like all inventions, it could be manipulated.

He didn't have a lot of friends, though. Not anymore.

"We follow all matters concerning the Maze," Hunter said.

"So Mr. Pen and Paper to the rescue." Freddy flipped a pen at him.

"Something like that."

Hunter settled back. The pen worked. His reading glasses were in the first pocket he searched. Freddy sighed.

"This is redundant, Mr. Montebank. I already submitted the report. There's nothing new to tell you."

"Understood. But we're the federal government. Redundancy is our middle name."

"Right."

"Ms. Sunny Grimm walked into the police station three days ago at about noon." Hunter consulted his notes. "She made a statement that her son was in her apartment, using a punch with the Maze logo stamped on it. He was unresponsive to physical stimuli—"

"Mrs."

"I'm sorry?"

"She's a Mrs. Not Miss."

"Says here she's divorced."

"She called herself Mrs."

"Okay." Hunter made a point of writing it down. Not because he gave a shit, but it would make Freddy Kaleb Billingsly hard if he won the little battles. "Before coming here she visited a place called 511 South—"

"That's the address."

"It looks like the name of the business."

"Doesn't have a name. That's how they do it uptown."

"It's located on the south side. Isn't that downtown?"

"Uptown around here, Mr. Montebank. Do you know where you are?"

Crankiest city in the world? It didn't sound rhetorical, though. Freddy sounded like he was really asking, like Hunter didn't have a clue. He was sort of right. Hunter didn't know much because, quite frankly, he barely gave a shit about these cases. They always ended the same, no surprises.

It felt like he'd been doing the same thing for a thousand years.

"Duly noted." Hunter scratched the back of his head. "She goes uptown because someone named Ax told her they could help. The people at 511 suggested she come to you."

"That's what the report says."

"What's at 511?"

"Body augments, sensory inputs. That sort of thing."

"Submersion technology?"

Freddy drummed his fingers. "Probably."

"You don't know?"

"They're licensed and bonded, Mr. Montebank. They're in compliance with federal regulations. I don't read the inventory of every business in the city."

"Okay."

Hunter scribbled on the notepad. *Freddy is a shitty detective and very annoyed with me right now,* he wrote. *He would like me to go away, so I am looking busy writing.*

Almost everyone Hunter investigated was fearfully compliant. Freddy was putting up a fight.

This is actually fun.

"So, you took Miss... excuse me, Mrs. Grimm's statement and escorted her to the apartment and found..."

"It's in the report."

"It says here you found nothing."

"That's what it says."

"The apartment was empty, bed was made. No son. No punch. No Maze. No nothing."

Freddy nodded along.

"You gave her a ride back to the station and put out a missing persons alert. She left somewhat distraught, I imagine. It says here that she hasn't been back to work since the incident."

"Goddamn it." Freddy dropped his feet. "She didn't come back to the station or file a missing persons alert. Where do you get your intel, gossip feeds?"

"Your office forwarded it."

"Bullshit."

"So her coworkers say that's unusual for her to be missing work?"

Freddy was staring at the ceiling. He threw his weight forward and leaned on his desk. "Put down the pen, Mr. Montebank."

Hunter stopped doodling.

"Let's be honest. Mrs. Grimm is emotionally unstable. None of her story could be corroborated. There was no evidence of anything she said. And now she and a coworker have disappeared. A lot of stranger things happen in the city than a woman and her coworker running off together."

"She and—" Hunter held out his notes "—Donny were a couple?"

"None of my business. I'm sorry to waste the taxpayers' money flying you down here to read me my report. So if that's all?"

"Maze incidents are very low in your city."

"Damn right they are."

"I mean really low. Like, unbelievably low for your demographic."

Freddy fell back in his chair. His eyes went up to Hunter's forehead then stared through him. Hunter resisted scratching his head.

"What do you want from me, Mr. Montebank? Crime is down in our city. Citizens are happy. You can write that down if you want. We're compliant with all the government's requests, file all the reports. But if someone wants to run off with a coworker, they're going to do it. If someone wants to commit suicide, we can't stop them.

"If some rich asshole wants to sacrifice himself to the Maze and make his family wealthy, he's going to do it. Perhaps it's a selfless act that saves her son or a selfish one to make money. I don't care. The money these people make while going insane is probably more than their life is worth. Who am I to judge?"

He jabbed at Hunter's forehead. "I don't know where you come from, but over here we have individual rights, Mr. Montebank. If someone wants to punch a hole in their head, that's their business."

"I'm a citizen, Freddy."

"You don't look it."

And he's racist, Hunter scribbled. "Did you know he was gay?"

"What?"

"Mrs. Grimm's coworker Donny. He was a homosexual. Or is. No one knows anymore because he's missing, but it does sort of shit on your romantic angle a bit."

Freddy sniffed. He knew the man was gay. It wasn't in his report because he stopped caring. A lot of stranger shit happened in the city than a missing queer.

"Are we done?" he said.

"I'd like to see her apartment."

"Help yourself. You're the government."

"You work for the government, too."

"I work for the people."

Hunter wrote that down. *Freddy the racist homophobe works for the people.* He finished it with an emphatic period and underlined it with a smiley face and got up to leave. If this was the only exchange he had, the entire trip was worth it.

Hunter's hand was starting to quiver.

"You understand what I'm talking about, Mr. Montebank. Don't you?"

Hunter turned in the doorway. Freddy was smiling. It was grim and knowing, spreading up to his eyes. He pointed at Hunter, then thumped his forehead twice.

"You mean this?"

Hunter pulled off his cap and pushed his hair back. A small scar was centered on his forehead, the lump of a dormant stent sealed beneath it, an old-fashioned brand left behind when the needles were large and needed a sleeve to be inserted.

"Folly of youth," Hunter said. "In fact, I only survived the punch because someone took it out of my hand and made me quit. Sort of what I do for people now. *You* should understand that, Freddy."

"Ever jones for another taste? The lick of the silver tongue?"

"You sound like a man that's been there."

Freddy massaged a tiny circle on his forehead, clean and smooth. No lump where a stent would be. No scar where the needle would kiss. It didn't mean he hadn't tasted newer technology. Punches like Sunny Grimm reported on her son had micro-needles.

"Plastic surgery can work wonders," Hunter said.

"Then why do you still have a scar?"

"A badge of honor. I've been down the rabbit hole and back. Who better to help those still down there?"

"Addicts helping addicts."

"Something like that." Hunter shoved his quivering hand in his pocket. "Good luck with your city."

"Enjoy your stay. You're going to get wet."

Get wet? Hunter didn't know if that was a threat or if that was what the kids called punching the needle. Or maybe Hunter wasn't up on his racial slurs.

"By the way." Hunter dialed through his phone and lit up a photo. "Do you have any more pics of the mother and son? Maybe something a little more current?"

Freddy squinted over his desk. "Where'd you get that?"

"Came with the report."

Freddy stared a few seconds longer then shook his head. Obviously, he'd never seen the photo. He'd stopped caring way before Hunter got there.

He was halfway across the station, counting his steps, thinking of food and checking into a hotel, when he realized he was still carrying Freddy's pen. When he looked back, the office door was still open, but the old woman was sitting in the chair again.

He decided to keep it.

[5]

Hunter
After the Punch

"Ever stop raining around here?"

"It did once," the driver said without turning.

The emotional impact of weather was well documented. Suicide rates increased under the long-term assault of dreary skies and bleak forecasts. A place like this should have suicide rates spiked to the ceiling. Either that, or emotional augment technology cured the blues.

Legal or not, if there was anywhere in the world that deserved a free pass to ride the Maze, this was the place. Anything to escape the hopelessness hanging over this city was an act of compassion.

Hunter unfurled the umbrella as he stepped into a puddle. His socks were already soaked, so it mattered little. Everything aside from his underwear was wet.

The building manager met him on the third floor. "ID?" the middle-aged woman asked.

Hunter gave it to her. She examined the photo sans the ball cap, looked back and forth, tried to read the small print, but who was she kidding. Anyone with a false identification would make it past her.

"You know where you're at?" she asked.

"I just need to look around."

She unlocked apartment number 300. He thanked her. She waved her hand and wobbled down the hall.

The apartment smelled odd.

It was moldy and pungent. Like something spoiled in the back of a cave. The entire city smelled like that, like a forgotten basement with open containers of bleach. But the apartment especially did. The air was turned off and there was the hint of rotten food. The trash was probably due.

Hunter unfolded his notebook. The pages were damp. He ripped Freddy's interview off the pad. The notes were fun, but useless. Before going any further, he captured a few shots with the holo lens in his right eye. Freddy didn't know he was being recorded.

The notepad diversion almost always worked.

His hands were still shaking, but now his legs were, too. A dull ache had joined the itch in his head. His stomach insisted on investigating the kitchen first. The refrigerator had milk and orange juice inside, pickles and lunchmeat. He snatched a loaf of bread and took the heel. No one cared about the heel.

He grabbed aspirin from above the oven, the time blinking in green. Three pills would buy him enough time to get back to the hotel. He took four.

The bedrooms were the same as the kitchen, all normal. The one on the left was obviously the kid's room. A stack of notes was on the desk, a research project for school. He couldn't help but notice the title page. *A Trip to Foreverland.*

"What the hell?"

This was beyond coincidence. Hunter was too familiar with the details of Foreverland. He wasn't just knowledgeable about that incident. He was a source. It wasn't impossible that he was researching it for school. The Foreverland incident was a fascination that possessed the world. Hunter was glad to disassociate from it. Freddy hadn't recognized him because he was a shitty detective. Hunter skimmed through the kid's handwritten notes and noticed the phone and a tin box with stickers—one with a circling snake eating its tail.

The scales were finely detailed, the fangs clamped on its own body, forked tongue out. An ancient symbol of infinity, the cycle of life and death. A scrap piece of paper was beneath the box.

Only the reflection, you'll see. Of the one you seek.

Only then you will be, the one who is free.

An amateur poet. Nothing wrong with that. Something rattled inside the box. He started to pry it open when his phone buzzed. Another text.

Who is this?

He cussed under his breath. It was the same number, the one he thought he'd blocked. He blocked it again.

The laptop was sticking out from under the bed. Before he could reach for it, his bowels insisted he investigate the bathroom. They were pushy. Hunter found the bathroom and politely closed the door.

Here's the deal. All of this probably happened just like she said. She found him in the bedroom, went to the police, something-something, game ended, the Maze people relocated him to the Bahamas or somewhere you can at least see the sun. Which is anywhere but here.

Or she was nuts.

Maze players got wealthy. It would also psychologically wreck the kid. A mere glance at survivors would support that statement. He would be lost in the Maze as long as his body was breathing.

There were those in his department that questioned whether the mind needed the body. Some rumors suggested the Maze freed them from their body and they lived in an alternate reality as real as the toilet he was sitting on. These rumors usually circled conversations about parallel universes and horseshit that had not one shred of proof.

Back in this reality, the one of flesh and bone, you lived as long as you breathed. When you stopped, you ended. Game over.

Of course, with reports of time dilation, the kid might have lived a thousand lives in the Maze and woken up an hour later on his bed and split before his mom got back. Maybe he won and took his money to a sandy beach. Although that doesn't explain where the mom is, but baby steps.

He washed his hands and face and dabbed his cheeks with a towel. He pushed back his coarse black hair. The circular scar looked like a third eye of scar tissue. Unlike his almond-shaped eyes, it was perfectly round. Hunter had lied to Freddy about it. He'd survived punching the needle, that much was true. But he didn't volunteer. Someone else did it to him. Hunter had never been in the Maze, but he'd argue it was a skip through Candyland compared to where the old bastards had sent him and the other boys.

He kept the scar so that people would know he survived the punch.

If you didn't have a scar, that meant you never punched. But maybe one day you would. So who better to investigate a case involving a punch than someone like Hunter? Someone who had been there.

Ever jones for a taste?

There was a knock on the front door.

Hunter listened. It came again, softly. The door handle turned. He went to the front door and pulled it open. A slight man jumped back, a manicured mustache twitching beneath an angular nose. Thin lips pulled back to expose perfectly square teeth.

"Who are you?" he said.

Hunter fought the urge to punch the man in the mouth. His hate was instantaneous. It was the face, the jittery mustache, and oily eyes. He reeked of disapproval, wearing it like a cheap cologne.

Hunter flashed his ID. "The super let me in."

The man studied it like he was preparing for an exam. He looked over Hunter's shoulder. "I'm Sunny's husband."

"She's divorced."

"Ex-husband. I'm just stopping by to see if—" He looked past him again.

"What?"

There was some haggling. Henk was his name. He didn't expect someone to answer the door nor someone to hand him a federal ID. It was all happening so fast.

"She doesn't answer my calls," he said. "I was worried."

"Why do you think that is?" Hunter pulled out his notepad.

"Are you writing this down?"

"Why are you here?"

"I told you I'm worried." He shook his head, took long paces into the apartment and around the couch, glancing at the kitchen. He looked in the bedrooms. He stopped at the bathroom and grimaced. It wasn't professional to shit at a potential crime scene, but the police weren't treating it like one. And it had already been established Hunter wasn't professional.

"My wife was nuts. Her head was a rock and it never changed."

"You're divorced, Henk."

"Ex-wife. Whatever."

"You fought a lot?"

"You could say that."

"You ever hit her?"

He twitched. "What? No, listen, she was tough, that's all I'm saying. She had it hard growing up and I don't think she was ever getting past that. You know there's only so much changing a person can do."

"So this was her fault, what happened to your son?"

"You're a cop?"

"What happened to your ex-wife?"

"Ran off with someone probably. She was always looking for something better. The queer probably flipped her."

"You think she's gay now?"

"I wouldn't be surprised."

"Because you're an asshole?"

"Are you kidding me with that? Can I see your ID again?"

Hunter flipped it open. Most people were a bit surprised he was a federal agent. He enjoyed watching their disbelief transform into puzzlement.

"Your ex-wife and son are missing. Do you care?"

"Why do you think I'm here?"

Henk wandered around the kitchen, trying to look casually at the open box with the address ripped off. He hesitated, even glanced back as he looked inside it. Henk noticed the bread crumbs and opened the refrigerator. Hunter had already confessed to using the bathroom. He wasn't going to admit to raiding the fridge.

"Do you use?" Hunter asked.

"What?"

"Mood-changers? Mind-benders? Drugs?"

"No." He sniffed. "She did, though. All the technology my wife had access to at work, like a junkie working at a pharmacy."

"She worked in manufacturing." Hunter was surprised he remembered that. Henk was making it sound like she worked at 511.

"She wasn't using a punch," Henk said. "But there are other ways to get out."

"Get out?"

"You know." He knocked his head. *Awareness leaping.*

"You sound jealous."

He suddenly went still. His eyes narrowed. Steely resolve finally bubbled up from a dark deep hole in that coward's yellow belly. He suddenly felt like a threat.

"What's your name again?"

"Hunter Montebank."

"Mr. Montebank, do you have family?"

"Not that I know of."

Henk shook his head, glaring. "Mr. Montebank, let's get something straight, all right. I'm not here to entertain your wet ass. I'm here because my son is missing and my lesbian bitch of an ex-wife is missing. Pardon me if I'm a little uptight and unpredictable right now, but my life went into the shitter a month ago."

"A month ago? This happened a week ago."

"A week, whatever!"

He walked slowly across the room and stood too close to Hunter. He was several inches shorter, and unless he possessed some hidden strength or misleading ability, Hunter was positive he could break the shit stick in half. Doing so would be a new level of unprofessionalism.

Even for Hunter.

"Am I a suspect?" Henk hissed.

"Just an asshole, Henk."

"That ain't against the law."

"I don't know the law, Henk. I'm not the police. I investigate cybercrimes. Whether you toss off to donkeys is not my concern. If your son and *lesbian bitch of an ex-wife*," he gritted through it, "were involved in Maze activity, then I'm your man. And if your bank account suddenly spins like a pinball machine, then I'm your man. I'll be back to investigate you. That's why *I'm* here, Henk."

Hunter clicked his pen poised over the notepad. "So why are *you* here again?"

"Fuck you."

"Fuck... me..." Hunter punctuated the two words. "Anything else?"

"She went to 511."

"The address place?"

"That should tell you everything you need to know."

Henk stepped back and finally blinked. The testosterone surge dried up. He went from unpredictable supersecret ninja to reluctant and more than slightly bitter divorcé. He started for the door.

"I hope you find him," he said. "Really do."

"Who?"

"Who are you looking for, Mr. Montebank?"

"Your son."

Hunter flashed his phone, the photo of Grey and Sunny Grimm. They looked to be hiking, a waterfall behind them. The boy wasn't smiling, but he looked content. It seemed a little outdated. He was maybe ten years old. Now he was eighteen.

"I could use a more current photo," Hunter said.

Henk's smile slid wide. "I hope you find him."

"Hope your bank account doesn't spike."

"Do you even know what the Maze is?"

"It's my job."

Henk turned at the door. "It's not a game, Mr. Montebank."

"Winners and losers, Henk. Sounds like a game to me."

"You forget who you are when you're inside. You become someone else. When you die in the Maze, you're reborn again and again. It goes on and on, forever and ever, until you remember who you are. If that sounds like a game to you, I assure you it's not."

"You sound like an expert."

"I do my research."

"You don't seem concerned that your son is living and dying, forever and ever."

"I'll cry later, if you don't mind."

Hunter grabbed the door before Henk could close it. He searched the man's face for a hint of guilt. Maybe he was just thrilled his son had somehow taken the plunge, an investment that would pay off. How could he be guilty when only the willing could enter the Maze?

Maybe he's just a shitty father.

Hunter stood in the quiet apartment. So far, this case was the highlight of his questionable career. He should probably tell Freddy about Henk and his weirdness, but the detective wouldn't do much about it. There was no evidence condemning the man and it wasn't against the law to be an asshole.

He went back for the other bread heel to ease the outset of the shakes long enough for him to reach the hotel, where he could put his agitation down for a few days.

His head was growling.

[6]

Hunter
After the Punch

Hunter entered the hotel lobby with his shoes in hand and socks stuffed inside. His fingers danced on the counter as the clerk checked him in. The shakes were lurking. His stomach was twisted and empty, but food would have to wait. A different hunger demanded his attention.

The sky was a darker shade of gray, the sun a dull disk falling between buildings. In his room, he pulled the heavy curtains closed—couldn't look at the steel sky another second—and double-checked the door lock.

The bed was standard. He'd be a little sore in the morning. He'd done this on yoga mats and thick blankets over concrete, even a park bench, waking up brittle and broken. A bed would be just fine.

He travelled with two bags. One for business, the other for this. The one for this was smaller and, for all intents and purposes, normal. It contained a foam horseshoe pillow that he positioned at the foot of the bed, designed to lay facedown for twelve hours. Or more. Next, there was the laptop. Nothing out of the ordinary there.

The last item was hidden in a seam. He began to salivate.

The jones is real.

Hunter checked the door a third time, shut off his phone and turned the air conditioner as low as it would go. Then stripped naked.

He washed his face. The back of his head quivered, the itch clawing through tissue, sinking its teeth into the soft underbelly of his brain. The scar on his forehead pulsed, the dead and buried stent still jonesing for a spike. It had been decades since it felt the steel kiss. Long ago, he'd considered plastic surgery to cover the stent that was still dormant, but the scar reminded him of where he'd been. How he'd become this. How he'd changed since the Foreverland days.

And how he didn't.

Hunter threw the bedspread back and crawled over the sheet. He readjusted the foam pillow, plugged the laptop into the wall and connected a thick cable. He lay on his stomach, test driving his position for a minute, sliding pillows under his feet. When he could wait no longer, when the demand had become a burrowing beast, he reached into the secret pocket of his bag to find a long vial.

Then his fingers searched the back of his head.

[7]

Grey
Before the Punch

Family Dental Center was wedged between a Laundromat and a bagel shop where some of the city's finest graffiti was on display.

Candace was twisting her hair behind the counter. His dad had hired her out of high school. She was only a few years older than Grey and had even sat next to him in study hall a few years ago. She didn't care about him then, either.

A Zen waterfall was in the corner, a plastic molding of gray slate set in a basin of Mexican pebbles. It dripped onto the carpet. No one seemed to notice.

"Lock the door," Candace said.

Grey turned the latch and crossed the lobby. Candace finished typing before buzzing him through. Somewhere in the back his dad was laughing, the kind of laugh that started and stopped like an unreliable car. He was the kind of dentist that buried all his fingers in a patient's mouth and then asked a question.

Ha-HA.

His office smelled like mouthwash, the medicine kind. Grey popped in his earbuds and watched bubbles stream around a bloated goldfish. The body bobbed in the turbulence like it was attempting to live again. The milky eyes said otherwise.

Grey sprinkled food in the tank anyway.

Dr. Henk Grimm looked inside his office, thick magnifying glasses perched smartly on the end of his nose. The neatly groomed mustache wriggled like a caterpillar. His lips were moving, but the words never made it past the ongoing musical assault on Grey's ears. He nodded. His dad went toward the lobby.

Grey pulled out his earbuds.

Candace's laughter played beneath his dad's dead-car laugh. She was probably bending over to turn off the space heater because her naked toes were always cold. His dad's laughter stopped because she was probably hanging halfway out of her blouse. Then there was murmuring. Another giggle. It was the start of a cheesy porn.

His dad paid her more than an electrical engineer. It was a sex loophole that only Dr. Henk Grimm could exploit—pay a marginally skilled receptionist to manage the office and work late hours when needed.

And other duties as needed.

His dad was a mediocre dentist with two pending lawsuits, both botched extractions that resulted in chronic pain. His teeth were perfect, but a bald spot was growing on his head, which would soon be remedied by the most recent hair treatment.

His dad flopped down at his desk. "Need you to look at this computer, bub. It's slow as hell. But not now."

He scrolled through his email, laughed at one of them, watched a video of a fat guy falling off a bike and laughed again. Grey sprinkled more food on the goldfish.

"Ready?" His dad was out of the office before Grey could answer. "All right, we're leaving, Candace. Have a good weekend, okay? Look forward to seeing you Monday."

He clicked his tongue.

"Have fun this weekend," she said. "Drive safe."

Grey threw his hoodie up and followed his dad past the graffiti. He was already three storefronts ahead of him, taking long antelope strides while thumbing his phone.

"We going somewhere?" Grey asked.

"Not we. *Me.*"

"Where *you* going?"

"None of your business at the moment." He started the car and jerked into traffic.

"Why don't I just stay with Mom, then?"

"Because it's my weekend to have you."

"That doesn't make sense if you're leaving."

His dad shook his head while stroking his lip. Exasperation leaked from his nostrils. His parents' divorce was a beautiful thing. Not only did Grey never have to floss again, he only heard that exasperated sigh every other weekend. Marriage went rotten, but not divorce.

"We'll hang out tonight," his dad said. "I'm leaving in the morning. You'll have the condo all to yourself. I'll be back on Sunday."

Then his dad took a call.

Grey inserted his earbuds and leaned back. He woke up in the parking garage. His dad had already taken the elevator. Dad-son bonding time turned out to be pepperoni pizza and texting.

Grey zoned in and out of sleep until 11:00 a.m. The condo was quiet. There was a note taped to the refrigerator.

Feed the fish.

A white card was clipped next to it. It was stiff with sharp corners. Two parallel creases marked it lengthwise, like his dad had folded it neatly into his pocket. Now it was flattened out and positioned on the freezer, a thick exclamation point in the middle with today's date.

Unlike the office, the condo fish were still alive. Grey dashed food on top and took in the view from the ninth floor. The blue sky passed clouds between glass buildings. The river that split the city was deep and dark, winding under bridges that connected the two halves.

His dad couldn't afford this place.

His debt was massive. Grey went through his mail when he wasn't around. His dad could barely make the monthly interest. *But why save for tomorrow when you have today?*

The Henk Grimm motto.

Grey cranked the stereo and finished the leftover pizza. He texted Rach to come over. She texted back she didn't have a ride, which was bullshit. She had a car. When he offered to send a car, she had already made plans. The refrigerator was sparsely loaded—half a block of cheese, yogurt and peanut butter. He found a box of energy bars in the pantry.

Then he went through his dad's closet.

Plundering his old man's privacy was like a treasure hunt. He did it because he was bored. He did it because he was curious. Most of all, he did it because his old man deserved it.

The revolver was still behind the giant red suitcase. The adult movie collection was next to it—guns and porn. His dad still wasn't hip to the Internet. He indulged in a higher class of degradation. He referred to them as *art films* when Grey was around, like he was spelling out words a five-year-old wouldn't understand.

Grey went through the desk drawers, looked under the bed and in the storage closet. He made a new discovery when he pulled out the bottom dresser drawer. A hole had been cut out of the divider. Grey retrieved a Ziploc full of weed.

"Bingo."

He texted a pic to Rach. *Party, anyone?*

He booted up the computer and waited for her reply. The

computer was clogged with spyware and Trojans. It took minutes to load a simple webpage. The inbox was mostly spam, no naked snaps from Candace. Nothing in the cache either.

He was scrolling aimlessly when Rach texted back. Even a bag of weed didn't tempt her. He pondered how to answer that. Maybe he just needed to lay it out for her, let her know what he was feeling. First he had to figure that out.

Emotions were treacherous ground in the Grimm camp.

He was about to turn off the computer when one email grabbed his attention. It was dated three days ago. *CONFIDENTIAL.* Seemed like if something was confidential, you wouldn't scream about it, but his dad wasn't a thinker. Neither were his friends.

The sender was curious. There was no name, just an exclamation mark.

!

Normally, that screamed spam. But he'd just seen that exclamation mark on the creased postcard stuck to the freezer.

Reservation confirmed, the email read. *A new universe awaits.*

Maybe it was spam, one of those vacation time shares had suckered his dad into a free presentation. He already couldn't afford the condo he was living in, why not commit to a time share on the beach? *Live for today!*

Only there wasn't a link.

Spam always had links to siphon personal information from the user's computer, or asked for passwords or social security numbers or a prince that needed money ASAP. This was just a short note. It meant something. Or it was the worst spammer in the world.

Grey sat on the couch and studied the postcard. It was just an exclamation mark and that day's date. It must've been where he went, but no address or map. There was nothing else for Grey to go on.

So he smoked half the bag of weed.

His dad returned on Sunday, just after lunch. The clock flashed 12:45 when the front door opened, his dad's keys hitting the counter. Grocery bags rattled; the refrigerator opened.

Grey lay in bed, flipping through a mental inventory of the apartment as a blender fired up. There was no memory of cleaning anything up or turning the stereo down. He pictured an empty pizza box and dirty dishes—the residual of a boring weekend. He'd get an earful—*you're a slob, have some respect, grow up*—but at least the computer was turned off, history wiped, and the Ziploc returned to its dark hole.

"How's your trip?" Grey stood in the bedroom doorway in only his boxers.

"Good. How were things here?"

I smoked half your weed. "Boring."

"It is what you make it."

Maybe if his dad had left the stash out in the open, Grey would've asked what his dad was doing with weed. But having to explain why he pulled out the drawers was a future conversation he wanted to avoid at the moment.

His dad wiped the counters while whistling. He handed the rest of a fruit smoothie to Grey, smacked his chest, and told him to get some nutrients. He smelled weird. Kind of like an open wound, the soft flesh that puckered up around the edges.

The shower started.

His dad was mellow that afternoon. And he was like that the rest of the way home, saying very few words but smiling and whistling. What he did say was chill, as if the stick had been surgically removed from his ass. He was just a regular guy with perfect teeth and trimmed eyebrows.

"You going to tell me where you went?" Grey said.

Big smile. "Nope."

"There was a postcard on your refrigerator, the one with the exclamation mark. It had this weekend's date on it."

"That was just something someone sent me."

Oh, they also sent you an email, said a new universe was waiting for you.

That was another conversation they would eventually have.

[8]

Grey
Before the Punch

THE SYSTEM UPGRADE WAS SLOW.

One of the cables was faulty. Grey swapped it out, reattached the headset to his laptop and double-checked the wall outlet. Music thudded from puffy headphones.

Good school grades got him the high-speed connection he needed to run virtual environments. What would he have to do for auditory implants, the outpatient surgery that inserted microscopic Bluetooths next to his eardrums?

Probably cure cancer.

He watched the update's progress and remotely tested the VR headset. If the new cable didn't work, he had a few more ideas.

A cold hand squeezed his shoulder.

Grey jerked around. For a moment, he imagined boney digits slipping from a wide, black sleeve and a long sickle in the other. His mother motioned to his headphones. Her bristly hair was red with dashes of gray. No makeup, no jewelry. Just a pair of safety glasses in the front pocket and a yellow bandana around her neck.

"I'm leaving."

"Okay."

"Dinner's in the fridge."

He nodded, the headphones bleeding guitar riffs.

"You have homework tonight?" she asked.

"Done."

He wasn't lying this time. He'd finished the paper for ethics class ahead of the deadline. It helped that he got to choose the topic. He'd become obsessed with the Foreverland incident, the body-swap ring that shaped technology laws. He'd read everything written, watched all the documentaries and followed the lives of the survivors. Sometimes he wished he was one of those boys that woke up on a tropical island. Everyone had to die, why not have some fun doing it?

"Clean up after yourself, all right?" She looked at the empty cups. "I don't want a mess waiting for me. How you getting to school in the morning?"

"Bus."

"Okay. I should see you before you go." She grabbed a handful of hair. "We need to cut that."

Grey put the concert back on his ears. The update was finalizing. He pretended to scroll a webpage, waiting for her to leave. She stood in the doorway.

"What?" he said.

She shook her head, fussing with the bandana. Sometimes she did that, just looked at him before she left. When the front door finally closed, he went to the kitchen for something to eat. Her vanilla-scented candles were still smoking, wisps still rising from black curly wicks. She rarely left a room once, always returning for keys buried in the basket.

When he returned to his bedroom, he kept his eyes on the front door as he reached under the desk for a crude sleeve made from a plastic soda bottle. The edges of duct tape curled around it. A slender phone was tucked inside, a high-res model modded for virtual environments.

There were very few things he hid from his mother. She went through his stuff under the guise of collecting laundry or dirty dishes, but he knew she nosed for electric cigarettes (which he quit, sort of) or other contraband. He rarely cleared the history on his laptop, surfing incognito when needed. He wasn't doing anything wrong most of the time. The few things he did hide, though, were monster.

It was better she didn't know.

He tapped out the security code. A code he didn't write down, a code he told no one. Not even Rach. He locked the phone into a visual headset, slid motion sensors over his fingers and unplugged the headphones.

When everything was in order, he turned off the lights and lay on his bed without pulling back the covers, and adjusted the pillows. There were times he went into the VR headset for hours, coming up with neck pain that lasted a week.

The VR headset fit snugly. An initial retinal scan—a red laser line —verified his identity, one last layer of security to keep out strange eyes. Images danced and a periscope into a virtual gaming environment opened.

The projection filled his periphery. Earbuds snugged in place, he ignited the environment with a flick of his wrist. Fog rolled in. Trees as large as buildings emerged, gnarled branches reaching for him, vines dangling. Moon-cast shadows ran over mossy logs and a thicket of leaves.

The scarred hands of a warrior appeared as Grey lifted his hands, jewels gleaming on knobby knuckles. He was no longer a shaggy-haired loner, but a hunter that stalked the forest with no particular mission, just a leisurely stroll that usually ended in a solid bludgeoning.

A word blipped in space. *Hey.*

"Hey." His auditory text formed a balloon.

What are you doing? Rach texted back.

"Homework."

Leaves crunched below him. A sagging cottage emerged off the narrow path. He leaned against a tree, slippery lichens beneath his hands, the damp smell of soil. He would feel better if this was real, this wooded earth filled with trolls and bandits.

If this was Foreverland, he thought, *I wouldn't have to leave.*

What are you doing this weekend? Rach texted.

"Dad."

Sorry I didn't come over last time.

He didn't answer. They hardly saw each other at school. She returned his texts after an hour passed, sometimes two. And then it was usually about plans she had, they would catch up, maybe next time.

Or some bullshit.

Just get on with it, he thought.

A dwarf opened the cottage door. He stacked weapons against the wall and didn't see Grey lurking behind the banyan tree.

"Go on," he said. The words typed out.

What?

"You know."

There was a long pause. *Just need some space, that's all.*

"Whatever."

That all you got to say?

"Guess so."

He killed the connection and blocked incoming. Enough with words. A massive emptiness opened in his gut; an elephant climbed onto his chest. When the dwarf arrived with his third cache, Grey stepped into the open; fallen limbs were crushed beneath him.

The warrior dwarf was armed and ready, but not for what Grey brought. He funneled all his rage. The battle was over quickly; the dwarf's braided beard dangled from his peeled face. Sticky blood stained Grey's rings. He whistled for a pack of wild dogs and fed them the remains, then plundered the treasure and set fire to the cottage.

It was virtual. None of it real.

Some of the characters he destroyed were merely computer constructs, programs that walked and talked, acting human or humanlike. Sometimes he felt guilt for punishing them for no good reason. *That's your human condition,* someone once explained. *You're programmed to feel empathy for hurting something, even if it isn't real.*

He wondered if there was something wrong with his programming. Because he still destroyed and he still felt guilty. Somewhere in the world, someone watched their carefully constructed dwarf sim be pulled apart by wolf beasts and his elaborate hut turned to ash. He didn't feel Grey's fists or the snap of his neck, but it hurt just the same.

Grey didn't feel better for doing it. But at least he felt something. And no one got hurt.

Not really.

MIDNIGHT, he got something to eat.

His mom had made a bowl of pasta. That was third-shift dinner. Easy to make, easy to keep. Grey ate it night after night without complaining.

He had ditched the VR headset and watched video torrents. He'd opened an email from an unknown sender. It came with an attachment. Usually, he pitched something like that right to the trash. This one intrigued him.

The file name was an exclamation point.

Maybe it was a coincidence. The sender might have been from one of his encrypted pirate accounts. Grey downloaded tons of videos through them, but viruses were rampant. He ran the file through security and it came up clean. It was still inadvisable to open, best to trash it. But curiosity got the best of him.

Like usual.

It was a video that started with a stage, a big production of lights and announcements. He knew the setup, he'd seen Maze events. But this was new. Ten tanks were in the center, a soft spotlight for each one. They were tall and transparent, light refracting through the prism of clear liquid, something thicker than water. Almost like gel.

A body floated in each one.

Some were completely bald. For the non-shaved, hair floated out like the vacuum of outer space. Respirators covered their faces.

Both genders. All races.

The sound was blotted out by music. Grey didn't need to hear the announcements, didn't need the commentators to describe the risks. Nine of them would barely survive. One would be greatly rewarded. All of them would never be the same.

A symbol filled the screen.

MACABRE SCENES of mayhem followed the opening ceremony, as realistic as the tanks. Grey knew of their experiences, read of the awareness transport into virtual worlds as real as the skin on their bones. When a wild dog tore them open or a warrior pulled their head off, they didn't die. But they felt it.

Over and over, they felt it.

Every game was different, some more bloody than the next. Others were cerebral challenges to follow clues to a secret exit. Sometimes they had no idea they were in the Maze, a complete memory wipe. They would be lost in a different dimension of time and space. Some claimed to have lived a thousand lifetimes in these alternate realities, even though their bodies were only submerged for months. Sometimes weeks. Or, as impossible as it seemed, only hours. Time was not synced between the Maze and the flesh. A time dilation sped up life.

The investors got wealthy from the black-market spectators. It was illegal, which drove up the price to watch it live. And it didn't scare off advertisers. Even family-friendly restaurants threw in product placements.

Due to the time dilation, spectators watched condensed highlights. The boring and mundane parts were clipped out, the everyday living that no one wanted to see. The climaxes were expertly edited for maximum adrenaline or heart-wrenching drama.

The players paid the biggest price.

They paid it for escaping the tanks they willingly entered. Their flesh unaltered, unharmed, but their psyches mangled. All except one. A lucky winner would escape the game intact. Some victors claimed to be enlightened, that the experience had stripped away the illusion of separateness, that they had indeed found their true selves.

They had captured the secrets of the universe.

When they emerged, they had a peculiar smell. After months of living in the solution, they came out with a scent that would remain with them the rest of their lives. Rumor had it you could smell a player in the next room.

Grey advanced the video to the end, skipping the highlights until a heavyset woman pulled herself out of the tank. Stripping away the respirator blocking her entire face, she looked up with the eyes of a newborn, as if seeing the world for the first time. Maybe she was enlightened.

Or maybe just relieved to have escaped.

The Maze symbol pulsed in the background as she was winched out. The mucus solution stretched from her toes, pooling on the stage in sticky puddles. She wiped off her face and began to weep.

To play was to risk prison if caught. He'd seen these endings before, read the stories of riches that followed, the Maze creators hiding from authorities sometimes in plain sight, as if no one really wanted to catch them. The players were given new identities.

The losers came out wide-eyed and paranoid. The ones that could talk barely made sense. He was almost asleep when he heard one of them babble. It was nothing new, but it reminded him of something he'd seen at his dad's apartment. Something he'd read in an email. He said it over and over, as if they were the only words left in his vocabulary.

"A new reality awaits."

"I WANT TO GO WITH YOU."

His dad was in his office, an iPad on his lap. "Close the door."

Grey stood with his thumbs wedged beneath his backpack straps. The office smelled more like a dead fish than mouthwash. His dad slid his eyeglasses between his teeth, sucking on the plastic end.

"Go where?" he said.

"The place you went."

"Where did I go?"

Grey shrugged.

"You don't know, but you want to go?"

His dad's laughter broke Grey's knees. This wasn't the dead-car laugh, but an eloquent one that words could not capture. It said you're an idiot, a moron. *You want to go, but you don't know where I went? God, you're stupid.*

Grey didn't know where he went, but he had an idea of what he did. It was that peculiar smell described by those that experienced immersion reality. Obviously his dad didn't go into the Maze, but he'd been awareness leaping. He had dropped into a tank and left his flesh behind, returning to the glow of happiness, the kiss of an angel, the breath of God in his lungs.

That's what I want.

His dad stood up slowly. His leathery smell filled the room, no longer tainted with the putrid tang of a few weeks ago. He sucked on a breath mint.

"You must have an idea."

"I just want to hang with you."

He half-turned, aiming a squinty eye. "Try again."

Grey kicked at the floor. He didn't want to tip his hand. Vagueness was the best way to approach his dad, let him feel like he had the upper hand, all the power. Besides, he learned everything from snooping through his dad's shit. He'd give himself up if he said too much.

"I don't know. It just looked like you had fun. You seemed... happier, I guess."

"You guess."

It was the truth. Work it right and the truth could manipulate as well as a lie. *Or better.*

"So you have no idea what I'm doing or where I'm going?"

"I'm just asking, that's all. If it's fun or something I can learn, then I'd like to do it. I don't want to sit around your apartment another weekend. Boring as hell."

"Smoking my weed is boring?"

Grey looked at the floor. Best to fall on that grenade. "Sorry."

"You go through my drawers, my closet; you destroy my privacy with one hand and ask for a favor with the other?"

"No, I just... I knew you kept the weed somewhere. That's all, I swear."

"You didn't water down the whiskey?"

Grey was stepping on landmines now. His dad was lighting them up. Now was the time to shut up.

His dad looked in the fish tank. The goldfish stared back with one bloated eye. Hands on his hips, he spoke to the ceiling.

"You want to tell your mom I have weed, go ahead. She's no angel. You want to tell her I'm leaving you at the apartment with a refrigerator of food and neighbors complaining about music, be my guest. Because if you have any ideas of blackmailing me, son, you best know I don't lean that way." A darting look came his way. "Understand?"

"Yeah."

"You sure?"

"Look, I'm eighteen. Leaving me alone in your apartment is a bad idea, you know that. I'm just saying that you're doing something cool and I want to do it with you. I'm your son. We should be doing things together."

The sarcastic laughter returned, this time more of a soft slap than a knee-breaker. He crossed the office with long, slow steps. He was slightly shorter, but he felt bigger than Grey. His soft, clean hands pressed against his cheeks, the smell of lotion and antiseptic. Hands that spent decades in peoples' mouths gently slapped him.

"You're clever. But you don't know shit."

Hands dropping to his shoulders, his dad bored a stare through his head, a spotlight seeking the truth. Grey didn't know what he was doing that weekend, he just wanted to be part of it. Now that Rach wasn't part of his life, there was nothing else to do.

Why not risk it all?

"It's expensive, what I'm doing."

"Okay."

"You'll have to pay your own way."

"I can get a job."

"No. You can't mow a couple lawns. This ain't that kind of money."

"I've got a college fund."

Bingo. Grey pulled victory from the jaws of defeat. He *had* a college fund. His mother didn't know it was gone. Grey wasn't supposed to know, either.

His dad, the brilliant dentist on the Upper West Side, had left the mail on the desk one afternoon. Grey had rifled through it, as was his habit, and saw the massive withdrawals that turned his college fund to ashes. He assumed he was paying off gambling debts or boning the secretary on lavish cruises. Turned out he'd used it to take a month-long vacation on something called the Sessions.

Grey never found out what the Sessions were.

"It's my money," Grey said. "If mom asks where it went, I'll tell her I spent it."

The tone in his voice hinted at the truth. It wasn't an outright threat, but enough to make his dad pause and reflect. His mom might not give a shit about weed and whiskey, but she'd want to know where her son's future went.

A final swat to the cheek. "I'll see what I can do. No guarantees."

"Understood."

Grey hiked the book bag on his shoulders and left the office. Candace locked the front door behind him and turned the closed sign.

[9]

Grey
Before the Punch

Mom was asleep on the couch.

The vanilla candle burned. She rarely made it to her bedroom. Her bag—the one she slung over her shoulder, the one that could hold a week's worth of food—was crumpled under her arm. A big bowl on the floor, the remains of unpopped kernels were at the bottom. She often fell on the couch after third shift, sawing off several hours before getting up.

He carefully packed a duffle bag.

If she woke up and asked where he was going, he'd say it was Dad's weekend. She'd remember and ask why he was packing so much. He rarely took more than a toothbrush.

You were right, he would say. *I need more clean underwear.*

That wouldn't explain why he was packing computer gear. He didn't know where his dad was taking him or what he might need.

Luckily, she never moved, not a thin eyebrow or a lip smack. Not even when he dropped a cup in the sink.

He left the laptop in his room and wiped the history this time. She might snoop this time and there were too many breadcrumbs about the Maze and something called the Sessions. The Maze led in plenty of directions. The Sessions search went nowhere, unless his dad was interested in channeling a new age spirit that lived under an oceanic volcano.

Her teeth were grinding a hard plastic plate, jaws flexing. This was the kind of pressure that could chew through braided cable. Had her dad not fit her with a bite guard, she would've already ground her molars down to nubs.

There was a bagel with cream cheese and orange juice on the counter and a flyer for a local homeless shelter where she sometimes volunteered. It was civic duty, helping those less fortunate than her. She had made the breakfast for him before crashing. He chugged the juice and snatched the bagel so she'd know he ate before leaving.

She would want him to wake her up, tell her he was going. But he hated doing that. Sleep was the best part of her day. She deserved to rest, earned that little reprieve. *Sometimes life is like that,* she would say.

That wasn't Grey's philosophy. If you don't like it, then get out. He could change things, not end up like his parents or anyone in his family. There were ways to change the brain, ways to control destiny.

A new universe awaits.

Maybe this weekend was one of those ways. He'd figure out a way to bring his mother with him. She deserved to glow. Not the dentist. If he could write all that in a note, she would understand. He went back to the kitchen and scribbled on a scrap of paper.

Gone to Dad's. Love you.

"WHAT?" Grey dropped his bag and followed his dad into the bedroom. "You promised."

"I said I'd look into it."

"I'll pay whatever I have to, I already said that." He tried to keep the whine from his words and failed. "Mom doesn't know about it, either."

His dad continued packing.

"I thought this was something we were going to do?"

"We'll do something else. How about fishing?"

Grey's voice rose. "Look, I'm good at computers, I know virtual reality environments. I brought all my gear. I know more than you. I can help."

His dad stared at a ball of black socks. "I thought you didn't know what I was doing?"

"I don't."

"You been on my computer, son?"

"No, Dad... I was guessing. I was researching and, you know, hoping you were... but I don't know."

"I let you stay here, feed you and everything a dad is supposed to do. Have some respect, that's all I'm asking?" He paused, then pointed. "All right?"

"Yeah."

"Now this isn't kid shit, you know. I'm not letting you go for your own good. Life ain't a video game, Grey. You don't hit restart; you don't respawn all fresh and new."

Liar. If he was awareness leaping, that was exactly what you do. You go into a false reality, you make mistakes, you die, *and then do it again!*

His dad threw socks and underwear into a suitcase along with pants and shirts. His movements were stiff and jerky, a far cry from the glowing angel that came home the last time. Either he was having withdrawal or someone got to him. Maybe he asked about Grey coming and pissed someone off. Adults sometimes shit their pants like children when they got slapped.

Especially when it's another adult.

"I'm doing this for you." He left the suitcase open and started the shower. "I set up security cameras in the apartment, so don't be going through my shit. I'll know about it. You can smoke the weed if you want, I don't care. I'm a shitty dad, so what's it matter?"

You're not a shitty dad. Just not much of a dad.

His dad winked, flashed a perfect smile and closed the door. Grey waited until he was in the shower before grabbing his dad's phone. It asked for a passcode when he swiped.

0-0-0-0.

Of course it was. His dad was lazy. When he came out of the shower, Grey was in the kitchen, eating cereal. His phone was exactly where he left it.

GREY WOKE EARLY.

He lay in bed, occasionally dozing off. When his dad bumped a chair or dropped his suitcase, he would force his eyes open and listen. Finally, the front door closed.

Grey snooped around the office for security cameras. His dad was bluffing. It had that tone, the one that told him Santa was real and the Tooth Fairy was broke. He decided to risk it. If he was wrong, he'd catch hell.

Nothing new.

Another white card was clipped to the refrigerator. The edges crisp. Today's date was stamped above a thick, black exclamation point. Suspiciously void of information, there were only random black lines on the back.

The first invitation was still clipped under it—white and crisp, the date from a few weeks back and an exclamation point. The two creases were flattened out.

Grey hovered over a bowl of cereal and tapped through his

phone. The Find a Phone app was loading a map. Two black icons appeared several miles apart. One was labeled Grey.

The other Big Daddy Dentist.

His dad barely knew how to operate his phone. How would he know the GPS was linked to Grey's phone? Not in a million years.

Three bowls later, Big Daddy Dentist was on the interstate south of the city. Grey turned his dad's computer on then went to the bathroom until his legs fell asleep. The car was still moving southbound when he finished. He was off the interstate, travelling on Route 66 toward Lake Mansour.

The hell is he going?

The computer was locked. A password had been installed.

So he knew Grey had been snooping through the emails and thought he'd teach him a lesson. Grey tried the word *password* and *11111*, but neither worked.

His dad once had a secretary he didn't trust, an older woman that drank coffee by the barrel. She was also happily married and dressed warmly. He kept his office computer password-protected because she was nosy, he'd said. He wrote them down so he wouldn't forget. Grey had suggested where his dad could keep it.

He flipped the keyboard over.

A few minutes later, he was scrolling through email. There was nothing new as far as he could tell. The inbox was loaded with spam and dating site weirdness such as *Sugar Daddy* and *Just 15 Minutes*—invitations from future dental secretaries with bright smiles and promising measurements.

The previous email from *!* was gone. It wasn't in the trash or filed in a folder. Even a search of the entire computer turned up nothing.

But there was an invoice for scuba gear.

Shit.

His dad was a hundred miles away and heading for Lake Mansour. This was a bad sitcom of double-talk. Grey had it all wrong. He wasn't doing some sort of underground illegal immersion reality trip. Grey would've bet his college fund (if there still was a college fund) that his dad was dabbling in awareness leaping and it turned out he was hiding out at a hedonistic resort on the water.

His dad wasn't looking into new ways to explore reality; he wasn't risking everything to become wealthy or enlightened. He was just a fornicating asshole spending his son's college fund on water sports and strange.

He slammed the keyboard. *Who's the bigger asshole?*

The plastic cracked. He pounded the seat and collapsed. This was worse than being left behind. Now there was no hope of awareness leaping. None. Zero. He was stuck in his life.

Get the grinding plate ready.

There was only one icon on the GPS. His dad had dropped off. Grey followed the route back to his last location. He'd disappeared sometime in the last ten minutes, about ten miles from the water. It appeared to be a long private drive that led to a sprawling house.

Either he'd turned off his phone, which was impossible, or he'd figured out he was being tracked. Equally impossible.

What did it matter? Let him find out he was being followed. Grey would rather get super stoned and listen to music than scuba dive off a wave runner with a bunch of fake assholes.

Grey torched up a bowl, turned the music up and ate more cereal. He took a second tour of the bathroom, watching videos until his legs were numb again. He streamed the same ones from the other night, the highlights of Maze competitors, mucus gel dripping off their toes.

A new universe awaits.

Mid-afternoon, he took a shower. A respirator was hanging on the showerhead.

That's weird.

Why would a respirator be in the shower? And why didn't he take it with him? Unless there was equipment at the resort. A rubber disc was next to the soap, the type used to plug the tub. Maybe he was practicing.

Something's lining up.

His dad was too nervous before he left. This was adult stuff, he had said. But not the adult stuff that involved hedonism. He was sort of scared.

And he was practicing scuba diving in the bathtub.

Grey rinsed his hair, washed away the pleasant buzz and slowly dried off. Something occurred to him with an edge of hope. With the towel wrapped around his waist, he left a damp trail to the kitchen and tore the white cards off the refrigerator.

It was the one on the bottom he looked at, the first one. The one with the creases. This was more than an invitation. His dad hadn't folded the card to put it in his pocket. They were crisply lined up, perfectly parallel.

Grey folded the card.

They closed like shutters, the edges falling just short of each other, keeping the exclamation point exposed. The random black lines on the back of the card aligned with the thick exclamation point. He dropped it on the floor. Swallowed hard.

He'd heard of this.

He'd heard of people getting invitations in the mail, ivory cards with very little information, nothing that could be tracked. No return address, just the recognition that you had been selected. Hope had returned.

It was staring up in the form of a symbol.

THE SESSIONS

A room without windows.

There was a door on each wall but no windows. And next to each door was a monitor that pretended to be a window. The images were of a lake. The opposite shore was too far to see. Dr. Henk Grimm assumed it was an ocean, not a lake. Nonetheless, they were not windows, they were images on monitors, so they couldn't be trusted.

Was there really a man in a boat with his son?

Henk was sent to the room upon arrival and locked inside. For the privacy of others. That didn't make sense. They all saw each other the first night of the month-long Sessions retreat. There were no masks, no mystery. No plates of blow, no orgies at the end of the night. They knew why they were there.

So why lock us in?

His room had two couches and a coffee table. No matter where he sat, he was looking at a monitor with a lake and a father and a son in a boat. The sun was just off the horizon, early morning. That was another thing, there were no clocks.

Time is relative, Micah said. *Be here, now.*

If Henk wanted a Zen teacher, he would've gone to the mountains and saved a fortune. He'd paid for technology magic, not belly-gazing bullshit.

He sank into a couch with a tepid cup of coffee. The robe fell open, his genitalia running wild. He left it that way. If someone was watching, *enjoy*.

The door behind him opened. Henk spilled the coffee, staining the white robe. He quickly stood, wiping his hands on the lapels.

"I'm so sorry, Mr. Grimm," Rema said.

"*Dr*. Grimm."

"My apologies, Doctor. I did not mean to startle you."

Rema was Indian—*dot not feather*, his father would say. She was also gorgeous. Silky black hair, olive complexion, with a sexy English accent. He had a taste for blondes and blue eyes, but he was willing to explore new pastures. Exploration was why he was there.

"I expected you earlier," he said.

"Are you comfortable?"

"I'm showered and ready. How about you?"

"I am always ready, Dr. Grimm."

I like it already.

She sat on the opposite couch. Her clothing was loose and slipped off her shoulder to expose a bra strap. Her teeth were a good color, but the left central incisor was twisted. If he went back to his practice, he could fix that for her. He'd taken the month off for these Sessions. His partner had taken over the client load. He'd told them he was going hiking to clear his head, that sort of thing. He hadn't told them that if everything went well, he wouldn't come back.

At all.

Rema unpacked her bag of pill bottles and equipment—a respirator, headset, stethoscope and other fancy gear.

"You're not wiping my memories." He pointed at the leathery skull cap.

"Of course not, Dr. Grimm."

"I know what that does."

"You're only preparing for a short leap. It will be a temporary disassociation with your body. There is no memory wipe; you will return as yourself. There is nothing to worry about."

She chuckled, truly entertained.

Her adorable smile and intelligent accent put him at ease. Honestly, he wasn't opposed to losing his memories and starting over. That was sort of the point of the Sessions. So why was he scared?

Because when it came down to it, memories were a security blanket, his identity, who he was. His memories made him *Dr.* Grimm, not *Mr.* Grimm. It wasn't easy giving up the blankie.

There was no reason to hang onto his identity. He wanted to forget it, to start new. *Born again*, as the Christians would say. What would it be like to program new memories, fabricate a past that would lead to a *new* Henk Grimm?

Not a new Henk Grimm. A new me.

He would drop his name because it was already tainted. He would pick something else, forget who he was entirely, believe a new past, whether it was borrowed or fabricated.

I would still be me.

"This is to help you relax," Rema said. "Your vitals are slightly elevated. I expect you are a little nervous about today. That is natural. Have you been practicing mindful breathing?"

"Yes, of course." That was a lie. He didn't see the point in breathing on purpose. The body had that under control. "When can I get some fresh air?"

"You're here to maximize your time, Dr. Grimm." Rema adjusted the straps on a respirator. "We are not interested in what's out there. We explore in here."

She touched his head. It was the same line, the same gesture Micah had done during the welcoming event just before they were locked in their rooms.

"Take this." She handed him the respirator. "Breathe deep."

She urged him to lie back. He was stoned within minutes. Whatever they were pumping through the mask put him on the ceiling.

"What's in this?"

"We are elevating your oxygen levels. There are some minor additions to help you relax. Are you feeling them?"

He heard her moving behind him and began to fantasize she was getting undressed. If she climbed over the couch and wrapped those brown thighs around his head, he would forget about all the money he'd invested.

I didn't come for that.

Sex he could get without mortgaging his life. This was a spiritual journey into new realities. The only unanswered question was how far did he want to take it?

He didn't have to enter the Maze, not if he didn't want to.

They didn't pressure him. In fact, they hardly spoke about it. Everything he knew was hearsay. There were rumors of players turning into gods, of never returning to their bodies, of new realities and endless dimensions. He didn't have to enter the Maze to experience that; he could awareness leap recreationally and call it good.

But very few were satisfied with that.

Junkies start off small and slow. They nurture the high, nurse the needle until they fall in love.

Henk couldn't afford more than the one month-long Sessions. He would have nothing left after this. He would return to work and hold off the lenders as long as possible. And then it would be over.

I'll end up in the Maze.

He hadn't even made his first leap, but he knew it. He would enter the Maze and get rich or go crazy. If he went insane, at least they would wipe his memories. He wouldn't know any better.

Does it hurt if you don't know any better?

He was feeling light and porous when Rema took his pulse. Her touch was sweet, but the horniness had left him, replaced by something more spiritual. Not so grabby.

"Are you ready, Dr. Grimm?"

He nodded like a dopey patient coming out of surgery. She unclipped the respirator and led him to one of the doors. It was difficult to know which one it was. The room was perfectly symmetrical. It could be the bathroom.

There was a bubbling tub of semen.

He gagged. The roiling liquid popped like a six-year-old blowing snot bubbles. And the smell stung his eyes, clearing out the euphoria.

"I thought we were doing the—"

"The vertical tank is a bit more advanced." She sat on the edge of the tub and raked her hand through the liquid. "This is easier for beginners, Dr. Grimm. You will lay horizontal for a very short trip. And trust me, you will get used to the smell."

The adorable laugh was lost in a haze.

"This is a nutrient-rich solution, non-oxygenated. You will wear a respirator during this trip. Once you master the vertical tank, you will no longer need it."

"No respirator? How the hell will I breathe?"

"Sit, Dr. Grimm. Think of this as a hot tub. You will find it pleasurable."

She stepped into it, hands inviting. The bubbling goo burped around her knees, staining the fabric of her dress. He took her hand and stepped in.

It was warm and silky. His legs were being licked with hot tongues from all directions. His revulsion vanished. He wanted that sensation all over his body. Rema guided him into a sitting position and stepped out to fetch the respirator. The liquid clung to her calves.

"Once inside, you will experience a dream, Dr. Grimm. One you cannot distinguish from reality."

He was melting. If this was an elaborate ruse to melt his flesh and repackage it as bologna, then it was totally worth it.

"For most people, the leap is generated by a memory or a wish. It is often unconscious willing." She test-fit the respirator before pulling it off for minor adjustments. "Your experience with time will not match the time that passes in this room. I expect you to remain submersed for an hour. Your experience, however, may feel *much* longer."

It was hard to say where Henk ended and the world began. His flesh was permeable; he was breathing through his skin. In a few minutes, he would simply pour himself into the tub and mix with the greasy stew of fat that bubbled and farted. He no longer smelled it, no longer cared.

"This is a sensory deprivation respirator." Rema stood over him with the hooded mask. A corrugated hose extended from the cone that would cover his mouth. "Imbedded probes will hijack your senses and read your mind. You will forget this vehicle you call your body."

She rubbed his shoulders. Her touch was slimy.

"The real you, Dr. Grimm, your true self, will make the leap. Are you prepared?"

He must've nodded.

She covered his head in silence. It was black inside the hooded respirator. The air was stifling at first, and then a blast of cool comfort filled his nostrils. There was no sense of sliding beneath the liquid, but he could feel it on his shoulders, under his chin. Soon, that sensation disappeared.

There was only the humid feel of his breath.

Colors moved.

A rush of excitement shot through the dark. He wanted to fly, to leap off cliffs and swim in the ocean and soar through outer space. He wanted to explore all those dimensions of another reality Micah had promised.

Henk stood on the brink of that doorway.

He would leap into a new universe, explore an inner dimension of consciousness, go somewhere he could do anything. Be anyone. God or angel, demon or animal. Technology would launch him from this flesh, free his mind to explore. It was new. It was exciting.

He waited for it.

His breath was hot again. The air slowly turned thick and began to feel suffocating. There were sounds. Not the gluey burps from the tub but actual sounds of people laughing. Not Rema's lovely chortle, but more than one person laughing at him.

And there was pressure. A weight on his chest.

He struggled to get it off. Rema wasn't that heavy, but there were others. Two, maybe three people were sitting on him, pressing a pillow over his face, the fabric stuffed into his mouth.

Henk tried to shout, but nothing came out. And then he recognized the voices. Those were his brothers'. They were choking him until he couldn't take it; sometimes he passed out and woke up bloodied and bruised.

He wasn't in a tub, he was there. He was little again, and his brothers were back. They would choke him until he blacked out and there was nothing he could do about it. He didn't want to be little. This wasn't where he wanted to go. Henk kicked and screamed, but it did no good.

It never did.

A warm gush of liquid filled his nostrils; it rushed into his lungs. An acrid sting set his head on fire. He attempted another breath only to draw a deeper gulp and sink further to the bottom.

Rema pulled him out of the tub.

She laid him over the edge. Greasy vomit slid down the side as help rushed in. He felt her holding him, the world spinning in a painful vortex.

He didn't remember ripping the respirator off while he was still under, didn't remember vomiting. He remembered suffocating, though. That was an old reality.

Made new again.

PART 2

THIS PARTY STARTS

[10]

Sunny
After the Punch

"Hey," someone shouted. "You look lonely."

A hefty woman leaned into Sunny. Her bicep was clammy. A cloud of perspiration enveloped her. Sunny avoided shrinking. The woman introduced herself as Fran.

"Friends bail on you?" Fran said.

"For now."

Sunny rocked her head. The wall pulsed with music, tickling her ears. Fran waved two of her friends over. One of them had a striking resemblance to Tinkerbell. They smelled of booze and close quarters and smiled imperfect smiles. A gold necklace stuck to Tinkerbell's neck.

The conversation rolled around Sunny, carrying on without having to respond. She'd been there most of the night by herself. A waiter that looked barely out of Boy Scouts leaned into the conversation.

"What are you drinking?" Fran shouted.

"Petron."

Sunny pointed at a little man leaning against the bar with a taller, thinner man half his age. The little man's high-pitched laughter punched through the music. The waiter nodded. He knew the deal.

"Honey, you're pitching to the wrong team," Fran said.

"Paying it forward."

"Paying what?" Fran asked.

Sunny didn't answer.

She watched the waiter deliver another shot to the end of the bar. The little man looked around with a sloppy smile, lifting the glass before throwing it back. He didn't know who was sending them or why, but he drank them nonetheless. Someone was getting him drunk, but that was why you came to the Glass Jar—to take advantage of someone, or the other way around.

Either way.

Sunny had slipped into the club without notice. Her cropped hair was in line with most of the women there. Her starchy work shirt—a penlight still clipped inside the pocket and yellow bandana stained with sweat—was two days on her body and smelled worse than Fran. Sunny looked like someone needing to blow off a tanker full of steam, Glass Jar style.

"Why are you feeding Barry?" Fran asked.

"Barry?"

"That little bear you just sent a drink to."

A devilish smile turned the corners of Sunny's mouth. *That little asshole's name is Barry.*

She wasn't sure why she disliked him so much. It was a deep-seated hatred that had nothing to do with sexuality, height or misplaced snobby fashion. Her dislike was primal, instinctual. Like she'd known him all her life.

"What are you drinking?" Fran elbowed her.

"Water."

"You're no fun."

"Not right now, I'm not." *Maybe never.*

Tinkerbell and girlfriend raised their drinks and howled. Barry flopped on his seat and raised a tumbler. His glazed eyes roamed the room and, for a second, landed on Sunny. She stepped into Fran and the big woman's damp armpit wrapped over her shoulder.

The dancing continued. The drinks flowed.

Two more shots went to Barry's end. He begged to know who was sending them, that he'd suck everything in the place, soft or hard, until he found out.

Tinkerbell was kissing her girlfriend, her tongue deep in her throat, hands crawling through her hair. A tattoo was exposed on her neck, black-inked lines of something she'd seen before, something between Grey's eyes. Sunny ground her finger and thumb into her eyes until the room stopped turning. When she looked again, the tattoo was a Chinese symbol.

Not the Maze.

Barry fell off the stool. His flimsy partner picked him up in fits of laughter. They staggered through the crowd.

"Want to go back to my place?" Fran's cigarette breath was in Sunny's ear. "Or we can go out back."

Barry made his way toward the restrooms, slamming the door open. Sunny handed her water to Fran.

"Be right back."

There was no plan. She'd arrived to confront the man that Donny had called over to the apartment, the one who'd passed her the note with Micah's name on it. Her weak plan had made sense until she saw him at the bar; then it was obvious a conversation about the Maze would go nowhere.

There was no backup plan.

She had hid and watched, had fed him drinks until his knees poured into his shoes. It was now early morning and he was barely coherent. Sunny followed him into the bathroom.

The tang of urinal cakes and piss stains was pungent. There were puddles on the sinks and floor. Sunny tied the bandana over her head. Her feminine features wouldn't pass in the men's room, but no one paid attention.

Barry saddled up to one of the urinals, a ship buckling side to side. His partner held him steady with one hand. Sunny stepped next to him and unzipped her pants. The digital watch began beeping.

Barry leaned his forehead against the cool tile and rolled dead fish eyes at her.

It was three in the morning. She couldn't get it to turn off. Barry sighed as he relieved himself, not seeing the woman with the bandana or hearing her digital watch. He began licking the chrome handle.

Sunny turned away.

What now, Sunny? What now?

What was she going to do, ask if he remembered her? He couldn't remember his own name. What kind of real information could she get besides slurry phrases?

It's time was stenciled into the grout followed by a phone number.

"You're pissing on the floor." Barry's partner shook him. "Come on."

They stumbled out, propping each other up. Unless they injected Viagra directly into their genitals, no one was getting laid. That wouldn't stop them from trying. They fell against the bar long enough for one last shot.

Sunny called a car and stood on the curb. She held the driver until Barry and his partner dumped themselves into the back of another car. They arrived at his building at four o'clock. Sunny slipped into the building with her arms around them. The doorman didn't give it a second thought.

Barry didn't even notice.

"The hell?"

Sunny was yanked from a deep hole. She pulled herself out of a chair, kicking the comforter on the floor. Pain crowed in her neck.

Barry flailed.

His hands and feet were bound by nylons she'd found in the closet along with leather straps and toys. Everything but fucking handcuffs.

"Who the hell are you?" His tongue was swollen, eyes puffy.

Sunny shook off the lead of sleep. It was almost noon. Sand filled her head. She went to the kitchen and started a Keurig. Curses continued from the bedroom, followed by violent yanking that only cinched the knots tighter. She couldn't remember how she'd learned to tie constrictor knots.

She sank into the doughy chair with fat armrests, something stylish, cartoonish. The room was chic and smelled like hard sex. She huffed the cinnamon hazelnut coffee, closing her eyes.

This is insane.

It was somewhere between tying his hands and feet, as he laid stone-cold passed out, that she realized there was no going back. Judging by the inventory in the closet, this wasn't the first time Barry had been tied up. By a desperate woman, maybe, but not the first.

What choice did she have?

Henk thought she was crazy. Most everyone else did. Now she was relaxing in an overstuffed chair with a man tied to his own bed while drinking his coffee. The judge and jury would close the case on her. And she was fine with it. Her old life was days behind her, a closed book. This was a new chapter.

It was starting with a bang.

"Do you remember me?" she asked.

"What?"

"You were at my house a few days ago. Do you remember?"

"No."

"No?"

"I'm a little fucking distracted!"

"I mean you no harm."

"A bit late for that."

"I just need to ask a few questions and then I'll leave."

"Are you kidding me? Where's Hamlet?" He craned his neck. "What'd you do with Hamlet?"

"He went home."

She thought he'd start screaming for help about then. It seemed likely and she couldn't blame him. She'd stuff a sock in his mouth. It would start to feel like a crime at that point. Technically, she'd already crossed the line.

"What do you want?" he grumbled.

"You came to my apartment. My son had something around his head, something with a needle and the icon of—" she gestured to her forehead "—the Maze."

His head popped off the pillow. Recognition spread from his eyes into his bloated face. He stopped struggling.

"My son is missing," she said. "So is Donny. You sent me to a place called 511 and told me to speak with Micah."

"I didn't tell you shit."

"You wrote it on a piece of paper." She dug through her pocket. "You said he could help my son."

"No. No, no." He shook his head. "I didn't do that."

"Where are they?"

"Look, I don't know you. I barely know Donny. How would I know where your kid is?"

She placed the coffee on the dresser, picked up a studded belt and lashed him across the stomach until he cried an apology.

"I thought you and Donny were friends."

"We met at the Glass, hooked up a few times. I must've kissed and talked about what I do, I don't remember. He called me about your boy. I never should've answered."

"What do you do?"

"I know people."

"Like Micah."

"Like Micah, sure."

"Where are they, Barry?"

"How do you know my name?"

"Where's my son?"

"Listen, I'm sorry. I truly am. Your son was young and confused. Shit, I'm old and confused, but I know better than to... than to shove a fucking needle in my head. Especially one labeled with the Maze."

He whispered the last part.

"You afraid they can hear us?" Sunny sat down. "Maze! You think they'll hear that, they'll come running? Is that what you think? Maze! Maze!"

"Shh-shh... goddamnit. You don't know what the hell you're doing."

"Then tell me. Where do I go next, Barry? I want to find my son. Who do I talk to? I went to 511; I asked for Micah. I went to the police. Where do I go, Barry? Where?"

He collapsed like a punctured balloon. Sunny bounced her foot. His cheeks were flush. He was moaning about a headache and a dry throat while twisting his wrists in search of a way out of the nylons. She wasn't much of a knot-tier aside from her shoes, but she'd fashioned those knots better than a crusty sailor could make.

She went to the kitchen and returned with a couple of white pills and a glass of water. He gladly swallowed them.

"I got to piss."

"Not yet," Sunny said.

"Look, I don't know what to tell you. I'm nobody. I party with important people; I know a few names. All those people connected with the... the Maze..." Again, he whispered. "They're crazy. Certified. Your son probably thought it was a game. It happens all the time. I'm sorry, but I can't help you."

"What happens all the time?"

"Kids, they think it's a game."

"What is it?"

He picked up his head. An artery throbbed on his forehead. "Are you serious?"

She knew the Maze was dangerous, knew it was a felony, but it was clear she knew less about it than everyone in the world.

"Do the research. Find out what your son got you into and then run, that's my suggestion. Now can you untie me? I'm the least of your problems."

"Who is Micah?"

Again, he collapsed, this time with laughter, rocking his head into the pillow. She was almost done with the coffee and was prepared to make another cup.

"He's someone," Barry blurted. "I met him at a party. He was a little weird, even for me. Someone said he was god, that's all I know, I swear on my dead dog's grave."

"You sent me to him."

"Yeah, well, I wasn't thinking straight. Don't go back." He yawned, smacking his lips. "I can't help you, really. Even if I could, I don't want to. It's your son's fault, tie him to a bed and make him piss himself."

The sheets around his midsection were soaked. He'd relieved himself and didn't care. The smell of urine mixed with various lotions and past sexcapades.

She decided to make that second cup.

When she returned with a vanilla espresso and the laptop she found in the next room—the logo brightly lit—he was singing a dance tune, rolling his head and hands, tipping his feet. She sat back and listened. He was oblivious, laughing through a jumble of words, his lips fattening with each syllable.

The roofies were starting to kick in.

There was a bottle of them in the bathroom. He thought she'd given him aspirin. How many times did he use them on someone else? Her guilt for tying him up had vanished the moment she found them.

He went silent when she started tapping the keys. "What're you doing?"

"Learning about Micah. And the Maze."

"No, no, no, nooooo... no, no. Not on my... don't do that. Don't, don't. I swear, please don't type that search. There's a... look, I have a jump drive of... of Mazes you can take. Just... untie me and I'll—"

"Where?"

He threw his head back into the pillow and growled.

"Where is it, Barry?" She tapped the keys randomly. "Where?"

"Desk drawer. Red drive."

She could drag him to the desk before he passed out and let him sleep it off. Sunny sipped the coffee while he sang another song; this one she didn't recognize. Drool seeped from the corner of his mouth.

She went to the office and searched the desk drawers. There were several jump drives, but only one red one. She took them all.

He was still singing when she returned with a kitchen knife, the words blurred into one long slur, and untied one of his hands. He was completely unaware she'd put the serrated blade on his chest, but he'd find it when he woke and cut himself free.

"*If you want to find me,*" he sang, "*I'll see you at three, but not a minute before, you walk through the door. You won't find me, so you can't be free...*"

He sucked in a long breath, arching his back.

"You can't... be... *freeeeeee—*"

"Shut up."

She was going to slap her hand over his mouth, maybe even sit on his chest until he passed out. But the knife had slipped off his chest. It was in his free hand. She had a vision of him sticking it in her stomach with a stupid grin on his face. He would call the police and they would take her to the hospital before Barry pressed charges for kidnapping and torture. She'd go to prison and they would never find Grey.

Maybe she was feeling paranoid, but that thought felt more like a memory that came from the same place her hatred for him was born.

She kept her distance.

"What's that mean?" she asked. "The song."

"He's not coming back," he sang.

"Why do you say that?"

"He's just not." His eyelids were heavy. "And even if he does, he won't come back. Not really."

For a moment, she thought the truth would slip from his drugged-soaked brain, that his secrets would leak out. She sat at the foot of the bed with an empty barbell in her hand, far away from his free hand and the knife. If he attempted to cut himself free, she'd break his kneecap.

Whatever it takes.

"Where did they take him, Barry?"

"I don't know," he breathed. "You won't find him, but they still want you to look. That's why you're here."

"Here?"

"It's why you came here, to look for him. They want you to look."

"Why?"

"To keep it going."

"Keep what going?"

His drug-fueled laughter rattled down the tracks. He muttered the song again, barely arching off the bed now.

She clutched the bedspread. It was stupid to put the knife near him. She wanted to shake the answers out of his mouth, smack him until he bled the truth. She imagined bloodstained pillows and gory laughter, saw herself lost in a rage that would hurt him far more than she wanted. He had answers and he was taunting her. She dropped the barbell. It landed with a heavy thud.

Maybe she'd put that knife there to protect them both.

"*If you want to find me,*" he slurred. "*I'll see you at three...*"

Sunny rinsed the coffee cup and placed it in the sink. He was grinding his teeth when she returned to the bedroom. Sweeping the laptop under her arm, she started for the door. She would look for her son, Barry was right about that. She would find him, too.

It was why she was here.

[11]

Sunny
After the Punch

Sunny held the elevator open.

The hallway had grown longer. Her rain-soaked clothing rubbed between her thighs. Barry's laptop was tucked under her arm. It might not work after the downpour. She listened outside her apartment door. A cat meowed in Mrs. Jones's apartment, the hallway still empty.

Sunny opened the door.

Her apartment exhaled a stale breath. She hesitated outside Grey's bedroom, closed her eyes and uttered a childish wish that didn't come true.

She pulled food from the pantry, aspirin from above the stove and went to the shower to wash off days of sweat and worry, hot water cleansing weary skin. She closed her eyes, the water running to her toes, and sang.

There were no words in the song, just a rambling hymn vibrating in her head. It was soothing, relaxing. She'd done that when she was a kid, following the melodic rhythm of a music box while a ballerina turned on top. She still did it to calm her nerves in the shower, when she was cleaning or driving or just alone.

She grabbed full handfuls of hair. It had grown a full inch.

Wiping steam off the mirror, she dried off in front of it, noticing how the skin stretched between her ribs. The jagged scar throbbed across her forehead. Her fingers trembled over it, the raised flesh sensitive. Her gums were receding; vivid green eyes with lighter bands like a wagon wheel stared back from hollows. Her mother used to talk about her eyes, said they were magical—the outer rings dark and focused, the inner irises streaky green, almost metallic.

No one has eyes like you, Mama would say.

Something fell.

It was a bump on the wall or floor. Sunny's senses perked up, those emerald eyes laser tight. She held as still as prey.

"Grey?" she called.

Nothing was in the front room. The deadbolt on the door was still in place. Rain spit against the window. Clean and alert, she put on fresh clothes, ditching the uniform. Might as well throw it away. She wondered if Donny was at work. Had he tried to call? Did he stop by?

Where is he?

There was a wallet in the back pocket of her uniform. She didn't carry a wallet; neither did Grey. It was filled with cash. The name on the driver's license wasn't familiar, but the face was. His real name was Trevor Martin.

Hamlet.

There had been a party somewhere on Barry's floor the night she'd followed them back. She stepped onto the elevator with them and slunk in the corner as they fell against each other. Hamlet melted onto the floor. She offered to help. Barry stumbled ahead, barfy sounds sliding out of him. That was when she heard the party somewhere on the floor, when she dragged Hamlet into the hall.

Why do I have his wallet?

There was three hundred dollars inside it and a business card. City Shelter for the Homeless. She knew this place, had volunteered there a couple times when Grey was with his dad and she had nowhere else to be. Maybe Hamlet was a resident, was just using Barry for a hot and a cot and a roll in the sexatorium. There was a symbol on the back of the card, something she'd seen before.

A snake eating its tail.

Panic seized her by the neck. She had to get out before someone came looking for her. The man in the black coat, the person on the phone had warned her to leave. *What am I doing here?*

She grabbed Barry's laptop and stepped into the hall. The cats meowed from the old woman's apartment. Lightly, she tapped the door.

"Mrs. Jones?"

The door was locked. Maybe the old woman was sleeping. She only wanted to say thanks for the other day and ask if anything suspicious had happened since she'd been gone. If anyone had called.

Had she seen Grey?

Sunny waited for the elevator. When it arrived, she could still hear the cats.

COFFEE BEANED WAS for hipsters and introverts.

Sunny grabbed a fashionably scarred wooden chair in the corner. Trinkets, local art, and old movie props were on display. A long bull-whip was coiled on the wall, the leather tassels dangling above her head.

Sleep deprivation was bending the corners of the room.

If she closed her eyes, she'd drip onto the floor. This sometimes happened at work when they were behind schedule, when they stacked shifts. Bolts would wiggle out of steel plates and jump like exposed earthworms until she blinked them back into reality. She'd learned to ignore it, to plow through it.

It was how she lived her life.

She would never admit, deep down, tragedy was a welcome change from the monotony. When the trapdoor popped under her feet, at least she felt something. Even if it was terrifying.

Just not Grey. Don't let anything happen to my Grey.

She would give anything to trade places with him, to give him a chance. Her life was half done. He deserved more. She had already dealt him a shit hand of genetic predisposition to soul-crushing depression.

She wanted something different for him.

"Soony?" someone called.

She raised her hand.

The man who had taken her order delivered a muffin. She devoured it and shut her eyes, the chaos of the café driving her down a melting pot of sleep, where rich aromas carried her into a dreamless nap. She awoke to a fresh crowd of people and the laptop warming beneath her cheek.

It was fully charged but choking on viruses. The jump drive contained exactly what he said it would—a long list of video clips, each with cryptic labels and symbols. All of them inside the Maze.

She didn't want to watch them, didn't want to imagine her son in some sort of animated death match where he respawned again and again, dying over and over. Some videos were simple smash and dash competitions. Others were a bit more complex.

All of them psychologically irreversible.

She opened a browser and typed a search: *survivors of the maze.*

It sounded like research, not an inquiry into participation. Whatever alarms crawled the Internet, she hoped it wouldn't set them off. It was an illegal, black-market operation, but these kids were somehow finding the clips without getting arrested.

The first link was a winner. *Stopthemaze.com.*

Sunny tipped the screen and clicked. The infamous icon faded onto the screen—the thick black lines contrasting with a stark white background.

While the menus loaded, her heart sank into the refreshed memory of Grey lying peacefully in bed. Mission statements, personal stories, up-to-date newsfeeds from law enforcement, videos and links to report suspicion appeared.

She wasn't alone. There were others fighting back. Sunny clicked the "About" tab—

"What is the Maze?"

Quickly, she muted the sound and stopped a video, not that anyone would hear it over the music. She read the transcript.

Why does the Maze exist? Money. Power. Those are the big ones. Participants are guaranteed a handsome payout, win or lose. Nine out of ten will, in fact, lose and have no understanding of their winnings that eventually goes to their families. Some see this as a means to help out desperate people in need, but the sad truth is that the Maze feeds on despairing souls to deliver power to the few behind it.

It's gambling with your mind.

The winners, it is said, emerge with clarity of mind described by some as a state of enlightenment, although these claims have been disputed. Because winners are rarely heard from upon exiting the Maze.

Grey could win.

Sunny would benefit from his winnings. She couldn't care less; money was not the cause of her suffering. But would Henk receive those winnings, too? That bastard would revel in that treasure whether Grey was a bodhisattva or a basket case.

What am I thinking? He's been kidnapped. And winners are rarely seen again.

What was worse, seeing him drooling nonsense or never knowing what happened? Her hope continued a slow march to the gallows.

Perhaps, the transcript continued, *one of the most appealing draws of the Maze is something beyond fame and wealth. Some suggest the Maze is a spiritual journey, one that allows the true identity to escape the mortal coil, to be free of the desires inherent in the flesh. The creators of the Maze are rumored to be gods that created humankind as a vehicle to give birth to the mind and, in turn, imagine alternate realities as real as earth and stone. That the games and wealth and entertainment of the Maze are simply a means to deeper realization.*

Not all of the Maze games are blood and guts. Some are psychological thrillers designed to erase the personality so that the players find themselves in the Maze. And thus find the god-spark of creation.

The true purpose of the Maze is a gift to set us free.

Sunny wondered why a site devoted to stopping the Maze sounded more like an advertisement. There was nothing selfless about the Maze. The website's personal stories segment proved that—tales of men and women, boys and girls, all losing out to a game, lured by the promises of money and everlasting peace.

One story caught her attention, that of a single mother finding her son comatose. She had returned from work. He was on his bed. The mother managed to enter the Maze in search of him.

Sunny rubbed her eyes. The names were not Grey and Sunny

Grimm; the faces were different. The people different. It never said if she found him.

She clicked the next link—*ARE YOU A VICTIM?*—but it circled back to the homepage, flashing the Maze icon before reloading the menus. One of the cooks was approaching, his greasy apron dangling around his neck. He balanced a small plate with a scone in one hand, a coffee cup in the other.

Sunny nearly closed the laptop. He stopped just short of her table, turning to an old woman reading a book. She made room for the delivery, nodding her approval. She was bundled in an old coat, a multicolored scarf wrapped around her neck and a silk one around her head.

Black saucer sunglasses.

"Mrs. Jones?"

She looked like a blind cancer victim, but deftly handled the knife and fork to cut the scone. It was the same floral scarf around her head, perhaps even the same clothes as the last time Sunny had seen her in the apartment. A bit more wrinkled.

She slowly chewed a wedge, dismissing the cook with a nod, and thumbed a page of a hardback book. A queer quiver rode a wave of gooseflesh down Sunny's back. Perhaps Mrs. Jones was a regular at Coffee Beaned. Sunny was a first-timer. It felt like she was being followed by the old woman.

Or someone.

"You should be careful." Mrs. Jones jabbed the fork at the wall.

Sunny looked over her shoulder. A hazy mirror hung loosely on a rusty wire, the angle aimed at the laptop and the logo filling the screen. She slammed it closed. A young couple looked in her direction.

The mirror hadn't been there when she got there, or had she been too caught up with the bullwhip? Her focus was fuzzy, attention drained by sleep deprivation.

"A bad idea in public," Mrs. Jones said.

"I was just..." Sunny trailed off. Any explanation was too much.

And Mrs. Jones wasn't interested in one, returning to her book. "Have you seen anything?" Sunny said. "At my apartment?"

Her apartment already felt like someone else's home. *If it's not my home, where do I belong? Where have I been?* She'd lost track of time, unsure how long she'd been away, what day of the week it was. She slid the laptop under her arm. Self-conscious, she preferred to be where no one recognized her.

"What do you wish to accomplish?"

Mrs. Jones pointed with the fork, this time at the laptop. Sunny's twin reflections looked back from the old woman's large black ovals. A whirlpool swirled in Sunny's head, the disorientation that followed an extended ride on a merry-go-round, the curse of vertigo. She held the edge of the table, poised to start walking, when the floor settled beneath her feet.

"Will you watch my apartment," she said, "while I'm gone."

She choked on the words, forcing them through a thicket of emotion. Mrs. Jones couldn't call her; Sunny didn't have a phone. She didn't have anything.

She teetered for a moment, leaned toward the exit and let her momentum carry her forward.

"It's not there," Mrs. Jones said. "What you're looking for."

Laptop clutched to her chest, Sunny stopped at the table, frowning back at the old woman cutting another dry wedge off the scone.

"What?"

The cook returned to the table and leaned over Mrs. Jones's shoulder. She told him the food was good, that she would like another coffee in five minutes. And to bring Sunny a cup, too. Both black. That was how they liked it.

Dutifully, he returned.

The chair opposite Mrs. Jones slid out, the toe of her boot nudging it. Sunny pushed it back under the table.

"Do you know something?" Sunny said.

Mrs. Jones dabbed her mouth with a napkin and thoughtfully

returned it to her lap before sipping her coffee. When she looked up, Sunny's twin reflections stared back.

"I lost my son to the Maze," Mrs. Jones said.

She didn't whisper, didn't cringe. She threw the word out like she'd said daisy or belt buckle. The laptop made tiny popping noises in Sunny's tightening grip.

"What?"

"It's true. Curiosity, ignorance, the folly of youth—the things that define an adventurous young man are the reasons why they get caught in trouble they can't escape. I'm sure you know what I mean, Sunny."

She forked another bite.

"They have to be willing to enter the Maze. My son was tricked. I know it sounds like something a mother tells herself late at night, and I did that often, but this is true. He was manipulated into the Maze. The young are so trusting sometimes. Adults too ruthless. Innocence is a troubling time, wouldn't you say?"

"Your son." Sunny nodded at the book. "He took the punch?"

Mrs. Jones looked down, having forgotten she had been reading, perhaps. She slid it off the table, placed it in a large bag by her chair, but not before revealing the hardcover.

Foreverland.

It appeared to be an investigative work on the incident. She knew about it; the entire world knew about it. It was also the very same event Grey had been researching before he...

"He was lost," Mrs. Jones said, "like so many before him. The mind is vast and endless."

She adjusted the silk scarf, pulling it over her eyebrows. *Did the needle hurt? Was it as painless as anesthesia, instantaneously clipping out a segment of time, transporting him to another place?*

Those were the thoughts Sunny had, the thoughts she imagined Mrs. Jones had entertained night after night as she cupped her coffee in both hands.

"Did you find him?" Sunny asked.

"I went looking, of course. A mother can't help feel sorrow, a certain degree of regret and responsibility. It's unimaginable, the pain. Of course, you know that."

The cook returned with two cups of coffee. Mrs. Jones thanked him. Sunny stared into the steam, the surface as black as the old woman's glasses.

"Do you know what I found?" Mrs. Jones said. "The Maze is an unsolvable mystery, what the Buddhists call a koan, a question that can't be answered. All those silly games people play, the ones where they shoot and kill and rape, are just masturbation. The Maze is truly a swirling riptide of existence, an eternal free fall. It's illogical, a series of contradictions, one fallacy after another meant to pull apart conceptions. It's a place where time stretches into a never-ending moment, an immortal cycle of searching. It's a mouse on a wheel."

It sounded a lot like that website. *How could there be anything redeeming about all this suffering?*

The old woman chuckled without smiling, the wrinkles along her ashen cheeks deepening. "Mind buggery," she said.

"Why?"

"There are lots of Mazes, I'm sure your search told you so." She waved dismissively at the laptop. "Much of what happens is simply entertainment, greed—battles that consume simple minds, the carnal thrill of removing the enemy's head, the sort of thing that fulfills a child. Perhaps if my son had entered one of those sorts, it would've been easier to accept."

Sunny shook her head. "Where was he?"

"I couldn't save him, Sunny." She adjusted the sunglasses. "He'd entered the Maze of contradictions, a destroyer of concepts and identity, an endless dream that would free his mind or destroy it. Only he could save himself; only he could escape. Even if I found him and led him to freedom, it would do no good. He had to find himself. Only he could do that."

For a moment, it appeared she would remove the sunglasses.

Perhaps she wanted to, thought better of it, and pushed them up her nose instead.

"Did you find him?" Sunny asked.

Mrs. Jones returned to staring into her coffee, turning the cup as if the future swirled in its contents.

"There are three questions to be answered," she said without looking up, "before this particular Maze could be resolved. Who am I? Where am I? And why?"

She said resolved, not escaped.

Sunny waited for an explanation, a conclusion that continued hiding in mystery. When she prodded the old woman, there was no answer. Perhaps that was the answer, that her son never found his way out; madness ensued. *Perhaps she went mad.*

Slightly haggard, an ancient presence that could be mistaken for a homeless soul, Mrs. Jones still had knots in her life. Regrets. Maybe helping Sunny was her penance.

"When the time comes," Mrs. Jones said, "don't run. Open the door."

Sunny felt the heat of suspicion fall on her, the intensity of someone watching, someone following. Had their flippant talk of the Maze finally drawn attention? People were still lined up at the counter; dishes clattered in the kitchen. Conversation rambled on the hard floor. She was exposed, standing at the table, laptop cradled to her chest. No one was looking, yet she felt the pressure.

Then saw the black overcoat.

It hung on a rack by the front door, rain drizzled on the shoulders. Mrs. Jones was watching her.

Sunny shuffled back a step. "I..."

She rushed to the back of the room and found the bathroom, locked the door. The laptop teetered on the sink then crashed on the floor. She grabbed her hair, swallowing a string of curse words. The screen was cracked, the corner shedding shattered fragments.

"Goddamnit."

She took a deep breath, braced on the sink and closed her eyes, humming her childhood song, allowing it to soothe the panic standing on her chest. The scar was throbbing. She cupped a handful of water to her face.

It was so much. Too much. The world rushed at her with the ferocity and hunger of a predator. She needed space to breathe, to think. *But then what? Where do I go?* All paths were dead at the end. And the old woman, suspicious or not, seemed to know something.

She wanted to tell her something.

They had to leave the café, go somewhere quiet, somewhere private. She needed Mrs. Jones to tell her what to do. *Because I lost my son, too. And you know it.*

She exited the bathroom without the laptop and stopped. Stared. The table had been cleared. The remaining scone, the coffee mugs, the book and bag were gone, the chairs pushed in. Table clean.

The rain continued to fall on the front door. The coat rack next to it was empty.

The black overcoat, gone.

[12]

Sunny
After the Punch

Sunny stood behind a massive pillar. Blisters chafed her heels. Rain fell on the library steps. She peeked out from the shadows. No one was in sight, but she could feel it, could feel their eyes. She was on stage, the spotlight heating up.

Someone is watching.

There was a mysterious caller and the man in the black coat outside her apartment, her missing son and Mrs. Jones. Sunny had walked through the rain until her paranoid thoughts caught up with her.

Then she ran.

Someone coughed. A little sound escaped Sunny. A homeless woman shifted in a tattered sleeping bag, curled up against the wall. Her lungs were wet gutters. A plastic yellow flower was stuck in her hat, the petals dingy and broken.

Automatic doors slid open. Sunny entered the austere halls of the public library. She needed to sit and think. She also wanted to hide.

The main lobby smelled like floor cleaner and old paper. The circulation desk was wide and inviting. A host of librarians were looking down at whatever business was below the counter; quiet mutters passed back and forth.

Despite the open floor, it felt claustrophobic. Like the sleeves of a shrunken sweater. She headed for the computer cubicles. There was a free one in the corner. She pulled at the monitor, angling it away from the slight man at the help desk.

"Can't do that," the lady next to her said. Her cheeks shook like molds of cherry Jell-O. "They know what you're doing."

Sunny didn't care about the librarians. She didn't want the eyes around her sniffing around. Once that Maze icon went up, everyone would be watching.

And she was tired of that feeling.

She typed *stopthemaze.com*. Hit enter.

There was no icon this time. There was nothing. The website didn't exist, it said. She checked the spelling and tried variations of the phrase. According to a search, the organization didn't exist.

Never did.

The librarian was helping someone with a pink cast decorated with graffiti on his left arm, a sleeve of Sharpie tattoos. He was staring at Sunny while the librarian was busy with his computer. His hair was matted, blue eyes bleached and vacant and aimed directly at her. His body odor had baked into the shredded edges of the cast, a tangy mix of salt and grime.

"Excuse me?" Sunny raised her hand.

The librarian was a thin man of Asian descent. Dandruff spotted his inky hair. He stooped over and whispered, "Is there a problem?"

"Can I search for, um." She whispered behind her hand. "Maze queries?"

Cherry Jell-O stopped typing. Her ears rolled back.

"You may search," he said, "but you may not inquire. Maze-related activities, whether it be inquiries or downloads, will suspend your account."

"I'm researching."

"Be more specific, please."

"Historical, how it started, known arrests. Things like that."

"That's fine."

"Is there another computer?"

Cherry Jell-O's head turned like the turret of a tank. Her eyes were the color of algae set deep in the shade.

"There are some nooks upstairs." The slender librarian was off to help someone else.

Sunny clicked out. Pink Cast watched her walk to the stairwell. A video of a drowning woman played on his computer.

The upstairs wasn't as modern as the lobby. The shelves were tighter and taller, the books hardbacked and frayed. The smell of dust bunnies and long-dead authors haunted the corners.

The computers were taken. She was about to return to the first floor and invade Cherry Jell-O territory once again when a nook was being vacated—an elderly woman pulling herself out of a deep chair that faced a wide window. Sunny reached her in time to help her to her feet.

"I got that next," a girl said.

"No, no, you don't," the old woman said. "She's been waiting."

"Bullshit." The girl glared through slits.

"Watch your language."

She patted Sunny's hand, her fingers knobby and papery. The loopy brown curls of her cheap wig fell over her forehead, the hairstyle made for a woman in her twenties. A chill went through Sunny when she touched her, like the comforting reminder a parent gives her child. *It's all right, Sunny.*

Sunny fell into the seat. It was the most comfortable place in the building, perhaps the most coveted. Slitty-eyes crossed her arms.

"I'm going to be a while," Sunny said.

"I can wait."

"Somewhere else, you can."

Sunny stared until she huffed off, muttering a trail of cuss words. Any other day, Sunny would've dragged her down the steps by the earlobe. Today was not that day.

A computer to herself, she had a prime seat in a public library that overlooked the city. Puddles were still on the sidewalk, but the sky had cracked—a jagged yellow slice bleeding sunlight onto the buildings. She pulled the keyboard closer.

Stopthemaze.com.

The browser spun a moment. The website still didn't exist. She tried another variation. Maybe it was *stoppingthemaze* or *survivethemaze*. Every attempt ended with the same response.

How can this be? It existed in the café.

The search engine never heard of the organization, but it didn't see into the dark web where the Maze operated—an entire world of seediness existed in the virtual universe, none accessible without a password or encrypted link. A world of drugs and crime, out of reach from law enforcement.

She looked around before typing *local maze activity*. No one came rushing at her with a red flag, demanding she turn over her library card. The computer didn't die. But nothing came up.

The city was clean.

The police had no evidence of any organization or citizen participating in Maze-related activity. *That's impossible.*

The way those cops listened to her story, she wasn't surprised. They didn't care. She was hysterical. Pissed off. She had wanted to rub their smug noses in it when she took them to the apartment. Instead, they thought she was crazy.

Maybe they're right.

She typed another search, this one for awareness leaping.

Some hits, finally. Awareness leaping was still practiced in the city. The federal government had put an end to casual use of the technology. Nowadays, only the most extreme cases of psychosis received permission despite the growing research that supported the benefits. A list of licensed tanking professionals was compiled. First line, a boutique vendor was named.

511.

Of course. Their wares in the front room lent themselves to something like this. They were probably fronts for the real technology in back.

Tanks.

There was no way to schedule an appointment, said one page. It could only be accessed through referrals from a short list of psychiatrists. A brief search of their bios made it seem impossible to schedule an appointment within the next decade. Most clients were court-ordered, said one blogger.

Bullshit.

The psychiatrists were shills for the real money, appointments set up with a fake diagnosis. Or sidestepped altogether. How closely were the appointments monitored anyway? Money always found a way to get what it wanted, whether it was government money, corporate or private.

It all spent the same.

A few more searches and she accidentally stumbled onto a blog that, by all means, should've gotten the librarians' attention.

Find your way into the Maze.

She looked over her shoulder. There were a few computer nooks to her right, an older couple combing the shelves to her left. No one seemed interested.

She clicked the link.

It was for aspiring fans of the Maze, should they one day want to get in the game. The odds were good that they would come out insane. *But, hey, it's better to burn out than fade away.*

Death, the blog confessed, was better than the psychological torture they would experience in the Maze, but that didn't shorten the lines. People wanted in. They wanted the money; they wanted the challenge.

Sunny wanted her son.

A list of websites with known Maze connections was listed. It seemed doubtful they were legit given how easily she accessed the list and how little anyone cared. They were probably spammy, virus-infested websites that took advantage of desperate searchers.

The requirements to enter the Maze, the blog continued, were money, of course, and the ability to tank. The nonrefundable entry fee was slightly less than the average citizen's retirement account. If they dropped you in a tank and you were one of the few that couldn't handle it, you didn't get your money back. Not everyone could tolerate the claustrophobic experience of being pickled in a glass jar.

It was a gamble. No secret there.

Now, you could see if tanking was part of your skill set at venues like 511 and their extended training sessions, which brought her back to the psychiatrist problem. You couldn't see if it was in your skill set or schedule a training session unless you were referred. Or knew someone.

But there is another way to enter the Maze, the last section said.

She knew the other way. She had seen it lying on her son's bed, a surgical steel conduit driven through the skull. There were no laws that allowed that technique, not anymore. It didn't matter if you were a homicidal schizophrenic and the punch was the only way to cure you, there were no exceptions.

The needle was part of an outdated technique called computer-aided alternate reality, or CAAR. The results of needle-induced leaping were well-founded, not to mention the well-documented abuse. Foreverland ended the needle's use.

The needle was a form of alternate reality that was globally banned under all circumstances. Perhaps had the Foreverland incident never happened, the stigma wouldn't have torpedoed the technology.

But who wants a hole in the head?

A drip of water splashed on the carpet. There wasn't a stain on the ceiling, no leaks. It wasn't even raining. But there was a spot on the carpet.

The next blog launched her into the blogosphere of paranoid conspiracy. The Maze was simply a recruitment tool for a much greater purpose. It wasn't to make money, even though its investors reportedly made trillions. It wasn't for the thrill of competition. Even though most people were said to pursue it for one of these two reasons, they still weren't the true purpose of the Maze.

It had to do with new universes and gods.

You'll receive an invitation in the mail, the blog said. *A standard white postcard with very little information. It's said the symbol varies, but it typically requires some problem-solving skills to see the infamous icon.*

There wasn't a card in Grey's room. She assumed the dreaded needle arrived via post; maybe the card was thrown away or was in his pocket. But he would've received it before the box arrived.

Right?

These were questions for Mrs. Jones. What clues were left behind from her son? How did he get in? *Didn't she say he was tricked?*

All Sunny knew was her son was gone. And someone had told her a man named Micah could help. She searched 511, but there was no website. They would have no use advertising to the general public. Their clientele found them.

Just like Sunny did.

Micah, she typed. The computer spun its search.

The ceiling dripped again. She leaned over, put her finger on the dark spot, and sniffed it for some reason. It was pungent. *Like something other than water would drip from the ceiling?* Another drip. She saw this one disappear into the tight blue carpet.

Something splashed under the nook.

Her feet were soaked. She pushed back. An inch of water was sloshing under her chair. The spots on the carpet disappeared beneath a rippling sheet of water.

The computer nooks behind her were empty.

She jumped up. No one was at the shelves. Papers were floating in a current that swept up debris. She didn't know whether to run or call for help. She did neither.

Did someone forget me?

A geyser was bubbling up the stairwell, a frothy wellspring of gray, churning liquid that spilled between the shelves and swallowed the desks. The water had risen to her waist, lifting the chair off the floor. Books bobbed in the current, old covers stained and spread open, the pages swelling as they fled the incoming current.

"Help!" She paddled against the tide. "I'm still up here! Someone help!"

The current dampened her words, pushed up to her chest, and slammed her into the window. She kicked off her shoes, treaded off the floor, and banged her fists on the glass. The streets were flooded, the cars submerged. The ceiling bumped the top of her head.

She punched out, but the window rang against her knuckles. The current pressed her against it. Tiny bubbles streamed up the glass. She was trapped inside. Her lungs burned, sinuses stung—

"Ma'am?"

Sunny yanked around in the chair, gulping. The librarian jumped back, hand to his chest.

"I'm so sorry," he said.

Sunny looked around. No water, no flood. Not a drop on the carpet. Everything was dry; nothing had happened. She had fallen asleep again.

"The library is closing."

Sunny pushed herself up.

The librarian followed her to the stairwell, where a gurgling geyser did not exist. Her shoes echoed in the large hall. He walked her to the front door. Dusk was less gray than usual. Even slightly cheery.

Homeless men and women were on the front steps, wrapped in

sheets of plastic or damp blankets. The yellow flower lady was gone, but Pink Cast was smoking a butt.

She turned in the other direction, feeling his eyes on her. She needed to find a safe place to sleep.

Even waking was beginning to feel like a dream.

[13]

Sunny
After the Punch

Sunny's apartment door was locked.

She was searching her pockets for the key when she noticed Mrs. Jones's door was cracked open. A black, silent gap shrouded the opening. It was closed the last time Sunny had come back. *Did the cats escape?*

"Mrs. Jones?" She tapped the door. "Hello?"

The couches were still buried with scarves, the curtain blocking more light than before. She tugged it aside, letting the last remains of a gray day into the room. A dusty haze of cat odor swirled in the dull sunbeam.

"Mrs. Jones?"

Something was off, something strange. Sunny had never noticed Mrs. Jones across the hall until now, but the apartment looked twenty years lived-in. The smell of microwave popcorn was still fresh. Why did she leave the café so suddenly? *Where the hell are all the cats?*

The kitchen was empty, the counters cluttered with dirty dishes. The bathroom was open, the shower curtain pulled aside. The bedroom was infested with knickknacks, the sort that filled resale shops and rummage sales, dusty trinkets and empty picture frames.

Sunny hesitated in the bedroom. She was stepping up her invasion of privacy, peering around the old woman's inner sanctum without her consent. She told herself she was concerned, that something wasn't right. The old woman had left the café so suddenly and the door was open.

The cats were missing, too. Maybe that was the weirdness: the dead silence hanging on the walls. Litter boxes were in the bedroom with wet spots and piles of buried treasures. The smell of ammonia watered her eyes. She pinched her nose, holding back a sneeze.

The nightstand was crowded with silk kerchiefs and knitted scarves, a box of cheap sunglasses, more empty picture frames, and a pair of scissors. Several paper dolls were folded and propped around an alarm clock like marching soldiers. Instead of two legs, they had three. When she wasn't knitting, she must have been cutting these weird little things to keep her company. More had fallen on the floor; others were randomly placed on the dresser and bookshelf, little tripod paper dolls with flat arms wide and waiting for a hug.

There were at least a hundred of them.

Sunny couldn't remember who lived in that apartment before Mrs. Jones. They were shut-ins, as far as she could tell. And it appeared Mrs. Jones moved into their clutter. Maybe they were family. *I should leave now.*

There were photos taped on the dresser mirror. Sunny was drawn in for a closer look. She breathed through her damp shirt, her own body odor wafting out. Pictures were taped on top of pictures, a photo album circling the perimeter of the mirror. Her reflection approached the center.

She had a son, so Sunny assumed she was married. Very few of the photos, however, included people. They were mostly shots of landscapes, spectacular views at nightfall or birds in flight. She didn't recognize any of the locations, certainly not tourist attractions but stunning nonetheless.

She was quite a photographer-turned-paper-doll maker.

Only one photo had people. It was in the upper right corner of the mirror. It was at a state park. There was a waterfall in the background and the faint glimmer of a rainbow rising from the mist. Sunny knew where it was because she had taken a photo just like that, had set up a tripod and tripped a timer. She ripped it off the mirror.

That's Grey.

He was standing on an iron-stained boulder with his thumbs wedged under his backpack. He was ten years old. A woman was behind him, hands on his shoulders, a spontaneous peekaboo moment. Her hair was strawberry, down to her shoulders. That was before she started cutting it.

What the hell?

Sunny had used her photo as a screensaver for a long time. It was her favorite, a digital photo she never printed, but here it was on Mrs. Jones's mirror. It was even an old print with worn edges, the kind that looked developed from film.

There was a noise.

"Mrs. Jones?" Sunny held the photo.

The front room was still empty. No cats. Just the stink of them. The noise came from the hall. She pressed her eye to the peephole.

Her heart punched against her breastplate.

A man in a black coat went into her apartment, closing the door behind him. His face was partially obscured.

Sunny slid the lock on Mrs. Jones's door in place.

She would wait for her to return and ask her to explain the photo. Maybe the old woman was taking her trash down to the chute.

With all her cats.

A WRISTWATCH DRAGGED HER AWAKE.

Sunny woke on the same couch she had slept on the previous time. She stared at the ceiling, searching for her name and then the day of the week. The days bled like watercolors. She pushed all the buttons on the wristwatch to make the alarm stop. The masking tape Grey had wrapped around it was curled on the edges. *For mom* had faded. The buttons were so tiny and complicated. Every night it went off.

Outside, the silence was complete, the city still asleep. The beeping finally stopped.

"Where'd you come from?" She reached down for a purring Siamese cat. "Mrs. Jones?"

The cat trotted toward the kitchen. Sunny checked the bedroom. The bed was still empty and the paper dolls standing guard. A hole in the grouping of photos reflected her tired eyes. Sunny remembered the man sneaking into her apartment across the hall. She'd stood at the peephole, waiting for him to leave, waiting for a chance to see his face. Eventually, she'd grown tired and lay on the couch, listening for the door across the hall to open.

The Siamese was calling.

Empty bowls were under the kitchen table. Sunny went through the cabinets. The cat pawed at the one below the sink. A bag of dry food was rolled up next to a jar of popcorn.

The cat food smelled good. *How long has it been since I've eaten?* The refrigerator was stocked with expired milk and thick orange juice. The cheese was moldy. She was afraid to crack an egg.

A box of granola bars was in the pantry.

The cat rubbed against her legs as she finished off a third bar, chasing it with water. She was fully aware that she had snuck into her neighbor's apartment and slept on her couch and was now eating her food and feeding her cat. Mrs. Jones would understand. She'd lost a son.

But how did she get that photo?

Sunny felt better, less shaky. The sleep helped. And this apartment felt like the only safe place in the world. Slowly chewing the last couple of bites, she savored the sweetness, feeling the fullness, staring at a magnetic yellow flower on the refrigerator. The petals were plastic, the edges curling on a dry-erase whiteboard.

Shaky lines were scrawled in red.

WHO ARE YOU?
WHERE ARE YOU?
AND WHY?

THAT WAS FAMILIAR.

Mrs. Jones had said that in the café, the three questions that needed to be answered in order to escape the Maze. *Did she say to escape the Maze?*

Something else, though. She'd dreamed those questions, too, dreamed of actually writing those words. Sunny could see her hand, the skin was spotted and knuckles knobby as her crooked fingers gripped the marker in a fist.

There was a number on the board.

She took the last bite, the food turning stiff in her mouth. It was a familiar ten-digit number. She had dialed it before, and that wasn't a dream. It wasn't Grey's phone number, not Henk's. She hardly remembered phone numbers since they were programmed into her phone, but this one she had dialed before. She found the corded phone and punched the numbers. It rang three times.

"Welcome to Hadron Technology. If you'd like to continue in English, press or say one."

The phone slipped down her cheek. What was that number doing here? Was this the mystery caller that had told her to leave the apartment the first time?

"If you'd like to continue in English—"

"One."

"Thank you. Your call is important to us. Please listen to the following menu items, or say your extension at any time."

"Fabrication."

Pause. "Hold, please."

A dull silence filled the phone. The Siamese purred against her leg, arching her back. Sunny stared at the dry-erase board.

Who am I? Where am I? And why?

Tears filled her eyes that refused to blink, a thousand questions prying them open, but one rose above all the others.

Why the hell is my employer's phone number on Mrs. Jones's refrigerator?

Maybe they were looking for her at work and left a message. But why call Mrs. Jones? How would they know her? Unless it was the same person from the first time, the one she said sounded from far away. But none of that made sense.

Nonsense was the only constant in her life.

The silence stretched out. It was taking too long. Maybe she shouldn't be calling. The man in the black coat might still be in her apartment. Did he have Mrs. Jones? The phone number was just a—

"Dawkins," someone said.

Sunny stared at the phone like a tongue darted out. She almost dropped the phone.

"Hello?" Dawkins grumbled.

"Um." She held the receiver to her mouth. The words wouldn't come out. She swallowed hard, cleared her throat, took a deep breath and pushed. "Is... Donny there?"

Dawkins didn't recognize her voice. He distantly mumbled to someone. For a moment, she thought he forgot she was on the line or was about to hang up. There was laughter, the scratch of whiskers against the phone.

"Donny punched out early," he said. "He just left."

The phone hit the floor.

[14]

HUNTER
After the Punch

HUNTER MADE a run for the car.

Something warm and salty spread across his lips. His nose was leaking. He leaned back and pinched his nostrils, blood clotting in his sinuses. He'd never had a nosebleed before. But he was older now and things were changing.

For better or worse.

The car carried him across the city. Hunter wiped his bloody fingers on his wet socks where his pants would hide the stains. It was the best he could do. His destination, blurred in the downpour, was approaching. The driver pulled up to the curb on the one-way street.

"Can you drop me off on that side?" Hunter asked.

"No."

"Go around the block and try again, I'll pay extra."

"You get out now."

Someone was waiting for the door to open. She had an umbrella.

"Give me a second."

He didn't need the time, just wanted to stick it to the driver, who would be warm and dry in this little sweatbox for the remainder of the day while Hunter marinated in wet underwear.

He leaned back to apply a few eyedrops. They were always dry after a long night facedown. His body had essentially shut down for twelve hours. A reboot. He blinked, tears streaming.

"Get out now," the driver said.

Hunter stiffed him on the tip.

He jumped around the woman and hid in the doorway to a café and adjusted a water-resistant stocking cap to keep his head dry as well as hide it. The fewer questions about the scar, the fewer distractions there would be.

Across the street, a big window was brightly lit. Someone was inside, an elderly woman with a peach-colored sweater. She was slightly hunched, her back to the window.

Hunter had an appointment.

In fact, he was late. The person he'd spoken to sounded much younger than the peach-sweater woman. If he was waiting for a break in the weather, he would miss his appointment altogether. This city was going in the ocean and he wanted to get out before it hit the bottom.

By the time he crossed the street, his shoes were filled with dirty water. He pulled the glass door open. The room was quiet. The steady drip from his sleeves filled the silence. The floor space was wide open; product displays were along two walls. There was no reception desk or cashier.

The old woman was gone.

She had exited through the door in the back wall. A shiver ran up his back and lingered in his neck. For a moment, the back of his head quivered all the way to his forehead. The scar hidden beneath his stocking cap stung for a brief second, a quick stab from an imaginary needle.

That happened from time to time. A phantom jab would pierce

the dormant stent whenever a memory was jarred loose. Maybe it was the technology that reminded him of the Foreverland days. Or the peculiar smell. Although he couldn't recall anything that smelled like that in Foreverland.

A polished steel stand was a few steps inside the door. It displayed a stack of postcards. Ivory white, the address was embossed in the center. It resembled the minimalist décor. A tagline was stenciled below it.

Find a way to please yourself.

The door opened. Instead of a peach-sweater grandmother, a slender woman in heels crossed the room with quick, hard steps. She carried a bone-white towel that contrasted with her ebony skin.

"My apologies for the delay, Mr. Hunter."

She spoke with a South African accent that was sophisticated and alluring. He immediately wanted to listen to her, let the words softly fill him, as if just hearing them would lift his social status. She handed him the towel.

"You must hate our city. May I take your coat?"

"I'm fine. Thank you."

A puddle had formed around him. He wiped his face and adjusted the stocking cap. She stood back while he wiped down the sleeves. Her smile was bright red and plump. Her eyes, chocolate. Hair closely cropped. Her smell was melodic.

"You mind?" He gestured to the stand of cards.

"Be my guest."

"These are business cards?"

"More like brochures."

He flipped it over, studying the random pattern of black lines, an explosion of ink. "Doesn't tell me much."

"It says everything it needs to." A slight turn of her head, a devious smile. "Take two. You might need them."

Hunter slid a pair inside his overcoat and looked around the sparse line of products. "Commercial minimalism. Don't see that much these days."

"Simplicity, Mr. Hunter. We believe the most elegant products are quite simple."

"And who are *we*?"

"This."

"What do you call *this*?"

The devilish smile returned, painted red. She walked around the room, heels clapping, calves flexing beneath smooth and shiny flesh. She called out the products with a thick accent while he stayed put, following her legs.

"What are you lacking, Mr. Hunter?"

"What?"

"Our mission is to enhance the human experience. What are you lacking that we may enhance?" She spread her toned arms.

"Dry socks."

"Maybe if you found the joy of having wet feet, you would not be lacking."

"Says the person with dry feet."

"Change what you believe, Mr. Hunter, and reality transforms."

"Reality is relative?"

"We perceive what we believe."

"And if we don't believe?"

She strode diagonally across the room, legs crossing in runway fashion, arms swinging. Eyes daring. Hunter had not moved from his puddle. He'd seen products like these; they were nothing special. And that was the problem. Anyone could purchase this online. *Why all the pretense?*

"Problems don't exist, Mr. Hunter." Her scent wrapped around him, the allure of oils, a touch of pheromones.

"Tell my ex-wife."

"You're not married?"

"I come with baggage."

"You appear to pack light."

He handed back the towel, trying to suppress a smile. He wasn't accustomed to a come-on. Not particularly a handsome man, lacking game, he always settled for whomever was willing to talk to him when the party was over. And he didn't go to many parties.

"Are we flirting?"

"I'm being friendly, Mr. Hunter. Are you?"

Her smile said otherwise. If she was friendly, it had benefits. She draped the towel over her forearm.

"I'm investigating a Maze incident. Believe it or not, it's led me here."

"I am aware of your intentions, Mr. Hunter."

"You are?"

"You've been with the FBI most of your life. A career man."

"Very good. How many years, exactly?"

"Twenty-seven."

Hunter frowned. "You investigate all your appointments?"

"We're quite thorough, Mr. Hunter."

"*We?*"

"Do you know where you are, Mr. Hunter?"

"What did I have for breakfast?"

"A bagel and orange juice."

He stiffened. Twenty-seven years with the FBI wasn't hard to find on the Internet. A crafty middle schooler could learn that. *But breakfast?*

She began laughing, a melodic chortle that sang off the walls. When an uncharacteristic snort erupted from her slender nose, she covered her mouth and smiled with her eyes, *undress me* stenciled around the pupils.

"You're staying in a hotel, Mr. Hunter. I assumed you ate the complimentary breakfast and there aren't many options. Bagel was a high-percentage guess, you see."

"Sunny Grimm came to your business," he deadpanned. "She said you could help her, that her son had used a punch to awareness leap and suspected it might be Maze related."

"That is true."

"Why do you think someone sent her here?"

"I'm afraid I won't be of much help, Mr. Hunter. You already know everything. She arrived hysterical, said the Maze emblem was on the punch. I feared for her safety and suggested she report this to the police. There was no one in her apartment, I'm told. I'm afraid she may have suffered from schizophrenia."

"I'm sorry, did she pass away?"

Her smile faltered. "Not that I'm aware of."

"It's just, you used past tense."

"It was unintentional, Mr. Hunter."

"How did you know her son was not in the apartment?"

"The police came to us. They asked questions. Perhaps you should talk with them. They will be of more help than we are, I'm afraid."

"I thought you would know I already talked to them."

"Perhaps I do." She winked playfully.

"Who is Micah?"

"There is no Micah."

She adjusted the damp towel. The corners of her smile sagged. *Her first lie.* But did she want him to see that? Want him to know she was telegraphing a falsehood? Deception was the mission statement of this setup, including the woman in front of him. *A lie within a lie.*

"I didn't catch your name," he said.

"I am Dova."

"Dova? Lovely name. It means dove?"

"Morning dew."

"Very nice. When will Micah be here, Dova?"

Her smile was genuine, unperturbed. "Can I offer you coffee?"

She walked to the lonely door at the back of the room, steps measured and decisive, and returned with a cup. The oils swirled on the mocha surface. He wasn't in the mood, but sipped out of curiosity. Cream, no sugar.

Just like he took it.

"We are very sorry for Mrs. Grimm," Dova said. "We understand why she would come here, of course."

"Because you have connections with the Maze?"

"We deal with high-end technology, Mr. Hunter. Sensory enhancement. Naturally anyone in a state of hysteria would seek out an establishment such as ours."

"She was told to ask for Micah."

"You've made that clear."

"Did you forget that I'm with the FBI? I can look him up, find him in a database. When I do, I'll come back with friends. We won't have coffee."

Her smile grew on one side, eyes walking on him. A faint tickle fluttered over his scalp, the harbinger of something deeper, more insistent. He didn't break eye contact, resisted blinking. Her smile deepened.

She went to the glass wall, observing the crawling traffic. He wondered how many accidents she'd caused just by standing there.

"Micah is an associate."

"Your boss?"

"He controls such things."

"What *things,* Dova?"

"All things are connected, Mr. Hunter. Events, people, natural phenomenon... they are intertwined like fabric weaved together. Pull a thread and the effects ripple throughout existence."

He shook his head, clearing his throat. "What did he do with Grey Grimm? That's all I want to know."

"He did nothing. You must ask Grey what he did to himself."

"Where is Grey?"

"I believe you are asking questions to which you already know the answers."

Her allure returned to wrap around him, tentacles that suctioned tightly, penetrating his senses, his brain. His groin. The image of taking her on the bamboo floor unreeled, a pornographic display for those stuck in traffic.

"I would like to show you our products. You have made an appointment. Perhaps there is something that will interest you."

She took the coffee from him and placed it on the floor, then hooked her arm around his and guided him around the perimeter. Their lazy footsteps echoed. She pointed out the latest iterations of cochlear implants that connected with brainwaves for thought control as well as Wi-Fi speakers; there were visual enhancements that did something similar, purporting to project informational holograms with depth-of-field touch capacity. A mind net, she described, was the newest line of nervous system modulations. It put the user in control. Pain could be dialed back. Pleasure heightened.

She squeezed his bicep. "I am boring you."

"I'm more interested in seeing the rest of your products."

"It is what you see that we have, Mr. Hunter." *The smile.*

"You show only by appointments to high-end customers. This here is just window dressing." He waved at the room. "Pretend I'm wealthy and know nothing of the FBI. What would you show me?"

"I'm showing you everything, Mr. Hunter."

"Show me what's back there." He nodded at the back door. "The awareness leaping tanks."

"I'm afraid those are rumors, Mr. Hunter."

"You mean a psychiatrist can't send a wealthy patient to you for a little dip?"

"Don't believe everything you read."

"Indulge me, then. Just crack the door, let me take a peek. I won't even walk inside."

"We could accommodate your request, but not today."

"Then tomorrow."

"I can let you know, Mr. Hunter."

"I know it sounds like I'm asking, Dova."

She let go and stepped back. "We have nothing to hide, Mr. Hunter. This is what we offer. It is for you to see."

Her smile remained. The back of Hunter's head began to tingle; a faint itch niggled beneath the scalp and reached for the scar on his forehead, stabbing it with a phantom needle. He flinched. Even made a little sound. A valve in his sinus opened.

A warm salty gush flowed over his lips.

"You're bleeding, Mr. Hunter." She pulled a folded tissue from her bosom like grown men came in with bloody noses all the time. It smelled of sweet perspiration.

He tipped his head back. The ceiling was white and curved at the corners, lending it the illusion of endless white sky. Eternity.

"I can take you there, Mr. Hunter, through that door," she whispered. "But it's not what you want to see right now."

"And what do I want to see?"

She cradled the back of his head, wiping the blood from his lip. She stepped back, palming the tissue. "I would like to invite you to a demonstration party."

"Here?"

"No." She shook her head. *Don't be silly.* "I will send a car. You'll see everything you want to see, Mr. Hunter. I assure you. Afterwards, if you are not satisfied, you can make your calls to walk through the door at the back of this room. I won't waste your time."

"There won't be a need to go through the door. You will have made arrangements by then."

"Perhaps." She took his arm and walked him to the front. "A car will pick you up at the hotel."

Hunter stopped to take another card from the stand. He pocketed it with the others. *Find a way to please yourself.*

"Can I ask you something?" she said. "What does your name mean?"

"It's just a name. It doesn't mean anything."

"Is that right?"

"Names don't mean much where I'm from."

"And where are you from?"

"Nowhere."

"Interesting," she said. "I look forward to seeing you tonight. And I will show you everything, Mr. Hunter. Perhaps you can show me something in return."

He could be mistaken, but her double-talk was telling him something entirely different. If she thought he could be distracted by her slim figure and dangerous curves, she was right. This was unusual for him, out of his normal experience. People went out of their way to avoid a federal agent, especially those that peddled technological trade. They made great efforts to cut conversation short.

The rain had given way to a light drizzle.

Hunter stood on the steps. Her footsteps echoed through the glass door. When he looked back, she had already made her way across the room. The itch in the back of his head had calmed down, but something still bothered him. A lot was bothering him, actually, but something in particular was front and center.

Perhaps you can show me something.

He could've sworn she glanced at his forehead when she said that.

[15]

Hunter
After the Punch

A call arrived from the front desk.

Dova had said they would send a car. He'd never told her where. It still bothered him that she knew his breakfast. A bagel and orange juice wasn't exactly original, but slightly beyond a lucky guess. He was being watched and she wanted him to know it.

He arrived in the lobby, waited with a clear view of the street, and pulled a postcard from his overcoat. The *brochure* Dova called it, something that carried less information than a fortune cookie. An address, a tagline and a bunch of random lines.

You see what you see.

There was a challenge in it, something he wasn't seeing. It reminded him of those colorful static posters that contained three-dimensional images. To see them, you had to look at it differently, focus just right and the image would emerge. Some people had an easier time than others.

Hunter wasn't one of them.

He looked at it from various angles, blurred the edges, crossed his eyes, put his nose in the center, placed the card on the other side of the room. Even took a picture and converted it into a negative.

"Mr. Hunter?" the clerk called. "Your car has arrived."

A black sedan was at the curb. Hunter pulled his stocking cap down to his eyebrows. He checked his nose for blood. Two nosebleeds in one day. Perhaps it had something to do with the weather.

Or something else.

The driver waited at the back door. He was Caucasian and middle-aged, a freshly shaved scalp. Tiny flecks of moisture drifted about, a thick mist settling on the waxed hood of the car.

"Where we going?" Hunter asked.

"We'll arrive in approximately ninety minutes."

This was unusual, a federal agent attending a function like this, but they invited him. Perhaps he was walking into a trap. *Or maybe I'm already trapped.*

The driver didn't say a word during the trip. His hands remained on the steering wheel. No radio to pass the time, just the countryside. It was dark when they pulled down a narrow road.

The massive canopies intertwined, blotting out the stars and moon, a cage of knobby branches. His phone had dropped reception at some point during the trip.

Strings of lights greeted them at the end of a winding road. A sprawling oak was draped with dappled light, the kind of tree found in southern climates with moss and resurrection fern, certainly not something he expected to see in these parts.

The driveway swung around the tree. There was a one-story ranch, a green metal roof and a generous porch where ceiling fans turned lazily and people milled about. Someone opened the car door. Hunter stepped out with umbrella in hand, but the air was humid and the sky was clear. It was the first time he'd seen the stars since arriving in the city.

"Recording devices are not allowed." The man that opened the door was not large, but the edge of his voice was sharp. His complexion was the color of putty.

"I was invited."

"Of course you were, Mr. Hunter. We ask that you make no attempts to record the weekend."

The weekend?

"Mr. Hunter." Dova descended the wide stairs in a long red dress, a color that matched her lips and nails. "Welcome."

Hand on his forearm, she rose on her toes to kiss his cheek. He remained stoic and professional, but if she slid her hand to his crotch, he wasn't sure he could stop her.

"I didn't realize this was a party," he said.

"Oh, do not worry. This event is for many people."

"Do your friends know I'm with the government?"

"Ah, you met Blair." She smiled at the man, who was harassing the next car in line. "It is a formality, that is all. Your technology won't work; it is impossible to record. You may tell your friends at the bureau everything you see here, we just prefer you not record the details. Trade secrets, you see. You will probably find this boring, you know so much already."

She winked.

"Then why invite me?"

"You want to see, Mr. Hunter." She hooked his arm and guided him to the front steps. "Would you like a drink?"

They climbed the steps. The house was wide and luxurious, but the single story seemed out of place for the implied opulence and number of people. Most were speaking English; there were various accents and a few foreign languages. They drank martinis and scotch and wine. A few took sips from longneck bottles of beer.

He recognized no one. And no one was interested in him.

"Strange crowd," he said.

"How so?"

He hinted at the beer, the man laughing at a bawdy joke. "Thought you only catered to real money."

"We are not prejudiced, Mr. Hunter. Our mission is to help everyone."

"Who can afford it."

"We are a business, yes."

"That's doing quite well."

She squeezed his arm. "Perhaps you chose the wrong line of work."

"I don't like seeing people get hurt."

She reminded him of the nervous system modulation product line, the promise of pain control and heightened pleasure. This was the next step in human evolution, no longer slave to primal urges and outdated nervous responses. He'd heard that argument for technology before. He wasn't buying it.

He'd seen too many people hurt.

He was one of them, at the mercy of others when he was a child. The scars were still raised, the wounds still raw. *The itch still real.*

"People want to matter, Mr. Hunter."

"And that's why all these people are here? To matter?"

"Among other reasons." She stopped at the front doors and stepped back. *Isn't it obvious?*

"May I take your coat?" a woman in formal attire asked.

Hunter stripped off his black overcoat without breaking eye contact with Dova.

"Your cap?" the woman asked.

"No. Thank you." Rude or not, he was keeping it. His past was advertised on his forehead, something that rarely mattered to him. But here, it seemed prudent to keep it secret.

"Have you eaten?" Dova asked.

"You tell me."

She laughed. "Breakfast was a lucky guess, Mr. Hunter."

"And the hotel?"

"I called around, yes. I suggest for future anonymity you use a different name when checking in."

"Is that all I have to do to remain hidden, change my name?"

"Perhaps."

She pushed the doors open to enter a ballroom. The floor reflected a massive chandelier. White-clothed tables were stationed in the corners with displays of seafood, salads and desserts.

A woman from the staff whispered in Dova's ear. Hunter caught the syllables of another language. "If you will excuse me, Mr. Hunter, I will only be a moment. Please enjoy the food and surroundings."

She was ushered to a doorway on the left.

People gathered in small groups, drinks in hand or small plates. Hunter stood like an introvert shoved on stage for the very first time. Various works of art were displayed on the walls, sculpture on the tables. A large piece was centered beneath the chandelier, a larger than life depiction of Zeus holding a lightning bolt. The Greek god, the ruler of the skies, the father of gods and men.

He moved around the room, stopping at paintings, feigning interest as he looked at faces, memorizing details. He paused at the doorway Dova had gone through, a metal railing spiraling down a stairwell.

A painting grabbed his attention.

It was to the left of the door. A similar one was on the other side. He wasn't interested in the arts, certainly not abstract, but there was something different about this one. Slashes and drips of vivid colors camouflaged a pattern of lines.

Hunter reflexively felt for his coat pocket.

The pattern was the same as the one on the back of the postcards. There was no address, no tagline hidden in the seemingly random spatter of paint. Long lines of yellow were among the dashes, like a chalk line of paint had been snapped across the canvas, a fractured element breaking up space.

Or hinting at it.

"Fan of the abstract?" Dova was at his side.

"Who lives here?"

"The business."

"The business that has no name?"

"Is a rose not a rose?"

Dova cracked the seal on a bottle of water. She did it slowly, let him hear it, let him know it was new. She took a sip and put it in his hand.

"Let me show you something."

Bifold glass doors were open along the back. A breeze gently fluttered the tablecloths. It smelled of earth and water. Dova took his arm and led him to an expansive balcony. The glass railing did not hinder the view to an endless body of water, the horizon sharp and flexing beneath of darkened sky. It couldn't be the ocean, but there was nothing to say otherwise.

"I love it out here." She closed her eyes, inhaling. "Much better than the city."

"Why did you bring me here?"

She paused for several seconds, gazing at the stars in the water before turning her dark eyes on him. "It is how a relationship begins."

"I'm the government."

"Why do you continue reminding me?"

"Because this is unusual."

"We have nothing to hide, Mr. Hunter. Everything is for you to see."

He chuckled. "You want me to see, is that it?"

"What do you see, Mr. Hunter?"

He looked around. Men polluted the air with cigars. Women laughed. An elderly woman was leaning on the railing, drinking in the view. Three stories below, there was a pool. Palm trees rustled in a rogue breeze. *Palm trees don't grow here.*

Dova dug through a tiny purse to find a thin cigarette. She cupped her hands to light it. The smell of cloves streamed from pursed lips.

"When the mood strikes, I smoke." She took another drag. "Have you experienced that, Mr. Hunter? When the mood cannot be denied. You must have it. Like an itch that must be scratched."

He felt like a child who had wet his pants, attempting to hide behind his hands. That was not a lucky guess. There were parts of Hunter's life that he kept hidden, even from himself; memories he locked away to forget. Parts that itched from time to time, that wanted to be remembered. That needed scratched.

A bell rang.

The patrons on the balcony extinguished their cigars and began walking inside the ballroom, forming a line that led to a spiral staircase on each side of the room. The elderly woman remained on the balcony.

"You're ready for this, Mr. Hunter." Dova ground the cigarette beneath her heel. She said it as if they'd been waiting for him, that the time was right. That all of this was for him, despite the crowd.

He lingered outside, unsure whether to follow or not. He was being played, the moves laid out for him. Only traps were at the end of those paths. But he wanted to know; curiosity had sunk its hooks. And all these people couldn't be in on it.

He checked his phone. Still no signal. The agency wouldn't know where he was. But there would be clues if something happened.

He was the last one on the balcony. Hunter found Dova at the back of the line, her hand open and inviting, slipping her fingers between his.

THEY DESCENDED at least three stories, a cacophony of footsteps that measured the plunge to a cool, damp room. A hint of something pungent, slightly spoiled. He expected to see iron bars around the corner, the elaborate joke finally up.

It was another large room, this one subtly lit with dark corners and round tables. It resembled a small nightclub. A circular dais was shrouded by a black curtain. Dova led him to a standing table, a candle flickering on a white tablecloth. She excused herself with a gentle squeeze and left him with his bottle of water.

The crowd was less than fifty people, but how many of them

were business associates pretending to buy whatever they were selling?

Despite the air-conditioning, hot flashes were flaring inside him. He slid the cap off his head, bunching it in his hand. Sweat beaded along his forehead. The air felt stagnant. He could hear his own breath.

He checked for a nosebleed.

Dova was not in the room. In fact, fifty people was a small number based on how many were mingling upstairs. Each of them was welcomed by someone when they arrived. Dova was his invitation.

Or recruiter.

Someone had entered the room and made their way between the tables, occasionally stopping to shake hands, kiss a cheek or share a laugh. They seemed to recognize him, a celebrity among them. Maybe this wasn't their first time, or they'd heard so much about him. His gait was graceful, fluid.

"Welcome, everyone," he said above the chatter. "Welcome, welcome. We can get started, finally. I know we're running a little late, but time is relative, yes?"

There was laughter. Hunter wasn't in on the joke. He knew about time dilation inside the Maze, but they were laughing at something else.

The man climbed onto the dais, his back brushing the curtain. His hair was as white as his teeth, his smile a heat lamp. Hunter could feel it in his stomach, a pleasant sensation that mingled in the heat of claustrophobia.

He clapped his hands. "We're glad to have you."

Hunter drained the bottle of water and mopped his forehead. No one else was fidgeting. They wore big smiles while sitting at attention, every word driving dead center, bull's-eye. Maybe they were all business associates and Hunter was the only real customer in the room, all of this for his benefit, orchestrated to make him feel safe, to lure him deeper into the trap.

All of them watching him.

"Why are you here?" He paced around the dais. Some answered the rhetorical question; his smile never wavered. "You want something better. You know you're more than who you are, you can feel it. Am I right?"

Agreement murmured throughout the room.

"How many of you dreamed last night?" Three silent steps, hands together. "Where did you go? Did you leave your body? Go to Peter Pan's Neverland? Did you experience Foreverland?"

Hunter flinched. Dry heat exhaled through his pores. *Did he say Foreverland?*

"Who are you?" the white-haired man asked. "When you dream, do you become someone else? I speak of a convincing dream, one you feel and smell and hear, a world as real as this."

Several people nodded along, reminding Hunter of those megachurch gatherings.

"Your body is merely a vehicle, not much different than a car. Your body only carries you to your destination. You care for the body, you feed it and bathe it, give it medicine to keep it working. But you step out of the vehicle when you arrive at your destination. So what are you if not the body?"

There were several answers.

"The mind?" The white-haired man nodded along. "I believe we're more than that, my friends. We know the world through our five senses." He counted them off. "Is that all there is? If we are born without sight, how do we know such a thing as seeing even exists?"

The man straightened the curtain behind him. The silence hung as thick as velvet.

"If your body is a vehicle, where is it taking you? I think you have come to the right place with that question, my friends. Each and every one of you has a destination. You are going somewhere, but you don't know where. You don't know how." He took calculated steps around the dais, hands out. A wide smile. "You don't know why."

Hunter leaned forward, waiting for the next words. They came out in a whisper but reached them all.

"My friend, you are blind and cannot see."

The hook was set. They were on the edge of their seats, leaning on the table, against each other. Every word was a turn of the reel, a little closer to shore where the white-haired man waited with a net.

He said friend, not friends.

Hunter sniffed. Sweat seeped into his eyes, smudging details, streaking lights. The white-haired man disappeared on the other side of the curtain. Hunter's pocket buzzed. He jolted with surprise and reached for his phone. There was a text, even though he still wasn't getting service.

Who is this?

He ignored it and looked for the white-haired man. The business with no name was about enhancements, about improving the human experience. Making it more. But this was something else. Something more. He should leave before he felt worse. A swamp of perspiration spread between his shoulder blades. It trickled down his back. He needed some air.

Why did they invite me?

"You didn't come here for money or fame. You have no need for carnal pleasure or simply to dream," the white-haired man said. "*You came to create.*"

Hunter's elbow slipped from the table. An iron tang filled his throat and rang in his head. He wiped his nose. A crimson streak smudged the back of his hand.

"For the first time in your lives, you will know the true purpose of being human. You will truly *see.*"

Hunter's past rushed up from the deep, a leviathan sinking teeth into his mind, tearing away the walls that hid his past, the events that left a scar on his forehead, enslaved him to a lifetime of yearning for something else. Something more. His haunted past had branded him with unobtainable desire. The tropical island where he was first introduced to the needle.

"The universe, my friend, is indeed—" the man raised his hands "*—endless.*"

The black curtain dropped.

Hot air scratched through Hunter's throat, scorching his lungs. He fell into the table and went to the floor. Only the people near him noticed. The rest of the room saw only what was center stage. Hunter caught a glimpse of the upright tank before rolling onto his back. Bubbles streamed up the sides.

A body inside.

He fell onto warm sand and smelled the ocean, went deep into memories that were down but never forgotten. When he hit bottom, the past was waiting.

Foreverland was calling.

[16]

Hunter
After the Punch

Where am I?

Hunter looked through a glass wall that was slightly curved, a horseshoe-shaped building a few stories below. Beyond that was a large green field, a college campus lined with palm trees with giant white birds.

Foreverland Island.

He was a kid when he woke up with a headache and a scramble pot of memories, memories the old men programmed in him, confused him. Memories he believed, he trusted.

Memories that weren't his.

Is that what we are, memories? A record of past events, each one a building block forming an inescapable foundation? Blocks cemented beneath us in childhood, blocks that support us, convince us who we are?

Even if the memories aren't mine.

His memories, the ones before the island, were of a loose childhood. He lived with adoptive parents that disciplined often. Their weapon of choice was an old car antenna that sliced the air before stinging the backs of his legs, a blazing line burning his thighs. His mom slept most of the day. His dad was usually gone.

Hunter ran away when he was young. He didn't plan it, just left school one day and didn't go home. It was the next morning they noticed he was gone. It wasn't long after that he woke up on the island with no memory of how or why.

The old men brought him there and boys like him. They scrambled their thoughts and locked them in cells, made them uncomfortable, and instilled a mad desire to escape their bodies. Eventually, they did. What was left was a young, healthy body with nobody home. The old men in their sick and failing bodies were waiting.

It was the needle that was erasing them. They strapped on a punch and welcomed the needle as it drew them out of their suffering bodies and sent them to a dreamland where every wish came true, a place of make-believe they never wanted to leave, never wanted to return to the agony. Like all the other boys, Hunter embraced the needle, craved its kiss, clung to its escape. Even though it was erasing him, he reached for it when it was offered.

We all did.

He'd survived the island only because the authorities arrived, but it taught him one thing: memories couldn't be trusted. He kept them at arm's length, regarding them with suspicion. Who he was—his identity, his core existence—was something more than just memories; he believed, like all sentient beings, he had an essential nature that used memories to form an identity but didn't require them to exist.

He'd escaped the island, was rescued from the old men before they stole his body, but part of his mind never left.

The island is inside me.

The jungle began to fade. An off-white ceiling replaced the sun and sky. His vision was obscured by a damp cloth over his forehead.

He wasn't looking down on the island. He was lying in a chair and struggled to sit up.

"Shh-shh." Soft, thin fingers stroked his arm. "Slow down."

His body was heavy, a mold filled with wet sand. He dropped his head into a pillow. Water was running down the walls to his left and right. The wall in front of him was transparent. It overlooked a great lake. Unlike the island, this glass wall was not curved. The moon hung above the horizon.

"What..." His throat jammed up.

"You're in the healing room," Dova said. "Many find it soothing to be here after an overwhelming experience." She smiled down on him, pupils large.

His front teeth were numb and slightly loose. He ran his tongue over his lower lip. The taste of clean iron and the sting of a neat gash were near the tip of his tongue.

"You fell before we could catch you," she said. "I never should've left you alone. Your reaction wasn't unusual. It just came a little faster than anticipated."

She dabbed his cheeks.

He pushed onto his elbow despite her resistance. The chair folded to his new position. A full view of the lake was below. She offered a bottle of water.

"You drugged me." His words were long and slurred, heavy and wet. They put something in the water, uncorked all those memories of Foreverland, things he wanted to forget. *But she opened it in front of me. Took a sip.*

"I assure you, Mr. Hunter, you were not drugged. Others have had a similar experience. It is why we escort our clientele. It is quite overwhelming when first exposed to the possibilities."

He shook his head. That wasn't it. He knew all about tanks and awareness leaping, of the alternate realities they experienced. He'd seen that show a thousand times. It was his head. It had begun to itch. The residual was still in his skull, a creeping worm that inched its way up and down the dormant stent buried beneath the scar, scratching the gray matter in search of a way out, dragging him back to the island.

"There is a certain energy," she said, her full lips curling, "that fills the room during these moments. You experienced this."

It was illegal, what they were doing. And they knew it. Recreational tanking was what they were selling. The sales pitch suggested something more than mere entertainment, though. To create.

Create what?

They wanted him to see it, an agent of the federal government. But why? He twisted around. A door was in the back wall.

"You are free to go, Mr. Hunter." She chuckled. "You need a few moments to recover, get your strength back. Your legs are weak. Another fall like that and you'll lose a tooth."

"What you're doing, you'll all be arrested if I leave."

"We are doing nothing illegal."

"You're peddling awareness leaping to paying customers for recreational purposes."

"That is not what we're doing, Mr. Hunter."

"What are you doing?"

"Teaching people to see."

"I have to report this, Dova. Your operation will be shut down, I promise you. You will be detained. An operation like this will get you… arrested. Prison, most likely."

Guilt twisted his stomach. He didn't want to do it, didn't want to report this. He knew why. She had cast a spell and he was lapping it up.

"You've seen what we do, Mr. Hunter. You know our potential." She dabbed his swollen lip. "And we know yours."

He stopped her from caressing his cheek. Her wrist was slender, the tendons rigid. He imagined the taste. He threw his weight forward. Blood surged in grainy waves, pixelating his vision. A black tunnel rounded the edges. He took a moment before standing, swaying in place.

He made it to the glass wall with his hand out. They were two stories above the pool, the water clear blue. The top floor and balcony was above them. *Weren't there palm trees?*

He was certain he'd seen them. Palms didn't grow this far north. But now there was only the pool and big pots spilling flowers. A sudden urge to vomit buckled his knees. He held himself up, his damp palms pressed flat.

"What have you done to me?"

"We have done nothing." Dova put her hand on his waist. Her touch was delicate. Sensual. "You chose this."

Her fingers trailed up his back and slid over his shoulders. She wrapped her arms around his chest and stroked his chin. Her touch sent shivers through his neck, around his head. Her fingers traced the creases above his eyebrows and stopped on the tiny scar where a stent used to be.

You chose this. Was she talking about Foreverland? Because he didn't choose that.

"We know who you are," she said.

"And who am I?"

Her breath was in his ear. Her hand worked through his hair and found the secret on the back of his head. A queer sensation knifed through his brain. He jerked away and found himself leaning against the wall. Water spilled down his arm, dripping from his elbow.

He worked his way to the door and turned the handle, surprised to find it unlocked. The hallway was empty. Dova remained across the room, his prints smudging the glass wall next to her. She did nothing to stop him. She didn't have to.

We both have secrets.

They knew his addiction, the one he kept hidden from the world. *But I didn't choose this.*

Addiction was forced upon him, but it was his now. If the government knew, he would be ruined—an employee that compromised their entire purpose. He would be singled out as a mole, an informant. As part of the problem.

I'm worse than that.

But he only hurt himself. These people were doing something worse; they knew what they were doing and disguised it in some greater purpose. He just didn't know what that greater purpose was.

"Consider our proposal, Mr. Hunter."

"And what is that?"

The itch flared in his head. He knew what they offered. *Peace. If you join us, you'll have peace.*

"Sunny Grimm," he said. "Her son. Do you know where they are?"

Her grin was pleasant. "*You* know where they are."

"I want to speak to Micah."

"When it's time, he will find you."

He looked down the hall. He could ruin them. He wouldn't even have to run; they would let him walk out and he would make a call and ruin their entire operation.

Dova strode across the room. "Freedom, Mr. Hunter, cannot be forced upon you. All we can do is offer. You must see it. You must choose it."

"I didn't choose this." He clutched the hair at the back of his head, clenching his teeth. "*I didn't choose this.*"

His addiction, his compulsion lived inside him. It demanded of him. The old men did this to him. *But I'm the one feeding it.*

She took his hand and walked him through the door. The hallways were empty, her footsteps sharp. A car was waiting outside, the back doors open. The grounds were empty. *Where is everyone?*

She climbed inside and pressed against him. Hand on his thigh.

"What if I tell my superiors?"

"You are free to choose, Mr. Hunter."

Of course he was. They were prepared for this. He'd stepped into something much bigger than he imagined. Even now, he had no idea.

The stars disappeared as they drove to the city. They stopped in front of his hotel, rain dancing on the hood. She opened the door, then walked him to his room and laid him on his bed.

The brain itch had grown into the serpent inside his head. It was hungry. Dova slipped off his shoes. She removed his pants. His shirt. Her hands kneaded the knots from his shoulders. She climbed on top.

Her flesh warm. Muscles taut.

In the morning, she was gone. For the first time, the brain itch had disappeared without being fed. It just disappeared. He woke bright-eyed and clear-minded. A new man with a taste of peace. They had him.

Whatever they wanted from him, he would give.

[17]

Grey
Before the Punch

Coffee Beaned was a long café, separated into a front and back room by an open grill and bathrooms. Grey stood next to the men's room and watched a group of girls around a laptop. He texted a message. One of the girls looked at her phone, then turned it over.

That was Rach.

Officially, they weren't boyfriend-girlfriend anymore, not since the textathon letdown just before a warrior dwarf lost his head. But they'd been friends since the third grade. In fact, she was his best friend before her boobs came in. Then there was high school and the whole kissing thing and now she was dusting off his texts because once you traded in the friend card for a roll on the couch, you couldn't go back.

"Can I get a small coffee?" he ordered.

"A petit?"

"Just a small."

"You want a pour over?"

"Yes."

He had no idea what a pour over was, but it cost three times more than a crime. He went back to the bathrooms, cup warming his hand. He took a sip, the first and last, and waited. Rach was still involved with the laptop. He thumbed his phone.

I'm at Coffee Beaned. Watching you.

He deleted the last part. A bit stalkerish. So was the first part but whatever. It didn't matter. She didn't even pick up the phone this time. He could stand there and wait and stare and let it get weirder.

Or nut up.

Petit pour over in hand, he started for the corner table. Anna elbowed Rach. Three of the girls averted their eyes as if a hunchback was about to ask them to the prom. Rach was the last to look up.

"Can we talk?" he asked. "Just for a minute. Over there."

"Awkward," one of them sang.

Rach excused herself. The girls were muttering before Grey passed the bathrooms. He stopped at a stand-up bar along the wall, a dusty mirror revealing his moptop of curls and her short bob. His sheepishness. Her confusion.

"What are you doing here?" she said.

He kicked the floor. The coffee was scalding his hand. The lid had fallen off at some point during his escape.

"You all right?" she asked.

"Yeah. Yeah."

"Sorry about, you know, breaking up with a text. I didn't think you'd care, to be honest."

"No, yeah. I get it."

"Oh, good. Glad it didn't bother you. At all."

"Look, I'm a shitty boyfriend. It was a good call."

"You're not... listen, we're not good that way. We tried, it didn't work, that's that. Can we just go back to the way things were?"

"How about tomorrow?"

"Okay. That's quick."

He put down the coffee. *I hate this shit.*

He didn't know if he meant the coffee or the coffee shop or the music or the fact that she was hanging out with fake-ass girls who were talking about him. She wasn't that way. Even if she wanted to be, she wasn't a cardboard cutout.

"It's about my dad," he said.

"What about him?"

"He's doing something and I just want to... listen, I'll give you gas money."

"For what?" She shuffled back.

"We won't see him, I promise."

The promise was a stretch. He couldn't guarantee his dad wasn't going to be waiting wherever he wanted to go. The odds were long, so his promise was in his favor. It was far from a lock.

"I need a lift."

"So you're using me for my car?" she said.

"Yeah."

Her blond hair shook off her neck, revealing the tattoo she got one day after school. He was with her, held her hand while she laughed and cried, said it hurt worse than having a baby, not like she'd know. It was a tattoo her parents still didn't know about.

"My dad is up to something."

"You just said we won't see him."

"We won't. I just want to follow up on what he's doing."

She sighed. "Call yourself a car."

"It's too far." He shuffled with his head down. She'd know he was lying. She was the one that told him he shuffled when he lied.

"I don't want to be alone," he said. "Not right now."

"Grey, listen—"

"I'm not saying we get together, creep. I just... I need to follow up on something. It'd be cool if you were with me. That's all."

"And you want to use my car."

"That too."

She looked at the corner table—the trio of teenage vampires

watching them—and jutted out her jaw, tapping her teeth. She knew when he was lying, but she didn't know he knew when she was about to give in and just needed a nudge.

"You did break up with a text." Grey shrugged. "Just saying."

RACH PICKED him up at the curb. He jumped into the front seat.

"Did it have to be so early?" she asked. No makeup and thick-rimmed glasses, she just woke up. He handed her a disposable cup. "What's this?" she said.

"Coffee."

She stared for a long moment, considering the motive. He was a shitty boyfriend, but not a bad friend.

"What for?"

"Just because." He mounted his phone on the dash. The GPS started a route. "Okay."

"Want to tell me where we're going?"

"Not really."

"Just not with your dad, right?"

"Promise."

She heard the sliver of doubt—he was 99.9% sure—but pulled away from the curb anyway, sipping the coffee. He'd even put creamer in it. That might have saved the morning.

His dad had been her dentist when she was little. *He's a little weird,* she would say. *Leans on me funny.*

He never tried anything with her, didn't grab her or invite her to do something. It was the way he hugged her too long when she came by the apartment before Grey's parents divorced; it was how he kissed the top of her head and smelled her hair. *It's old man creepiness, that's all,* Grey thought. *The kind that's inappropriate but innocent.*

He did put her under anesthesia once. Her mom was in the waiting room when she had her wisdom teeth extracted. The door was open when Rach woke up. She talked her mom into changing dentists after that.

He just creeps me out, was all she ever said.

He wasn't always that way. Grey still remembered the dad that came home with video games, the dad that pulled all-nighters to beat campaign mode and spent weekends in online tournaments. Sometimes they watched horror movies. Mom would go to her bedroom with popcorn and read a book while they fell asleep on the couch.

He listened to hard rock. Threw New Year's Eve parties. He was a cool dad. Until Grey was seven.

The divorce changed him.

Mom never said anything, but he was up to something. It wasn't until Grey was older that he understood the looks he passed around the room. The new cologne, the cars he bought, and the closets of expensive clothing.

The way he leaned into his clients when he drilled cavities.

Mom wasn't perfect. She didn't drink, didn't fight. Didn't do much of anything. When she walked into a room, it dimmed just a little. Her smile looked more like a frown. She'd slip off to bed long before the party was over and no one would notice.

But she didn't deserve what he was doing.

"Where the hell are we going?" she said. "It says another hour."

They reached the city limits, the freeway aiming for the green countryside. "Just follow."

"I'm not driving two hours for nothing." She shouted, "I swear to God I'll turn this car around."

She threw glances at him, each time driving onto the shoulder. Even with both hands on the wheel and eyes ahead, she was a horrible driver. Staring holes into the side of his head was going to launch them into a guardrail.

He pulled out a white card.

"What's that?" she asked.

He folded the worn creases like shutters, the sides nearly meeting edge to edge. The thick lines on the back of the card lined up with the exposed exclamation mark.

"It's an invitation."

"For who?"

"My dad. I think."

He explained the white cards on the refrigerator, his weekenders, the way he smelled when he got back, the way he looked. The strange emails, the respirator in the bathroom.

"I turned on his phone one weekend." He pointed at the GPS. "He went there."

"Where is that?"

Grey shook his head. He wasn't sure exactly. His dad's phone had shut off. A search of the area led in several directions, but he had an idea.

"If this is what you think it is"—she tapped the white card—"you don't just walk up and ring the doorbell. You sure about this? Your dad just doesn't—"

"Seem like the type?"

The same doubts nagged him. His dad didn't know much about technology. Maybe he was bored and had indulged himself into complacency. The Maze was a challenge. And there was the money.

And the missing college fund.

"So where do you think we're going?" Cars were passing them. "Exactly."

"To the lake."

"And then what?"

She continued to stare. He wondered if she forgot she was driving. He pointed at the road. She looked over just as the tires kissed the shoulder.

"If you get us killed..." She sped up. "I'm going to kill you."

Grey scrolled around the map. He hoped there would be something obvious when they reached the point where his dad turned off his phone. Then he realized he had no reception. Not a single bar.

They were in the country, but not a desert. The lake wasn't far away. Somewhere, there was a house on the water. A big one. They were on the road that led to it, a two-lane highway in need of repair and not a side road in sight or a house in the trees. Pretty soon, the highway was curving inland.

"Think that's it?" Rach asked.

"What?"

"That little road."

He didn't see it. Rach turned around in the middle of the highway. They hadn't seen another car in twenty minutes. The little road turned out to be a couple of ruts buried in a forest. About fifty yards off the highway, a cast-iron gate was anchored to brick columns; a sign in neon orange warned they were trespassing.

Rach turned the car off. They stared at the sign, the thick bars. There was no fence beyond the pillars, just a barrier to keep someone from driving up the road. But not from walking around it.

"We'll just walk a little ways, see what's up there," he said.

"What if they got dogs?"

"They don't have dogs."

She was twisting the wheel. Unblinking, staring. Tears welling in dry eyes, not from fear or sadness, but throat-gripping adrenaline. That was how she looked when they gamed all night. *And what could be more serious than what was beyond that gate?*

"Goddamnit," she whispered.

That was why she drove him, why he wanted her to come along. All those Maze videos they'd watched growing up didn't seem real. Deep down, they never believed people were going insane. The Maze was an urban legend. Not anymore. The gate wasn't anything special, could've been some wealthy introvert staying off the grid. But his dad had come out here. Grey knew there would be something to see, something to climb or walk. And he needed Rach to come with him. That simple little gate cast aside all doubts. She felt it, too.

The Maze is real.

"What do we do when we get there?" she said.

He shrugged. He hadn't planned anything beyond looking at

it because his hormone-fueled brain held a little secret fantasy that when he got there, he would ring the doorbell and they would answer. They'd be pissed at first, wonder how he found the place and then for some unknown reason invite him inside. That was when they'd see how passionate he was about gaming, how he studied awareness leaping, how he downloaded all of their torrents and even solved the mystery of his dad's invitation.

They'd know that he was worthy.

A truck came up the road a little too fast, bright lights piercing the forest. It jerked to a stop just on the other side of the gate. He snapped out of the daydream just as Rach reached for her door.

"Wait." He put his hand on her arm.

A man and a woman got out of the truck and waited for the gates to swing open. They were casually dressed—no bulges in a business suit or black stretchy pants. They approached cautiously and signaled for them to roll down their windows. The man came around Rach's side.

"This is private property."

"Sorry." Grey leaned over. "We're almost out of gas and our phones are dead. We were hoping someone could help."

The guy took out his phone. The woman was at the gate, holding up her phone. She was taking a picture of the car. Grey wanted to lift his arm to block the camera, but it was too late for that. The man stood back

"You need to turn around."

"But we're almost out of gas," Grey repeated, a lie that would hold up until they looked at the gauge, after which he would say that was broke, and then get punched in the face or stun-gunned.

"Not my problem."

"Just let me call my dad," Grey said. "He'll pick us up."

He looked for a sign of recognition when he said that. *My dad.* It came by way of a sly smile on one side of the man's mouth. Maybe they didn't know who Grey was when the gate opened, but he did now. Instead of pulling the gates wide to make room for Rach's car, he pointed at the highway.

"Turn it around. Now."

Grey reached for his door. He was getting out, was going to talk to them. Have some mercy. They were from the city; they'd be stranded. They just needed to make a call. You know, talk to someone. This wasn't what they thought it was.

Rach popped her door open. The man slammed it closed. Gripping the frame with oversized hands, he bent down and looked inside the car. His cheeks had the texture of clay with childhood pockmarks. He didn't bother looking at the dashboard where the gas gauge sat just below empty.

"Back the car up, and don't come back."

His words tumbled into the car. He didn't pull back until Rach dropped into reverse. A curt nod, he took three steps back and watched them back up the rutted driveway. The woman watched from between the truck's highbeams. The glare obscured her face, but it was unlikely she was smiling.

Rach swerved onto the soft shoulder and jerked the car into the opposite lane before getting back between the lines. Her hands were shaking on the steering wheel. They drove in radio silence for a mile, only the sound of rubber grinding asphalt between them. Rach was squeezing the steering wheel, eyes flicking in the rearview then to Grey and back to the rearview before speaking.

"Your dad is so in the Maze."

[18]

Grey
Before the Punch

"You KNOW what I don't get?" Rach said. "Why they were using phones."

"What do you mean?"

"I mean, if they're connected to the Maze, shouldn't they have all the sensory upgrades. You know?" She sipped at the cold remains at the bottom of her coffee cup. "They should've been grabbing screen shots with a retinal lens."

"Maybe we should've asked."

"I'm just saying don't you think that's a little off."

He didn't know what to think. According to his best guess, his dad had been heading for that driveway when his phone lost reception. There were no other houses or driveways for miles. Maybe whoever was beyond the gates owned it all. That would go along with illegal awareness leaping. It didn't prove the Maze was back there.

The invitations did.

"What next?" Rach said.

Grey looked over and frowned. Her lofty tone of hope was unexpected. In fact, it scared him a little. There was no going back to the front gate, not after that. And she was the one talking about dogs and doorbells. Now she wanted to know what next, as in *you're not giving up, are you?*

Grey's pocket vibrated. He pulled the phone out and quickly tucked it between his legs.

"Is that him?" Rach said.

"Yeah."

"You should answer."

His dad rarely called his phone. He next left a message. The phone had buzzed three times since clay face ordered them to get the hell off their property. Now there were three messages.

Grey didn't listen to any of them.

"What do you think he wants?" Rach said.

Those people took pictures. They'd captured their faces and Rach's license plate. Maybe they had all the sensory augments going, too. If they did, they had access to facial recognition databases or even the department of motor vehicles, if they were connected. It wouldn't be hard to identify them. After that, they would make the connection to his dad.

This was coming together, but not exactly like he thought because he had no plan. *Just drive up and ring the doorbell* was pretty much it. The city loomed ahead. The buildings hadn't come over the horizon, but the haze was creeping toward them.

"He knows," Grey said.

"How?"

Grey turned a lazy stare on her.

"What do you want to do?" she asked. "You can stay at our place. My mom knows what your dad's like."

He'd been running all his life and could never outdistance his problems. Even when he managed to get some breathing room, found peace and equanimity in a boring moment, he managed to fuck it up.

It was like he couldn't stand swimming with the current. It was too easy to just drift along. Why not go against the current and make things interesting?

Only this wasn't interesting. And he was tired.

He took his phone off silent and scrolled through the messages. Besides his dad's waiting messages, there was a text from his mother.

Where are you?

With Rach, he answered.

A minute passed. *Your dad's trying to reach you.*

Grey typed a message and deleted it. Typed another and deleted that one, too. There was only one way out of a tailspin. It wasn't going home to Mom or hiding at Rach's apartment. Even if they had enough gas money to keep on driving, his problems would come along for the ride. So why not just keep swimming into the current?

"Come up with me," he said.

GREY STOPPED OUTSIDE THE ELEVATOR. His dad waited outside his apartment door. Hands on his hips and a dad-pooch pushing against his belt, he blocked the hall.

"You," he said. "Get in here."

Two teenagers were on one end, a bowed-up dentist on the other. It was a showdown of teenage angst and failed parenting. He chopped his arm at the open door.

"Now!"

The dad-voice had been engaged. It reached deep into Grey and snatched the five-year-old still hiding inside to the front line. The legs cooled a few degrees. A year ago, it would have bullied his ass down the hall and sat him on the couch. Hell, maybe even a month.

Not anymore.

"Let's do this out here," Grey said.

"What did you say?" His dad took a step. "What did you... get down here, you shit. Get down here!"

A door opened halfway between them. Mrs. Nichols peeked out, her robe revealing fuzzy pajama bottoms that matched her slippers. She looked in both directions, a casual observer caught in a gunfight but too fascinated to find cover.

Grey started the walk, slow and even. He greeted Mrs. Nichols with a smile.

"Rachel, go home," his dad said.

"She's coming inside."

Grey stepped into his dad to screen her. He was almost half a foot taller than his old man, with eighteen-year-old muscles to back him up. His old man had dad-power, a special skill that made children brush their teeth and do their chores. But that universal power was dimming. They touched bellies as Rach snuck into the apartment behind Grey.

His dad took a moment to explain things to Mrs. Nichols, said it was fine, you know how kids are these days. They never listen.

Or listen to the wrong things.

His dad's cell phone was in three different pieces. His footsteps were as measured as his words. He shut the door gently and propped his thin arms on his hips again.

"What do you think you're doing?"

Grey stood a half step in front of Rach. Suddenly, this seemed like a bad idea. He was certain he could pin his dad to the ground if it came to that, but he didn't factor in the instinctual dad-rage that kicks in when the young bull steps up.

"Answer me!" He kicked a chair and raked a stack of paper off the table. "You followed me, is that what you did? You followed me and... what?"

"What were you doing out there?" Grey said.

"I gave you a home, gave you food and clothing and you rape my privacy, you savage! I have to install security cameras on my own son for real?" Hands on hips, he paced. His breath scratched its way in and out. "Answer me!"

Grey slammed the invitation on the counter with an open palm.

The flaps hinged open, but the symbol was still apparent. His dad stared, eyes flickering to the refrigerator and back. Then he laughed.

"Is that what you think?"

"What else is it?"

"A *game*? You think I was driving out there for that game?"

"Then what is it?" Grey slapped the invitation over and over. His dad watched his tantrum peak. The more heated Grey became, the calmer his dad appeared.

"The Maze is a poor man's desperation," his dad said. "Nothing more."

"There were some sick motherfuckers that met us at the gate and turned us around. What are you doing?"

"You wouldn't understand. You're a kid." His slender finger darted at Grey. "And you betrayed me."

"I betrayed *you*?" The top of Grey's head was about to explode. "What are you doing?"

"It doesn't matter."

"What were you doing?"

"It doesn't matter!" His dad's delicate fingers curled into fists. "What I was doing depended on confidentiality and not my son dragging his girlfriend to their front door. What I was doing is over because of you."

He took a strong step in their direction. Grey braced for his old man's rage then watched him go to the refrigerator and wipe everything off. He picked up the second invitation off the floor, the one Grey left on the freezer, and tore it into pieces.

"Done! Everything I worked for is done because you had to stick your nose in it, Grey. Couldn't let me have a moment, could you?" Spit bubbled in the corners of his mouth, lips pulled over perfect teeth. "All my money, gone. Wasted. Because of you. *Because of you!*"

"*Your* money?" Grey snapped. "That was *my* money you wasted. My college fund, my savings. You took it; you spent it. That was my money, you say it! Who betrayed who, Dad? Huh? Say it, that was my money!"

His dad stiffened. A flash-frozen expression of shock snuffed out his rage.

"Yeah, I know you spent my money," Grey said. "It doesn't take a genius. You put Maze invitations on the refrigerator, leave bank statements on the table, tape your passwords underneath your keyboard. My college fund went to zero when you went on that month-long *vacation.* Or, more specifically, the Sessions."

His dad looked at the kitchen table, his bedroom and rested on the floor as he recounted all the carelessness. Of course Grey was snooping. He'd just had no idea to what extent. Until now.

"I know what you do, always. Your emails, your weed. Your porn. You scatter breadcrumbs like a child. The respirator gear." Grey pointed at the bathroom. "You were practicing for the tank, weren't you? You were getting used to long-term submersion, the way it felt to breathe underwater. Why else would you keep it in the bathroom? It's like you want to be caught. And then you blame me."

His dad rubbed his mouth, still staring at the floor. A trapdoor had just swallowed all his plans. Maybe his dad was just a glutton and the Sessions was just a month on a tropical island. Maybe this was his last attempt to make it up, win the Maze and start a new life.

He shuffled to the giant glass wall that overlooked the bright city. "Get out."

"Tell me what you were doing."

"Get out of my apartment."

The iron grip of guilt or shame or hopelessness that was just there moments ago vanished. He spun around, grabbed Grey by the throat, and slammed him against the window. An inch of glass was between him and a nine-story plunge. Grey seized his dad's shirt, bunching it in both hands. Rach shouted, pulling at their arms. His dad leaned in until their noses were almost touching. Minty breath mingled with his lotioned hands.

"Get out of my life," he hissed.

He shoved Grey into Rach.

The secrets were exposed. The empty bank accounts, bankrupt

morals and bottomless self-doubt. And his dad had more to hide. That was what was behind the rage and panic. These secrets were out. *But there was more.*

"You were tanking," Grey said. "Practicing awareness leaping, admit it."

His dad said nothing.

"You strapped on a sensory suit and dropped into a tank. Your senses were transformed, your awareness pulled into an alternate reality where *a new universe awaited.* You came home stinking of it. You think I'm an idiot?"

His dad turned his hollow stare back out the window. Perhaps he was rethinking everything—the Sessions, the marriage. His son. If it would all go away, he would be happy; if he could just create a new reality, escape into another universe, then he could start a new life. He could be happy again. At least for a weekend.

"You couldn't do it, could you?" Grey said. "You failed to drop in the tank, so you bought the respirator to practice. But the tub ain't like the tank, is it? It doesn't have the same claustrophobic feel, doesn't have the walls, the finality."

The Internet was filled with failed attempts. Tanking wasn't scuba diving. The long-term respirator for awareness leaping fit deeper into the mouth. Even if the user didn't have a gag reflex, there was the coffin-like experience, the tightness of being buried alive.

Users would thrash against the glass, claw at the cable attached to their backs, ripped the respirator out as they were winched to the surface, crying as they hung over the edge. Some of them were frightened, caught in a reaction they couldn't escape. Deep down, though, they all wept because they couldn't do it. They knew they wouldn't be able to awareness leap.

And they wanted it more than anything.

They hated this world. They wanted out. Wanted a dream that felt warm and fuzzy. And if they had a taste of a new universe before the panic set in, if they visited a new reality that made them happy for just a moment before failure ripped it away, they went full-on manic. They would never escape who they are.

And this world is dull and lonely.

"Where were you leaping?" Rach asked. "If you weren't joining the Maze, where were you going?"

"He was training, Rach. That's what that place on the lake is. You get invited, they train you for the leap, then commit you to the Maze. Isn't that right?"

"You're just a kid." His voice leaked out.

"Then tell me. You're my dad, tell me what you're doing. Maybe I can help."

"Not everything is a game, son. Sometimes it's life and death."

"What does that mean?"

He rubbed his chin, contemplating thoughts that seemed to evaporate just beyond the window. He dropped his hand and casually, as if he suddenly needed a nap, started for the bedroom.

"Close the door behind you and don't come back. I'll tell your mother that we're done now, she can deal with you. I'm a shitty dad; you're a shitty kid. I'll take responsibility for both of us. Just get out."

"I'll get you back in there," Grey said. "I can tell them it was an accident, that I didn't mean to go out there."

Grey grabbed his arm. His dad yanked away. This was all a mistake. It wasn't supposed to end like this. They were supposed to get things off their minds, air out the dirty laundry then sit down and fix things.

"Don't do this," Grey said.

"I didn't. You did."

"Let's figure them out."

"What you did is final. They terminated my access. I'm finished. Because of you. So you win, Grey. You and your mother. I'm a piece of shit that spent your money, ruined your childhood. That's that. Nothing can be fixed or changed. Ever."

Grey wanted to say it wasn't true. There were fond memories of them in the distance, of late nights watching movies and being perched on his shoulders. They were faded and fragmented, but they were there, the building blocks of a relationship that fell apart. They had to mean something.

So why didn't he say that?

Because that distant life was covered in a muck of shit that hurt. Hurt him. Hurt his mother. The man that locked himself in the bedroom deserved this life. He built it. Who was Grey to take it away?

That's that.

[19]

Grey
Before the Punch

Mom leaned into the room with a toothbrush, white foam in the corners of her mouth. "Not going to your dad's?"

"No."

She waited. "What's up?"

Her radar was picking up trouble. Her instincts for misfortune were finely tuned. *You look for trouble,* a therapist once told her. *If you look for it, you'll find it.* She never went back to her. Instead, she visited a psychic that read her past lives—thousands of them—where she'd done terrible things and was now balancing the karmic scales.

His mom had bought that one.

She just had to hold on until this life was over, pay her debts and hope for something better the next time around. If you believed that sort of thing.

"He's not feeling well," Grey said.

That was close to the truth. He didn't say his dad was sick, even though that was dead on true—sick in the head and sick in the heart.

"He's not returning my texts," Mom said. "Or calls."

"You surprised?"

She nodded with the x-ray vision beaming through him, a spotlight in search of the truth. Grey gave her his full attention, let her look, hoping she wouldn't see. She didn't need to know about the bottomed-out college fund or his dad's state of mind. She didn't believe her opinion of him could get lower.

The truth was hidden for her protection.

Maybe his dad would change his mind, call him one day and invite him over. Grey was accustomed to the absentee-dad thing, but what if he got access to the Maze again? Grey wanted that. The college fund would be worth it.

I am a selfish shit because the nut doesn't fall far from the tree.

His mother finished brushing her teeth at the kitchen sink, gave final instructions to clean up, don't make a mess, don't do drugs and see you in the morning. She tied the bandana around her neck and was off to work.

Just another Friday night.

A small bowl of popcorn waited in the kitchen—his mother's nightly gift, just in case he was hungry. Grey ate while he whittled the hours away on his phone, watching tank drops. Not everyone could drop into a sensory tank without blowing a circuit. His dad was one of them. The respirator in the bathroom was just a guess. The look on his face confirmed it.

He can't do it.

Sensory tanks started out as horizontal deprivation tanks. Black walls, buoyant saline solution, and the complete absence of the five senses created hallucinations. The brain didn't evolve to be ignored. When deprived of input, it made up its own reality.

Even if it was a dream.

The shift to vertical tanks began when manufactured sensory input was substituted for the absence of reality. Instead of letting the brain wander through a miasma of fragmented dreams, computer-aided realities were created by hijacking the latent five senses.

The subject could be monitored through the glass. Weightless in a viscous solution, a nervous system hijacking was achieved through a skinsuit. The brain was fooled into believing its environment when nerve endings were stimulated. The user would see, hear, smell, feel and taste what it was being told to see, hear, smell, feel and taste. The experience was no different than the real world. Their thoughts and awareness were integrated into a computer-animated reality with an auto feedback loop.

Awareness leaping.

The technology was used to correct brain deficiencies as well as mental illnesses—PTSD, traumatic childhoods, etc. It worked well for decades, for those who could afford it.

And then came reality confusion.

People were coming out messed up. They couldn't trust their senses, didn't know if they were in a dream or the real world. Even the word *real* was becoming subjective. If reality is determined by our five senses, then what was real? But assholes were jumping off buildings. In the tank, they could fly. In the skin, they were water balloons. *That's real.*

These reality-confused users assaulted others, raped and robbed and looted because in the tank none of that mattered. You could treat people like meat puppets when you were in the tank.

Rach texted. *Sleeping?*

Yes, he typed.

It was past midnight. She wouldn't fall asleep until after two o'clock and get out of bed at noon. That was Grey's schedule, too. There had to be a way they could sleep together without sex. Friends *without* benefits.

Can't stop thinking about it, she texted.

She had more questions than he did. She was fuel to his obsession. Whenever he forgot about his dad or the people at the gate, she was in his ear, on his phone, wondering how far his dad got, if it really was the Maze.

Nothing we can do about it, he texted back.

Except go back.

Go back?

To the house.

In a way, it was a relief to have it over with, to be done with his dad. It was like a death in the family, without the guilt. And inheritance. But it was clean and final. His dad was an asshole. So was Grey. It ran in the family. Whose fault was that?

He wants you to go back, she wrote.

He rolled his eyes. It was like she didn't witness the rage-a-thon.

He left the clues in the open, she texted.

Because he's an idiot.

Or he wanted you to find out. He's not stupid.

Grey hesitated. *Why would he want that?*

He wants help?

If he wanted help, why would he excommunicate Grey from the apartment. Why didn't he just ask for help instead of leaving out clues? Besides, they weren't obvious. Grey did some major snooping to put it all together. *Maybe he underestimated me,* Grey thought.

Let's go back, Rach texted.

That guy clearly wants us to.

We don't go in the front door.

Parachute into the backyard?

Head sunk in his pillow, he waited for a reply. His arm got tired. He dropped the phone and turned the music up, head thumping. Sometimes she fell asleep before finishing a thought. It was best just to forget the whole thing. Go back to school, study hard, get a job, pay some bills and then die. There was a song that went like that—birth, school, work, death.

Exactly, he thought.

The phone vibrated. He tipped it up. *Pick you up in the morning.*

She wasn't giving up.

The sun was setting. A warm glow was cast upon the parking lot litter. Styrofoam cups and paper bags and empty cans were flattened on the asphalt. Similar trash floated near a boat ramp.

A shirtless man was steering a two-person Sun Dolphin toward shore, his shoulders bright red. One hand on the wheel, the other wrapped around a beer, he shouted at the truck backing down the ramp.

"Rach—"

"Shhh. We're doing this," she said. "You want to. I want to. Stop crying."

She had picked him up that afternoon. Half an hour later, they arrived at her grandparents' farm. An hour after that, they pulled off with a johnboat. Now they were watching the driver attempt to back the trailer down the ramp for the third time. He didn't look old enough to have a license. His dad kept the boat steady, waving him down.

Rach's grandfather's johnboat was about the same size as the Sun Dolphin. It was big enough for two people and a cooler. It was also older than both of them. Many holes had been patched over its lifetime.

It was a very big lake.

Somehow she'd determined the house beyond the gate was on a piece of property that stretched along twenty miles of shoreline. That explained the lack of houses in the area. They could take the boat to shore, she explained.

"Then what?" he had said.

She shrugged. "See what we can see."

If they saw something interesting, whatever that meant, they could hike toward the house, say they ran out of gas, got lost, or something. Of course they would recognize them, they had photos of them pulling up just a few weeks earlier. They had called his dad within minutes. They could call him again if they wanted. What was he going to do, disown him again?

"Aren't you the one that said we can't just ring the doorbell?" he said.

"We're not ringing the doorbell."

"This is worse."

"They don't own the water."

"They own the land, Rach."

She stared blankly. "Look, you started this. You want to quit now?"

If he was honest, this was why he'd asked her to drive him out the first time. If his nerve wavered—and it was doing a major dance right now—she would be there to set him right. He wanted to quit, to turn around and go home. Driving to the house was crazy, but this was suicidal.

"Don't give up." She took his arm. "We just take a look, see what we see. It's just a ride across the lake, that's all. It's not like you had plans to do something else tonight. We're just a couple of friends enjoying the great outdoors."

It wasn't the best speech, not the most convincing, but he heard what she was saying. She had been there when his dad called it quits. She never liked him, but her father wasn't winning parenting awards, either. Maybe that was it.

It's just a boat ride.

The boy finally backed the trailer down the ramp. When they were tied down and out of the water, Rach swung around. Her grandfather's army green johnboat teetered in the water.

"Is that going to make it?"

"*Hamburger Hill*?" She pointed at the boat. "She has never leaked."

"Always a first."

"It's just water, Grey. There aren't sharks out there and you can swim."

"Not across a lake."

"We got life vests. You get the orange one."

"How about gas?"

"How about a pacifier?"

She left the truck running and didn't ask for help, released the boat into the water by herself and backed away from the ramp. A cloud of blue smoke puffed from the engine. Grey parked the truck and waited on the dock. The sun had dropped behind the trees.

"We get there at dusk," she said. "Look around, that's all."

The water was calm. Grey imagined he could see the other shore, imagined maybe it was closer than it really was. He climbed aboard, sitting on the life vest. The engine roared and the boat leaned. Rach steered with a smile and the hair off her face.

It was just a boat ride.

GASOLINE.

The ridged hull rocked like the belly of an aluminum whale, bloated and still. The prop slapped the water.

Grey couldn't feel his fingers.

"Rach!" He wiped his face, a warm sting on his lip. "Rach!"

He kicked the black water. His jeans were heavy. A sock wagged off his foot. He was missing both shoes.

They were full throttle when the cliff came into view, a rock wall of iron-laced stone that plunged into the water. Points of light dotted the top. Grey was pressing the binoculars to his eyes—a three-story mansion coming into focus—when the boat lurched.

Rach didn't see the old post lapping just below the surface, a remnant of a forested town when the manmade lake was flooded. There were markers they didn't see in the dark.

The water hit them like concrete.

"Rach!"

The boat rocked on the waves, catching his chin. The blow opened a gash and slammed his teeth together. A bell rang between his ears, a high tenor that refused to fade. He drifted from the hump-backed boat, legs numb. Water filled his mouth, nipping his chin where the flesh hung open. The sound of the slapping hull faded as he went under, the green wash flushing his eyes.

Fingers clamped his wrist.

He was yanked up. The hard edge of the boat was in his hand.

"Hang on." Rach put his other hand on the hull. "Don't let go. You got it?"

He pushed his hair away. Her eyes were big and white, hair slicked back. She swam away before he could say anything, returned with a cushion and shoved it between his legs.

"You all right?" she asked.

He rubbed his face. His nose was slick. He felt the slash beneath his chin, raw and wet. "I think I'm bleeding."

"Don't touch it."

"Are you..." He swallowed. "Are you okay?"

Her chin was quivering. She didn't look scared, but the lake was sucking the warmth from them. They clung to the boat, huffing, shivering. There would be no turning it over in the deep. The shore was far off. If they took their time and traded off the cushion, they might get there before hypothermia set in.

"What happened?" he said.

"We hit something."

Grey knew what had happened, knew boats hit posts and trees all the time, usually inebriated captains or distracted teenagers that had to be pulled from the water and wrapped in towels. Sometimes they were arrested for drunk driving, but they were saved. Always saved.

That was during daylight.

"Just hang on." Her teeth chattered. "Someone will pass by."

The only lights were perched high on the cliff, too far away to see a couple of bodies on the water.

"No one's coming," he chattered. "We should start swimming."

Rach ducked below the surface. Grey panicked for a second, thinking she was giving up or leaving him behind. She popped up several yards away. He heard splashing and saw her retrieve more debris. Where was she finding the strength to swim that far? He didn't like floating in black water, let alone swimming in it.

This is all too stupid. All of it. Starting with Dad, the email, the white cards. The Maze. I never should've got her involved. It was selfish, should've gone alone on this.

The stars were out and a pleasant numbness had begun creeping inside him, warming him to the thought of sinking to the bottom. Perhaps it was just as well.

She returned with two orange vests, stuffed one under his arms, and put the other between her legs. She rose above the surface, a blonde buoy scanning the water.

"Rach." He squeezed her hand. "I'm sorry."

"Shhh. No. Don't say that." She squeezed back. "Someone will come."

"We should swim or something. Before it's too late."

"Hang on, just a little longer."

He grabbed her, leaned into her, their foreheads touching. It wasn't fear or sadness. Selfishly, he was glad she was there. An unceremonious ending shouldn't come alone.

"It'll be all right." She swam around the boat again.

He considered following her. The high-pitched ringing in his head dulled the outside world. He was already disoriented, the moon hiding behind a cloud cluster. He cursed his cowardice, hated that he couldn't let go of the boat, convinced himself that staying put was a good idea while she retrieved another floatation.

"Hang on." She hugged him from behind, their chattering bodies in sync, her chin on his shoulder, wet and warm. "Someone's coming."

It sounded like lost hope, what destined victims tell themselves to stave off panic, clinging to optimism as the branch was breaking. He was too cold to care. It would be so much easier to do this if she wasn't there.

He closed his eyes and bumped his head against the boat.

The ringing droned louder. He turned sluggishly, stupidly, toward a cluster of lights. Perhaps he had already left his body, had floated above the lake, was staring into the mansion that overlooked them, dreaming he could fly onto one of the cantilevered porticos and sip wine or whatever rich people did.

The light grew brighter.

It sliced over the water, illuminating the lapping waves. For a moment, it blinded them. Then the sound of a motor cut through the ringing.

It was coming from the cliff.

[20]

Grey
Before the Punch

His chest hurt with the dull ache of a large boot standing on him, holding him down, pushing the air out of his lungs. Burning and crushing—Grey thrashed awake.

He lunged to escape black water. He inhaled long and loud. Pain spread across his ribs. Blood surged between his eyes.

A rhythmic headache settled into harmless ripples. Shipwrecked memories rose to the surface. They bobbed just out of reach, chaotic and nonsensical, faded photos, snapshots distorted with a vintage filter.

There was the lake. And then what?

The room was odd, futuristic. He lay back in a lounger that reminded him of a dental chair. There was an empty hard-backed chair on a shiny hardwood floor. Sheets of water trickled down slate walls to his left and right, disappearing into narrow troughs at the bottom. A white wall was behind him.

He faced a glass wall that reminded him of his dad's apartment. Instead of a view of the city, an orange glow highlighted a large body of water. It was early morning, the sun peeking above the horizon.

Memories began falling in line, an unwinding of chaotic thoughts snapping into their rightful places. The lake. The boat.

The house.

He was wearing a white robe, the sleeves wide, the belt long. The white terrycloth was soft and clean. The flesh over his ribs was raw and tender. He explored a numb spot on his chin. Some sort of glue had been used to patch the open wound.

"Hello?"

His voice echoed off the floor and in his head. Water clogged his ears. He thumped the side of his head. His forehead screamed. It took a few minutes to settle.

Where am I?

He and Rach had been stuck in the water, cold and alone. And then the boat, a bright light. And now he was in a strange room.

The house. I'm in the house.

The glass wall was spotless. He reached out to touch it before coming closer, his swirling fingerprints fading. A swimming pool was a few stories below. Vertigo clutched his belly. He remembered a time he bungee-jumped from a tower, how the cord yanked him upside down, blood surging into his head like it was now. He hung like a dying yo-yo, his friends hollering from the tower.

Wait. I've never bungee-jumped.

The door opened. He jerked around too quickly. Nausea turned his stomach in circles. He braced against the glass wall, forgetting about the drop below, his attention consumed by a barefoot woman. Her hair was short; her dark skin contrasted with the ivory white summer dress. One of the narrow straps fell off her shoulder.

"Good morning," she said with an accent.

"Where's Rachel?"

"Your friend is well and rested, as are you, I hope." She placed a breakfast tray on the hard-backed chair. "You are hungry?"

A bagel with cream cheese and a glass of orange juice. The coincidence escaped him, that he ate this every morning for breakfast and there it was in this strange room. She stepped away, surrendering, afraid to frighten him—a trapper not wanting to scare the bunny.

"Where am I?" he said.

"Where were you going?"

He eyed her with suspicion. His stomach overpowered his sense of wariness. Base instincts compelled him to reach for the tray. She crossed her arms, fingernails polished red, watching him keep the lounger between them.

He snatched the plate like a runaway child. His head filled with chewing noises as he attacked the bagel. A pleasant grin rose on the horizon of her eyes.

"This is my favorite room in the morning, when the sun is just about to rise. You know it's there, promising another day, a harbinger of hope."

Her toes wiggled against the hardwood. A thin orange slice peeked above the sharp horizon, setting fire to the water. It glittered in her eyes.

"Why are you here?" she asked.

He wiped his mouth and considered lying about why they were on a course for the house on top of the cliff, how they were just looking for a place to fish off shore. But he knew nothing about fishing to even make it sound feasible. It seemed a lie wouldn't work if he did.

"My dad was out here."

She was looking at him in the window's reflection like a parent who already knew the answers and was just giving him a chance to confess. Or lie.

"Why are *you* here?"

He cleared his throat. "Where's Rachel?"

"She's at home."

"At home?" He dropped the last bite of bagel. *Why am I still here?* "Is she safe?"

"Of course."

"How do I know?"

"I am honest with you, Grey Grimm. Perhaps you can do the same."

She knew his name. Of course she knew his name. He was at the gate a few weeks ago; they'd called his dad.

"What do you want?" he asked.

"What do I want?" Her cherub smile flattened out. "You have trespassed upon this property twice. You recklessly brought your friend across the water, where you both would have died. This is all fact, Grey. It is truth. It is not what *I* want that is the question. What do *you* want?"

It wasn't clear what she was asking. The question was simple, but it was multilayered. What did she really want to hear? A thrill of hope sprang inside him, a hopeful twist that all his dreams would come true. *You've passed the test. Welcome to the Maze!*

"You know why I'm here," he said.

Her smile found him amusing. She approached with soft steps. She reached out, delicate fingers trickling down his cheek. He pulled away.

"You were drowning before we found you, Grey Grimm."

The sun rested just above the horizon. Her complexion glowed. She poked his ribs and he winced. A hot flash filled his head. He instinctively moved closer to the waterfall wall. Adrenaline drove his heart into passing gear. Cool air drifted from the trickling wall, a humid breath on his neck. He swallowed hard, working up enough courage to leap.

"You're the Maze," he said.

She didn't react. Anger, agitation, or impatience could be hiding beneath her smile, but he saw no sign of them. She stepped back and looked toward the lake and the rising sun. A ripple of tension rode across her shoulders.

"And what do you know about the Maze?"

"Everybody knows about it."

"What do *you* know about it, Grey Grimm?"

He had the major competitions memorized, had seen the most gruesome deathmatches, knew the names of all the repeat victors. Even watched most of the lesser known games, the ones not promoted but equally gruesome. But that wasn't what she was asking.

What do you *know?*

He told her about the invitation on the refrigerator, the weekends his dad drove out there, the way he tracked him, the money he was spending, the scuba gear he was using. All the while, she listened with her back to him.

Her hips swayed in the white dress. The sharp outline of her body, the indention of her belly button, the snug gap between her thighs rigged him in place. The water wall wet the hair on the back of his head.

She leaned into him.

"*How* do you know?" she whispered.

"I'm sorry?"

"Your name," she said distantly. "The day, the time. When you wake in the morning, how do you know who you are?"

She turned her head, searching. The conversation had taken a hairpin turn and he sailed through the guardrail. She lingered, sweetly. The early morning kissed her cheeks, her shoulders. She hugged herself.

"What you see, hear, taste and smell. What you feel. Your senses are the windows to reality. You flipped your boat last night; you plunged into cold water. You clung to the edge, the feeling deserting your fingers, your toes. Your ears were ringing. Your reality was very different than it is now."

She gestured to the window. "Do you trust your senses?"

The memories of the past twelve hours were coming together like foamy trash clinging in the river's current. There was some semblance of the events—launching the boat, the cliff, the spill—but the memories had gone through a blender and poured back into his head.

His throbbing head.

"Where's Rach?"

"She beat you to it, Grey Grimm. She dropped into the Maze an hour ago. You're late."

"What?"

His hand slipped down the waterfall wall. He staggered a step. The woman caught him before he crashed. He shook her off; the robe pulled off his shoulder, bunching around his arms. He slid away from her until the glass wall was at his back.

I never should've brought her.

She began laughing, hiding behind her hand, red nails fluttering across her cheek. Grey pushed into the corner, where the glass met the opposite waterfall wall. The back of his robe grew heavy with water.

"Grey, stop," she said.

He felt himself sliding to the floor, water draining beneath him, pooling between his thighs.

"Shh-shh-shh." She squatted near him, gently stroking his bare foot. "She's not in the Maze, Grey Grimm. Your girlfriend is safe. She's at home and perfectly fine. As if none of this happened, she's asleep in her bed."

"What?"

"I was teasing you. But that is what you think, correct? That there is a Maze in this house?"

"My mom knows where I went. She'll come after me."

"Of course your mother will. She loves you. We would expect her to do so, but you're not in any danger, Grey Grimm. We saved you from drowning. We're not keeping you here. You are free to go."

"Why am I still here?"

"I apologize for the starkness of my teasing, but life can be uncomfortable, can it not? When you seek adventure, you risk falling. You may be hurt. There are things out of your control, the laws of physics, gravity. The lake cares not if you are young or innocent, whether your friend is involved. It will drown you. There are prices you pay for living. Fair or not, they are paid in full."

She gently pulled him away from the waterfall and lifted him on his feet. Her strength was surprising. She slid the robe from his shoulders. It bunched in a puddle around his feet. The reflection of a teenage boy looked back from the glass, a boy in boxers with long hair and a sickly yellow patch of a future bruise over his ribs. He coyly folded his arms.

The woman returned with another robe, this one dry and warm.

"I like you, Grey Grimm." She wrapped the robe around him. "You're smart, funny. Fearless."

He watched her fuss with the collar, cinching the fuzzy belt around his waist. *How could she know anything about me?*

"There are people that love you," she said. "There are those that don't. There is great advantage to having both of these people in your life. Disadvantages, as well. Sometimes, it's not simple to know which is which."

She brushed the hair from his forehead. He jerked back, her touch gentle but his head tender—the result of kissing the lake, full throttle. There was no memory of hitting the water, only the turbulent aftermath.

The price paid in full.

"Understanding is your freedom, Grey Grimm. The hunt *is* the destination. Know where you are, where you are going. And knowing why. Only the willing truly live. Do you understand?"

He shook his head. Even frowning sent aching waves through his brain. This conversation was speeding ahead of him.

"Life has you now," she said. "We cannot intercede again. You drown next time, Grey Grimm, so go home. There is nothing here for you. Return to life; understand your risks. Only the willing can do so."

She tightened the collar around his neck, rose up on her toes and kissed his cheek. A sensual shiver warmed his face, soothing his aches.

"I wish you luck."

He listened to her bare feet. She closed the door quietly and left him alone with the rising sun and the peaceful water. He wondered what the hell just happened, what was she talking about? Why did it seem like she had been expecting him?

And why did she wish me luck?

The driver waited for Grey to get out.

He hadn't made a sound the entire trip, even when asked a question. Vomit streaked the car's rear quarter panel. Grey had hung out the window to unload his stomach, a sad dog with knotting hair and a sour taste. Maybe the driver was pissed about that.

Grey checked his phone.

Service had returned shortly after leaving the country. He texted Rach six times. Called twice. It was too early for her, but her phone was never far from her reach.

"She's already home." It was the only time the driver spoke, waiting with the door open. He said he'd driven her home the night before. "She's fine. She's safe."

That didn't help.

Grey's apartment building was shrouded in fog. Humidity clung in microscopic drops. The lobby was empty and musty. Grey leaned against the elevator door. The vibrations stirred the headache to life, his brain throwing stones around his skull.

Seasickness swung him like a limp towel.

He didn't know her name, but he wouldn't forget her face or the way the dress clung to her. She'd told him not to come back, in so many words. And wished him luck.

What did she really mean?

He opened the apartment door, threw his keys in the little basket and listened for his mom. It was Sunday morning. Sometimes she got home early when they were ahead of schedule.

He downed four aspirin.

His memories were making more sense. Taking the boat across the lake at night? There were few moments in his life that were more stupid. Shoving wires into an outlet came close.

We should be dead.

They'd saved them. They didn't have to come for them, pull them out of the water. They didn't have to dress him, let him sleep it off in some waterfall room. But they wouldn't do it again. *Life has you now? What the hell does that mean? Would they watch from the cliff if we dump the boat a second time?*

Only the willing live.

His mother threw the front door open with a bag of groceries and dragged the weight of a third shift behind her. She tossed him a weak smile.

"You're up."

"Couldn't sleep," he said. "You're home early."

"Some repairs and an early shift change." She put milk and orange juice in the fridge. "I asked you to clean the dishes last night."

"Sorry." He started unloading the dishwasher.

His mother hovered over the toaster, watching the coils turn orange. Wispy threads of smoke wafted out. She ate the toast dry while blinking slowly. Her eyelids moved like lead.

"What happened?"

He froze in place. Had her question had a flatter tone, he would've confessed on the spot. Instead, she reached for his chin, frowning.

"Oh, nothing. I slipped in the bathroom and hit the sink."

"You cut it on the sink?"

"Yeah, it's nothing."

"What's the stuff?" She stroked the medical glue.

"Rach had it. She stopped over last night, had it in her purse along with a hammer and a crossbow. She has everything, you know how it is. How was work?"

"It's over."

She continued chewing. That was a lot of lies to untangle. Nothing momentous and she didn't have the energy for them.

"Talk to your dad?" she asked. "Why aren't you doing weekends with him?"

"He doesn't want me to."

"Why?"

"Does he need a reason?"

She wiped her mouth. "When's the last time you talked to him?"

"I don't know, a week?" he lied again. It had been a month.

"So he's alive?"

"Does it matter?"

"To you, it should."

"Yeah, well."

She said the right thing because it was her duty. If his dad died yesterday, it wouldn't bring her any tears. Grey, either. Then again, he hadn't been around many dead people. His grandparents had passed before he was born. Death was a foreigner. He didn't know how he'd answer when it came knocking.

Maybe he'd sob like a toddler.

"I'm going to take a shower." She tapped his chin. He tried not to wince.

A TEXT ARRIVED AT NOON. *What's your problem, creep?*

When did you get home? Grey texted back.

Last night. You?

This morning.

Ooo. Party boy, not rude boy.

He erased several messages before sending a reply. How much should he say through the phone? His heart was suddenly jacked on speed, his fingers tense.

They brought me home, he finally sent.

They?

You sore?

A little. She paused before adding, *Headache.*

Grey followed the four aspirin he'd downed when getting home with two more and then another two. The ache was spreading like a stain. At least it wasn't throbbing anymore.

Meet for coffee? he wrote. *So we can talk about last night.*

I'm in trouble for the boat.

How were they going to explain the boat at the bottom of the lake? Unless the rescuers dragged it out with them. But the trailer was back at the ramp. So was her car.

How'd you get home? he texted.

I drove, ding-dong. How high were you?

Your car is home?

Are you trippin?

She was safe. She sounded normal. Too normal. They just about sank to the bottom of the lake, the chill still in his bones. They were holding hands while clinging to the hull and she was still tired from too much sleep.

Pick me up for coffee, he texted.

I have to fix the dent.

What dent? He quickly typed a follow-up. *Wait, you have the boat?*

Several minutes passed before she responded. The jokes about getting high had run their course. He was officially on her nerves.

Yes. I have the boat.

Grey paced around his room, trying to piece this nightmare together. It was fairly simple for a while. The people on top of the cliff were good people, normal people. They'd saved them from drowning. Obviously, there was something going on up there, Maze activity or gang-related drugs or something. They weren't bad people or Grey would be bloated and blue by now. But now the story just went crooked. *They saved the boat?* he thought.

What did you tell your gpa? he sent.

What happened.

You told him we crossed the lake? he wrote.

What?

He typed slowly, his fingers turning cold. *What happened last night, Rach?*

There was a long pause. Twice she started writing something. Finally, she sent *Seriously, are you trippin?*

He started to reply, but she followed up before he could send something. A knot rose in his throat. Grey dropped the phone. His tongue seemed to swell and the room began a slow turn. *Do you trust your senses, Grey Grimm?* he thought as he looked at it from his bed, not daring to touch the radioactive words.

We didn't cross the lake, creep, she texted. *That would be stupid.*

THE SESSIONS

Five men, five women.

They walked along the narrow hallway, wearing robes of various colors. Their flip-flops snapped. The motley crew of strangers from all over the world had only one thing in common.

They were completely shaved.

Rema had assisted Henk before escorting him to the group. His skin was soft and warm from a shower. She used a laser shaver to remove the hair from his head, arms and legs. It certainly would've been pleasurable to have her do the rest, but it wouldn't have led to any sort of gratifying completion. In the two weeks she'd been coming to his room, he learned his exorbitant fee included everything.

Except sex.

They entered a large room, one that resembled a small warehouse. Pipes and conduit ran in complex patterns along the high ceiling. The smell of nutrient solution took on a vinegary tang, slightly different than the taste of the small tubs. Henk couldn't gargle the flavor out of his throat, even when he flushed his nostrils with warm salt water. It was like putrid ink that seeped into the skin.

Black curtains hung from cables. There was plenty of room

behind them. Men and women joined the group as they entered. They were dressed in simple clothing, each of a solid color. One of them was Rema.

"Welcome." A tan young man with short black hair greeted them. "And congratulations on your progress."

He began clapping and the assistants followed his lead. Henk's multicultural companions joined in. Henk waved Rema to come over. She pretended not to understand, having eyes only for the young man addressing the group. He spoke with a Spanish accent.

"I hope your assistants have attended your every need?"

Not quite.

Another round of clapping. Some half-bowed. They were all very grateful. Rema ignored Henk's pleas. He just needed a word.

"Up until today, you have experienced solo awareness leaping into a computer-assisted reality. While it is limited in function, it has allowed many of you to master the basics. Today you will be introduced to the vertical tank and the networked reality."

The Spaniard clamped his hands behind his back.

"However, you will soon learn there is a certain degree of synergy that occurs when several people leap together and weave an integrated alternate reality. The boundaries between you and me and the illusion that we are separate fall away when you experience this unified reality. We experience something much greater than any one of us can contain."

"Excuse me." Henk raised his hand. "I'm not supposed to be here."

"Of course you are."

"No, I mean—"

"We're only demonstrating the process, Dr. Grimm. You are exactly where you need to be."

Exactly where you need to be... more Zen bullshit.

This asshole knew exactly what he meant. Henk wasn't ready for vertical tanking. In the days that followed his first disaster, he had regressed. Rema came to his room and lured him into the tub like a frightened dog to water. Each session ended in terror. Every time he went down, the world collapsed. He thrashed out of the tub in horror. Tremors would last for hours. Rema would hold him until they stopped.

"There's another way," she had assured him. He didn't think she was talking about vertical tanks.

"Phillipe will be our leader," the Spaniard said.

Another man stepped forward, this one a freckled Caucasian. He most likely had bright red hair, but like the rest of them, he had shaved down to his pale skin.

"Phillipe is wearing a skin suit," the Spaniard explained. "It is a supple replication of flesh imbedded with complex electrical relays that act much like a secondary nervous system."

Phillipe dropped the robe around his ankles. He was wearing a black suit that formed to every curve and wrinkle. A rank smell wafted out of the disrobing, something like congealed ozone.

"The shaving," the Spaniard continued, "is to maximize contact with your skin suit so that all sensory flow is unimpeded. This is first-generation technology, I'm sure some of you are aware, but we find it useful to start your first vertical experience with the skin suit. By the end of your Sessions, many of you will experience more advanced techniques."

Rema had told Henk about the oxygenated water when she thought it was the claustrophobic effect of the respirator. The advanced methods involved jumping in nude and breathing water. It took a little practice, but she was sure he could do it.

He was sure he couldn't.

Two assistants came to Phillipe's side. One of them guided a cable dangling from the ceiling to the small of his back.

"Are there any questions?"

"Yes, um." Henk cleared his throat. "Really, I don't think I'm ready for this."

He swallowed spastically. Heat sweats were breaking out beneath his arms and across his chest. His legs were already quivering. Everyone was glowing with anticipation, the wide-eyed wonder of children in a chocolate factory with endless possibilities. Henk was staving off a panic attack.

Rema pulled him from the pack. "Dr. Grimm—"

"I'm not ready."

"We're just observing."

"I can't."

"You don't have to do anything. Trust me, I've seen it benefit people greatly to watch."

How many times had he failed? Watching someone succeed wasn't going to make it better. It would only bring more shame. He'd spent all of his money, much of which wasn't his to spend, and he'd failed.

"You said there was another way," he whispered. "Besides this."

"We can discuss that later. It's important you know the process."

One of the curtains dropped. A clear cylinder was gurgling with thick bubbles of solution. Henk gagged on sight. The assistants fitted a specialized mask over Phillipe's head. He bit down on a tube that would slide into his throat, then climbed a rack of steps anchored on the side of the tank. The cable sagged.

"It will be important to relax," the Spaniard said, then followed with a large grin, "and breathe."

The others found the humor. Henk tightened. He'd sucked enough lungfuls to fill a barrel.

Phillipe reached the top of the ladder. The cable reeled out the slack and hoisted him above the rim. He dangled like bait.

"The cable is for support," the Spaniard added. "Should an emergency arise, it will lift you from the tank within a second. The skin suit monitors your vitals. There is nothing that can't be addressed should it go wrong."

"*Puis-je poser une question?*" a heavyset gentleman asked.

"*Oui*," the Spaniard answered.

The gentleman continued in French. The Spaniard listened patiently.

"Mr. Moreau very astutely asked where Phillipe will be going. In the network, you will experience a different sort of leap. Computers are involved but more as sensory modulation. The new reality in this room will be a collaborative effort, but will hinge primarily on a host."

The Spaniard gestured to the large curtain behind him. It appeared to be concealing an eleventh tank, one slightly larger.

This would be an organic host, a live human being whose dream was the foundation upon which others would leap into. Their input would help shape the new reality in which they existed. They would be like Greek gods, but the host would be the final word.

Zeus.

"*¿Se requiere ninguna memoria?*" a woman in a maroon robe asked.

The Spaniard conversed fluidly in his native tongue before addressing the group. "Miss Martinez asked if this requires a memory wipe. It does not. Only for participants entering the Maze is a memory alteration applied. We are simply awareness leaping."

Phillipe placed his toe into the bubbling goo. The cable gently lowered him inside. The viscous solution surged around his thighs like corn syrup.

Henk reached out for Rema. She held him with both hands. A sour burp burst in his throat. He swallowed down an acrid tang.

"Phillipe will remain in the tank for an hour, but he will experience time differently where he goes. Depending on the laws of the universe he helps create, he could experience a lifetime during that period, a phenomenon known as time dilation."

Phillipe's head sank below the surface and lolled in the swirling agitation. His arms drifted from his sides. The cable fell slack.

"I can't do this..." Henk slurred.

Rema supported his weight.

"Phillipe has already vacated his skin. With practice, you will find it just as effortless."

Henk swayed forward. His stomach twisted in a wet coil.

"And when you complete the Sessions—"

Henk pushed through the crowd, clawing the colorful robes off their shoulders, pushing them off balance. They were too engrossed to be offended. Rema pulled on his collar. He tripped forward and splashed on the concrete.

"You will no longer need assistance," the Spaniard finished.

The other curtains dropped. A tank behind each of them. The host tank was at the end, wider and taller, the solution vigorously brewing. The man inside looked more like a preserved specimen than a living being. He was nude and mostly hairless. Tendrils drifted in the solution, surrounding his body, massaging it. No respirator. No skin suit.

A blanched, pickled human being.

Henk painted the floor with his breakfast. That was the moment he knew something so completely that it would be his reality until death.

He was never going to tank.

PART 3

OBJECTS MAY BE CLOSER THAN THEY APPEAR

[21]

Sunny
After the Punch

The hookah café was on the Lower East Side.

The window was marred with grease pencil advertisements, today's specials that pretended to end but never did. Inside, the patrons were lumped in a blue haze of hookah smoke.

Sunny avoided a puddle. Her feet were puckered and sore. She'd ditched her socks at Mrs. Jones's apartment, but her shoes sloshed as she stepped into an aroma of apples and cinnamon.

Donny filled the back corner, his shirt untucked, a square name tag stitched above his right breast. He read the newsfeeds from a tablet and pulled white smoke from a tube. A mint infusion jetted from his nostrils.

There he was, just another day after a late shift, hitting the hookah before heading home. All was normal. All was good. And Grey was still missing.

She approached like a ghost, an undead victim newly awakened, a stranger in a foreign world. Several patrons looked up. Smoke leaked from Donny's lips.

"Holy shit."

He grabbed her before she could say anything, pressing her damp shirt that smelled of sweaty plastic. His embrace was the only thing that kept her from falling.

"Grimm," he said, "the hell have you been?"

She was shaking. Breaking down. This mad ride finally hit a stretch of sanity, a hopeful plane of familiarity. A sense of home. Donny, her longtime peer, the closest thing to a friend, the man that watched Grey as she went for help, the man that disappeared doing it. He was there; he was all right.

Hope lifted its sleepy head. *Hello.*

"You all right? You look worn out... like you ain't slept in a month. Sit down." Donny pulled out a chair and waved at the counter. He pressed her hands between his palms like warm skillets melting a thin sheet of ice. She was cold through her bones, damp and shriveled.

"I tried to call," he said. "I stopped by. Your voicemail isn't working; it just keeps ringing. What the hell happened to you?"

"Where'd you go, Donny?"

"I'm right here, Grimm. I'm not going anywhere." Someone dropped off a glass of water. Donny asked if she was hungry and ordered toast before she could answer. "You look like you been put away wet, Grimm. Rode hard, first."

She pressed his hands against her cheeks. He smelled manlier than anyone in her life. He put his arm around her, letting her sink against him.

"Hey, hey, lady. It's all right. You're all right."

She didn't make a sound; tears wet his factory-stained shirt. He patted her shoulder and kissed her forehead. Tension fell away in pieces, unraveling around her, her springs overwound. The world was safe again; it made sense. This wasn't a dream; she wasn't crazy. He was here. Donny was here.

She wiped her eyes. "Where have you been?"

"Picking up your slack. I've been working doubles since you bailed. Denice hired your replacement yesterday. He sucks, but not in a good way."

"I... I didn't quit."

"It's been six weeks, Grimm."

Six weeks? "It hasn't been..."

"It's all right. Not a big deal."

"Donny, you came over to my place."

"Yeah. I called, too."

"Grey had the... the *thing* on his head." She looked around and whispered, "Maze."

His brow furrowed.

Her voice cracked. "You stayed at my apartment while I went for help."

"Um..."

"The other day!" She waved her hands. The days melted together. It could've been three days or three months. Tension reclaimed her, resuming an armored suit grip. Donny leaned back. "When your... your friend... *your fucking friend, Donny...* told me to go... I went to the police and came back and you were... you and Grey were..."

She lost her breath. The chair was sinking into the floor. Donny reached back for the hookah.

"Take a hit, Grimm. Loosen up."

"Donny, where'd you go?"

He looked around and chuckled. Everyone was watching, all listening. They heard the Maze thrown into the conversation. All ears were on deck. Blood rushed in her cheeks. She shook convulsively.

"Is Grey all right?" he said softly.

All the words, all the happiness, all the relief disappeared like a thick white cloud of smoke blown into the wind. Nothing was safe.

She gulped for air.

"Where have *you* been, Grimm?"

She shook her head, didn't know how to answer that, couldn't really remember where she'd been or for how long.

"You said my *friend* told you to go somewhere," Donny said. "What friend?"

"The one from the Glass Jar."

"I haven't been there in a lifetime. Who was it?"

She ran her hand over her head, avoiding pulling her hair. "His name was..."

There was no need to finish. His expression was caring but empty. She should've known better. Was Donny her friend? She'd worked with him for how long? A year? Five? She couldn't recall. She didn't have friends, didn't know what qualified as one.

This is a mistake.

She shouldn't have come here, shouldn't be talking to Donny. She should be looking for Grey, pounding on the right doors, not talking to a man she thought was a friend because he was part of this tragedy, recommending his friend, pretending to stay with her son.

She was unwinding into a ball of loose threads, a mop of yarn kinked and scrambled.

"Did you come to my apartment last night?" she said.

"What?"

"When did you come to my apartment? Answer the question."

"Relax, Grimm. Talk to me. Tell me where you've been—"

"Is that yours?" She nodded at the chair behind him. A black coat was thrown over it, rain still beaded on the shoulders.

"Grimm." He looked around the room. "Look, I don't know what's going on here, but you need—"

"Is that your coat, Donny?"

"Please," the man behind the counter called. "Watch your language."

"Where is he?" Sunny grabbed Donny's shirt. "Where's my son?"

He threw his arms out. His doughy cheeks quivered, blotchy patches glowing beneath his eyes. Hands were suddenly on her, pulling her away. She threw them off, kicking over the chair. Donny was blubbering, begging them to be careful, she was having family problems.

Sunny wheeled on the café owners.

"You need to leave," the man said.

"Wait." Donny stood up and grabbed the tan coat on his chair. The black one she'd seen behind him, the one with dripping beads of rain, was gone.

She ran.

"Grimm!" Donny gave chase, his arms swinging side to side, his belly hanging out the bottom of his shirt.

"What the hell is going on?" Her voice squelched. "You came to my apartment, Donny. Grey had gone into the Maze... he used a fucking thing on his head and went into the Maze! Do you understand me? You were there and now he's gone and you're acting like everything is okay and it's not, Donny. It's not okay!"

Donny cringed. Bystanders turned toward her.

"My son is in the Maze, do you hear me? And no one cares. I don't—"

He reached for her. Sunny pulled away, stepped off the curb, and nearly tripped into traffic. Blindly, she walked into the street with no idea where she was going, less certain of where she had been, what was happening.

She ran along the dashed line, traffic swerving. Cursing. The rain came down, blurring streetlights. Rubber skidded on the pavement. Sunny weaved through a sudden traffic jam. She leaped onto the sidewalk with a spike in her side and a fire in her lungs. Pedestrians jumped aside. She didn't look back, barely looked ahead and ran until her legs vanished and her ankles burned.

Lost and running, a mouse on a wheel, tirelessly sprinting to nowhere, not looking back, not seeing ahead. The world streaked past, the city smeared in a landscape of grays, and swallowed her.

She came to rest beneath the awning of a café, her back against the window. Rain seeped from her hair, briny with perspiration, nose leaking onto her upper lip.

The jagged scar a fresh slash.

Across the street, a storefront window offered a generous view to an empty showroom. Lights softly lit products along the wall and a number on the glass door.

How the hell did I get here?

This was where she started. It all began on this avenue, in front of that vendor. And here she was again, staring at the starting line, no closer to the finish, no closer to her son. This had become a hopeless race through eternity, where nothing made sense, the rungs of the mouse wheel coming around again and again.

Sunny pushed herself up, walked across the street, and ignored the traffic that braked to avoid her. Transfixed, she climbed the steps and pulled at a locked door. She tried with both hands, braced her foot on the wall, and hammered the door. The glass rattled. She was prepared to break it.

"Come out!"

The floor was empty. The stand of cards alone.

They had something to do with this. Donny didn't disappear one day and forget what happened. They did something, she could feel it. They were high-end tank dealers, licensed awareness leapers. They had answers and gave her silence.

She closed her eyes, slammed both fists into the glass, braced for a shatter, cringed for shrapnel. Her blood would run down the steps and stain the concrete, dissolve into the rain. The blood they deserved.

The blood they wanted.

"Answer! Goddamnit, answer!"

Cars slowed and she continued her assault. When no one came to the door, she was sure the police had been called. They would come to haul her away. There would be a restraining order, charges filed. An investigation into her claims of a son that never existed because they would erase him. They took him and erased him from existence, would convince her he never existed, that she was chasing ghosts, she needed real help.

She searched for a stone or a loose brick. A trash can she could heave through the plate-glass window, bury it on their showroom floor. She wanted attention, someone to talk. She wanted someone to know. Fists clenched, throat raw, she screamed until the words tore at the cords.

"I want my son!"

Pedestrians looked; they stared, but didn't care. They walked around her radioactive behavior, casting their glances away until she collapsed on the steps and clawed at the glass.

"Where are you?" she muttered.

Inside, the floor was empty. So was she.

Sunny laid her head on the unforgiving steps and closed her eyes. Nowhere to go, nothing to find. This was her last stop. They could call the police, have her locked up. Someone was going to hear her. These people were going to see her desperation. Someone would help. They had to.

Please.

"They'll come for you."

Rain popped on a sheet of plastic.

Sunny's eyelashes refused to unclip.

Through a crust of sleep, a yellow sun moved on her like a headlight, not warm or promising, just cold and wet. The rays transformed into the petals of a chrysanthemum tucked into the rim of a hat. An old face, like that of an aged apple, smiled behind a pair of sunglasses. An old woman was hiding beneath a sheet of clear plastic. The droplets dribbled from her gnarled knuckles.

Mrs. Jones.

"They don't like you sleeping here."

The edge of a concrete step bit into the small of Sunny's back. She sat up, wondering if she'd fallen asleep. It was still daylight, but the rain had subsided to a drizzle. Mrs. Jones looked older. She was still wearing the same clothes as the last time she'd seen her, only now they were frayed and filthy.

"Why are you here?" Sunny croaked.

Mrs. Jones reached into a large bag slung over her shoulder, the fabric torn and wet. The bulk of her treasure was settled at the bottom. She produced a neatly folded square of plastic and placed it in Sunny's hand.

"You'll need this." The gummy smile widened.

Sunny took the plastic, assuming it was a kind gesture to escape the rain, but the weather had already soaked through three layers of clothing. Her flesh was soggy, possessed by a cold that turned her bones brittle. What use was it now?

She looked around, the surroundings suddenly unfamiliar. "Where am I?"

"Stop running." Droplets spotted the oversized sunglasses, a distorted reflection looking back at Sunny.

"Running? I'm looking for my—"

Horns blared. The grind of rubber on wet pavement ended with the abrupt crack of metal. Sunny cringed, eyes closed, fists clenched.

Cars worked around a center-lane fender bender. The drivers in the accident were out. The woman in the front car hurled curses from beneath a red umbrella at a man that held a black book over his head. Across the street, pedestrians threw hurried glances at the showdown. One of them stopped briefly before rushing against the flow of traffic. He hunched beneath a black umbrella.

The collar of his overcoat was pulled up.

"Hey!" Sunny threw herself off the steps. "Hey!"

She walked through puddles and traffic without looking. A slow-moving Volkswagen crawled in front of her, gently nudging her thigh. The horn wailed. She was oblivious, eyes aimed at the overcoat. The man sensed the attention, glancing over his shoulder without noticing.

He heard the footsteps and turned in time to put up his forearm just as Sunny swung on him. His briefcase spilled papers and folders, a shotgun of rain splattering the print. He cried out in surprise. She latched handfuls of his coat and threw her weight into his chest. He hit a storefront window and dropped the umbrella.

"What the hell is wrong with you?" He recovered from the ambush. "Are you out of your mind!"

"Where's my son?"

Sunny stumbled backward and dropped the square of plastic Mrs. Jones had given her. His cheeks flush with anger, he adjusted his coat and knelt down to pick up the contents of his briefcase. They flopped like rags. He balled them up and stuffed them in like trash.

"The police are coming." He held up his phone. "I don't give a goddamn what's wrong with you, this is assault, the police are coming."

She grabbed the papers closest to her. There was nothing secret about them, no discreet photos of her around town, no investigative evidence of her son or the Maze. They were legal papers that had nothing to do with her or Gray or Donny or nothing or anything.

He snatched them from her. There was a distant siren.

"Don't move," he said.

Sunny knocked his hand away. He pushed her against the wall and she took a swing, tripping over her own feet. He backed off but barricaded her escape, briefcase in both hands. Trapped like a loose zoo attraction, bystanders crowded around, jeering the man in the black coat for pushing her. He was attacked first, he said; he was just holding her until the police got there.

The sidewalk had scuffed her palms. She'd lost a shoe when she fell, droplets of blood oozing from her big toe. The nail broke in half.

"Here." A woman held an umbrella over Sunny, rain popping on the fabric. "Do you want your plastic?"

She thought Sunny was homeless, the sheet of plastic her only shelter. The plastic had spread on the curb, a pile of translucent folds holding small puddles. A white card was stuck to it.

The woman with the umbrella dragged it over. Someone helped her fold it back into a square. Sunny pulled the card from one of the folds. It was soggy. She thought it had come from the briefcase, but it appeared to be stuck inside the plastic. A section was torn from the middle.

"Where'd she go?" Sunny said.

"Who?"

"The woman who gave me this." No one knew what she was asking. They hadn't seen Mrs. Jones wake her on the step, didn't notice Sunny cross the street, only saw her attack the man still holding his briefcase.

Sunny described her, the bag, the plastic sheet, the sunglasses. "A hat with a... a yellow flower."

"You mean Marie?" the woman with the umbrella said.

Sunny shook her head. She didn't know Mrs. Jones's first name. "How do you know her?"

"She's always here. She's homeless."

The siren was getting louder. Traffic nearly gridlock.

Homeless. Sunny knew where the shelter was. She had volunteered there many times. *And the card she found in Hamlet's wallet, the one with the snake eating its tail. The sticker on the tin box in Grey's room.*

But it couldn't be Mrs. Jones. She must be mistaken. The old woman lived across the hall. She had cats and little paper dolls and a picture of Sunny and Grey on her mirror. And she'd been wearing the same clothes ever since the day Grey strapped the punch around his head.

"Stop her!" the man with the briefcase said.

Sunny kicked off her other shoe and ran down the sidewalks, cold puddles splashing over her feet, the pavement rough and unforgiving. No one ran her down or got in her way.

She clutched the white card.

The 511 card wasn't something new, it was the way it ripped, a bite taken from the 511 tagline—*Find something to please yourself.* What was left of it spoke loud and sent Sunny running.

Maybe it was a coincidence, just a random occurrence and a mistaken identity. Maybe it was just an old woman that looked like Mrs. Jones that gave her the plastic and filled her days picking up garbage, a good soul, a warm heart that reached out to Sunny and offered her protection from the rain. Maybe the card was on the steps and accidentally stuck in one of the folds when she picked it up and tore out the middle words of the tagline unintentionally. Maybe this was all a coincidence.

Or maybe she was trying to tell her something. It was crazy to believe that. But everything was. Sunny was ready to listen.

Find... yourself.

[22]

Sunny

After the Punch

A line had formed.

Men and women took refuge beneath sheets of plastic and soggy cardboard. Most stood numbly in the open, with scant belongings as wet as the gutter.

The city's punishment.

At the front of the line, beneath the sky blue awning of the City Shelter for the Homeless, a woman shrunken by time and gravity stood hunched over with a tattered bag on her shoulder.

A plastic flower in her hat.

Sunny's feet were bleeding. She paused on the sidewalk, hands on hips, a long needle in her side. She walked past the men and women waiting for dry beds and a dinner bell, cupping cigarette butts in gloved hands, eyeballing her beneath dripping hats.

"Where you going?" a bone-thin lady said, her receding gums holding blocky teeth. "Cutter!"

One by one, they turned. Bitterness brought them renewed life, zombies smelling fresh brains. The message of a cutter fell through the line like racing dominos. Sunny was perhaps twenty steps from the sky blue awning when a heavy man blocked her way.

"Back of the line."

"I'm not in line—"

Somewhere beneath a crop of brows, eyes as hard as stones fell on her. Even in the nomadic world of homelessness, there were rules. There was order.

Church bells gonged in a spire stabbing the sky. It was five o'clock.

The doors opened.

The line queued up, a centipede shuffling forward. The heavy man, however, cared less about the line than her place in it. Mrs. Jones was first in line. She bent in slow motion to pick up a silver gum wrapper to put inside her giant bag.

Sunny wasn't homeless. She had an apartment. She had a job and a son. A purpose. *Where am I?*

She queued up. The heavy man watched her the entire way, slipping back in line once she started the centipede shuffle. One by one, the building swallowed them.

"Marie's always first." The man in front of her was missing a molar. His face sagged with sparse whiskers. His winter coat was soaked, the hint of a pink cast peeked from the sleeve.

"You were at the library," Sunny said.

"She's always first."

"Who?"

He placed his hand against his forehead, wiggling his fingers. *The plastic flower.*

"Welcome." A preacher greeted them at the double doors, his hand on a shoulder. "Welcome," he said. "Welcome."

Sunny had volunteered infrequently. The staff rotated often and wasn't likely to remember her. Not anymore. The preacher must have been a new director. Although she didn't recall the shelter being an affiliate of the church.

The building exhaled a mixture of warm bread and wet hair. A few of the needy hustled inside, but most of them responded to the preacher with gratitude. Sunny shivered beneath the awning as a young man conversed, continuously shaking the preacher's hand, nodding as words mushed from his cracked lips.

"Thank you, thank you. Thank you."

Rain trickled down the brick columns that supported the awning. They were decorated with graffiti and tinges of algae. Flyers were disintegrating in the rain, stickers sun-faded and peeling. A large circle had been painted on one of the columns, an outline of a snake.

The preacher took Sunny's hands between his own—warm, promising and steady.

"Are you lost?" he said.

Was it her hollow stare, the violent shiver? Rain seeped through her brows.

"The old woman in front of the line," she said. "The one with the flower. I need to talk to her."

"This is the first time you've been here. I never forget a face. Do you?"

"I'm not staying. I just need to ask her a few questions."

"You're safe here."

"No, I—"

"You're holding up the line." He gently guided her inside.

Sunny resisted at first, but the tug of a dry room drew her in. Her face flushed with warmth, pulsing in the jagged scar along her hairline. The lobby spun with a sense of déjà vu. She was familiar with the layout, where the rooms were located, how the kitchen worked. There was something new, though. A smell.

Freshly opened air fresheners. Evergreen.

"There are warm clothes." A woman held Sunny's arm. "You can change over there."

Sunny grabbed the social worker, suddenly dizzy.

"Are you all right?"

"Yes, yes... there's a woman here... her name is—"

"You feel feverish." Her hand was cold against Sunny's forehead.

"I'm fine. Dehydrated, I think. Can you—"

"There's bottled water over there. Change out of your clothes, at the very least."

"No, can you—"

A chair crashed in the big room. Someone had fallen over. Others helped him up and began wiping the floor. He was tired. A red spot was glowing on his cheek.

The big room was lined with folding tables. A clock was above the wide doorway. The red second hand pointed straight up. The rules were posted to the left of the big room. No alcohol, no drugs, no violence. All residents would follow the rules or sleep in the rain. She remembered the rule board.

The clock was new.

"Excuse me." Sunny grabbed a volunteer. "Do you know where—"

"Dry clothes over there." The stout man guided her to a side room and left before she could ask about Mrs. Jones.

They gave her a sweatshirt, a pair of cargo pants and a ball of fuzzy socks. She used to fold the clothes and organize them, hand them out to those in need. Now she was taking them.

Her skin was pinkish-gray. She threw the wet stuff away and quickly stepped into the warm clothes. The boots were black and slightly big. But dry.

When she stepped out, the big room had already been converted to a cafeteria. The residents were parked over plastic trays of food. They looked up, almost in unison, and stared at her. The next moment, they were digging into their supper.

A thousand eyes followed her into the big room.

"You look lost." The preacher's checkered shirt was tucked into a clean pair of khakis. "Why don't you get something to eat?"

"I need to speak with Marie."

He was as unmoving as his smile, gesturing to the clutter of the big room. "The cafeteria will be closing. We'll fold the tables to make room for beds, for the overflow. A lot of people in need. You'll be sleeping in here tonight. The women will be on the right side."

Wide-eyed, reluctant, she looked at the clock above the doorway. The hands hadn't moved. She had lost all sense of time. No longer knew what day it was, what month—stuck in a churning moment.

The preacher smiled at the clock. "Please, before the food is cold."

She moved into the big room, with his hand on the small of her back. The residents watched him guide her inside. She ate a dinner of chicken fried steak with lukewarm gravy and a side of grainy sweet corn. It was thick and tasteless. She ate it anyway.

And they watched.

They began breaking the room down, flipping the tables and kicking the legs. The cots came in, thin and squeaky. The residents began claiming their turf, tucking in sheets and fluffing flat pillows. Some talked to each other, familiar faces in a familiar place. Some kept to themselves.

None had a flower.

Sunny considered leaving, but the weather had grown severe. She would stay the night, but just this night. And just until she found Marie. Maybe she didn't know anything; she was just an old woman that looked like Mrs. Jones.

But the picture. How did Mrs. Jones get that picture?

She went to a bare cot in the corner. A stack of sheets sat on a thin pillow. She sank into the springs, laying her head in her arms. Her feet hurt, ankles ached. The walls of desperation were truly slippery.

The pit deep and dark.

The cot next to her squealed in protest. The ramblings of a large person sank into the springs. Her back was to Sunny, a thick fuzzy hat, a kind that could be described as Russian, was pushed over her head. Her clothes were damp. A sour cloud of booze and stale cigarettes hovered over her.

The preacher wasn't around. None of the volunteers, either. The residents knew the routine. Sunny left the sour smell of Russian hat behind.

The bathrooms were on the other side of the facility. They smelled like cleaning solution and wax. The sinks were spotless, mirrors free of smudges. An emaciated woman looked back at Sunny, the green shine of her eyes gone but the jagged scar still there. She stroked it gently. Felt it pulse, a hot cinder buried beneath her skin.

She felt eyes follow her into a stall and watch her leave. She stared at her boots, one large step after another. There was laughter down the hall. And something else.

Sunny stopped.

She wanted to go back to the cot, curl up like the woman in the Russian hat and forget this day ever happened. Forget this life ever existed, at least for an hour or two. But the familiarity of a song pulled her back.

Someone was singing.

It was a hymnal, a wordless song that vibrated in someone's throat and warmed her heart. It resonated in Sunny. She could feel it in her own mouth.

Her childhood song.

It was the one she sang in the shower, when she washed dishes, when she was bored or anxious. *The ballerina song.*

It was coming from the end of a hallway.

Sunny passed open doors. The rooms bunked men and women, longtime residents with dibs on more private quarters. Most of them had bedded down for the night. Some were still up, conversing, laughing. Eyes rheumy as they watched her pass. The humming cut through the chatter, overplaying the volume of televisions and radios when it shouldn't have, like an amplifier was in her head.

The scar blazed.

The door at the end of the hall was different than the rest, a vintage door made of solid wood, paint peeling from the inlaid trim. The knob was burnished brass and dented, with a scuffed plate with a large keyhole.

She put her hand on the cracked surface. The song trickled through her fingers.

The song continued. A music box plinked along with it, the kind wound by a key, the tinny notes an undercurrent of music.

"Hello?" Sunny knocked gently.

The hallway behind her was empty. No one had come out to stop her. She gently turned the knob. The latch clicked. The door popped and the song gushed into the hallway, its arms wrapping around her, tugging her inside. It wasn't a bunkroom or a bathroom. Not an office.

It was a kitchen.

The kind of kitchen found in a house, not a shelter. There was a center island and faux wood cabinets. The laminate countertops were enormous and set at eye level. But not just any kitchen. Sunny knew this place. She'd been there before.

I grew up here.

The countertops weren't oversized. She was small. Sunny was wearing a faded nighty. Her bare feet poked out from the hem. Her little toes were painted turquoise, her favorite color.

A man was at the table.

He was eating cold pizza. His mustache was thick, his whiskers unshaven. It was a bristled chin that would scratch her face when he kissed her goodnight. He would smell like alcohol and musty fabric, a toxic mix of loud nights and slamming doors. Her mother would be crying.

But not that night.

Sunny had been sleeping. She woke up when something shattered. It was another fight. Only this time her mother wasn't screaming back. She wasn't telling her father to get out, she wanted a divorce, she hated him and always had. Her mother was quiet this night. Someone was on the floor.

The toenails painted turquoise.

It shook Sunny hard, filled her eyes and blurred the details. Her father turned, chewing his food slowly. She didn't wait for him to tell her to go to her room. She spun around to get out, to run away. To never stop.

The corner of the countertop caught her forehead. It sank deep into her flesh, tearing a jagged chunk from her hairline. A warm flood spilled into her eyes as she fell.

She never hit the floor, never encountered the flash of light that followed the collision, the concussion that ached in her head. She never saw her mother wake up or her father taken away.

She just kept falling.

[23]

Sunny
After the Punch

"What time is it?"

Sunny was locked in a heavy place, a body soggy and leaden. Dense and motionless. She had fallen into a deep black sleep.

Metal table legs snapped into place.

"What time is it?"

She jerked awake and nearly rolled off the edge of the mattress. Eyes wide, she clutched the sheets. The room was big and airy. Blankets were stripped from mattresses. People moved around with stacks of linens and pillows, orderly chaos that emptied the room of beds. Many had already packed their belongings for the city.

The young lady that clothed her, now wearing a sweatshirt that said COLLEGE, approached. "The shelter is closing soon. You'll need to clean your area."

Sunny's eyes burned. She couldn't get them to blink, fearing the return of something awful. She clung to the bed.

"Hey, it's okay. You can return tonight. I promise there will be a bed for you."

The walls were still slowly spinning, the world unstable.

"Fifteen minutes!" someone shouted. "Fifteen minutes!"

The woman reached for the covers. "I can help—"

"No."

She forced her feet to the hard floor, jolting her tender ankles and knotted calves. Her boots were open, socks waiting. There was no memory of returning to the bed, no memory of taking off her clothes. Just the memory of that day in the kitchen and the cut that required stitches. The scar was thumping her forehead.

"What is this place?" she muttered.

"You're at the shelter."

COLLEGE woman was still there, off to the side. Sunny needed space to sort this madness out. She had heard singing, a music box. She opened a door and walked into... *walked into a memory.* And woke in a bed with someone reminding her there was still room for her when night came.

"What time is it?" It was the woman with the Russian hat, the one that slept next to her. No one answered when she called out, "What time is it?"

Sunny laced her boots.

"Clear your cot!" someone shouted at her. "Hey!"

Sunny blended into the crowd that shuffled to the exit, where the preacher wished them a blessed day, where staff members provided job opportunities and support. Sunny turned toward the bathrooms. The dorm rooms were open, the bunks cleared out.

The door at the end was ajar.

Her heart fluttered. There was no smell of air fresheners like her daddy put in the car. Just floor wax and wool blankets. She shuffled ahead, pushing against the wall.

"Five minutes!" someone called.

The hustle continued. Sunny remained halfway between leaving and exploring. She nudged the door at the end of the hall open.

The room was empty.

Blood rushed into her ears, the ocean crashing in her head. There was a bed in the corner, the sheets stripped off; the pillow was bare. It looked like all the other rooms, quarters recently vacated until someone returned that night. Carefully, she put her fingers on the door frame and held her breath, bracing for something unexpected.

She braved a step inside.

There was no black hole in the floor, no endless pit. No kitchen island or her momma's feet. Toenails painted turquoise.

Just a music box.

It was in the middle of the room. A ballerina poised on top, balancing on a pointed toe. Hands gracefully above her head in fifth position.

She'd gotten a music box when she was little. Her grandmother gave it to her as a birthday gift. She would wind the key and open the lid, metal tines hitting the keys on a metal cylinder until the tension gave out. The figure dying in place, hands above her head.

The hair had been colored red with a marker.

A shadow filled the doorway. The preacher waited patiently. Sunny's eyes darted around the room, searching for an explanation, a reason for the irrational. This was not a hallucination. She was here, touching this, feeling this. Hearing it, seeing it.

The door was different than all the others.

When she was a child, she would peel strips of paint from the molding and scrape them into piles, pretending it was firewood for the mice. She would peek through the vintage keyhole—the kind that took an old skeleton key—and pretend another world was on the other side. If she could just crawl through it, she would go there.

She didn't make the connection the night before, seeing the door at the end of the hallway. It didn't match the others, was out of place, some sort of doorway to a place that held secrets and memories. *And a song from childhood.*

"Where am I?" she said.

The preacher held out his hand. It was unaccustomed to manual labor. He offered a smile meant to be kind and supportive.

"It's time to leave."

"Where's Marie?"

"Marie?"

"The woman with the yellow flower. She was in line last night. You greeted her."

He shook his head.

"No, no, no... don't pretend. She was the first one in the shelter. She was in that room, right there. I heard her singing. I felt it." Sunny thumped her chest. "She was trying to tell me something."

"The shelter is closing."

"Don't act like I'm crazy. She was here; everyone saw her. Don't do this to me, *don't do this to me!*"

"Come back tonight. If there's room, you can find who you're looking for and—"

She weakly attempted to pound his chest, to grab the collar of his checkered shirt, to shake him into a confession. Because this couldn't be happening. People didn't disappear and not know it. They didn't walk into a memory and go back to bed.

"Don't do this, Sunny."

"How do you know my name?" She struggled to get loose.

"We all have a name."

"How do you know it?"

His eyes were empty, but everyone was watching. She looked to the ceiling, to the walls. Paranoia seeped through the cracks, empowering toxic thoughts.

She broke away from his grip.

"That was my room when I grew up. My room. That's the door, the doorknob, the keyhole. And this!" She shoved the music box ballerina at him. "I painted the hair with a marker to look like me!"

"Thoughts can confuse reality."

"What?"

"You're tired. You're hungry." His tone was soothing. "You're under a lot of stress."

"That door is real. You touch it." She thumped it. "That was my door!"

"Memories are unreliable."

"I know what I remember. I grew up in a one-story house. We ate dinner on a scratched table with crooked legs. My momma painted my toes. She was there. She was in that room!"

The preacher approached with calming grace. "Where was your house?"

Sunny spun away from him. His back was to the bedroom door now. She rubbed her face, pulled her hair. Where was her house? What kind of question was that? But she couldn't remember where it was, just the details of her room, the nights of terror, the toys in her closet, hiding under her bed.

Where is my house?

"We only see what we want to see," he said. "But often what we need to see is right in front of us. It always has been. You're welcome to stay a bit longer until you're—"

"What do I need to see?"

The preacher's smile began to falter. He looked behind her. One of the staff members stopped. Sunny put her back against the wall before someone jumped her. She was a wild animal, hair bristling on her arms, tendons rigid.

"Am I crazy?"

"You're confused."

"The door, the room. The memory. Am I losing it, is that what I'm supposed to believe? Am I supposed to run off and fall apart? Go to the police? Talk to my ex-husband? Run in circles until I unravel? Is that what you want?"

"I don't want anything, Sunny."

Sunny turned her hands over, stared at the lines in her palms, looked at the stained ceiling where water had dripped from an overflowing bathroom on the floor above it, the scratches in the walls from a fight that expelled both residents.

How do I know these things?

None of this made sense. It wasn't supposed to.

"How did I get here?" she whispered.

"You're lost, Sunny."

"No. How did I get... *here.*"

The creases deepened in the corners of his eyes. He knew what she meant. She didn't say the word, didn't clarify her realization, but he heard it.

The clues were all around, people were telling her. Every day made less sense than the one before it. She couldn't trust the past, couldn't trust the future. Couldn't trust her memories. All of this confusion, this illogical sequence of events, was meant to throw her into madness, to pull at the seams of sanity and unwind her.

I know where I am.

"What time is it?" Russian hat shouted from around the corner. Two volunteers escorted her toward the exit. "What time is it?" she railed.

"How do I escape, preacher?"

"Escape?"

"You're a man of God, I assume. Help a lost sheep."

"God helps those that help themselves."

"If I shove this ballerina up your ass, will God help you pull it out?" She held it like a dagger. A note plinked inside.

"You will be arrested for assault. It's the way the world works."

"*This* world? Is that how this world works?"

"All are God's worlds."

"How did I deserve this?" She wanted to bounce the ballerina off his head, open a gash at his hairline and leave a jagged scar. "I just want my son back. I want nothing else, just my son. Keep me here forever, I don't care. Just give me my son. Please."

"He'll have to find his own way." The smile returned to the preacher, one laced with a whiff of the devil.

"You can help me." She stepped closer with the ballerina cradled in both hands. "Show me how to find him."

He closed the bedroom door and paused with his hand on the knob. "It's time to go, Sunny Grimm."

The staff had cleared out the shelter. Now they approached. Were they lost, too? *Are they even real?*

"Perhaps you'll find what you're looking for another day," he said.

The preacher's long steps parted the gathering crowd of staff members. He disappeared into the big room. One of the women gently reminded Sunny that it was time to vacate the premises, that she could return at dinner.

Sunny clutched the ballerina and looked back at the bedroom door, the details of her childhood staring back.

They walked her outside and gave her advice where she might go for the day. Rain dripped through a rip in the blue awning. A cruel wind blew her off-balance. She wrapped her arms around herself and shivered.

Mrs. Jones had posed three questions when she was in the café. She said three questions had to be answered to escape this particular Maze. Sunny had now answered two of them. She knew who she was, and now she knew where she was. But she didn't know why. She thought of a fourth question as she stepped into the rain.

How did I get in the Maze?

[24]

Hunter
After the Punch

The phone lit up.

Call me now, the text said. It was followed by *where the hell are you?* There was a voicemail from the main office, too. His superiors were insistent.

Hunter had been due back weeks ago. He had texted at some point that he was sick, got the flu, was going to ride it out at the hotel and didn't know when he'd be back. Someone had called every day since, but he didn't answer because he was sick.

I'm incurable.

The itch had become a full-grown dragon.

For decades, he'd kept his addiction hidden, protected it, and fed it. What choice did he have? If he told someone what he was doing, he never would've gotten a job. He had to pretend to be normal, pretend he loved his wife and his house and his dog. He was the poster child of what was possible after tragedy, that a wrecked past could be left behind.

He had to keep it secret.

No one could blame him. Foreverland was a tattoo that faded over time but never disappeared. It was a mainline of heroin that ignited pleasure centers that never forgot. Deprivation of that beauty transformed into a brain worm that crawled around in his skull in search of gratification.

The old men had planted the itch. They'd marched him with the other boys and tempted them to reach for the needle with pain and suffering. Once he saw where the needle took him, a beautiful alternate reality, he didn't need to be coaxed anymore. He reached for it on sight. He was a kid.

It's not my fault.

There were people that tried to help when he was younger. There were doctors that wiped his memories after being rescued from the island, deleted the worst parts of his life, told him that he was safe now, that he wouldn't go back. He could start over, start fresh.

But they couldn't erase everything.

He maintained fragments of the island, little sections of memory like he was reading about someone else's life, like he wasn't the one running on the beach. He wasn't the one that saw the chimney smoke when another boy had been deleted. It wasn't him that saw the old men collapse en masse when Foreverland died. Sometimes he wondered if he actually saw the Coast Guard arriving on saving day or just remembered someone talking about it.

But the body remembered.

It knew the damage done, even if the brain did not. His adoptive parents were happy to have him back when he was rescued. They were thrilled to receive compensation for his pain and suffering, the Foreverland fund that supported the survivors. But in his late teens, it was clear he hadn't completely escaped. That was when the brain worm had grown from an annoyance of facial tics to a creature of panic disorders and hallucinations.

At night, he scratched until his scalp bled. Scalding showers sometimes worked long enough to sleep a few hours. He turned to cutting tiny red lines that let the worm breathe. He started on his arms then moved the razor between his toes, behind his ears.

It worked for a while.

The Foreverland fund put him through years of cognitive therapy, mindful awareness and psychotropic remediation. All of it helpful. None of it the cure. Hunter was still a minor, but he knew the root of the problem. No one would believe him if he told them, but he knew deep down what the worm wanted.

Foreverland was calling. It wanted him to come home.

After all the touchy-feely nonsense had failed, he found a way to quiet the compulsion. He had searched for a way to do it so that when he turned eighteen years old, he moved out and took the Foreverland fund with him. He would use the money to quiet the madness.

The procedure was experimental and, of course, illegal. The needle had been declared a felony, thanks in large part to the island. It was nearly impossible to find a way to awareness leap through a needle, but not where third-world governments took a cut.

The needle accessed the front lobe through the forehead, which left a noticeable mark, one that was hard to hide. He already had the stent and there were prosthetics to camouflage it, but he wanted a permanent solution, one that he could hide.

A true addict.

It happened somewhere on the other side of the world. He didn't speak the language, but his money answered all the questions. He was alone when they wheeled him into an open surgical room. A goat was bleating in a far corner. People were weeping behind curtains.

He was awake for the procedure, heard the saw open the back of his skull and stared at the lights as the men behind masks spoke another language, the tone a bit too conversational for his comfort, the laughter too genial. When they were ready for the insertion, the surgeon pulled out the sleeve that would put a dagger through the worm.

They showed him a graphene stent.

It was the size and shape of a straw, the barrel several inches long. When they slid it between the left and right hemispheres of his brain, positioning it in the exact location needed to access the frontal lobe from the back, he distinctly remembered smelling popcorn and seeing the color blue.

Then they revealed the dagger.

The needle was encased in a tube of gel. A thin wire ran to a bank of computers in another room. They waved it in front of his face, then carried it out of sight. When they broke the seal, the translator explained it would be inserted into the graphene stent.

He knew exactly when they did it.

It went in like an icicle. The worm that had been rooting through his brain all those years suddenly vanished.

Somewhere behind him, the translator relayed questions. The temperature fluctuated. Colors broke across the room, faces and balloons and animals came out of nowhere. The sound of an ice cream truck was under the table. A clown hung from the ceiling.

"Where you go?" The surgeon's English was broken behind the mask. "You choice."

Hunter knew how this worked. Visualize your destination and the needle would take you there. That was how Foreverland worked, how all alternate realities worked. The universe wasn't even your limit. Your imagination was.

Only one destination would cure the itch, one that had followed him most of his life, one that demanded he return.

Do I have a choice?

He closed his eyes and felt the sand on his toes, the salt on his cheeks. He returned to the island of Foreverland, the place of promises and horrors, where the old men stole their bodies and erased their minds. He went back to the place that took his childhood, a paradise he swore he would never see again.

Until now.

All these years later, he sweated through a hotel bedspread. The worm had matured. Now he floundered under the weight of a dragon. Nothing had been solved, the addiction not satisfied. He could only manage it by feeding it, which had only served to fatten it.

Do I have a choice?

He reached for his luggage. Quivering, he arranged his pillow and broke a new needle from the vial. Face down, he felt along the back of his head until his fingertips touched the hidden stent. Parting his hair with two fingers, the tip of the needle hovered near the opening. In one fluid motion, he stabbed inward.

The needle's kiss.

His awareness was yanked from his body like a log chain ripping a tree from the earth. He dreamed a dream and for the thousandth time felt sand beneath his toes, salt on his cheeks. The laptop was hardly enough to support the alternate reality he craved—he couldn't walk around, couldn't explore—but he could sit on the dune. And that was enough.

The dragon would sleep for a little while.

He was a victim of greed and the long shadow of abuse. Hunter couldn't trust his thoughts and memories, and perhaps that was the deepest wound struck by the old men. That lash separated him from his own self. Now he lived for the needle to survive. What choice was there?

If there was a way to slay the dragon, he would pay the price. If Dova could do so, he was powerless to stop her. Foreverland wasn't of this world. And he lived his entire life as if he belonged there, not in this life, not in this skin. He would pay any price to get off this wheel.

That scared him more than anything.

[25]

Hunter
After the Punch

The old woman was in the office.

Hunter quivered with déjà vu. She had been there on the day he arrived, sitting in the detective's office, and now she was there again. And Freddy wasn't.

His phone buzzed. *Who is this?*

It had been a while since he'd gotten one of these cryptic texts from the same number he'd blocked a dozen times. *How is this prick doing it?* The phone number seemed familiar. There were a lot of things he didn't care about anymore. That number was one of them, familiar or not.

Your mother, he typed back.

"Can I help you?" a young officer asked. He was handsome, hair as black as his pupils. His shirt was tucked in, belt buckle shiny and Gutierrez was on the ID around his neck.

"I have a meeting with the detective," Hunter said.

"He got called out, be back in an hour. He expecting you?"

Hunter had spoken with Freddy on the phone, told him he was still in town and had a few more questions. Freddy wasn't thrilled, sighing long and hard into a stretch of silence before agreeing to meet with him.

Hunter had moved to a hotel on the other side of the city and checked in under an assumed name. No one would find him. Not his employer, and not Dova. He needed to get his head right, get control of the situation like he'd done for the last fifty years. But the stent was beginning to ache. He was using every day now. Something had to change and he didn't want it to be Dova's people.

"You can wait," Gutierrez said, "or leave a message up front; he'll call you back."

If Hunter went back to the hotel, he'd go facedown. At least outside, he broke the ritual of pulling the drapes closed and indulging.

"I'll wait."

Hunter remained standing, briefcase over his shoulder, looking much the same as he did the first day he arrived. *And she was there.*

He'd seen the old woman before, and not just in Freddy's office. The more he thought about it, she was at 511 when he first met Dova. And she was on the veranda at the lake house while Dova smoked a clove cigarette.

She's following me. He didn't expect an old woman to spy on him, to find him at the hotel, watch him eat breakfast, learn where he was going. She had to be working for Dova.

She always gets there first. How does she know where I'm going?

He sat on the corner of an empty desk, arms crossed. Folders were spread over a keyboard with papers spilling out. One was labeled Foreverland. The cops were doing research. Why would they have information sitting out like that?

They're all watching.

He realized the absurdity of that paranoid thought. There must've been more than ten thousand old women with white hair in the city. And everyone knew about Foreverland. But he was looking for a reason to explain this city and what was happening to him. Everything had fallen apart since arriving.

It was the same report on Foreverland: the advanced technology, the sophisticated network, the kidnappings. They'd been printed right off the Internet. A list of victims was paper clipped to one of the folders. It was long and alphabetized. Hunter pushed the other pages around, expecting to see his photo or name, a background check or something. There were plenty of photos, but none of them were him. His name wasn't even on the list of victims.

"Weren't you here a ways back?"

Hunter had been caught reading the file, but Gutierrez didn't seem to notice.

"FBI, right?" he said. "Looking for the Grimm woman. Sunny Grimm, right?"

"Yeah."

"You find her?"

Hunter shook his head.

"The city has her now," Gutierrez said. "Stay here long enough and you learn that. People come for the bright lights and just melt away."

"I didn't realize giving up on a missing person was police procedure."

"I get it." He nodded along. "You think we don't care, right? But hang around, you'll see. People are going to do what they want; you can't stop them. Some, they don't want to be saved. That's why they come to the city."

"To melt away?"

"You got it."

"So just let the Maze have them."

Gutierrez bristled at first. "You mean the Grimm boy?"

"Him, others. Whomever. You don't care if they punch a needle; that's their choice, right?"

"You've been here, what, six months?"

Months? Gutierrez waited for an answer. Hunter didn't have one. It was a strange place to be, not knowing how much time had passed.

"City's an evil bitch." Gutierrez laughed, genuinely laughed like a joke that struck him dead center. "Once you know that, you can live with it. You fight her and you melt away like the Grimm boy." He pretended to perform a magic trick. *Where did the quarter go?*

"Look the other way, is that it?" Hunter said.

"Don't piss the bitch off and maybe you'll get out."

Hunter reached into his briefcase. Fingers on the folded piece of paper, he hesitated. Gutierrez stood quickly. Maybe he thought he was reaching for a weapon. Hunter pulled the folded piece of paper out slowly, no quick movements. He held it like a badge. Once a thick, off-white card, it had been cut and folded in a dozen directions, the black lines on the back matching up to form a piecemeal ransom note.

The Maze symbol.

Gutierrez took the makeshift origami. He grinned at first, looking around, considered showing it to someone, but the office was relatively empty. He laughed, shaking his head.

"Go down to the corner and get one of those street performers to fold you a miniature flamingo out of a napkin." He held the symbol like a flashcard. "If all you look for is the Maze, all you see is the Maze."

"But if you don't look," Hunter said, "you won't find it."

"Can I keep this?"

"Get your own." Hunter snatched it back. "There's a stack of them at 511."

"Okay. Well, good luck. Don't make yourself crazy."

"Once I'm gone, another fed will come. He'll be in here asking the same questions, looking in the dark and rainy piss-poor corners of the bitch you're so fond of feeding."

"Oh, I know. There's always another one and he'll find the same as you." Gutierrez walked off. "Same as you, brother."

Hunter only wanted to speak with Freddy one last time, dig

around about Micah before getting out of the city. Maybe he'd ask why they were investigating Foreverland. After that, he'd fall off the radar for a while, call in sick and request an extended leave of absence.

Gutierrez was right about one thing, the city was hungry. Hunter just wanted to get lost, not consumed.

Is there a difference?

Freddy's office was still open. The old woman was gone. Hunter looked around before peeking inside; the desk was still cluttered, the computer asleep. He put his hand on the seat to see if it was warm where the old woman had been sitting.

"Mr. Hunter?"

A velvet tongue dragged over his brain. It sent a butt-puckering shiver down his spinal cord. Dova was behind him, wearing a silky black dress that matched her skin.

"You are coping well, I see," she said with a tight grin. "And haven't left us."

He cupped the back of his neck. A trickle of pinkish liquid oozed from his hairline. The city wasn't the only bitch. There was another one in his head.

"You have moved to a new hotel," she said. "And turned off your phone."

"Why are you here?" He looked around. "To stop me from asking questions?"

"We had a disturbance at the business today."

"More problems. Bit of a pattern with you."

"Problems are part of life. Why are you here, Mr. Hunter?"

"Sunny Grimm is still missing."

"And her son."

"And her son. Seems no one wants to talk about Micah."

"What do you wish to learn from the detective?"

"My decisions need to be well informed."

"You've already made your decision, Mr. Hunter. I believe you know that."

Her seductive grin vanished in a grim line. She believed he wasn't leaving the city, that he would hole up in the hotel until he couldn't take it anymore. The only question was how long he could avoid joining them.

"You are the Maze," he said quietly.

"I won't deny or admit that, Mr. Hunter."

No one heard her. Still, he jerked with surprise that she had admitted as much.

"The painting at the lake house," was all he said, wagging the card with the cobbled symbol of the Maze.

It was the abstract painting he had stopped to admire, the one by the spiral staircase, that tipped him off. It had the same display of lines as the card, but included faint additional lines throughout the canvas. He followed them from memory, treating them like dotted lines to be folded or cut. It was the third card he got right, the thick black lines coming together to build the Maze symbol and an altered tagline. *Find a way to please yourself* had become something much simpler.

Find yourself.

The Grimms were lost. And so was he. He'd been lost all his life. Maybe now he was just admitting it.

"I'm putting an end to this, you hear me? I'm calling this in and bringing more agents to shut you down. You can move around all you want, we'll find you and end it."

A smile crept across her face. His threats were hopeful but empty. They both knew it.

"We are many things, Mr. Hunter. I believe I told you that." She inched closer. She gently wrapped her fingers around his hand, lowered the makeshift symbol and slid it into his briefcase. Why were they recruiting him? Was it because he'd survived Foreverland?

They want me in the Maze.

"What happened to you as a child was a tragedy," Dova said. "We can take that burden away from you."

"And what do you get?"

"To help you get lost."

"Get lost?"

A bored officer approached with a handful of papers and asked Dova if she could step over to his desk so they could sort out whatever disturbance had occurred at 511. Her hands were still on Hunter.

"Your decision has been made." She squeezed him one last time and left him standing alone.

Conversations continued around him, a blur of words, snippets of dialog and laughter as if he didn't exist or matter. Dova spoke quietly to an officer, answered questions, and wrote out statements. Hunter fidgeted at the desk, staring at the Foreverland list of survivors and wondering if his name had been deleted. Were they making a folder just on him?

He left before she did.

Freddy wasn't going to return, wasn't going to answer questions if he did. No one could help him now. He returned to his hotel, ready to indulge his need, and discovered what Dova meant.

Your decision has been made.

[26]

Hunter
After the Punch

A drip.

It fell steadily on Hunter's forehead, trickling coolly down his face and beneath the collar of his overcoat.

A bus pulled up, air brakes hissing. The door folded open. A driver—a woman this time—stared into the shelter. Hunter blinked lazily. She aggressively chewed gum, glanced down at the needle wagging in his hand, then yanked on the handle.

The bus rolled off.

A dirty wave of rainwater sloshed over the gutter. Cars honked and swerved as the bus bullied its way into traffic. The tailpipes coughed soot, a thinning charcoal cloud between cars. A sane man would have gotten on the bus.

A rational man would fly home, get his job back, and live a normal life. A lucid man knew the city was consuming him, that the flies were already circling a corpse. A sane man would avoid the rain dripping through the shelter.

Hunter looked at the bent needle in his hand. *Leave now, Hunter. Or stay forever.*

His belongings were still in the hotel. The rest of the needles were in the room, bent and broken just the same as the one he was holding. They were scattered on the bed, thrown in the sink.

Your decision has been made.

He hated himself for not leaving, hated what he'd become.

Dova knew what was waiting for him in the hotel. She was at the police station to see him one last time, to look in his eyes, to size up what he would do. One look and she knew.

He wanted to hate her, too.

A man stopped outside the bus shelter. His slacks were creased, his leather wingtips tucked into rubber slip-ons that shed the rain. He folded his umbrella before stepping inside and filled the enclosure with a fresh scent, a clean smell.

His legs were dainty, twigs that folded one over the other, the top one rocking into place. He tugged at the rim of a charcoal fedora, a red feather splayed in the band. Chalk-white hair was sharply trimmed around his ear and across his equally powder-white neck. He looked in Hunter's direction, hands folded over the teetering umbrella, sharp blue eyes falling on him.

A long black coat falling open.

"You missed the bus." His accent was slightly British. Or was it South African?

"What have you done to me?"

"We all make choices, Mr. Hunter. The choices we make may have been given to us. The words on our lips and the thoughts in our heads may come from a parent or a teacher, perhaps an old man, but we own our choices nonetheless, whether forced upon us or not. These choices make us, Mr. Hunter. Fair or not." A small twisting smile aimed his way. "You made a choice."

"I didn't do this." He twirled the twisted needle.

"You made it your master. You fed it, nursed it, loved it until it became what it is now. Bent or not, Mr. Hunter, that was *your* decision."

"What do you want?"

"You, Mr. Hunter."

"For the Maze?"

The fedora-wearing man ran a finger and thumb over the corners of his mouth. Hunter dipped his head between his knees. The drip pattered the back of his head, soaked through his hair, and kissed the inflamed stent.

"I know what you are." Hunter held up the folded card, the Maze icon tattered and soaked, and threw it on the man's lap. "*Micah.*"

The man did not answer to the name, did not deny it, either. He studied the invitation with a tight twitching smile, turning it between his fingers. In return, he slapped another card on the bench. This one was square, not rectangular. The stock was thick and heavy, the corners sharp.

"The twisted minds you create," Hunter spat. "The horrors, the madness. Your Maze is torture for the entertainment of a few."

"A few?" His eyebrows rose. "The masses know exactly what we do."

"And you sit there as if no one gets hurt."

"Only the willing enter, Mr. Hunter. Remember, choices."

"You tempt."

"You would take away their freedom to choose?"

Hunter ground his palms into his eyes. The rain dripped down his overcoat. When he opened his eyes, the gray world slowly came back into focus. Between gaps passing in traffic, someone was watching him from across the street. Her white hair flashed like windows in a passing train. A sense of the familiar calmed him. He'd seen her so many times, but she had not looked at him until now. Even from that distance, he felt her warmth and comfort.

Micah followed his gaze. The amused smile dropped, the light snuffed from his eyes. The man accustomed to control, from the clothes he wore to the people around him, looked slightly troubled.

"Is she one of yours?" Hunter asked.

Micah twisted the handle of his umbrella. He did not answer.

"I never saw her, not before I came here. And now she's everywhere." Hunter faced the man sitting next to him, proper and grim. "What have you done to me?"

He tapped the metal point of the umbrella on the concrete. His back rigid, head postured as if a string was attached to his crown, he patted the bent needle in Hunter's grip. The shank was still slick with gel.

"You have choices, Mr. Hunter. Take your life and slay your problem. I believe you have entertained this option before."

Hunter had spun the barrel many times. If there was a god, he or she would understand his need to escape this life. He had every right to eat a bullet, even dreamed of times he'd done so. Dreams so vivid that he smelled the gunpowder and saw the flash. He heard the top of his skull pop as the bullet tore through his brain and decorated the ceiling. There were dreams he tasted the steely aftermath and the iron flood spreading across the floor. There were mornings he woke up and couldn't believe it wasn't real.

Yet here he was.

"You may leave the city," Micah said. "Go back to chasing the serpent's tail and the cycle will continue. I think you know that game doesn't have much time left."

The stent was weeping from overuse. Infection wasn't far away, if it hadn't already started eating through his gray matter. To continue the chase was the same as eating a bullet. A very slow-moving bullet.

"Or you can stop running, Mr. Hunter." He nodded curtly. "Let me show you your true potential. Let me show you that what you think of as a curse is an immeasurable treasure. Very few people know the true purpose of the game, Mr. Hunter."

"The game." Calling it a game sounded so innocent and fun. "Is this how you recruited the boy?"

Hunter suddenly felt sadness. An image of him strapping the

gear on his head crystalized in his vision, the feeling of hope just before the darting tongue pierced his forehead.

"Did you promise him riches, too?"

"We offered opportunity." Micah opened his hand.

"And his mother? What did you do to her? Where is she?"

Hunter's legs were dead and shaking, the flesh between his toes puckered and peeling. He stepped out of the shelter. The sky gently stung him with tiny droplets.

"Risk comes with reward, Mr. Hunter."

"And what are *you* risking?"

Hands perched on the umbrella's handle, the man pushed onto his feet. He put the folded card with the Maze symbol—the one Hunter had spent a day cutting and piecing together—into his coat pocket, then retrieved the thick square card he had slapped on the bench.

He took Hunter's hand and pressed the square card into his palm, the sharp corner biting into his flesh. It was cold and heavy, as if minted from a dense alloy. He could feel the raised black lines against his palm. On one side, the card was blank.

On the other, the Maze symbol.

"This is *my* world, Mr. Hunter," Micah said. "*I* am the risk. *I* am the reward."

Hunter quivered. The queer sense of déjà vu, the sinking feeling of an imploding dream. The quaint man with white hair was psychotic. He was calm, self-assured. The posture of an untouchable man of immeasurable power.

He thinks he's god. That this is his world.

A bus roared up to the curb, the brakes hissing. The door folded open. The driver, an old man with sagging eyes, looked out. Hunter didn't look away from the white-haired man and his sharp blue eyes. Rain pooled on the rim of his fedora, trickling onto his shoulders.

"My offer stands," he said, "to rid you of the weight you've been pulling all this time, to quell the hunger that lives inside you." He tipped the fedora and spilled a pool of water then gently tapped his forehead. "You have the potential to create your own world, Mr. Hunter. I can show you how."

Leaving the city was the same as eating a bullet. Had he been down that path before, taking the easy way out? And now here he was, asked to choose when there was no choice, only the illusion of one. Accept his invitation, or the end of his life.

Have I done this already?

The bus door closed and the air brakes hissed. Dreary faces peered from dark windows as the bus pulled away. A decision had been made.

Micah unfurled the umbrella and held it over Hunter's head. The patter of rainfall danced on the fabric. Streams dribbled from the spines like tiny faucets. It was a promise to protect him from the weather, should he accept the invitation.

A silver sedan stopped at the curb.

Micah opened the back door without breaking eye contact. He protected Hunter from the rain, inviting him to seek shelter from the pain.

The potential to create my own world.

Hunter grabbed the door, hand trembling. Dova had told him they wanted to hide him. Micah wanted him to create his own world. The offers were vague, their motivation cryptic. But the choice was clear. They would kill the dragon.

Before it killed him.

As he dipped toward the backseat, the umbrella following him, Hunter looked over the hood one last time. The old woman that followed from a distance was now in the open, watching him commit to the man that was presumably the Maze.

This is my world, he'd said.

And just as he lowered himself toward the safety of the car, a jagged line of static ripped the scene like an old photo. It popped in Hunter's ear, a high-pitched squeal that deadened the roar of traffic and the patter of rain. In complete and utter silence, the colors of the world flipped. The woman's hair was now black. The asphalt now bleached white.

Rain exploded on the car, giant droplets splashing in slow motion as raindrops glittered in a slow, silent descent.

Micah's hair was black, his coat white. He frowned at Hunter, the first sign of life since he'd entered the bus shelter. It was an expression of doubt and confusion. He looked around, then across the street. His mouth moved, but words didn't come out. He dropped the umbrella. His foot splashed in a growing puddle. Gray water was hurled over his shoe and spread over the wet pavement.

He reached for Hunter. His hand closed on the lapel of his black overcoat as rain dripped from a twisted snarl. The driver began to exit the car when colors flipped back to normal.

Gray then color. Color then gray.

Back and forth it went, each turn of the wheel slowing traffic, unwinding the rain. Each time the colors flipped, a crackle of static struck him with fingers of electrical current. Each time, the colors bleached lighter and the grays had less contrast. The buildings were still there, the road and sidewalks, too.

But the cars had vanished. Bystanders, gone. Micah was the last person to blip out of existence, his desperate reach merely inches from grasping Hunter's coat as they slowed to a stop. His eyes had grown wide. And then he was gone.

Blip.

The old woman was still there, hands at her sides. Raindrops had frozen around her. They had become liquid jewels hanging in space. Hunter stood alone on the curb. The silver sedan was gone.

The sky was clear blue. The sun beamed into a colorless world.

Hunter couldn't feel his body, wasn't sure he had one or where he was, whether he'd gotten in the backseat of the car and started to dream, if Micah had hit him over the head. Maybe he was lost in the needle and this was all a dream.

It is a dream, he heard.

All was light, all was right.

He hovered in that space between black and white, the existence between good and bad, here and there, only now with one last thought. A thought that was obliterated by the shatter of countless raindrops, the shrapnel of water molecules shredding all that was matter, including the old woman. Including Hunter. Including this world.

My world, Micah had said.

Until all was white. All was nothing.

That final thought went with him into nothingness, a thought that followed him into the light. The old woman that had been following him since the day he arrived in the city. She did not work for Dova.

I know her.

[27]

Grey
Before the Punch

The boat rested beneath a corrugated roof yellowed with age and algae.

Rach's grandpa sorted through shelves of paint and varnish. His glasses were gold wires, the spectacles stained like poorly washed glass. He slammed a can down with heavy hands, not out of anger or spite. It was just the way he handled things.

The engine was cocked at an angle. The seat cushions were fastened to the benches. The tackle, the life jackets, even the koozies were in their rightful places. Grey remembered them bobbing in black water, the boat turned inside out. Now it was put back together as if nothing had happened.

Except for the damage.

Hamburger Hill had had many holes over a lifetime of fishing trips, but nothing like the fresh wound now slashed across the hull. Gramps leaned over the side with a ball-peen hammer and hit the dent. The echo of metal on metal drove a spike between Grey's eyes.

Gramps handed her the hammer. "Tap it out."

He stood back. She clenched her teeth and popped the dent three times before pretending to examine her work. Grey's eyes were about to explode.

"Lucky you didn't hurt someone," Gramps muttered.

"Wasn't our fault," Rach said.

It happened at the landing, she'd told him. The wind was uppity and then some jerk sped through a no-wake zone and tossed the boat onto a rotten pillar. They lost a cooler of fish and damn near capsized.

Damn near?

"Were you drinking?" Gramps asked.

"Coffee."

"That why you both got a headache?"

She sighed. "I promise, we weren't drinking. It was an accident."

He stared over the wire-rims, lips silently working in his St. Nick beard. He told Grey to stir the paint, then pointed at the dent—hand thick and sun-spotted—before leaving for the house. Rach hit the hull until he was inside, each swing louder than the one before it.

"I can't do this." The hammer rattled inside the boat. "I'd rather buy him a new boat."

"You serious?" Grey whispered.

"You know how many times I helped repair it? It's older than you and me put together. God, no wonder he thinks we were drinking. I *feel* drunk."

"Rach." He looked out the window. "That's not what happened."

"You want me to tell him I let you drive the boat?"

"*What?*"

They hadn't talked much on the drive out to her grandparents' house. She had a blazing headache and refused to answer his questions. *Can we talk about this later?* she had said.

It was now later.

"He's going to blow an artery if I tell him you wrecked it," she said. "We're in enough trouble. Well, I am. You can do whatever you want." She pinched her nose. "Listen, it wasn't your fault. The guy threw you off course with his big-ass boat. I'm not sure I could've stopped from crashing."

Grey ran his hand over the dent. It was long and creased. That wasn't something that happened when a boat was thrown onto a rotten pillar. That happened when you hit it at full throttle. He told her so.

Then told her exactly what happened.

"You're still high." She laughed.

"We drove out to the house before that. You remember the gate, the man and woman that stopped us, pointed phones at us? Remember my dad flipping out in his apartment? It was your idea to take the boat across the lake and explore the house from the shore. We went when it was dark and hit something at full speed. We were in serious trouble, Rach. They saved us."

"Who saved us?"

"The people on the cliff. I woke up in there, but you were... they took you home already."

She was watching him talk. Memories collided in her pupils, attempting to latch on and make sense. Instead, they bounced like billiards balls.

"You're serious," she said. "Holy shit, are you experimenting with sensory gear or something? That will erase reality, you know that?"

"No, I'm not—"

The screen door on the house rattled. Rach wiped her forehead and swung the hammer, shaking her head and grimacing. Grey popped the crusty lid on a can of paint. Each swing rattled his teeth.

She took sixteen aspirin before they were done.

Gramps had brought the whole bottle from the house. Each time he went back, she snuck two more. Grey ate eight of them. Once the dent was out and the hammer put away, they flipped the boat to sand and paint.

Gramps didn't say much. She was a horrible liar. Her grandpa knew it. The whole family knew it.

That dent was from high impact, not a little misdirection at a loading ramp. Maybe he was just glad she was all right and would give it to her later. Or maybe he gave her a pass because she was selling the lie like the truth.

Because she believes it.

The sun had fallen prey to the city by the time they started home, the buildings knifing into the sky like fangs. She was singing along to the radio. Straps of hair were matted to her forehead; sweat stained her pits.

He'd tried to set the record straight twice more that afternoon. The third time she'd held the hammer like a weapon, said she would crack some sense into his skull if he didn't shut up. Her lips thinned when she was genuinely pissed and he could hardly see them. She was hot, cheeks flushed, hair sweaty. Irritated with him, with everything.

Maybe he was the insane one.

She stopped across from his building. She was drumming to the song on the radio, bobbing her head, staring ahead. Her cheeks were rosy.

There was a red spot on her forehead. Grey leaned closer.

"Whoa. We tried that."

"I'm not trying to kiss... just hang on."

He pushed her hair off her forehead. She was stiff and wary. A swift punch to the throat was on deck should he lick his lips or lean in. Instead, he jumped out of the car.

Mom was at the kitchen table with the laptop. He went to the bathroom and ran the shower. Breathing heavily, he pushed brown curls off his forehead, holding them on top of his head as he leaned over the sink. His breath fogged the mirror.

How did I miss it?

He'd seen it on Rach's forehead, a blackhead nestled into a red welt. Nothing out of the ordinary. A simple teenage blemish centered exactly in the middle. But Grey had one, too.

Only it wasn't a blackhead.

He knew what it was. The woman that had met him in the water room with the South African accent, she'd warned him.

Do you trust your senses?

Grey sat in the shower, hot water running over his tired aches. What he saw and heard, what he smelled and felt and tasted all determined his reality. Did he trust his memories?

Rach does.

[28]

Grey
Before the Punch

Class ended.

Grey sat on the front steps, one side of his shirt untucked. He'd lost the belt weeks ago. Now the blue Dockers sagged enough to receive a demerit. He would've got one had he gone to class.

He was falling behind in one of the top prep schools of the nation. An academic scholarship took care of most of the tuition. His mom took care of the rest. He couldn't care less about the school, but it kept him out of public education, where school was as dangerous as a civil war.

The front doors opened.

A flood of identically dressed students skipped down the wide steps, book bags swinging. They were all talented in some way—arts, music, or science. Future lawyers and doctors, future leaders of the world quickstepped their way to freedom. Most would succeed by society's standards. They would get married, retire early, and enjoy the finer things until they died with loving families by their sides.

Others would deal illegal wares, get arrested. They weren't thugs, weren't morally corrupt. Money did not guarantee happiness or success. Sometimes it bred greed and disillusion. And intelligence wasn't a guarantee to navigate the waters of temptation, where everything was promised and sometimes delivered.

Some of them would end up in the Maze.

Grey's talent was to blend. He could stand against a wall and never catch a second look. He would make a great homeless man. No one ever looked at the homeless on corners or stuffed into doorways. They were invisible. They wanted it that way.

But it still hurt.

A small group of girls squeezed through the crowd. Grey stood up to spy on the one with a pink book bag and oversized glasses, the frames thick and smart.

"Rach!"

She told the coffee bunch that she would catch up. They cast a glance at him then quickly forgot he was there.

"Hey, creep," she said. "Where you been?"

"Sick." He faked a cough. "We need to talk."

"'Bout?"

He looked around the crowd, his superpowers of invisibility fully engaged. "Let's take a ride."

"Sounds a little weird."

"I want to show you something."

"Weirder."

The coffee bunch waited, thumbing their phones with dumb, bored expressions. Rach looked their way. Her hair was pinned back, a short ponytail tied up. Just like them.

"New friends?" he said.

"Just people. You should try it sometime, talk to someone, make a new friend. It's not that hard."

It wasn't like that when they were little, when they were bound by their mutual fear of social situations. Anxiety was their common bond. Now she was sailing into new waters and he was clinging like a stubborn barnacle.

"Call me later." She gave the universal *call me* gesture.

"Does your head still hurt?"

"What?"

"Your head. Does it still ache?"

"A little."

Her rosy color blanched. A fringe of irritation appeared on her upper lip. Grey reached for the side pocket of her pink book bag and took a pencil from one of the slots. The eraser was new. Delicately pinching the sharp end, he gently touched his forehead.

A dull pain flared outward.

There was no longer a red welt. No longer a little blackhead. It only took a week to heal, but the pain was still there.

"When I think of that weekend, it hurts right here," he said.

The pain was hard to describe, a sort of straining resistance that bloomed between his eyes, a deep sense of injustice, like being forced to do something he wasn't supposed to do.

Or remember.

But he didn't have to explain it to her. The bitter resistance was in her eyes. He touched her forehead with the magic pencil. She knocked it out of his hand.

"We're not talking about the boat."

"I just want to drive tomorrow, that's it. I'll never bring up the boat ever again." He raised three fingers. "I swear."

"You're not a Boy Scout."

"How do you know?"

In the week since the accident, he had decided nothing could be trusted. Especially his memories.

SHE PICKED him up that Saturday.

It took three texts to wake her. Another one to get her going. It was three o'clock when she pulled up wearing her grumpy face. Grey handed her a lukewarm coffee.

"How long's this going to take?" she said.

Grey told her where they were going. She shook her head and bit down on some nasty thoughts. They made the drive in silence. Only the radio had something to say.

He'd been researching. In the mornings, he said goodbye to his mother to catch the bus. When it dropped him off, he passed the school and walked another six blocks to the library. All research was done on public computers. Not one search through his phone or laptop. He knew what had happened that night at the lake.

Just didn't know why Rach couldn't remember.

What happens when you learn that memories can't be trusted? What if it's deeper than that? What if everything is a lie and the rabbit hole is bottomless? There is no reality and there never was? This is just a dream.

Identity just an illusion.

He needed her to know the truth. The other questions could come after that. If he was the only one on the crazy train, then he was going over a cliff alone.

He'd taken a car out to the landing earlier that week but never got out of the car. He and the driver watched a man and his wife drop a boat into the water. Grey asked the driver if he saw what Grey was seeing. The guy, a little confused, agreed.

Then they left.

How do we know reality? I can't just tell her. She must experience it, must see that her memories are false. If she accepts that, she'll be treading on thin ice.

Even Grey felt it crackle.

"Now what?" she said.

"Park there."

They sat in the car and watched a pontoon boat chug past the dock, fishing rods bending at the rear.

"We dropped in at dusk. Remember?"

She nodded, eyelids heavy. Eyes bored.

"We crossed the lake, heading due west. We saw the house on top of a cliff. It was dark—"

"Insane," she muttered. "We crossed the lake in a johnboat."

"Tell me what *you* remember."

"You know what happened. I'm not telling you again."

He got out of the car. It smelled like dying fish and sour beer. Jet skis bounced past the shore, rooster tails behind them. Grey stopped at the top of the ramp. Water slid over the slimy concrete.

Rach sat in the car until he waved. They weren't leaving unless she got out. Or left him behind. That was a possibility he hadn't considered.

Reluctantly, she met him at the ramp.

"One last time," he said, "tell me what happened. I'll never ask again. Swear to God."

Shoulders slumped, she recited, "I backed the trailer down the ramp. You were driving when a boat plowed through the no-wake and tossed you on—"

She pointed. Brow furrowed, she looked around, trying to finish her thoughts, to make them come true, but the harder she tried, the more the thread unraveled.

"Hit what?" he said.

"There was a post right there. It... it..."

"We hit something on the other side of the lake, Rach. A post or tree just below the surface, we hit it full throttle. That's why the dent was so long. That's why your grandpa doesn't believe you. The dent doesn't match your story."

She wandered closer. The water lapped her shoes. Her eyes were locked on the post she remembered, the way the johnboat was launched onto it and tipped, the cooler dumping out their fish. It was old and rotten, the remnant of a dilapidated dock.

"It was there," she said. "Someone took it out."

"No one took it out, Rach. It was never there."

She was shaking her head, wrestling with the memory and the reality. She touched her forehead, where an ache was beginning to bloom. Grey felt it, too.

"They did something to us." He put a jump drive in her hand. "Watch the videos I downloaded. Don't go online, okay. Just watch and then call me. I think I know what they did to us."

She looked at the jump drive. It wasn't going to be an easy leap. But he needed her to do it. Because he couldn't ride the crazy train alone.

She looked up. "If this is true, why do you remember and not me?"

Why did they mess with her memories and not his? Why did they keep him until morning? Why did the woman in the white dress lecture him?

"I don't know."

THIS WASN'T LIKE HER.

When something confronted Rach, she didn't back off. If she was wrong, she apologized. If not, then get out of the way.

This time, she did neither.

He thought she'd settle after a day or two, laugh it off, tell him he was insane, whatever. But she knew something was off. Something deep down was messed up and she got a glimpse of it. She was wrong about her memories, but there was too much at risk to admit it.

There was no answer to his texts. No answering his calls. Did she even plug the jump drive in and look at the videos?

He approached her at school. "Let it go already," she said. "I don't care about it, the lake or that house. Neither should you. Can we move on?"

She slammed her locker. They stared for a long second. Her library glasses slid to the end of her nose. Her eyeliner was smudged. The coffee clique rounded the corner and she turned to follow.

"Get the latte," Grey said. "The vente or vagina or whatever they call it."

She lifted a middle finger.

He stayed by her locker and thought about posting a note to beg her to watch the videos. Maybe she did and that was the end of it. Instead, he shot her a text.

Sorry.

The worst part was losing her. He'd already screwed things up when he'd kissed her and then convinced her to give the girlfriend-boyfriend thing a try. Of course, he'd almost got her killed, there was that. Now she was drifting off and he was standing by her locker all alone.

When the weekend arrived, he did what every loner did—sat in his room. He used to whittle away weekends online, gaming or otherwise. Now it all seemed pointless. Who cared if jonnymcpothead69 won? There was no money in it. There was just teabagging your opponent. None of it made any sense.

Not after the lake.

What do they want?

He loaded a jump drive. Before entering the password, he looked out front. His mother was in the kitchen. Popcorn was dancing on the stove. She had a night off, which meant lying on the couch and talking to the television, telling characters not to open a door or repeating their lines until she fell asleep.

He left the door halfway open. She was twice as likely to come knocking if he closed it. He lay on the bed, laptop pointed away from the door, sound muted, and opened the jump drive. Thumbnail icons lined up. He'd been through them a hundred times.

Had Rach even seen them once?

There was no doubting what he researched. They might as well be documentaries. The first file was named *History of the Punch.*

Computer-aided alternate reality was first achieved with the insertion of a three-inch surgical steel needle into the middle of the forehead. This required an implanted stent for repeated access, which left an obvious port for everyone to see.

The needle accessed the frontal lobe, essentially networking the brain—what some referred to as an elegant organic computer—with servers. The five senses were hijacked, the awareness teleported to an animated reality, one in which the user couldn't distinguish between dream and flesh.

Grey knew all about the Foreverland incident, backward and forward. He was obsessed with the tropical island where boys were told they were in an accident, that their parents sent them there to be healed only to be lured into taking the needle and eventually erased from their bodies.

Grey often wondered what it was like to be one of those boys, waking up confused. Some of them were saved, but they were never normal again. The needle was illegal after that. But technology like that wasn't going to just go away. Heroin and meth were still a thing despite drug dealers clogging prisons and addicts overdosing. Because people wanted it.

So innovation prevailed.

The needle diameter was reduced to a tenth of a millimeter. Stents were not required. A trip into the needle went undetected. With the aid of the punch, the proper location was accurately located for the needle's insertion. Thoughts could be accessed; the senses expanded. Memories downloaded or uploaded.

Or changed.

Universities were proving the technique was effective for treating trauma victims of abuse or the horrors of unfortunate events. Legalization was close, according to reports. Means of monitoring the use of such technology was required to avoid another Foreverland.

But people wanted it.

He watched the insertion of one of these new age horsehair needles. There was no blood as it was pushed into the forehead. The participant's eyes were closed. Soon, they began the dance of REM, seeing dreams that came not from the imagination but whatever was on the other end of the needle.

Grey touched his forehead. It was still sensitive, slightly sore. They were able to relocate recent memories, reformat and upload new ones. They created a new scenario of a boat hitting a rotting pillar at the boat landing instead of racing toward the cliff.

But why just Rach?

"Hey." His dad stood in the bedroom. "You all right?"

Grey slammed the laptop shut. The door was still ajar.

His dad was wearing dark blue scrubs, fresh from the office. He looked down and grinned. "Had a late emergency, thought I'd stop by on my way home."

A late night affair wasn't out of the question, a little doctor-patient role play in the dentist chair, maybe. But this wasn't on the way to his apartment. It was in the opposite direction.

"What do you want?"

"Truce." He put up his hands. "Your mother let me in. We thought it would be good if you and I cleared the air, talked a little. How have you been?"

"You mean since you deleted me? Fair to horseshit. You?"

His dad stepped over dirty clothes, looked around the room but didn't say anything. He put his hands on his hips, glanced at the door and said, "I know about the boat."

Grey stared for a moment, waiting for more. His dad glared down. He didn't look angry. His lips weren't pulled across his teeth; his forehead wasn't tight. In fact, he looked like a man he'd never seen before.

Concerned.

Grey put the laptop down and gently closed the door. Mom was on the couch, the television splashing her face.

"What were you thinking?" his dad hissed.

"How do you know about it?"

"How do you think? You could've died out there. You would've if they didn't save you. Listen, I don't want anything to happen to you. We haven't always gotten along, I get that. Part of that's my fault."

All of it's your fault, Grey thought. But he knew that road went both ways.

"I could've been a better dad. A better person."

He sat on the pillows. The bed squeaked under his weight. He was nodding, thinking. Agreeing with himself.

"What are you doing at that house?" Grey asked.

"You know what I'm doing."

"It's my money you're using. I should have a say."

"I'll get you through college, don't worry about that."

"I'll tell Mom what you've done."

"You haven't yet." His eyes sparkled. "Why not?"

He called his bluff. Grey wasn't going to tell her for a thousand reasons. He didn't want to put her through it, sure. But more than that, he wanted to know what was happening out there. He wasn't welcome to go to the house alone, that much was obvious. He hoped, maybe, his dad would take him. It would be different if he did.

"I'd rather you not tell her," he said, "but I understand if you do. I've hurt you two enough already. I got us into this mess. I'll get us out."

He looked at the floor, elbows on knees.

"You're going into the Maze," Grey said. "Admit it."

Maze money wasn't what it used to be. In the beginning, it made the family rich, win or lose. That was when it was straightforward, a big production people could torrent. Now the money wasn't always a jackpot. But it still paid a lot of bills.

"I don't know what I'm doing," his dad said. "None of us do, Minnow."

A chill gripped Grey. Not because his dad sounded like he was about to weep. He'd called him Minnow. That was his nickname when he was little. *Load the game, Minnow,* he would say, *before your mom wakes up.* He couldn't remember the last time he heard him say that. He couldn't remember the last time he saw his dad struggling.

"Let me help you," Grey said.

"No. This is my situation."

"Dad, I can help, I swear. I know how the Maze works." Grey sat next to him. His dad shook his head and paused to say something before shaking it again. He took a deep breath and shuddered.

"Only if you don't go back," he said. "You understand what I'm saying? I'll let you help if you promise not to go back to the lake house. They'll let me in as long as you stay away, son. Don't mess this up. It's my last chance."

He was worn out. The stress had smacked him around and drained him. It added a decade of wrinkles. Grey hardly recognized him. He was a far cry from the days of Minnow.

"Look." Grey opened the laptop. "I've got a thousand videos on tanking. There are tutorials on how to awareness leap, how to relax into the drop. If you're still having problems going under water, there's a whole section on—"

"There's another way." His dad looked at his forehead.

Grey frowned. "What?"

"They say it doesn't hurt, that it's automatic, just sucks you right into the game. You can even do it from home. I need to find out more, but I think that might be the way in."

He still had the dad-smell, the manly musk that reminded Grey he was safe, that his dad was there to take care of things. He was the one that stopped the monsters under the bed. He had the answers to nightmares that kept him awake. As long as his dad was in the house, there was no need to worry.

At least when he was Minnow.

"Hey, creep."

Grey spun on the bed and, for the second time, slammed the laptop shut. Rach was leaning into his room, her hand on the doorknob. He hadn't heard the door open.

"Your mom let me in," she said.

Grey leaped off the bed. His mother was talking to the television.

He pulled Rach into the room and closed the door. This conversation wasn't for his mother.

He noticed she was relaxed. His dad always made her edgy. She didn't smile as much or talk when he was around. He sometimes wondered if his dad had done something that she just wouldn't admit, something she thought was better to bury than air out.

"You all right?" she said.

The bed was empty.

The pillow wasn't even dented. Grey picked up the laptop like a full-grown man might be hiding beneath it. He looked under the bed.

"He was just here, Rach. When you walked into the room..."

"Who?"

He rubbed his face. It was getting hard to breathe. His forehead was numb, the sides of his head tingling. He paced back and forth, struggling for air.

"How could you not see him?" he said.

"Grey, I—"

He grabbed her arms and squeezed too hard. She twisted out of his grip and pushed him against the wall. She watched him slide to the floor. He was afraid he would keep sliding and never hit bottom.

"No," he muttered. "No, no, no..."

He touched her. She was real. He could feel her, he could see her and smell her and touch her, and that meant she was real. He didn't touch his dad. *But I smelled him. I saw him and talked to him.*

"Are you real?" he said.

"What?"

"Are you real, Rach? Are you really here?"

She didn't know how to answer that. She only had false memories that she believed. They'd planted a fake scenario, making her believe she never crossed the lake. She just had wrong memories.

He was talking to his.

[29]

Grey

Before the Punch

Rach's fingers were like twigs, the kind that might snap if she cracked her knuckles. Grey had laced his fingers with hers before leaving the apartment. She promised not to let go. Squeezing like a man hanging from a ledge, he was afraid he might break them.

He hadn't slept in a while.

The floor would dissolve when he would close his eyes, the bed would rotate and the sheets would twist into serpents. He would jump out of bed, sometimes scream into his pillow, and pull on his hair to bring the world back to normal.

He had refused to come out of his room and would only answer his mom through the door. Maybe that was her on the other side of the door, her voice calling out, asking if he was hungry, if he was all right.

Maybe it wasn't.

Rach was all he had now. She was the only one he could trust.

His dad, the ghost, the make-believe person he'd had a conversation with, the hallucination that had called him Minnow, disappeared when she arrived. When Rach was in the room, the floor would stop rotating and the walls would quit melting. The sheets were sheets. She would sit on the bed while he paced, and asked questions he didn't hear.

When she was gone, the fun house was back.

His mom was starting to worry. He played off sick that week, pretending to sleep when she was home. That wasn't going to last. And she was still asking about his dad. At least, he thought it was her asking. He couldn't face another ghost parent of his imagination.

Grey still hadn't talked to his dad. That was the worst part. It wasn't the threat to his sanity, not the convincing presence of someone that wasn't there. It was that the ghost dad that came to visit him wasn't real. He never was. The caring, listening sort of dad, the support kind of man never existed. Grey really wanted him to be real.

The dad he always wanted.

"I just... I need to see him, talk to him," he had told Rach. "He can make things right."

"How?"

Part of Grey hoped the hallucination was more of a vision, that maybe his dad had changed. One look was all he needed. He wanted to believe the hallucination.

Grey was right about the needles and the lake, he was sure of it. All of that happened. They'd crossed the water and crashed near the shore, woke up with tiny holes in their foreheads and different memories. They'd done something to Rach.

What they did to him was different.

"What's your dad going to do?" Rach had answered.

"I don't know. I just need to see him."

That was the truth. He wanted to see him, talk to him. He was compelled to find him; it was all he thought about since the imaginary conversation. He dreamed of him, talked to him, hoped he would call him Minnow and play a goddamn video game with him or something.

Anything. But there were no answers to his texts, no messages from his dad.

An itch he couldn't scratch.

He paced the room faster, couldn't see any other way out of this trap, no one else to talk to. Not his mom. She was singing the other day. First time in a long time, she was shaking popcorn and humming along. His dad was the one who would help him. He knew the people at the house; he would know what they did to him and why. He was the only one who could get him out of this.

So he and Rach locked fingers.

"I'm heading out." His mother looked in the bedroom with her factory ID strung around her neck. "Make sure you clean up after yourself. I'll see you in the morning."

She glanced at their hands. She had always thought they were girlfriend-boyfriend, before and after they tried it. Her eyes lingered on him longer than usual. Maybe she was considering telling Rach to go home. Leaving them in the apartment all alone seemed a little risqué. She was a single parent and he wasn't a child. He wasn't going to stay in his room that night.

And he wouldn't see her in the morning.

THE FUN-HOUSE ENGINES were warming up.

Grey was attached to the elevator, banging his head on the back panel. The hallway was stretching, his dad's door getting farther away. If he didn't tear away from the wall, he would never reach it.

"Grey?" Rachel's knuckles were grinding between his fingers. "Hey, we don't have to do this."

Sweat broke on his lip and matted his hair to his forehead. His determination drained away. All roads led to his dad; this was where it started. He had emptied the college fund, went neck deep in the Maze, and Grey followed right along. Only Grey was in over his head.

I have to do this.

He shoved out of the elevator. He stared at the carpet, boots floating over the floor, the steady *bum-bum* of his heels beating down the hall. When he looked up, they were in front of his dad's door.

His breath was raspy.

He reached up and rapped lightly. The sound echoed and his arm tingled. He knocked a second time. She stopped him after the third.

"Do you have a key?"

Grey stared at the spyhole. His dad always took a peek before opening. The light never changed. He wasn't in there, but the door moved. A slight crack appeared.

Rach opened it. "It's unlocked."

Grey was drawn inside. Rach turned the deadbolt behind them. They stopped and listened. The kitchen faucet dripped. There was a box on the table, one of the flaps open.

"Dad?"

Rach peeled his hand from hers one finger at a time. His joints ached. His teeth hurt. She walked with him to the bathroom. The towels were folded, the drawers open. The scuba gear gone.

Sheets were wadded on the bed. Clothes were hanging in the closet, DVDs scattered on the floor. The giant red suitcase was gone. So was the pistol. Rach pulled open the chest of drawers, each one empty.

"He's gone," he said.

He'd packed the suitcase and enough belongings to get far away. He was scared. Something happened and he ran. He was good at that. He'd packed up and bailed, leaving his problems behind. Including Grey.

Not the first time.

Rach went to the bathroom. Grey's thoughts began to cycle. *Is he standing right in front of me? Is that Rach in the bathroom?* His senses were all he had to determine the here and now, what was around him. He had thought his dad had come to his bedroom, had even talked to him. Maybe his dad was in the room right now and he didn't see him. But Rach would see him. Unless they screwed her head up too and she just didn't know it yet.

Do you trust your senses?

He went to the kitchen for a glass of water, sat at the table—wide-eyed and tense. His mouth was dry, ears popping. Sooner or later, Rach would have to go home. She couldn't hold his hand forever. She would let go and leave him alone with his thoughts. What would he do if he couldn't trust himself? What if there was no way out?

He spilled the water.

It spread across the table and soaked the corner of the box. The address label had been peeled off. Grey pulled the flap open and reached inside. It was a velvet bag. He untied the drawstring. Chills trickled through him, settling like wet sand until he was heavy and full. What he pulled out had a strap and a knob. This time, the symbol wasn't disguised on a card.

It was right out in the open.

Grey had seen this thing used in video torrents. It was for those that couldn't stomach the tank. This was another way. And his dad was too chickenshit to use it. Maybe it was too real, or the thought of putting that thing on his forehead and imagining the silver tongue darting out was just too much. He'd packed up and never looked back.

"You ready?" Rach asked.

He didn't know how long he'd been staring inside the box or how long Rach was waiting or if she'd actually said anything. She'd gone to the bathroom; now she was next to him.

"You all right?" she asked.

"Yeah. Yeah, I'm ready." He extended his hand. "I'm all right."

"Sure?"

He stood without a problem. The floor didn't sway this time; the walls didn't buckle as they started down the hallway. Grey looked back at the apartment. He'd left the door open. There was nothing back there he needed.

"What's in the box?" Rach asked.

"Souvenir."

"What if he comes back?"

They stopped inside the elevator. Grey pushed the button, no longer shaking. The storm of thoughts had cleared away and the sky was blue. He closed the flaps on the box.

"He's not going to use it."

THE SYMBOL WAS CHILLING.

Grey sat at his desk and ran his finger over the embossed grooves. He'd seen that symbol flash a thousand times over grisly scenes of competition, seen it stenciled on the sides of tanks or photos of the wild-eyed players who emerged from them.

He'd never touched one.

The strap was wide and elastic. The knob was a smaller version of a hockey puck but heavier and glossy. The inner surface was slick and flexible. Somewhere there was a microscopic hole where a hair-thin needle would emerge when pressed against his forehead.

Did the Foreverland boys wear one of these?

The needle was thicker when they punched in. It required a surgically installed stent. He laid the heavy knob on his desk. A list of Foreverland survivors was mixed into his report. They had been rescued before the needle had permanently sucked their identities from their bodies, but some of them never really made it back to what they were like before the island. Their memories had been scrambled by a mental eggbeater.

The punch he was holding contained a needle that was barely visible to the naked eye. It might not hurt going in, but it could do just as much damage. Maybe more.

How many times did he wish he was one of those Foreverland boys? Didn't he want to be one of those people dropping in a tank to make a run at fame and fortune? Enlightenment? Grey was afraid he would waste away his life in his mother's bedroom.

If I'm going to end up like that, at least take a shot.

There was a time he went to an Olympic-sized pool with diving boards and concrete platforms. The big kids would leap off the high dive all summer long while Grey clung to the edge of the pool and watched them drop cannonballs into the deep end. The water would resonant with a deep *ka-thunk* and water would splash on the deck.

At the end of that summer, he was allowed to go up.

He climbed the ladder while his mom watched from the sidelines. The metal rail was cool and wet; the rungs bit into the soft soles of his bare feet. It was so much higher from up there. He wondered if he had climbed a different diving board.

His mom clapped.

Grey's toes gripped the end of the diving board as it wavered beneath his weight. His legs almost dripped over the sides. He had envisioned doing a slow walk and a double-bounce like the big kids would do, springing high above the trees with his fingers pointed and his toes curled as he executed a cannonball so perfect he would get his mom wet. He turned around instead. All the kids waiting on the ladder had to climb down.

"You were eight years old." His dad's voice was behind him. It sounded gruff and sandy, like those mornings after a long night out. "You came down that ladder and I made you go back up. You remember? I wouldn't let you quit because I knew you wanted to do it."

There was no shadow over his shoulder, but Grey could feel the weighty presence of his dad's voice.

"You went back there like a champ and walked off the end of that board with your arms glued to your sides. You fell like a stick in the water and came up with a smile. And what did you do after that? You went back up ten more times, didn't you? That first step is the hard one. The rest was easy."

Grey closed his eyes. "You weren't there."

His dad's voice was right. He'd faced the wrath of all the big kids and went back up the ladder and walked off the end of the board. But it was his mom who made him do it. She'd made him try again while she treaded water in the deep end even though the lifeguard told her not to.

Grey walked the plank once more. She was in the deep water, waving her arms. The lifeguard was blowing her whistle when Grey stepped off the end and dropped just like his dad said—a terrified stick. Chlorinated water shot up his nose and burned his eyes. His mom was there before he came up for air. His dad never saw it.

Because he wasn't at the pool.

"You're not here, either."

"It doesn't matter," Henk said. "You did it, Minnow. And you didn't regret it. All it took was that first step."

"You're not real."

"Can you hear me? See me?" He gently squeezed Grey's shoulders. "Feel me?"

Grey could feel him, and he was certain if he spun around, he would see him and smell him; if he shoved him, he would hear him fall, feel his weight beneath his hands. *But he's not here. This isn't real.*

"I'm not letting you climb back down the ladder, Minnow. I want you to fly."

That first step off the diving board was a gut-launching thrill—the wind in his ears and the sudden impact on his feet. He did it ten more times that day with a smile that grew wider with each attempt.

"You want this." His dad's voice turned cool. "You've always wanted this. You do this and you'll wake up in the morning before your mom is even home, I promise. You're ready for this, Minnow. You've prepared for this your whole life."

The bed squeaked. Grey slowly spun around and saw his dad patting the pillow. He was wearing the white lab coat and looked happy and relaxed. But he wasn't at the pool. He couldn't have known all the details of that first drop off the diving board, but he did because he was inside Grey's head. He knew everything. Or Grey didn't remember it right.

Maybe he was there.

"You won't feel a thing," his dad said. "Just like last time."

Grey slid his phone under the desk. He wound up his earbuds and placed them in a tin box.

A box with no stickers.

"You'll be right back, Minnow—"

"Stop talking." Grey refused to look at him. "I'm not doing it unless you shut up."

He wanted him to be real. This was the dad in his head, the one he wished he had. The one that listened to him, recognized him and saw him.

"But you're not real," Grey said. "No matter how much I want you to be, you don't exist. So go away and I'll do it. I'll do it by myself."

When he turned around, the room was empty. What was worse, a dad that wasn't real or the dad he really had? Grey was going to do it. His dad knew he would. Of course he did.

He lay on the bed and stared at the ceiling. Somewhere a television was playing loudly. The tenants above him walked around. His heart was punching his chest as he pulled the strap over his head. The knob stood on his forehead. The inner surface undulated. Soon the front of his head was numb. Next, there were magnetic waves. He might not wake from this.

But that wasn't the worst thing that could happen.

"Sorry," he whispered just before the spike came.

THE SESSIONS

Sycophants.

The group sat in a circle. The chairs were generously spaced apart. They sat with backs straight, hands folded. The similar clothing, the postures, the patience all implied implicit serenity.

Henk had none of that.

He took a seat on the outer ring and slouched in an inherent sense of unworthiness. He had failed. A week left and he had nothing to show for it. A week left and he was broke.

Rema sat next to him.

None of the others had servants with them. He had come to think of them as such, personal servants that guided them into the tank, human training wheels that kept everyone upright.

"Good morning."

"Good morning," the sycophants responded.

The Spaniard entered the room, a slender tan man with chest hair perfectly displayed in an open collar. The lights dimmed. He approached the darkened center, touching their shoulders along the way.

Henk fidgeted.

Rema watched him. She didn't move to stop him, but would if he became disruptive. An outburst would bring escorts into the room. Henk would find himself in his room alone, staring at sunrises on monitors. He needed to behave this time.

"Sleep well?" the Spaniard asked.

There was agreement. Of course there was fucking agreement. They shared knowing glances. They had mastered tanking. Some were off the respirators, diving in super-oxygenated gel solution that allowed them to breathe liquid with wireless transponders leaping their senses. And the participants that weren't in the room, they had moved onto more challenging leaps. Perhaps the game itself.

"Your dreams," the Spaniard said, "have changed, have they not?"

He walked the spacious circle, hearing from his sycophants, bouncing his fingers. He wasn't speaking of dreams that come during sleep. He spoke of the lands that appeared in the tanks, the worlds where they leaped. Nightmares were waiting for Henk.

A silver cylinder about the size of a thermos sat in the middle of the circle. The Spaniard stepped over it.

"If you choose to indulge in your dreams and leave it at that," he said, "then you may do so. You may leave the Sessions and take with you the ability to entertain yourself with lucid dreams, a respite from your earthly toil. With time dilation, you may essentially live more life than someone who does not indulge in the dream world." He paused and smiled that wide, salesy smile. "There is nothing wrong with masturbation."

Laughter rippled through the room.

"There is just more to life than self-gratification. I believe you didn't come here to mentally masturbate. You came to the Sessions to find the true meaning of life. The purpose of human existence."

They were all in agreement. They wanted more than to jerk off with their minds.

"You are here for the next phase in human evolution, yes?"

Henk thought they had all come for the same reason, that dirty little word no one ever said out loud. The Maze. That was his sole reason for being there, the only reason he listened to these pretentious lectures. Why else would they spend a fortune? The Spaniard was right about awareness leaping for self-pleasure. Henk was no stranger to indulgence, but why would they go through the trouble of drowning themselves for lucid dreams?

"Does the dreamer create the dream? Or does the dream make the dreamer?"

A dramatic pause. He let that sink in with a lap around the silver object. *If the dream creates the dreamer, then what is the dream?*

"How did all of this begin? This world, this reality? Astrophysicists tell us it began with the Big Bang, but what existed before that?"

They were plunged into darkness. A few of the sycophants yelped with surprise. Henk stiffened in panic. He couldn't see Rema next to him or see his own hand as he lifted it to his face. The Spaniard's footsteps continued to gently pace in the center.

A sliver of white light ignited a slit where the silver object was located. It hovered in the pitch black—a sharp line of light. The slit became a white laser that beamed into the dark.

The sycophants rustled in their chairs to see what it was illuminating.

Shapes were in motion, strewn on the dark floor—planets, clouds, buildings, trees, people—but only those that fell in the laser's path. None of that was there before the Spaniard entered. Their smoke and mirror routines were impressive, but Henk was growing tired of them. He was in the minority.

"The world around us, what we call the physical world, cannot be manipulated." The Spaniard's voice floated around them. "It has rules that a physicist understands. There is gravity; there is space. There are those boundaries that we cannot cross if we are to exist in this reality. I think we can all agree with that.

"But I think you understand, at some level, there is an illusion we cannot see through. Our human limits do not allow us to see the truth easily, that there is no separation between the dream and dreamer. A dream that begins and ends... *with you.*"

Henk wasn't an idiot. He knew they were selling bullshit, claiming that the dream worlds in the tank were alternate realities, as in *actual realities*, earth and stone, that sort of thing. The dreams they were creating were the alternate realities they created *with thought*, a manifestation of creativity. These dreams were places they leaped their awareness, but not dreams like we'd come to understand as children. Dreams were just another place to exist, another room to enter. They were as real as the chair beneath Henk's clenched buttocks.

We create the dream and then become the dream.

"This is a dream, right here?" someone asked. It sounded like the heavyset woman that often smelled like powder. "Base reality, flesh and bone? Are you saying someone dreamed the world we live in now?"

"Humanity dreams during sleep," the Spaniard said, "dismissing those brief forays of fantasy as infantile wishes."

The white laser was imperceptibly moving. The objects and scenery were changing in the slim line of illumination.

"You have created dreams," the Spaniard said. "*You* created them. It is your mind that builds the universe you visit; it is your mind that solidifies an existence for your awareness to reside in. And your mind knows no boundaries. You can dream a universe that is unique and distant, or rebuild this very world."

There was a pause. Henk imagined he was sweeping his arms out in reference to the world around them. It seemed to be his favorite gesture during these talks, accompanied by the perfect smile, neither of which they could see in the dark.

"You can build a parallel universe that for all intents and purposes is identical to this one—your family and friends, the great wonders of the world, the moon and stars. You created this world as you have all your dreams, and when you do so, you become this reality. *You are the Big Bang.*"

The idea of environmental absorption had already been discussed with at least ten arm sweeps and a hundred smiles. Even the sycophants were incredulous to the suggestion that they could somehow know every gritty detail of the physical world without really knowing it and put it in a dream, as if it were hidden in the dark of the subconscious. The Spaniard had suggested that a parallel universe would look just like this one—every person, every animal, twig, building, and road could be mirrored in the mind. None of them believed it, the stuff of science fiction.

That was before they became sycophants.

"Why do this?" the Spaniard asked. "Why dream another world into existence?"

A form hovered near the source of light. The Spaniard appeared to be squatting over the silver object. His palms appeared to levitate over the beam like they were warming themselves.

"Human potential, my friends, is to create new realities. It is not the cycle of mental masturbation. And as the creator of your new reality, you will come to know that everything exists as a result of your mind. All possible pasts and all possible futures exist simultaneously and time is an illusion. Time is simply a limitation, a creation to experience only a sliver of what already exists. Time unveils what has already been created a little at a time. You cannot see what is outside the light of time because of your limitations."

He ran his finger through the beam. Dust particles swirled in the luminescence.

"In your dream, you will come to know that time is not a limitation. The past and the future are illusions. The present moment contains the entire universe. You are the dreamer; you are the dream. You are all things at all times. Time will not bind the dreamer. Because you are everything."

His hands vanished, but his form was still hunched over the light source.

"In your dream, you *are* the light."

The silver object that contained the light source was suddenly lifted off the floor.

The luminescence was blinding. Just before it bathed everything in white light, there were thousands of little objects surrounding the source—a miniature representation of earth and water, civilization and life. It all existed around the source. Time was the silver canister that contained the light, the single being that marched through the eternal presence of all things.

The great illusion.

He threw his arm up and blinked through swelling tears. The blanched details of the room slowly came into focus. The sycophants were shielding their eyes. Their mouths hung open slightly, gasping in awe of the bullshit the Spaniard had just slung across the room. He was holding the silver object like a cup with a smile almost as bright as the glowing light. The objects that it had previously illuminated on the floor—the miniature buildings and clouds and planets—were gone.

Henk began slowly clapping. Rema grabbed his hands, but no one seemed to notice.

The Spaniard won them in that moment. They were already committed. They would all abandon their previous plans of mental masturbation and follow the Pied Piper to become gods in a reality that they created with their minds. Whether that led them into the Maze or not, Henk would never find out. He wasn't going with them.

Because he couldn't.

One by one, they returned to their rooms. They would drop into a tank, network their minds, and absorb their surroundings if that was really possible. The Spaniard said it was.

Henk remained seated.

He was the last one in the room. Rema was still by his side. Henk contemplated the possibility of suing them for blinding him when footsteps approached. There was a hand on Henk's shoulder. The man he'd waited to see, the one whose company he'd eagerly requested, sat in the chair next to him. He moved like wheat before the harvest, possessing a sense of gravity that compelled all things to fall into his orbit.

His hair was white.

"In a week, I'll be broke," Henk said. "I'll have nothing to show for it. All of this will be for nothing. All of this promise will be wasted on me."

Emotion saturated his words. He clamped his hands to keep from trembling.

"Failure does not exist," Micah said.

"I don't care if it exists or not. I'll have nothing."

"If you are here now, you have everything."

"Stop." Henk spoke through gritted teeth. "Just stop."

He'd never been this close to Micah, had always seen him from a distance, more often on one of the monitors for prerecorded announcements. It was possible the man didn't exist, perhaps an animation with perfect composure and reassuring disposition. But there he was, flesh and blood. Charisma beamed in magnetic waves and made it hard to look away; it instilled a curiosity one might experience looking at a masterpiece, one of the great wonders of the world, or a beautiful woman.

Henk wanted to drink from *that* fountain.

"I don't care about higher callings or parallel universes. I gave you a fortune to enter the Maze." He didn't bother whispering. "If I can't do it, I want my money back."

"You purchased an opportunity to enter."

"No. I purchased an entry."

There was no legal recourse to this transaction any more than if he purchased a box full of sex slaves. A strong bluff was his only chance. Micah's lazy eyes expressed no need to blink. They rested on Henk.

"You may exercise that entry when you are ready."

"I can't. I'll never..." His hand fluttered at the tank.

"There are other ways."

Henk jumped up. Rema tensed for what he might do. Micah remained fluid. There was no security in the room besides Rema, and Henk felt certain he could get to the most important man in the room if he wanted. Yet Micah was unconcerned, perhaps confident Henk wouldn't do anything.

He was right.

Henk paced in the open space behind the chairs, hand to his head. He had a thing with needles. He was a dentist, put them in his patients' mouths all day long. Not his.

"I-I-I can't… I can't do that. I just can't—"

Micah raised his hand. The words were clipped off Henk's tongue. He stopped pacing. The quivering root of fear vanished.

"What do you want from the Maze?" Micah asked.

Henk wanted what everyone else wanted. He wasn't proud of it, but with a wave of the hand, Micah somehow cleared the fog and he saw clearly into his own desires. As ugly as they were, he saw them with great detail. He rubbed his fingers.

Money. I want the money.

Micah nodded. He'd understood before Henk did. Now they both did. And now that they were clear on his intentions, they could move forward. The details of how he would collect on his investment would be worked out, a proposal that would be given to Henk when the opportunity arrived. An opportunity he would accept, as ugly as it was.

Henk knew what he was, knew he was not a man of honor or dignity. What he would agree to was even beneath him.

PART 4

FOUND IN THE DREAM

[30]

Sunny
After the Punch

The doorway of a public accountant provided shelter from the drizzle. Metal bars covered a glass door and pressed into Sunny's back. She pulled her legs against her chest.

The line had formed at the City Shelter for the Homeless.

She recognized the faded colors and ragged patterns, the same hats and coats. Day after day, they were always the same. Mrs. Jones, however, wasn't there. Not since the first day had she seen her. Sunny had gone back to the apartment and found Mrs. Jones's door locked. No cats calling.

Sunny's apartment was locked, too. She knocked on the door, thinking someone might have moved in. She had no idea how many days had passed. When no one opened the door, not even a groggy Grey without the punch around his head, she knocked on her neighbors' doors. No one came out. She went down to the building super's apartment on the first floor and beat on the door with both fists.

People were staring. She screamed at them, shouting for the super who wouldn't open the door until someone called the police.

Sunny never came back.

No one in the line outside City Shelter for the Homeless said much about Mrs. Jones or cared that she wasn't the first in line anymore. It was one less person to wait behind.

A man on a corner seemed to be waiting for a ride. His hands were buried in the pockets of a long black coat, rain dripping from the brim of a black hat. A fringe of white hair was exposed. He didn't look across the street, not her way. Nor did a ride pick him up. He was there, watching.

They all are.

It was hard to gauge the season. The sky was continuously colorless, the only change was how hard the precipitation fell. How deep the puddles.

The cold gnawed at her joints, seeping into her bones. Breathing triggered a domino effect of aches; loneliness snuffed the brilliance from her stare. Her eyes had become the color of a dying pasture.

The church bells gonged. She checked the time on her digital watch. The masking tape long gone.

The line came to life.

The squatty woman, the one with the Russian hat, continued to stalk the hopeless and lost while presenting her watch like a badge or a crucifix to ward off evil. Sunny had tried to give her the time, but she would never look at her, always walking off to ask someone else as if that wasn't the answer she was looking for.

The line shuffled toward the sky blue awning, the building swallowing them, one by one.

If this world was false, if she was indeed in some sort of dream, some altered reality of the Maze—however she got there—then it was convincing enough to no longer be false. She felt every nuance of its realness, every second of its grind.

How do I escape?

She didn't know why she was in the Maze. She still doubted she was in the Maze, testing its cruelty by pinching bruises down her legs and leaping from walls until she sprained her ankles and the pain radiated through her hips. But there was no explaining that room in the shelter, no other explanation for Donny's amnesia or the strangeness of Mrs. Jones.

Marie.

If this was the Maze, it was not an ordinary dream, one in which she could will herself awake. There would be a way out. And she was convinced it was inside the shelter. The sign was painted on the pillar beneath the awning.

The snake eating its tail.

The symbol of eternity, or immortality. The cycle of birth and death. There was a sticker in Grey's room, too. It had been stuck on the tin box when she found the wristwatch. Sometimes, she wondered, was it the suffering that convinced her that the dream was real? Did anguish drive her to accept what was around her as reality, transform her into a mindless human that craved relief from the world rather than the truth?

She had considered climbing to the roof of her apartment building and nose-diving to an instant end, but she knew enough about the Maze that she would not escape. The symbol of eternity suggested that was true.

Find yourself.

The torn card she'd found in the plastic said *find yourself* beneath the Maze symbol. Maybe it was an accident. Or the way out.

She folded the sheet of clear plastic, a poor cushion that kept her bottom half somewhat dry, and rushed across the street. No one noticed her queue up at the end of the condensing line.

"What time is it?"

The woman cruised the line, the Russian hat propped on her head as she exposed the watch on her wrist, begging someone to read it to her and not satisfied if they did.

"Get!" a stringy woman shouted at Russian hat. "It's time to get!"

She yanked at her hat and kicked her leg. One of the shelter's assistants ran to help her. She asked if she was ready to come inside. Russian hat shook her head, hands clutched to her chin. The attacker was escorted out of the line and told to leave.

She did not go quietly.

The drizzle kept them wet. Sunny squeezed beneath the sky blue awning, arms around her chest. The preacher was greeting them with big white teeth

"Welcome." He smiled down at Sunny. "Are you lost?"

She didn't take his outstretched hand and ignored his false inquiry, the mocking smile. Every day at five o'clock, he welcomed her and asked if she was lost, guiding her inside for another night of wandering. He wasn't there to help.

Just maintain the madness.

The warmth of the shelter sighed. Men and women filed into the promise of a warm meal and a place to sleep, an escape from the cruel city. They took refuge on thin mattresses, huddled with their few belongings, removed their wet boots, and dried their cold feet.

Sunny stopped beneath the clock. Down the long hallway to her right, past the restrooms and dormitories, was the antique door of her childhood. Every night, it called her, beckoned her to enter, and taunted her with a stroll into another memory.

It started with the song.

Night after night, Sunny would go to it, would stand outside the door of her youth, the paint peeling, and imagine the twirling dancer on the music box, praying that this time was different. This time she would open the door to find her son.

This time she would wake up.

She would turn the old brass knob, let the ballerina song invite her inside to witness another memory: finding her brother after a suicide attempt with a serrated knife, relive the sting of her grandmother's switch, experience the time she was trapped behind the school by a group of boys. None of those memories hurt as much as knowing Grey was still somewhere out there.

And she was still here.

She was insane, doing the same thing over and over, going to the door and expecting a different result. But it was there, the escape was there. It had to be.

What if it's not? What if I die and start over? Will I find my way back? It has to be now. I have to find my way out now. The clock is ticking, I'm wasting away.

Supper was in full swing, the smell of turkey and mashed potatoes, the clatter of silverware. Sunny ignored the calls to eat, transfixed by the lure of the childhood door, straining to hear the ballerina, waiting for it to announce another opportunity, another.

Residents vacated the dining hall, dishes piled into plastic bins, tables wiped and broken down. They passed beneath the clock, bumping her as they went to the restroom, some continuing onto the suites down the hall, sheets snapped over the mattresses, clothes folded.

Russian hat stopped outside the women's bathroom, presenting her watch to anyone that passed, tapping the face, begging them to tell her what they saw.

"What time is it?" she called. "What time is it?"

The heavyset woman never approached Sunny. No matter what someone said, the answer never satisfied.

Sunny looked at the wristwatch around her wrist, the one she'd found in Grey's bedroom, the one for mom. The one she never took off. It kept the time. And the alarm went off every night at the same time. No matter how she pushed those buttons, it never stopped.

The same time every night.

Russian hat had stopped her obsessive search. Her hands were at her sides. The distant madness had faded from her eyes. All signs of desperation—the furrowed eyebrows, the pursed lips, the mad itch needing scratched by the time—had vanished. For the first time, she looked directly at Sunny. Without disrupting another person, she walked out of the shelter and into the rain.

What time is it?

The chorus of snoring was punctuated by gasps of sleep apnea and the banter of sleep talk.

Sunny stared at a water stain on the ceiling, her heart dancing beneath the blanket. Somewhere past the restrooms, a ballerina was singing, beckoning for her to come investigate her childhood, to see what memory was next.

It started about midnight.

First, she felt the song in her throat, the hum in her chest. The ballerina chimes followed. They grew louder, rising above the sound of slumber, the sleep of the disturbed and fitful. This was the call she heard every night. And every night she fell to the promise that it would be different; this time she'd escape. It was hard to resist.

Even now.

She dozed in and out while listening, clutching the sheets when she woke to stare at the water stain. The ballerina sang louder as the night grew longer—a puppet master tugging her strings, coaxing her out of bed. She closed her eyes, sweat dampening her pillow.

Beep—beep—beep—beep...

The room fell silent.

No snoring, no talking. No restless rustling. The night died at the beeping of her wristwatch.

She raised the lit face. Every night it went off. Every night she ignored it. Even if she pushed the buttons, it wouldn't stop. But it wasn't broken. It was calling.

What time is it?

It threw her feet onto the waxed floor. Someone else was in Russian hat's bed, covers bundled on her shoulder. The blankets didn't rise and fall with each heavy breath. She was as still as the pillow. Tempted to rouse her, to shake her shoulder, to see if she was breathing, Sunny resisted. She wasn't breathing.

No one was.

Barefoot, Sunny walked between the rows of the lost. Their eyes were closed, their mouths open and expressions frozen. Not a sound rose from the congregation.

Even the ballerina had stopped.

The digital heartbeat of the alarm bounced through the room, the numbers stuck in place. Not even the seconds rolled over.

All those nights waiting for the ballerina, she'd never made it to three o'clock. She would immediately go to the room and stand outside the door, wishing for something different. Sometimes she would squeeze the knob until lines were printed across her palm. She would open the door to another memory, waking in the morning with the faint recollection of the alarm.

But never had she waited until three o'clock.

Shadows streaked past the bathrooms. White light outlined the door of her childhood, the brassy doorknob glimmering gold. A ray of light shot from the keyhole, a white laser beaming down the hall. A thousand suns were behind the door.

Find yourself.

The knob rattled as she neared. Reaching out, it glowed iridescent orange, a red-hot coal that was about to begin dripping on the floor. There was no radiant heat, but still she hesitated.

"Please," she muttered, "don't be a memory."

She closed her eyes and grabbed it. No melting of flesh, no branding of her palm. The rattling stopped and the door popped in the frame. The keyhole laser began to swing across her belly. Light bled from the opening, bathing her in something warm, and a saline smell leaked from the room, a splash of something thick and claustrophobic.

She threw it open, shielding her eyes.

There was no kitchen counter or bedroom to see, no awful day at the playground or forgotten birthday party or accident alongside the road. It was light, pure radiant light, warm and inviting. Soft and embracing. Somewhere was the sound of tiny bubbles. It felt good, felt right. Like the sun on her face after a long winter night. A warm blanket on a cold night. A warm bath. *Mamma's embrace.*

It was intimate and knowing, formless and pure. This was the essence of Sunny Grimm. *This is me.*

Something tumbled across the floor.

A tiny white snowflake blew over her bare feet, tickling her toes as it bounced against the wall. The room's light threw a long sharp shadow behind it. This little white tumbleweed was the first thing that had moved. It came out of nowhere. She bent down to pick it up. It wasn't delicate, didn't melt. It was a paper cutout, an odd little shape with arms out.

And three legs.

Another one bounced over her feet and came to rest against the wall. More were blowing from beneath a dormitory door, the crinkling limbs forced through the gap, popping free to tumble into the open, some coming to rest on her feet, a papery snowdrift filling the corridor.

Why am I hesitating? Why?

The three questions Mrs. Jones told her in the café. She'd answered the first two. She knew who she was. The white light inside the bedroom, she was certain where she was. It was the answer to the third question she was doubting, the answer she felt certain she knew. She was here to find her son.

But why am I in the Maze? Only the willing enter, so I must have come here looking for him. Why would I escape if I came here to find him?

She turned away from the bright light and its promise of finding herself and what she assumed was the escape from the Maze. She reached for the door where the paper dolls continued spitting through the gap and collecting against the wall. A vanilla scent escaped the room as she threw it open. A flood of paper dolls spilled out and filled the hallway, piling up to her knees.

Mrs. Jones stood between the dormitory beds.

A yellow lamp threw soft shadows around the room, a contrast to the sharp white light. The scarves were around her neck, the kerchief over her head. She was hunched with age, much older than when she'd first met her outside the apartment the day this journey began. Sunny's reflection looked back from the black saucers of sunglasses; pale yellow light revealed her gaunt figure.

A large bag was at her feet, the one where she collected items from the street, the sheets of plastic and other detritus. Paper dolls were erupting from it like popcorn, climbing over each other to the floor and blowing around the room, some escaping into the hall—the same paper dolls in her apartment were now piled a foot deep around her.

When the time comes, don't run. Open the door.

She had said that in the café, when she told her about her son having to find his own way to a solution. Was she talking about this door? Of course she was. She guided me to the shelter, left clues in her apartment, the photo on the mirror, the phone number on the refrigerator.

Mrs. Jones unfolded her hands, fingers curled, skin delicate. The nails retained the faded hint of polish, a curious color. They were turquoise. She held them out as an offering, as if an answer was in her empty palms.

Sunny looked at her watch. Fifteen seconds before the alarm would stop. Fifteen seconds before the white light would end—the light that promised her an escape from this madness. But would it find her son?

Don't run.

Mrs. Jones—the woman that the residents of the shelter called Marie—reached out. A rogue wind burst from the ducts. The paper dolls swirled and lifted off the floor, a deafening sound of falling leaves engulfing them. Sunny stepped into the calm eye of the strange twister and found the old woman's hands. She slid her hands into her parched palms and felt the yellow light fill the room.

Outside, the white light vanished.

The walls disappeared. The old woman's voice hummed inside Sunny's throat. The beeping of the wristwatch was consumed by the swelling tide of rustling paper. The cyclone spun inside Sunny's head. Mrs. Jones held on tight.

"Let me show you"—the old woman's voice rose above the dry storm—"why you are here."

The floor vanished like it did every time she had entered her bedroom door at the end of the hall. But this time she did not fall into a memory. This time she fell into the truth, transported back in time to see for herself. Sunny chose to open the door, chose not to run. She knew who she was. She knew where.

But why am I in the Maze?

[31]

Sunny
After the Punch

Milk had soaked into the carpet.

Sunny was standing inside Grey's bedroom. She witnessed herself open the door and drop the gallon of milk. Grey was on his bed with his hands folded over his midsection. The punch was strapped around his head.

This was how it started.

She had come home from a late shift at work and picked up groceries, saw the mess in the kitchen and was going to raise hell. Instead, she found her son laid out like a funeral visitation. Even now, Sunny felt panic throw a fist into her stomach. She watched herself flutter for several seconds, a thousand thoughts jamming her nervous system.

"Grey? Honey?" she whispered. "What are you doing?"

She remembered he felt feverish. His shirt was damp and sour, but he was breathing. Very long, even breaths. This was where she searched the room and eventually called Donny. He would come over and tell her what that thing was around his head, tell her he had a friend. What she didn't remember was the card.

It was propped between his fingers.

Sunny watched herself search the room but instead of calling Donny, she grabbed the card and turned it over.

Find a way to please yourself.

There wasn't much to go on. She didn't know if that was a band or a skateboard or a bar. Sunny watched herself search it on her phone. When she found out what it was and what they did, she called. No one answered.

She left the apartment without calling Donny. A little man named Ax didn't come over. She went directly to 511.

Because this is what really happened.

Traffic was heavy that day.

Sunny saw herself watching it through a window of 511. She stood next to her own self. Her son's tragedy lay on her as fresh as a blanket of snow, wet and suffocating, untouched and vivid. This younger version of herself was different than what she was now.

I was hopeful.

This was the moment she saw her reflection in the window and had mistaken it for a homeless woman. She was waiting for the South African woman to return and watching the traffic, wringing her hands in hopes that someone could help. There was no Micah at that point, just the desperation that someone could explain the thing around her son's head.

Dova. Her name is Dova.

While she was waiting for her to return, she didn't call Donny in hopes that a miracle had happened, that her son suddenly sat up and everything was right with the world. Sunny didn't make the call because he wasn't there. No one was.

The door opened.

It wasn't Dova that returned with the news they couldn't help her and suggesting she go to the police. Instead, a slight man with white hair approached. His pants had a sharp crease down each leg. Sunny watched herself turn away from the reflection.

"Can you help me?" she said. "I… I don't have anywhere else to go. There was this card—"

"We've been expecting you."

She was holding the card out like that would explain her hysteria. The man ignored it. Instead, he gestured to the door.

"If you would follow me," he said, "I can explain. And we can help your son." When she didn't follow, he said, "Your son is waiting for you."

"He's waiting?" Her voice trembled.

"Please."

He gestured again. Sunny watched him lead her into a hallway, holding the back door open with a delicate hand on her back as he closed it behind them. Sunny did as he said because there was nowhere else to go, no one to help.

"Third door on the left."

There were several doors along a hallway that smelled intensely antiseptic. Her eyes had teared with a mixture of hope and the sharp, strange scent. Sunny watched herself turn into a tiny stark room. There was a table with two glasses of water and two cups of tea.

"He's waiting for me?" She looked around. "What have you done to my son?"

"Please." He pulled out a chair for her to sit. "Allow me a moment to explain."

The white-haired man sampled the tea and crossed his legs, waiting for her to join him. Sunny watched herself reluctantly take the seat at the table, remembering the cold armrests and the quivering flush in her stomach, how the relaxed disposition of the white-haired man disturbed her the most.

"I understand your pain, Mrs. Grimm. It's not that these sorts of things don't happen from time to time. Someone chooses to enter the game and his or her family members are left bewildered by the choice. But you must understand, your son has entered the Maze, Mrs. Grimm. He did so at his own discretion."

She flinched in the chair. Sunny remembered that feeling when he laid the facts out, cold and bare. She was familiar with the symbol that was embossed on the punch, but not until he said it did she believe that was what happened. It struck her like the tip of a spear and shivered electric.

"I don't care. I want him out, now. He's a child."

"He used a punch outside of a sanctioned facility. It was quite risky of him to attempt an awareness leap through an Ethernet connection. The odds were not in his favor, but I can confirm he transitioned safely. He is alive and well and waiting for you."

"Waiting for me... no, no. Get him out, now. I want him to wake up. Whatever you want, whatever it takes, get him out."

The white-haired man nodded contemplatively. He took a moment to sample his tea, perhaps so the moment could be filled with something other than words and emotion that filled her legs with a toxic trickle of rage and fear.

"What do you want?" she said. "Money? Sex? What do you want?"

His eyes remained compassionate. "He cannot be withdrawn, Mrs. Grimm. His awareness has been reassigned. If you pull the punch from him now, you will leave behind an empty body. It is that simple."

"I'll get the police. I'll shut this fucking place down, you hear me? He's just a boy."

"You may call the authorities, but I assure you time is a much more valuable asset to you at this moment." He pulled up his sleeve to glance at his watch. "Your son entered the Maze approximately twelve hours ago. That is flesh time, the base reality in which you and I currently reside. Time, though, is malleable. Comparatively, he is experiencing it much faster. In the hours that have passed, he has lived several years. In the moments since I looked at my watch, perhaps days have gone by. If you choose to go to the police, perhaps lifetimes will pass before we have an opportunity to speak again."

"Lifetimes?"

"Death does not exist in the Maze, Mrs. Grimm. It simply respawns another birth."

The snake eating its tail.

Were those icons clues to escape her entrapment, or a cruel joke at her expense, something for the Maze spectators watching the highlights of their hapless bumbling to chuckle through entitled smiles? Or was it just the hard truth?

"How could you let him do this?" she said.

"He was afforded the opportunity. He chose to take it."

"Who did this to him?"

"If it eases your anguish, he is not playing any sort of immortal combat, one in which the player suffers one gruesome death after another. He resides in a psychological thriller, one that caters to a more elite audience, those more interested in the outcome rather than the entertainment. He's the willing subject of an experiment."

"Experiment? There's a needle in my son's head!"

"He's been completely wiped of memories. His identity reassigned. His core identity—what makes your son who he is—is still intact. He simply does not *remember* who he is."

"What do you want?" This time it was a request, not a demand, not a threat. *I'll do anything.*

He took a long moment to sip the tea. She was about to come over the table and shake him until his delicate neck bones rattled. She slapped the table instead.

"What do you want?"

"He's waiting, Mrs. Grimm."

"Waiting for what?"

"For you."

It was the first and only time the son of a bitch smiled—a grim little twist in the corner. It wasn't compassionate, wasn't smug. It was more of a curiosity.

"There is a small group of investors that are interested in this experiment. They are not interested in money; they have all they will ever need. They're interested in human potential. Your human potential, as it turns out. And your son's. A place has been secured for you, Mrs. Grimm, with no fee for you to enter. You may insert yourself into the Maze in order to find your son."

"No. No, no, no... I don't want him in an experiment. Stop it, now."

"It's too late for that. It has already begun. Unfortunately, your son has committed you to the experiment. Of course, you don't have to participate, but you won't find him here." He spread his arms. "He's not in the flesh anymore."

"Where is he?"

"As I've said, his awareness has been reassigned."

"Who did this?" She stood. "Who?"

"Mrs. Grimm—"

"Who's doing this? Who gets the money when we come out? I know there's a reward if we go into the Maze." She gritted her teeth around that word.

"You will have all the money you will need, of course."

"If I come out. If *we* come out," she corrected.

"This is a discussion for another time." He tapped his watch, an inexpensive digital watch. An exact replica of the one Sunny would find on her son's desk.

For mom.

"In the meantime, your son is lost. The longer he wanders, the further from home he gets. Every minute that passes for us could be a year for him. He is changing as we speak."

Sunny kicked the chair, clutched her chest, and struggled to catch her breath. "You manipulative bastard. Is this how you get your thrills, preying on bottom feeders like me? Have you no empathy? My son is eighteen! He's a boy; he doesn't know what he's doing!"

"Should your son put his hand in fire, he will be burned no matter what age." His words gained a sharp edge before softening.

"These are the rules of our reality, Mrs. Grimm. If you are going to the police, I suggest you go now. Otherwise, let's continue."

This bastard and all the ones like him owned the authorities. Wealth ruled the world; it did so by making others think there was justice, to believe people like him could be stopped. Sunny knew better.

She paced that tiny room like an animal freshly packed into a zoo. There would be no saving her son if she went to the police. And if the time dilation was true—if her son had already experienced a lifetime or more—then she was already losing him.

"What do you want from me?" she said.

"It's not what I want."

"Whoever!" She raked the glasses of water and teacup against the wall. "What do the investors want?"

"For you to find him."

She pounded the table with both fists. The man leaned back with a placid expression. The stink of this building had crawled into her head. It clung inside her. She wanted to put her finger down her throat and vomit this day on the floor, wanted to scream, to rip her hair out, to throttle someone or something until they apologized. It wasn't fair.

Life is such.

"You'll pay for this." She leaned over the table. Her breath puffed into his eyes. "When I'm done, I'll find you and all the other ones who did this. Do you understand me?"

Dova entered the room, sleek and graceful, unperturbed. She stood in the doorway that led to the hall. The man slid his tea between Sunny's hands splayed on the table. He smelled clean. Nonexistent.

"Mrs. Grimm wishes to find her son," was all he said.

The man's ice-blue eyes remained empty. When Dova reached for her, Sunny yanked her arm away. She wanted to flip the table and plant her foot on the impeccable man who remained impassive as her life unraveled.

Dova escorted her out of the room to find her son. The white-haired man stayed at the table to finish his tea. No one could be forced to enter the Maze against their will.

But will could be manipulated.

She dangled like an inflatable doll, one leaking at the seams.

Sunny witnessed the event from the warehouse floor, watching as they hoisted her body over a tank of bubbling goo—a viscous stew of translucent liquid, rank and fermented. Blood trickled from nicks along her legs.

The strangeness of watching her own body was not lost on her, reliving memories they wiped from her, memories that now unfolded in her consciousness. She cringed at the factory-laden effects, mechanical moving parts.

Her body an ingredient.

There was no time to train for the submersion, every second precious. When given options on how to insert her awareness into the Maze, she could punch her way in like Grey had done. But there were risks, they said. The tank was a more inclusive experience, but she would need orientation. She told them to just drop her, she'd figure it out.

Or die trying.

Sunny witnessed her own self hastily shaving the hair from her body. First her head, then her legs and arms and vagina. The razor snagged flesh in the effort. Valuable time was consumed, but it was better than taking the needle.

"Your success is much improved in the tank," Dova had told her.

A harness was fastened under her arms and around her waist. She dangled nude for the world to see. There was no one in the warehouse, only curtains that hid what she assumed were more tanks. Hanging naked and alone, all sense of dignity shed away.

Her toes were the first in.

Sunny watched the oxygen-rich slime ooze up to her knees. She remembered the sensations—the bathwater temperature, the stinging bite where the razor had cut. A cool sensation passed through her flesh, a mentholated burn permeating her calves, penetrating her shins. A vapor leaked into her femurs.

I'm breathing through my skin, she had thought.

The liquid reached her groin. This was the moment it became very real. The walls of the tank were all around, the buoyancy of the solution releasing the pressure of the harness. Her breasts spattered with bubbles. The pungency filled her head, clinging to the back of her throat in a thick coating she couldn't swallow.

She lifted her chin and closed her eyes.

"Allow the tank to breathe," Dova said.

Sunny could feel her final breath beginning to burn. The liquid passed her lips, filled her nostrils and popped in her ears. It slid over her freshly shaved scalp.

The harness released her.

Sensation was lost in the floating darkness behind her eyelids. She held her last breath until instinct took over.

The liquid gushed into her mouth.

She opened her eyes, thrashing against the glass wall, the thick fluid slowing her panic, a liquid straitjacket of claustrophobia around her. The blurry world dimmed. Numbness filled her from the inside. Momentarily, she began to sink. Her arms lifted above her head.

A drowning ballerina.

A matrix of thin filaments was imbedded in the walls of the tank, a Faraday cage that would wirelessly hijack her senses. The tendrils reached for her, caressing her softening flesh like fiber-optic seaweed that would complete the connection. As her body succumbed to the oxygen-rich solution, a matrix of her identity was captured.

Her awareness leaped.

She was back home, staring at her son as milk soaked into the carpet. She would call Donny. He would bring over Barry. And the hunt would begin.

Sunny was still in the warehouse, staring at her floating body. The atmosphere began to shift. The curtains billowed; the ceiling darkened. She witnessed in elapsed time the lifetimes she would experience once she had been inserted into the Maze. All of her attempts to find her son passed through the dilated dimension of the Maze, each lifetime respawning at the moment of coming home with groceries. Each lifetime yielding no answers, finding no hope. She would die and live, die and live. The cycle of rebirth.

The snake eating its tail.

The highlights of her incarnations sped around her, the details of multiple deaths that happened in the streets or alleys, in rooms or hospitals. Some passings were more peaceful than others. But she never escaped, never saw the clues.

Never found what she came for.

She lost count of the lives she lived and the deaths she died. All the variations of suffering she endured, all the times she'd kidnapped Barry, the man named Ax. There were times she beat him; times she lost control and stabbed him. There were times he escaped and hurt her.

That was why she was careful with the knife.

"*If you want to find me,*" he sang, "*I'll see you at three, but not a minute before, you walk through the door. You won't find me, so you can't be free...*"

With each lifetime, she grew older and lived longer. The futility of her efforts were etched into the fabric of her consciousness, the memories wiped away before respawning to do it again, but never completely forgotten. Her efforts were indelibly branded into her soul.

She eventually surrendered to futility. Hope extinguished, she gave herself to the Maze and merged into the present moment.

A kaleidoscope spun, the speedy winds of time circling around the eye of existence until Sunny witnessed herself as an old woman withered by eternity and carved with wisdom. Slightly bent, the old woman stood on the city's corner. A peaceful smile dug through her wrinkles.

Her emerald green eyes glittered.

The moment of her enlightenment—the point where she embodied the wisdom of the sages, the harvest of grinding through lifetime after lifetime, when there was no separation between all those lives she had lived and no separation between her and the Maze —had arrived. How many lives did it take to reach this moment?

A pointless question.

Time, she had come to realize, was an illusion. It was the point of view taken only from the self. She didn't need to escape the Maze to find her son.

The grand illusion of time had revealed its true nature to her on that street corner, its unwinding bestowing transcendence of the mortal coil. She had become everything. The Maze was not a dream. It was a parallel reality as valid as the flesh reality. And she was not separate from it.

This realization transcended rational thought. She had opened the secrets of the Maze, understood the secret of time, and escaped the bindings of its illusion. She was not separate from anything; therefore she could choose to be anywhere.

Choose to be anytime.

On that street corner, she lifted her eyes to a clear blue sky and slipped through the fabric of the Maze. The buildings faded into pixelated clouds. The sidewalk and streets undulated into grassy slopes. A meadow lay across the land with willowy clouds on the horizon.

The old woman stood in a field.

She had transformed the stuff of the Maze into this peaceful setting. Sunny was next to her. Heavy snowflakes fell around them, dampened the atmosphere, and stuck to their hair. A smile touched the old woman's eyes, snow reflecting deep in her pupils and covering the world around her.

Sunny was holding her hands. She looked into her emerald eyes.

The old woman held a pair of oversized sunglasses that once hid her eyes. She had removed the silken scarf that had covered her head and the jagged scar near her hairline. They weren't in the snow-covered meadow anymore.

They were in a room.

Sunny was still holding the hands of Marie Jones, the old woman who lived across the hall from her. Marie Jones, the homeless woman with a yellow flower in her hat.

I am Mrs. Jones.

Jones, her maiden name. Marie, her middle name. *Sunny Marie Jones.*

A snowflake landed delicately in the old woman's cupped palm. The crystalline flake remained perched upright and did not melt. She curled her fingers around it.

Paper dolls were all around.

At the moment of enlightenment on that street corner, Sunny could have had anything she wanted, could have been anywhere she desired. She could have escaped the Maze. She came back to find herself, to guide herself to the truth, to close the loop, to stop the searching. *Because there is no search. Nothing is lost. I am the light that needs not to escape, but shines on everything.*

The last beep sounded off on her wristwatch.

Sunny was alone, hands out.

Footsteps echoed down the hall and slowed on the approach. The preacher stepped into the room. He was wearing a checkered shirt tucked into pressed khakis with black dress shoes.

"Most unfortunate," he said. "You seem to have missed an opportunity."

Sunny looked around the room; the beds were empty. She could hear the snoring of all the lost in the shelter, felt their breath in her chest. All had been revealed; nothing was separate. Not for Sunny Grimm.

He stepped aside and let her pass. The childhood door was closed. The keyhole was dark. She peeled a strip of paint from the trim and let it flutter to the floor. Nothing was singing inside the room.

Not anymore.

"Is that yours?" the preacher asked.

The bag was in the dorm room. One with a flower on the side. He picked it up, the contents rustling. A paper doll escaped. It was full of them.

"Are you real?" she asked.

"Pardon?"

She looked around with beginner's eyes, a child seeing the world for the very first time. Whether he was real or not depended on one's perspective. He believed he was real. If he was not, then neither was she.

"You know the way," he said.

He was referring to the moment she'd opened her childhood door and gazed into the white light. That was the way out of the Maze. She had found it but didn't take it. Mrs. Jones—her own self—had come to remind her that she didn't need to leave the Maze. One reality was the same as another. And she came here willingly.

She knew why.

Every incarnation Sunny had experienced in the Maze now held this knowledge. It was their moment of enlightenment. All of her incarnations would find it with the help of her own self. They would all know why they were here. There was no reason to escape, nowhere else to go.

There is just here and now.

The preacher walked with her toward the big room. They stopped outside the big room, beneath the clock pointing at three o'clock.

"Perhaps tomorrow night," he said.

He expected her to return to bed and sleep another night, to wait for the digital watch to signal another opportunity. Sunny unbuckled the wristwatch and gave it to the preacher. Confused, he watched her walk out the front doors.

Rain dribbled through a rip in the sky blue awning. City lights cast a gray glow on the night sky. She held her hand out to capture the rain. A small puddle splashed in her palm. When she looked up, the sky cleared. Stars danced on a celestial canvas. The road was streaked with streetlights and passing cars. The moon glowed in the puddles.

The snake graffiti was on the brick pillar with its tail in its mouth.

Sunny reached into the large bag and scatter the paper dolls. They fluttered like moths. She walked down the middle of the street with a cloud of magical paper dolls hovering overhead. The early morning traffic went around her without honking, without cursing. She simply wished for them to avoid her.

And they did.

This was the Maze. It was an experiment that only included her and her son. What the investors wanted to find out was not readily apparent to her. She came to find her son but found herself instead. She would thank them for allowing her this opportunity to find true freedom, but she still harbored anger. Willing or not, someone forced them into this eternal search. She would keep her promise to the white-haired man. Someone would pay.

But first, her son needed to awaken.

[32]

Hunter
After the Punch

The clouds lifted.

He ran his tongue over his teeth. Hunter reached for his chin, the stubble thick and stiff, grinding in his palm. His hand felt as light as a whisper, a phantom limb that floated toward him.

A beam of hard light cut between heavy drapes. Dust particles were effortlessly suspended.

Where am I?

He took for granted that memories awaited him upon awakening. The day. His name. Only emptiness and cutting sunlight greeted him this morning.

Sunlight.

It was gray where he was, where he'd been. It wasn't sharp. Not illuminating.

He sat on the edge of the bed, fully clothed. His shirt was damp with body odor. His head levitated on his shoulders. He gently rose onto his feet and split the heavy drapery, birthing the daylight on his cheeks.

Buildings and cars. People moved like insects.

An ache lingered behind his eyes and spilled into his forehead. He hid behind his hand, deep breaths soothing the pain. He searched for aspirin in his luggage, a loose duffle bag dumped in the corner.

His name came back to him as thoughts drifted out of early fog and landed with a delicate touch, presenting him with who he was and where. He grimaced. Something was missing.

The itch.

He couldn't remember how he got to his bed or the days preceding it, but he remembered the itch that had plagued most of his life. His hand crawled over his jaw, crept behind his ear and through his hair, searching for a place on the back of his head where once he slid a needle.

And found nothing.

A bump, perhaps. A mole. But his fingers did not find what they were expecting—the port of a stent that extended between the two hemispheres of his brain to reach his frontal lobe. He turned his hands over, as if the answers were tattooed on the backs, as if the bulging arteries would divulge hieroglyphic answers, when a text arrived.

Who is this?

It was the same number he'd blocked a dozen times. All the messages had been identical.

Who is this? Who is this? Who is this?

The aspirin lodged just below his Adam's apple. He went to the bathroom and scooped water from the faucet, spilling it down his shirt. He threw his head back to swallow and jumped.

He had expected a tired face with bags weighing down his almond-shaped eyes and frayed black hair. Instead, a vibrant complexion appeared. It was the distillation of happiness. He searched the mottled irises for missing memories.

And then he remembered them.

The needles were broken. It opened a trapdoor of withdrawal, a meeting with a white-haired man, the pulling away of a bus, and the reaching for a car. He was going to surrender to Dova and Micah.

But there was the old woman.

And then everything was consumed in a white background. Everything except her. She was still there because she felt like she was everywhere. Micah had said this world was his. Hunter didn't know what he meant by that. His statement was authoritative, as if he didn't own it with wealth but had created this world as if his hand was the hand of God.

It didn't feel like it anymore.

THE SMELL of flowers pervaded the elevator.

The doors opened. He went to the kitchenette, mouth salivating for the feel of breakfast, and returned to the front desk with half a bagel and a glass of orange juice. Faint conversations tumbled out of a back room. He knocked on the desk.

"Yes, Mr. Montebank?" A young woman appeared.

"Did I, um, check out?"

She looked down. Keystrokes peppered the background conversations while her lips silently moved. He stared at his phone while she searched. There were no missed calls, no messages. He punched the number for the cybercrime office, listening to it ring while the girl shuffled through papers. If he still had a job, he could explain the unexplainable. It was a hallucination brought on by the needle. He would have to come clean about his past, at which point he would definitely not have a job.

The call continued with no voicemail.

He reached for the back of his head. The mole wasn't numb or tender. It was just a slight aberration. How could the stent just disappear? How many times had he driven the spike into his head, waking to live another day without the itch? Could it have grown over?

Not overnight.

"How long have I been here?"

"Pardon?" she said.

"How long have I been in this hotel?"

She mumbled through another series of keystrokes and frowned. "Weird. Let me—"

"What's it say?" He stopped her from walking off.

"Um. I don't see a date when you checked in. I mean, you have the room, I just don't know how long you've had it."

"I never checked out?"

"No. Do you want to?"

"How did I get here last night? Did someone drop me off?"

"I wasn't on duty."

He finished the last bite of breakfast and wandered off, a man lost in a flurry of thoughts and slippery memories. The young woman was still talking as he drifted toward the sliding front doors. Outside, the sunlight had turned a dusty orange. The glimmer of daylight was fading into dusk.

How long have I been here?

The street was dry. No puddles or streaks. The air smelled lightning-struck.

He stood on the curb and thumbed his phone. The calendar was up to date. He'd had an appointment at the police station with inspector Freddy ten days ago. The days following, though, emptied rapidly. Only the one entry since then.

Dova.

The woman with curving hips and strong arms. The way her fingers slipped over his shoulders and pinned his hands. The promises she made.

The needles she broke.

"Mr. Montebank." The young woman from the front desk stepped onto the sidewalk and handed him an envelope. "This was at the counter."

His name was scrawled on the front. The flap was sealed. A

metal object was inside, the edges easily revealed. He tore it open and poured a key into his palm. It was nothing of significance. He held the envelope up to the dying light. Something was written on the inside as if someone had turned the envelope inside out.

Only the reflection, you'll see. Of the one you seek.

Only then you will be, the one who is free.

The refrain was familiar. Where had he seen it? His phone went off.

Who is this?

It was the number that couldn't be blocked. He tapped it this time instead of attempting to block it again. The dial tone rang. It clicked into silence after the fifth ring. A car locked the brakes. The tires skidded on the pavement as his thumb searched to end the call.

And then he heard the voicemail, an alluring voice that seduced the caller to leave a message. Hunter's thighs weakened. He knew that voice well.

She'd been texting all this time.

[33]

Hunter
After the Punch

The stars drilled a million holes between the staggered skyscrapers, a wisp of condensation smearing the backdrop. He'd forgotten the stars, the celestial jewels concealed by the city's humid breath, her steady exhalation of exhaust fumes and foulness. But they were always there, hidden away, now exposed.

Such beauty.

The headache still lurked between his eyes. It was a manageable nuisance that lingered in the background. Traffic streaked past him, brake lights glowing. Windows were squares of light scattered on the buildings' dark faces. Where once their spires hid in the mist of descending clouds, now they twittered like newborns.

He dialed the number and watched the large window across the street. He remembered the old woman was there when he first arrived. She was perusing the merchandise. But she was gone when he entered. He assumed she'd gone through the back door.

And then he dreamed of her watching him from across the street, when the world turned inside out and colors flipped and reality evaporated. He woke in the hotel. It was a dream. It had to be.

Dova's prerecorded voice began speaking after the fifth ring, her voicemail beckoning to leave a message, appointments only. He put the phone in his pocket. His appetite had returned. The café at his back was crowded. He considered a quick bite before crossing the street, looking at the menu posted on the window.

For a second time, his reflection startled him.

It was unfamiliar. He locked into his gaze, recalling the refrain from the note he'd received with a key, the same words written on a scrap of paper somewhere in Grey Grimm's bedroom.

Only the reflection, you'll see. Of the one you seek.

It was the musings of an eighteen-year-old, perhaps a poem for a girlfriend or a class project. Hunter leaned closer and put his nose on the glass. The couple sitting inside looked up. He searched the depths of his pupils for a hint of the one he was seeking.

"Excuse me." A woman bumped into him.

The sidewalk was crowded. The stranger had already blended into the flow without looking back. Despite the warm autumn air, she hid behind the raised collar of a black overcoat, slipping between the gridlocked traffic.

Emptiness haunted the softly lit interior of 511. The mysterious texts, the phone number that couldn't be blocked, were coming from there all this time. He assumed it was Dova that had been texting. She was the only one he'd ever seen inside the business. What was the meaning of it? Was that how she tracked him?

Only the reflection, you'll see...

He hustled across the street, hopping up the short flight of stairs. A white card was on the top step. The metal stand lay on its side just inside the glass door, the cards spilled on the bamboo floor. Random lines were scattered on the backs of them.

He'd solved the puzzle, cut and folded the 511 business card (*more like a brochure,* Dova said) until the Maze symbol was revealed.

A psychologist might remind him that any symbol could be found if you applied the right amount of delusion.

Find a way to please yourself was the tagline. After folding it, it became *Find yourself.*

That was more than a coincidence. 511 was an entrance into the Maze. Solve the riddle and you'll see. *It is what you see that we have,* Dova told him. The evidence was right out in the open. *You just have to see it,* she was telling him. And then she asked what his name meant and he said that names didn't mean anything where he came from.

And where do you come from? she had asked.

Hunter assumed she was referring to his Asian features, but he said he came from nowhere. *Why did I say that?*

The floor was empty; the door at the back ajar. He pulled the front door without expecting it to surrender. It swung on silent hinges. Filtered air embraced him. The first time he'd entered the store, he dripped from the sleeves and cuffs. Now he stepped inside as light as a ballerina.

Quietly, he turned the lock on the front door. Everyone on the street would see him now; barring the door would give him time should anyone investigate. He leisurely crossed the room. His steps echoed off the walls. He listened for an alarm or approaching footsteps.

A police siren whined in the distance.

He put his phone on silent and slipped through the back door. Wall fixtures threw light down a long hallway. The air was dense and cool with a hint of saline and something antiseptic.

His heart was very much alive.

Water dripped somewhere. Hunter proceeded cautiously, pausing after each step. The first couple of doors were open, inside each of them a small room with a table and two chairs and nothing else. Further down was a similar room, this one with a padded examination table.

The next couple of open doors appeared to be efficiency apartments. Hunter slowly inspected them with the light of his phone, holding his breath as he crept around without touching anything. Water was dripping in a sink. He let it run.

A smell grew stronger, a sickly smell of fresh wounds or the slime on fresh meat. It clung inside his nostrils and thumped between his eyes.

He swallowed hard.

The last doorway was an open set of double doors. He stopped outside of them and shut down his phone. Water was running. It was much more than a sink. The air had turned to fumes, penetrating his sinuses, punching the inside of his forehead. He couldn't place the odor, a distinctive haunt that could never be forgotten. Like that of a dead body.

Tears rested on his lower eyelids. He coughed into his fist, gut clutching. He pulled his shirt over his nose and blinked.

It was a small warehouse.

The atmosphere was pale and dense. The dank pallor of things old and secret. Faint lights glowed on black conduit lining an elevated ceiling. Large objects were set to the left and right, enormous cylinders that emitted syrupy burps, the kind floating from vats of tar.

He took a breather in the hall, listening for signs of life. This was what he was searching for, the bedrock of a Maze room. The furthest from his thoughts was the fact that he'd succeed in busting the city down a notch, taking from her the power to seduce her citizens, to slam a fist straight through her insatiable maw.

Sunny Grimm.

That solitary thought drove him through the fumes, forced him to breathe the foul air. His pupils had dilated, absorbing the details of the bubbling objects.

Tanks.

Dark objects floated inside them, lumps of drifting arms and legs, ghosts long since submerged. Heavy bubbles swung their limbs like seaweed, listless and empty.

His stomach clutched again.

The memories of all the times he'd seen tanks, how he'd helped winch limp bodies from the solution, pull them over the edge, wipe the mucus from their faces. But with all those memories, one thing was missing.

Why don't I remember the smell?

He could see the details of their lifeless expressions, imagined the soft flesh beneath his grip, the countless contestants that gave their life to the game. But he felt like an observer to his memories, a moviegoer. He didn't remember a smell.

And there should've been.

A tank was centered at the end of a very long stretch of concrete. It was larger than the others. The body inside was dimly lit from behind. As he approached, the nudity was apparent. It was a slight man with narrow hips and tender arms, the legs of someone on the verge of starvation, or submerged far too long.

Seaweedy tendrils stroked the body. Translucent microtubules slowly bent the elbows and knees, held the man's bobbling head. A swirl of white hair moved about his scalp. Thin eyelids were locked tight, the eyeballs rolling in a fitful dream.

Micah.

This was the man that had seduced him at the bus stop, called forth the car and promised to kill the itch, to lay quiet his suffering. And then the world turned inside out.

Was Micah really there? Or was I talking to a hallucination at the bus stop?

The man inside the vat had clearly been there for quite some time. He didn't climb out for a leisurely visit to recruit Hunter. But the car was real. It had pulled up to the curb and the back door was open. If he'd climbed inside, Hunter would've ended up a specimen in a vat of goo. Had the old woman not somehow saved him.

But it was a dream.

Nothing was making sense. And somebody from this place was texting his phone, had been since he arrived in the city. Why was the message so cryptic? Why not call? Why not explain what was happening?

Who is this?

Footsteps echoed in the dark.

Hunter spun around. A dark form stood in the open doorway. It entered with hips swaying. Lights on the ceiling slowly anticipated the woman's approach.

"Mr. Hunter," she said.

[34]

Hunter
After the Punch

Each step she took pulsed between his eyes, the echo of her heels bouncing off the distant walls. The large tank was at his back, the curving glass humming along his flesh. The body of the white-haired man drifted behind him like a ghost haunting the moment. The light of the tank illuminated a red smile creeping into Dova's perfect cheeks.

"This is what you wanted from me?" Hunter said. "To put me in one of these?"

That was the promise, that they would take away his suffering if he surrendered. And he would've, gladly. Just like everyone who entered the Maze, he would've done so willingly if the itch had not vanished.

Dova gazed over his head, catching the blank expression of the nude man behind him. "There has been an unexpected turn of events. The investors of this experiment, I believe, have gotten more than they expected."

"Experiment?"

She toyed a glance at him. "There are a variety of reasons people leap into the Maze, Mr. Hunter."

"The money is a constant."

"Currency is a formality. We reward all participants well. And the masses are entertained. We are generous, Mr. Hunter."

"You're bribing the human race toward extinction."

She stepped closer. Her fragrance couldn't penetrate the tanks' odor swirling in his head.

"Why climb the mountain, Mr. Hunter, or explore the ocean? They are risks, are they not? Why should we risk so much when we could live safely in a prison cell? Because we are human. It is our nature to risk and discover. The Maze offers an opportunity never before available to the human race, a chance to explore the limits of the mind. And unlike the mountain or ocean, you will discover it has no limits."

She leaned into him.

"The Maze is more than a game, Mr. Hunter."

He paced out of the eerie glow, partially hid in the shadows of one of the smaller tanks, the participant floating darkly.

"Have you heard of the multiverse, Mr. Hunter?" She pointed at herself and him and gestured to the tanks. "We are the creators of those realities. We create dreamlands from the stuff of our minds, a dreamland that becomes a reality."

"A dream is a dream, nothing more. The Maze is no different."

"It is as real as the air we breathe." Her knowing smile was playful. "As real as you."

"There's a room full of floating bodies and you think dreaming is a higher calling? Look around you! This isn't some higher purpose, it's a fucking graveyard."

"You came here for a reason, Mr. Hunter."

"To stop you."

"Maybe you came seeking salvation from your past, an escape from a self-centered dream, perhaps." She passed out of the bluish light, her face half-hidden in shadows. "The truth is a destroyer of delusion, Mr. Hunter. It will strip away your beliefs and destroy the monster that's eating you."

He backed into a dark tank. She stopped at the edge of its light.

"I'm going to call this in," he said. "You'll be arrested, Dova. All of you will go to prison for this, for what you've done."

"We've done nothing, Mr. Hunter."

"You tricked them into doing this to themselves."

"Tempt them, perhaps. But they reach for it, Mr. Hunter, willingly. They always do because they know, deep down, their human potential is to create."

"Create dreams that turn into reality."

"It is our untapped potential."

Reach for it. They did that on the island, the boys in cells forced to endure discomfort until the needle dropped from the ceiling. They reached for it to take them away from the suffering, to draw them into Foreverland. It was a place as real as earth and water and no one could've convinced him otherwise.

Why wasn't my name on the list?

"They come to the Maze for various reasons." She turned to face the large tank. A blank expression looked back at her, the white hair swirling in slow motion. A bluish glow turned her complexion sickly brown. "But mostly, they seek something greater than themselves."

She pawed at the glass. "This experiment, however, has been unlike any game."

"What experiment?"

She put both hands on the big tank. The light sparkled in her eyes, eyes that gazed with a mixture of sadness and admiration at the drowning man.

Hunter reached into his pocket and pulled out a thick square card. It was heavy and sharp, the raised lines of the Maze symbol upon it. He had seen Micah at the bus stop. He talked to him, accepted the card from him. Hallucinations didn't leave calling cards.

"Who is he?" Grey pointed at the tank.

"He is a god."

"A god?"

"What would you call the person who hosts a universe? It is his dream where players exist."

"You're saying he *is* the Maze?"

"It's not as simple as that, Mr. Hunter. But close."

His mind was the players' destination. They awareness leaped into his dream—a dream so convincing it became reality. *But I met him. I spoke to him. He was in front of me. He was real, and now he's floating in the tank. How is that possible?*

Dova turned with a smile that glowed inside him, an expression that warmed his chest. He resisted taking her in his arms and weeping.

"You haven't found what you came seeking, Mr. Hunter." She looked into the dark tank behind him. "A great sacrifice was made, one as unexpected as it was illuminating."

"Where is Sunny Grimm?"

She took the hand he was offering, then reached into his pocket to pull out the envelope from the hotel. "You are indeed lucky."

"Where is she?"

"Someone could've escaped the experiment. She could've escaped the endless cycle of birth and death and left you behind. She solved the Maze but chose to stay. In doing so, the experiment's investors were richly rewarded with her revelations. They learned more about the potential of the Maze than they ever hoped."

"Left *me* behind? Where is she? What did you do to her?"

She raised her hands and he didn't stop her. She slid them through his hair and caressed the place where once a stent awaited a needle on the back of his head. Her alluring fragrance finally beat back the room's pungency.

"Why were you texting me?" He fumbled for his phone. "Why did you give yourself away?"

"I didn't."

He tried to pull away, to escape her tender touch. The truth was in the open and he couldn't see it. She pulled him closer. He let her. Dova kissed his cheek. Her breath tickled his ear.

"Good luck, Mr. Hunter."

She strode away, her path suddenly illuminated by the glow of the tank behind him. Hunter's shadow stretched across the concrete. She slowed to a stop, looking around to drink in the room's details one last time. Her silhouette in the doorway, she fully turned.

"Perhaps we will see each other again," she said. "In another dream."

The sound of her footsteps suddenly vanished. The edges of his shadow began to sharpen. Micah somehow watched him turn despite bobbing in the tank with his eyes still closed and body limp. Hunter imagined he was watching a grand realization about to unfold.

Micah's invitation in one hand, crumpled envelope in the other, Hunter backed away from the smaller tank once darkened, now alight. She was nude. No skin suit to leap her awareness. No respirator to shuttle oxygen into her lungs. Mouth agape, she had inhaled the oxygen-rich solution and stared into emptiness.

A crop of reddish fuzz covered her scalp.

Before he could lift the phone and bring up the picture of the boy and his mother at the waterfall, the picture he'd received before arriving in the city—a picture he couldn't remember getting—and hold it up, he fell on his knees.

The phone clattered on the floor.

A deep well of sadness gushed into his chest, the pressure pushing into his throat and throbbing in his head. He gasped for air and doubled over like an acolyte giving praise to the figure floating angelic before him.

He found her.

[35]

Hunter
After the Punch

Hunter crossed the city on foot. A full moon lit the way, beaming newborn and alive. He arrived at his destination in the early hours, clutching an envelope.

Someone made great sacrifices.

He stopped outside the apartment door. The door across the hall was slightly ajar, a tiny piece of paper propped on the threshold. He picked it up.

A miniature paper doll.

He turned back to apartment 300, key in hand, and lightly knocked. Resting his forehead on the door, he knocked once more before fitting the key from the envelope into the lock. The teeth bit into the tumblers. The bolt snapped away from the door jamb.

Hunter turned the knob.

The smell of old furniture and burnt popcorn squeezed into his forehead and swelled inside his sinuses. He stepped inside, put his back against the door, and automatically dropped the key in an empty basket like it was something he'd done all his life. The shadow of a vanilla-scented candle reached for him.

A dead television hulked in the corner. The chairs were pulled away from the table where he'd sat down to speak with Henk Grimm. Green numbers glowed on the oven, the time still frozen. Hunter checked his phone.

It was one a.m.

Only the reflection, you'll see. Of the one you seek.

He was short of breath; his legs were weak. The package was still on the kitchen counter, the flaps open. The shipping label torn from the side. He rubbed his eyes and tried to focus.

Hand to his face, he went to the cabinet above the stove and found the aspirin behind an unwrapped candle. Cupping water from the sink, he downed four pills. He turned the water off and held still.

Music.

It was coming through the wall. It was a tinny, distant sound leaking from a neighbor or the next room. Quietly, lightly, he stepped into Grey's bedroom. Clothes were strewn on the floor, electric light dancing from the desk. Sharp shadows flickered from a laptop, where music bled from a pair of earbuds.

The sheets were rustled. The pillow, dented.

The air was thick and hot, as if he were breathing through a wool blanket. He sat at the desk.

Only then you'll be, the one who is free.

Pages of clutter stuck to his elbow and fluttered on the floor. A tin box rattled onto his lap. He shook the box, pried the lid open and dumped the object into his palm. It rolled onto the papers.

A tooth.

It was a molar, the enamel shining in the laptop's rhythm. It rested on a word typed across the top of one of the pages. *Foreverland.* Hunter spread the papers like playing cards. It was a technical report for school, red markings left by a teacher that remained uncorrected.

Grey Grimm had researched Foreverland.

He knew the details of that entire event. He knew what the authorities had found, was familiar with the rescue of the boys by the Coast Guard. There was a list of names on the desk, but no need to read it. Hunter's name wouldn't be there.

The truth strips away delusion.

He took a deep breath. The veneer of the moment was thinning. The dark truth was clawing at him.

His phone buzzed.

He dropped the metal box and spilled papers on the floor. Another text lit the corners of the room. He read the question from a familiar number.

He knew the answer.

Reaching beneath the desk without looking, Hunter slid a phone from a makeshift plastic sleeve cut from a soda bottle. He didn't wonder how he knew it was there, or how he knew it was loaded with virtual reality software.

It wasn't Dova who was texting me.

The screen responded to his touch. It requested a security code. He recalled the numbers from a dormant memory and punched them in. He didn't lock the phone into the VR headset. Instead, he held it in his lap. A red line passed over the surface and pierced his eyes momentarily.

Who is this?

A retinal scan was completed. The phone recognized his true identity. Images appeared on the screen.

Rach was smiling in front of a school locker. She pushed up her glasses. Scenes of coffee shops and late nights in front of the television played out. They were hanging out after school. There were weekend video games and long car rides—a lifetime of images that sank in Hunter's stomach. His hands shook. The pleasure of melting into long-lost memories welled inside him.

The images found their rightful places inside him and stripped away the delusion. Hunter Montebank was not on the Foreverland list because he was never on the island. He knew all about the event, knew how the boys had been kidnapped and their minds erased. He knew the tragedy that happened, had even wished he was one of them. He thought anyplace was better than here.

But Hunter Montebank was not one of them.

"Can I ask you something?" Dova had asked him when they first met. "What does your name mean?"

She was teasing him. He had accepted his very own name because it was what he remembered. He'd accepted the reality presented to him and never doubted it.

A pot banged on the stove.

The VR phone strained in Hunter's grip. Someone was humming a familiar song. Kernels were pinging off a metal lid. The smell of popcorn reached the bedroom. Hunter tested his footing before attempting a step toward the front room. His entire body was vibrating. He held the door jamb with both hands.

Sunny Grimm was at the stove.

She was swirling the pot and humming a song she always hummed—when she was sad, when she was happy, in the shower or cooking. A yellow bandana was around her neck, the stiff collar of a work uniform. Her hair was short and sweaty.

Hunter struggled to breathe.

The rapid fire of exploding kernels drowned out her tune. She shook it once more before dumping the contents into a big bowl then filled a small bowl—a bowl she always left for her son, just in case he wanted to join her.

Bright light jumped on the television. A slur of words streamed from channel to channel. She settled back and hugged the big bowl.

A balloon swelled in his stomach and leaked into his throat. He wiped his face and watched the light of a movie glitter in her eyes, the twinkle of a long day forgotten.

Someone made great sacrifices.

The truth was hiding just below his awareness when he saw her in the tank. His memories might have been wiped, but his soul couldn't be cleansed. Some part of him recognized her, knew what she'd done and who she didn't leave behind. Hunter had come to the city in search of Sunny Grimm.

Because she didn't deserve this.

He knelt next to her. She didn't see him because she wasn't really there. The image was a memory playing out in front of him, a memory he cherished now so far away. He swallowed a tide of emotion until it gave way to a single word, one that would change it all. One word that would allow the truth to finally emerge. Hunter Montebank would disappear.

"Mom."

She changed the channel, not hearing him. Not seeing him. Not there. A crystalized memory that played out a part of his life he couldn't leave behind, one that couldn't be erased. One he could witness one last time.

"I'm sorry."

It wasn't Hunter Montebank's voice that whispered the apology. Grey Grimm was kneeling next to the couch. He found himself in a violent web of sobbing, collapsing on the cushions as the memory of his mother talked at the television between handfuls of popcorn.

"You need to go," she said.

She was sitting very still. Placing the bowl next to her, she leaned forward to drop a business card on the table. She sat back without appearing to see anything, as if she was talking to the television and had found the card between the cushions. He wiped his eyes.

Three o'clock was stenciled on the blank side of the business card. Beneath it a snake was eating its tail. He stood on newborn knees and looked at the time and snake, then flipped the card over.

It was a homeless shelter.

INTERVIEW WITH GREY GRIMM

Freddy looks at his watch. He should've been home an hour ago.

"What if you woke up with different memories?" Grey says. "One morning you remember a different name in a different place. Who are you then?"

"You're talking about Foreverland."

Freddy's familiar with the tropical island incident. Everyone is. He knows it's true, has seen the photos of the island and the buildings. He's seen the footage of the Coast Guard rescuing boys who were told they had been in an accident and were being healed by some hi-tech technology. What Freddy doesn't know is how much of it is true. Rich old men body-swapping for a younger model seems a bit much.

"So what you're saying," Freddy continues, "is that you woke up a divorced Asian man in his mid-fifties named Hunter Montebank—" He holds up his hand to stop Grey from interrupting. "I know what it means."

Montebank is a fancy word that means imposter. *Fake hunter.* Freddy likes to think if he wakes up with a joke of a name like that he'll figure it out before he pours coffee. Then again, dreams are convincing until the dreamer wakes up.

"But a Foreverland survivor?" Freddy says. "That's a bit odd, don't you think?"

"I was doing a research paper on the event. I know everything about Foreverland. The knowledge was fresh when I punched in. I'm guessing they drew on that to build Hunter Montebank to keep me obsessed and distracted."

"Why?"

"To keep me lost."

"No, I mean what's the point? You're saying this was an experiment. There was no audience or sponsors to make money. I don't see the point of keeping you and your mom lost and confused."

"The Maze is more than a game."

Grey pauses to finish his water. Freddy is half-expecting Andrew to deliver another glass. When he doesn't, Freddy takes the bait.

"What is it? If it's not a game."

"You know how we're told the sky is the limit when we're kids?" Grey regards him with that heavy-lidded stare. Blinking doesn't seem to be necessary. "It's a lie, Kaleb. There is no sky. There are no limits."

Freddy clears his throat. The kid isn't trying to goad him with his middle name, but he's still tired of hearing it. Unless it's his mother calling, that's not his name.

"Dreams are real, is that it?" Freddy says.

Foreverland proved that assumption, or so the reports suggest. The boys visited a convincing dream that was limited only by their imagination. They felt pain and hunger, experienced pleasure and joy that were no different than the flesh world. It was how the old men got them to leave their bodies and not return.

However, the concepts of multiverses and parallel universes created from these dreams were above his pay grade. *People dreaming up a world that solidifies into reality would mean we could be living in a dream right now.*

Freddy is only concerned with this world, the one where he has to feed his children and pay his bills. If there's another Freddy out there, it's not him any more than a clone or an identical twin.

Even if his middle name is Kaleb.

"What about Hunter Montebank?" Freddy says. "Is he still out there?"

Grey appears caught off-guard. It's the first time he's blinked since they started. He looks up and left, contemplating the question. Perhaps he hasn't thought of it until now.

"Maybe."

"The investors, who are they?"

Grey shakes his head.

"Were they just some random billionaires that forced you and your mom into an experiment?"

"Only the willing enter the Maze."

"So how did you get access to the equipment?"

Grey frowns. Freddy feels the air grow heavy and damp; he takes a deep breath and rubs his face. It's been a long day.

"I was tempted," is all Grey says.

"So your mom finds you punched in and comes after you. They throw her in a tank; she saves you and drowns."

"She's not dead." His voice is thick and wavering.

"You're not convincing me."

Grey casts his eyes down. He slides the empty glass from hand to hand and grimaces. When he stops, he looks up without blinking again. His eyelids are heavier.

"I grieve for her suffering, Detective. She sacrificed a great deal for me, but she's free now."

"She might be free, but her body is dead." Freddy snaps his fingers. "Ah, the multiverse."

Grey is nodding.

The pieces are coming together. Freddy is beginning to understand what's happening here. The kid punched into the Maze, but he didn't come out sane. He's coping with his mother's death with the belief that she lives in another reality. Why he's treating Freddy's interrogation room like a confessional, he's still not sure.

"I know you're having trouble believing this," Grey says, "but you're not a child. You once were a child, but you're not anymore. Time is what separates you from the child. And time is an illusion."

This is a troubled young man. He's a little Zen master who's good with body language. *But he's not reading my mind,* Freddy thinks.

"Time is an illusion," Freddy muses. "And you lived a thousand lives as Hunter Montebank—"

"I don't know how many lives I lived."

"You lived more than one, correct? And then you woke up in your bed as Grey Grimm"—Freddy gestured to the kid—"only twenty-four hours after you punched in. Did you know your mom was dead?"

Grey hesitates. "I knew she wasn't coming back."

"From the multiverse?"

"As you said, her body is dead. She couldn't return."

"Where's your dad?"

"He is where he is."

Freddy doesn't know if he's more annoyed with the young Zen master act or his refusal to answer questions. His father has been missing since Sunny Grimm's death. He didn't show up for work that morning and hasn't returned since. His apartment was unlocked and hastily vacated. The drawers were out and the luggage gone. If he had anything to do with his ex-wife's death, the kid isn't going to help. Although the grim tension around Grey's lips says different.

Freddy is good with body language, too.

"If you know anything about him, it's best you let us handle it."

"He'll come talk with you sometime soon, Detective."

"Don't do anything stupid, Grey."

"I'm here." He chuckles. It's his first outburst of emotion since he sat down. "I've already confessed to the Maze. By all accounts, I've already done something stupid."

"At this point, I'll have to hold you and report this to the feds."

"I've already posted bail."

That seems unlikely since charges haven't been filed. But he seems prepared for whatever Freddy has to do.

"Okay," Freddy says. "Are we done here? Did you get everything off your chest?"

"For now."

Andrew comes in the room. Freddy figured he would've gone home by now. He holds the door open. Grey stops before leaving.

"Thanks for listening, Kaleb. I'll see you soon."

Andrew gives Freddy a strange look before escorting the kid to the back of the precinct. Freddy wants to hate the kid for being so flippant with his middle name. He's making a point about something and Freddy's patience with object lessons is maxed out.

The phone is still on the table. The water droplets have completely evaporated. That was the kid's analogy for death. His mom is vapor instead of water; she exists in another state. *Does that mean she's still the same person?*

Freddy takes the phone back to his office.

He's missed dinner. The kids will be getting ready for bed by the time he gets home. His birthday cake will be half-eaten with the candles blown out. They'll be sad he wasn't there. His wife will be pissed.

There's a yellow envelope buried in his inbox. He pulls it out and sees it's from his mother. She sends a card to his home address as well as his office. His full name is written out in loopy cursive. So everyone in the office probably did know his middle name was Kaleb.

The kid's not a magician after all.

He sits back in his chair and opens the card. He doesn't want to see the kid hang for this. His mother is dead, water droplets or not. Whether he made up part of the story or all of it, he just needs to get on with his life.

Later, when the feds send someone to investigate, he's relieved to find out the audio recording of the interview is faulty. The conversation is lost. Subsequent interviews lead nowhere and the kid is off the hook. Although it is mildly disturbing that the federal agent doing the investigation is Asian, Freddy believes it's just a coincidence.

His name isn't Hunter Montebank.

However, a few weeks later, Henk Grimm comes into the office just like Grey said he would. Freddy meets him in the interrogation room, where he gives a full confession.

This time the audio works.

[36]

Grey
After the Punch

Rach swerved into traffic while singing. She made up the words because she could never remember them.

Grey felt the car's loose suspension bounce. He smelled the slice of pizza a man was eating on the corner—pepperoni and Italian sausage. Senses heightened, he felt the angry conversation between the driver and passenger in the car behind them. It was strange, like he was breathing experience, inhaling sounds and sights and tastes, merging with the chaos without becoming lost in it.

When Rach slammed on the brakes, he braced his hand on the dashboard. His pulse quickened. A car cut them off on the right and ended up costing them the green light. Rach was texting when his brake lights lit up.

"Idiot." She went back to texting.

Grey took a deep breath. Despite what he'd told Freddy, death was final in this life. He was human. He couldn't magically leap to another plane of existence. This life demanded a body. This experience of flesh had hard rules. Flying through the windshield would hurt.

He didn't know what happened after death. Maybe there was reincarnation and he'd start over in the flesh. Maybe he'd go to another plane of existence, or heaven or hell or somewhere in between.

Or maybe nothing happened.

He wasn't going to test the theories. He closed his eyes and inhaled a mixture of fallen leaves and exhaust. A squirrel chirped in a street tree and a car hit the horn. It was all vivid.

I am Grey Grimm.

He reminded himself of his name daily, did a reality check by observing his surroundings and checked in with his senses. When he was Hunter Montebank, he'd believed he was a survivor of Foreverland. He remembered the visceral crack of the needle in his forehead and the greedy old men, the lavish environment of the tropical island.

How was he to know they had wiped his memories and planted new ones as real and vivid as the ones he now held? Now he was Grey Grimm, eighteen-year-old entrepreneur. How did he know that wasn't just another suggestion, a program to fool him into living another life in the Maze?

Is Grey Grimm just another dream?

"Is it this one?" Rach pointed at the stoplight. "I can never remember."

Tight-lipped, he pointed to the right, careful not to sound nervous about rear-ending another car. They caught another green light. If not for getting cut off, they would have caught every light, a statistical impossibility.

"Good luck charm," Rach muttered.

Even she noticed the unusual number of green lights when he was in the car. They weren't all green, but it was safer to limit the number of red lights she would undoubtedly run.

Grey couldn't explain how he did it.

He woke up with this expanded sense of awareness. There was an electrical field in the city. It was a web of pulses, something he could feel under his skin and taste beneath his tongue. It was the wireless communications, the technology in cars and buildings and the subway beneath them. He had a hard time tweezing apart the noise. It was a ball of multicolored yarn the size of a house, each thread representing an alarm system, a television or phone.

Or streetlight.

But if he focused on the light, he could convince the sensors to give them a green light by the time they reached it. It was a little tricky if the system was on a timer. That would require more manipulation, and that brought up an ethical question: just how much of his environment did he want to influence to his advantage? It was a slippery slope that was steep and long and only required one step to start sliding.

To improve his odds of survival, he turned as many lights green as Rach would see.

It was instinctual. He couldn't explain the mechanism that allowed him to lift his arm—the nerves that fired, the muscles that contracted—but that didn't prevent him from painting something wonderful.

It was the same for Freddy's interrogation room.

There would be recording devices to capture their conversation. Grey wanted to be frank with the detective. He wanted him to know the truth of what had happened to his mother and to prepare him for the arrival of his dad, when that day came. Keeping their conversation off the record, a conversation that could have legal consequences, was important. He was certain that he could speed up Freddy's heart rate if he wanted. He could induce an adrenaline dump and step on the panic button. After all, the human body relied on electrical impulses.

Could I induce a heart attack?

These were just ideas. They were nothing he had attempted since waking on his bed and removing the punch. But he was certain they were possible in the same way he didn't have to step on an egg to know he could break it.

How many people are like me?

It seemed unlikely he was the only one. But would someone be tempted to use these skills for their own desires? If Henk had access to another person's mind, he would be a super villain.

The odds were slim he was alone with these abilities. This was a question he pondered often. *Perhaps,* he wondered, *the only way to obtain this level is through some sort of enlightenment.*

Grey wasn't claiming enlightenment in the Buddhist sense of the word. But his experience of the world had broadened. There was a general lack of fear because he didn't sense separation. He was okay with just sitting in the car as Rach checked her phone while changing lanes. His heart would race when they nearly hit someone on a bicycle, and, strangely, that was okay. It was all right. Everything was exactly as it was supposed to be. This ability to say yes to his experience had been completely opened.

How could he abuse this ability?

It seemed impossible. In fact, this was beyond enlightenment. It was the end result of the experiment he had unwittingly stepped into when he strapped the punch around his head—an experiment that had unknowingly drawn his mother into a submersion tank. The sight of her gray skin and open mouth would remain with him until this life ended. The emerald sparkle in her eyes had been snuffed.

How was it not my fault?

That was a thought he struggled to work with, especially since it was tightly wound with sensations of sadness and grief. *Is this what the investors of the experiment want?* No one had contacted him since waking. There were no condolences or recognition.

The lake house was abandoned. The front gates were open when he had a car drop him off. No one stopped him from walking down the path or met him at the front door. The rooms were empty. But they knew his journey had been complete.

His bank account was proof.

The weekly deposits were enough to buy a fleet of cars. He attempted to trace the source of the mysterious donor, but that was fruitless and silly. One thought had haunted him since he awoke.

Is the experiment over?

"What did the cops want?" Rach said.

Rach had picked him up at the police station. She didn't know he had to post bail. She didn't know anything other than his mother had been found in a tank. All those lifetimes he'd lived as Hunter Montebank unfolded within the span of twenty-four hours of flesh time. He'd missed a day of school.

That was it.

"They just had a few questions."

"About your mom?"

"Yeah."

"They find him yet?"

Rach was convinced his dad had something to do with his mom's unexplained death. No one could understand why she was involved with the Maze or her tragic end. And when Henk Grimm was nowhere to be found, it was assumed he was involved.

It didn't take a detective.

Rach had no memory of their trip out to the lake house. She didn't remember driving out there and still believed they'd capsized near the boat landing. His hallucinations of talking to his dad, she believed, were stress induced. *Maybe you knew something would happen to your mom,* she said.

Grey left it alone.

The complete absence or manipulation of memories was for her benefit, he rationalized. That would explain why they had different experiences when they flipped the boat and were rescued by the people in the house. Rach was sent home for her own protection.

Grey was sent down a different road.

All Rach knew was his mom was dead and his dad was gone. Her sympathy was deep and genuine and moving. He could feel her pain because she loved him. Not in the girlfriend-boyfriend way. *Not yet.*

He couldn't predict the future, but it didn't take a detective.

"I'm taking this one." She squeezed into a parking spot a block away from the café.

They walked without talking. Sometimes they held hands and swung them between each other like they did when they were kids. The storefront next to the café was boarded up. It was a furniture store that specialized in resale items. Someone had purchased the business and boarded it up. Metal security gates had been pulled down and locked. *Closed for business* was posted on both sides. Graffiti artists had already started filling up the space between the signs.

"You want something?" she asked. They waited for traffic before crossing the street.

"I'm good."

"How long you going to be?"

"A few minutes." Grey stopped outside the boarded door of the old furniture store. "I'll be done before you get your coffee."

"When are you going to tell me what you're doing?"

"When I'm done."

She watched him feed a key into the door and cringed when he opened it. "Whatever you're doing, it stinks."

He stepped sideways into the open door and waved. Rach went to the café and he locked the door behind him. She didn't know he'd bought the furniture business and closed it down. He was simply investing his inheritance in the available space.

She really didn't want to know what he was doing.

There was another set of doors inside the front door. These had been installed shortly after he had the windows boarded. Some ambitious criminals might get past the gate, but they weren't getting through the second door. He didn't need the space much longer. It had taken six months to set it up and get it ready. A few more days, maybe a week, and he'd sell the property and relocate. He'd take a loss on the investment.

The smell would be a permanent problem.

The second door required a palm print, a retinal scan and voice recognition to open. Grey's forehead tingled in anticipation as he waited for the retinal scan to finish. Inside, the lights were out. Syrupy bubbles gurgled in the dark. A pungent odor filled his eyes with tears. A light came up in the corner. Watery patterns danced across the floor.

A cylindrical tank was softly lit.

Thousands of translucent follicles swayed in the dense solution like tentacles of an anemone. They massaged the nude and freshly shaved body of a middle-aged man.

It wasn't hard to find Henk Grimm.

Grey had accessed his credit card statements and followed the money. He'd found him at a beach resort. Getting him back to the city was the roadblock. His dad wouldn't be happy to see his son and he sure as hell wasn't going to follow him. Grey had the furniture store ready. Patiently, he considered his options.

Then he got a text.

His dad was in the passenger seat outside the apartment building. He was unharmed and unconscious, hiding beneath a stocking cap and a black overcoat. There was a wheelchair folded in the backseat. The timing was impeccable. Grey texted and called the number without an answer. Someone wanted his dad as badly as he did.

Later, he would understand.

He drove him to the furniture store at a late hour and wheeled him inside. His dad was unaware his vacation had ended. When Grey undressed him, he discovered he had already been shaved. All Grey had to do was dump him into the oxygenated solution and let the tank do the rest.

He came out of the groggy slumber as the solution reached his chest. When a mouthful of the foul solution filled his throat, his eyes snapped open. He thrashed at the sides of the transparent cylinder. The tank's tendrils gently wrapped around his arms and legs, stroked his midsection and cradled his head. Henk Grimm released his son's name with his last breath and then swallowed the first draught of liquid oxygen.

He survived the awareness leap.

Grey now stood in front of the tank, the limp body of his father swaying with seaweedy tendrils that had leaped his awareness and tended his vacant body—a body he would soon return to and live out his days.

But not yet.

Grey sat in the chair next to the tank. His forehead twittered with excitement. He reached for the clunky band. Stretching it over his head, he centered the circular knob on his forehead. Eyes on his dad, he relaxed into the headrest and felt the dull thunk.

He'd be back before Rach ordered her coffee.

[37]
HENK

After the Punch

3:00.

The pounding. The burning.

A brush fire roared through his lungs, scorching his throat. He swam through the pain. A migraine waited above the surface of waking and swung a big club when he broke through.

It hit Henk between the eyes.

He blinked away the dry burning. The popcorn ceiling was familiar. An old web swayed in the slots of a vent. A bag of wet sand, he was hungover. He was dead weight. Heavy and slow, there was no memory of drinking. In fact, there were very few memories at all.

Palm trees. Sand.

That was the last thing Henk could recall. He'd gone south and left the city in the rearview for warmer weather and freedom. But he was lying in his apartment on top of the comforter, wearing shoes and pants. And his white lab coat.

His finger throbbed.

A gold band was on his finger. He'd pawned his wedding ring the day he left Sunny. No sense in wearing money around his finger when he could be spending it. And now it was on his finger?

He sat up slowly, cradled his head and waited for the day of the week to arrive. He tugged at memories from the recent past.

Nothing but sand.

The drawers were open, the closet door. There were clothes on the floor. *I've been robbed.*

A chair dragged across the kitchen floor.

Henk strained to listen. Maybe the thieves were still there. He was passed out while they ransacked his room. Did he bring someone home? Candace, maybe? No, not her. She wouldn't be happy to see him. No one from the office would be happy to see Henk Grimm, not after he stole from the office. He'd transferred all the money into his account and withdrew it as cash.

Why am I here?

Henk leaned against the wall. Someone was at the kitchen table.

"Grey? What... what are you doing here?"

A box was on the table with the flaps open. *The package*. But that was months ago. Grey watched him shuffle toward the table and peer inside the box. The velvet bag was nestled at the bottom.

A gust of wind spattered the glass wall of the apartment. Rivulets raced in jagged lines. A gray sky consumed the skyline. Henk took a deep breath, careful not to wake the migraine. His lungs, though, were still hot.

"Brought you back a souvenir." Grey slid a tin box across the table.

"From where?"

Grey's stare was intensely uncomfortable. The crosshairs were on Henk's head. Henk palmed the metal lid and shook. It sounded like a rock. He pried it open.

"What's this?" He dumped the tooth on the table. "Where'd you get that?"

"Just a gift from some people. They left it for me, sort of like a clue."

The enamel was thin and yellow, the root intact. It was a strange gift, even for a dentist. If Grey had been to the office, then they'd know Henk was in town. He couldn't let them find him. Too many debts to pay. Debts that could never be resolved.

"What's this about?"

The tooth trembled between his fingers. The roots dug into his thumb. Grey sat stone-still, hands folded on his lap, his eyes lazy and unblinking. An x-ray beamed across the table, an illuminating glare that exposed Henk's soul.

"What's this mean?" The words gushed out of Henk.

Vomit swelled in his throat. He swallowed hard and rushed to the sink, hand over his mouth to hold back the bile. He puked from the bottom of his feet.

Balls clenched, stomach knotted, he purged a foul translucent slime. A string hung from his bottom lip and crept down the drain, a rancid pool of oily emulsion, a distillation of watery pus.

Grey watched with x-ray vision.

Through involuntary tears, the Maze symbol appeared on the refrigerator. The card had been cut and folded and taped together to reveal the secret. It wasn't the invitation Henk had posted, the simple one that came in the mail, the one he knew Grey would find, the one he knew his son would solve.

This was a card with a tagline. *Find yourself.*

"Goddamnit," he muttered and spit. "So you know, is that it?"

Grey silently watched.

"I couldn't do it, so there." Henk hunched over the sink. "I swear, I would've done it myself, it just didn't work. The tank was... I couldn't make it work. I tried, you know. And I spent all the money..."

"All of *my* money."

"You wanted it," Henk said. "You loved the Maze, don't fool yourself. You wanted to go inside, just needed the opportunity. I put it out there, but you picked it up. You have to be willing, you know that. I couldn't force you."

He wiped his mouth and threw the towel on the floor.

"I'm not an idiot, son. The passwords were simple and I kept them where you'd find them. You went through my email. You set up the GPS on my phone, not me. You took the invitation off the fridge."

He shook his finger.

"I put that box on the table and opened it, that's all I did! You looked inside; you took it for yourself. *You did!* You strapped it on; you punched in. You did, son, not me, so don't look at me like that."

Grey continued silently judging. His expression had already announced a verdict. A sentence was to be passed.

"I can't do needles," Henk said. "You got to believe me, I would've done it myself, but I just don't have it in me. You wanted it—"

He gagged. This time he sprayed a coat of stench on the counter. His forearms slid through it as he collapsed. He was lying though. He could've taken the needle; he didn't want to. There were ways to tank he hadn't tried, too. Ways that made him quake with fear. He couldn't do it.

Didn't want to.

"Why is the box here?"

Grey had taken that thing; he'd used it. Henk had gone to the apartment and seen his son lying on his bed, a funeral display still breathing, the black knob seated squarely on his forehead. That horsehair needle was licking his frontal lobe. It had slurped out his son.

He was so still, so peaceful. Like he was little again, slumbering in his crib. Henk had run out of the apartment, ran out of the city, took a few belongings and left it all behind. He would never come back, would live off the prize money when the Maze was over.

He dry-heaved.

"They came to me," he said. "They said there was an experiment that was perfect for a parent and child... a *willing* parent and child, mind you. I did the hard work, just so you know. I went to the Sessions and made all the connections. I spent all of my money and yours, too, so don't give me the puppy eyes. I spent it all and planned on doing the Maze myself. It just didn't work out."

He ran the water and sniffed back an acrid wad of saliva to spit.

"She didn't have to do it, you know," Henk said. "I didn't plan that. You went in and then she followed, that was her doing. I didn't trick her."

Like I tricked you.

He could've followed Grey into the Maze. The people at the house made the offer and he accepted. They would do the rest. He wasn't going to ask his son to participate. Grey would've, he was sure of it. But then he would have to follow. The experiment needed a parent. It didn't say which one.

All he had to do was put the pieces together, act enraged when he discovered his son had gone out to the house, follow the script to act like he didn't want them involved. He baited Grey to want more. And when he took the boat out, when he crashed it short of the cliff (which wasn't part of the plan, but worked in their favor), they seeded his son with confusion and made him more suggestable.

More willing.

Deep down, he knew it would work. He knew his ex-wife would go after Grey, would accept their offer to enter the Maze to find him, where they would erase both of their memories and let them wander through countless lifetimes in search of each other. What the experiment was about, he didn't know. Henk was promised a payout if one of them survived.

And that made it all the worse. Henk was a coward, the weakest of them all. When it came to facing the fear, he sent his son to battle and hid behind his ex-wife.

He still had nothing for it.

"Where's the money?" He slipped on the tiles.

Grey finally moved. He walked to the glass wall. Rain was spitting waves behind him. Henk twisted the wedding ring off and threw it. It tinked off the glass.

"I raised you, you know. Where's my reward?"

He reeked of bile. Blood streaked across the back of his hand. He stumbled forward.

"I deserve something."

He inflated his lungs and reached deep for the source of parental power, the innate strength given to fathers to wield over their sons. He assumed the same unblinking stare his son was giving him. He turned the x-ray vision back on his progeny. Grey's back was to the window.

The storm spat.

"You kept the money from me," Henk growled. "I know you did."

Grey slid his fingers under the white lapels of Henk's lab coat. He bunched them into fists and held tight.

"I'll give you what you've always wanted," Grey said.

The plate-glass window—an inch thick, impenetrable, unbreakable—teetered outward. Slowly, it fell away. The storm howled against them, stinging pellets scouring Henk's cheeks and poking his eyes. He leaned away, but Grey held tight.

His son's heels hung over the edge.

The carpet soaked around their feet. Henk's thighs turned to putty. The urge to vomit lodged in his throat. Grey pulled him closer to the edge. Henk flailed helplessly. His son was a pillar against the storm's rage.

"I'll give you," Grey said, "what you deserve."

And then he leaned back.

The unstoppable momentum of gravity pulled him into the sky. The white coat still balled tight, Henk went with him.

They fell like stones.

The rain stinging.

The concrete raced toward them. His scream bled into the gray wind. They struck the hood of an SUV. Henk hit the front end. His head snapped over the edge; a spray of plastic grill parts sprinkled on the pavement.

Henk inhaled deeply and desperately.

He scrambled across the bed, bunching the comforter over him, clutching a pillow. The air was fresh and new. He shook on the verge of tears. The taste of vomit lingered in his throat.

He wiped his eyes.

The room was the same—drawers open, clothes strewn about. And he was wearing the white lab coat. The wedding band, too.

The package was on the table, the flaps open, but Grey wasn't waiting. Rain slapped the plate-glass wall. An inch thick, still in place. He didn't move any closer to it, the memory of falling still vivid, the crushing edge of the SUV sharp against his skull.

A white card was taped in the exact spot where his son had been standing. It was cut and folded.

A symbol stared back.

"Hello, Henk."

The coat whirled at his waist as he spun around. His heart danced in his chest. His lungs were still heavy and burning. An old woman was sitting at the table. She wasn't there a second ago. Now she was hunched next to the open package. There was something familiar about her.

It was the eyes.

She stood up and slowly approached. She was smiling a smile that was more sorry than it was happy. She smoothed the wrinkles on his lapels. Her hair was pulled back over her head. Before her smile turned more angry than sorry, he recognized her.

It was the jagged scar near the hairline.

REVIEW THE MAZE!

If you enjoyed this ride, please drop a review on your favorite vendor. It doesn't have to be long and complicated. Throw some stars on it and write *Loved it!* or *It was really, really okay!* or *Meh.*

Reviews make the difference.

REVIEW HERE

WHAT TO READ NEXT?

The Hunt for Freddy Bills
Book 2
bertauski.com/maze

There is no escape. There never was.

Freddy Bills is retired. Back in the day, he was fishing people out of unreality tanks and pulling needles from their heads. That was when it was against the law. Now everyone is doing it, including him. In fact, he dreamstitches unrealities for droppers to ride. He's one of the best. His plans were to fade into retirement, just him and his dog.

That was before someone from his past appeared.

A string of clues leads him to dig up a past long buried and forgotten. As evidence mounts, he learns the truth about the Maze and its true purpose. There's no escaping his past or future. He was destined to solve the Maze.

He just has to figure out why.

The Hunt for Freddy Bills

Book 2
bertauski.com/maze

BERTAUSKI STARTER LIBRARY

FREE!

---

bertauski.com

ABOUT THE AUTHOR

My grandpa never graduated high school. He retired from a steel mill in the mid-70s. He was uneducated, but a voracious reader. As a kid, I'd go through his bookshelves of musty paperback novels, pulling Piers Anthony and Isaac Asimov off the shelf and promising to bring them back. I was fascinated by robots that could think and act like people. What happened when they died?

Writing is sort of a thought experiment to explore human nature and possibilities. What makes us human? What is true nature?

I'm also a big fan of plot twists.

•

bertauski.com

See more about the author and forthcoming books at http://www.bertauski.com

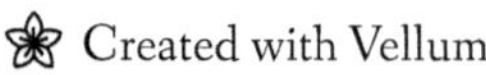
Created with Vellum

www.ingramcontent.com/pod-product-compliance
Lightning Source LLC
Chambersburg PA
CBHW051005180726
48291CB00006B/1984

9781951432140